The Wayward Wife

JESSICA STIRLING

The Wayward Wife

HODDER &
STOUGHTON

First published in 2013 by Hodder & Stoughton
An Hachette UK company

I

A CIP catalogue record for this title
is available from the British Library

Hardback ISBN 978 1 444 74459 0
E-book ISBN 978 1 444 74461 3

Typeset in Plantin Light by Palimpsest Book Production Limited,
Falkirk, Stirlingshire

Printed and bound by CPI Group (UK) Ltd, Croydon CRO 4YY

Hodder & Stoughton policy is to use papers that are natural,
renewable and recyclable products and made from wood grown
in sustainable forests. The logging and manufacturing processes
are expected to conform to the environmental regulations
of the country of origin.

Hodder & Stoughton Ltd
338 Euston Road
London NW1 3BH

www.hodder.co.uk

Contents

PART ONE

Tempting Fate

I

To ease the sting of losing her husband Vivian had invited Susan to lunch at L'Étoile. In fact, Susan hadn't 'lost' her husband at all. Danny wasn't dodging U-boats in the North Atlantic, digging in along the Maginot Line with the British Expeditionary Force or training to fly a Spitfire on an airfield in Kent. Flat feet, indifferent eyesight and a talent for editing had condemned him to a reserve posting with the BBC's monitoring unit in Evesham where the only thing he might die of was frostbite.

It had been a bitterly cold winter so far. The first few weeks of 1940 had brought no respite. Even within the restaurant the air was sufficiently chill to hold a hint of frosty breath mingled with cigarette smoke, a great cloud of which hung over the round table under the skylight where reporters and broadcasters met informally for lunch.

Susan and Vivian were seated at a corner table for two. Vivian had kept on her overcoat and fur hat. Taking a lead from the older woman, Susan too had retained her coat, a tweed swagger, and a pert little hat which, though chic, did nothing to keep her ears warm.

The men who commandeered the round table had checked in their overcoats and scarves and lounged, chatting and laughing, as if they were indifferent to the cold, though one of them, Susan noticed, still sported a battered, sweat-stained fedora that not so long ago would have had him evicted by the management.

'Well,' Vivian said, 'that didn't take long.'

'What didn't take long?' said Susan.

'For someone to catch your eye. Who is he?'

'I've absolutely no idea,' Susan said.

'They're Americans, aren't they?'

'The boys from CBS, I think. The slim one with his back to us is Edward Murrow, if I'm not mistaken. And that may be Bill Shirer, though I was rather under the impression he was still reporting from Berlin.'

'And the fellow in the awful hat of whom the *maître d'* so clearly disapproves, have you bumped into him in the corridors of power?' Vivian said. 'He's certainly giving you the once-over.'

'I'd hardly call Broadcasting House the corridors of power,' said Susan. 'In any case, if we had met I'm quite sure I'd remember him.'

Vivian sniffed and slid a menu into Susan's hand.

'You may have fibbed about your marital status to secure a job with the BBC but it must be all above board now they've removed the bar on hiring married women,' she said. 'Why don't you wear your wedding ring?'

'Because it's written into my contract that married women will be expected to resign the instant the war's over.'

'The war,' Vivian said, 'has barely begun. No one's naïve enough to suppose it'll be over soon and, if it is, chances are we'll all be jabbering in German and bowing the knee to Herr Hitler.'

'I'm sure you wouldn't mind that too much.'

'Now, now!' said Vivian. 'I may have taken tea with Dr Goebbels and had some of my books published by that Nazi, Martin Teague, but I've completely changed my tune since then, as well you know.'

'My brother, Ronnie, thinks you're a hypocrite.'

'At least I stayed in England. I could have fled to the United States like half the literary crowd – well, the fascist half anyway.'

'Fish,' Susan said, 'I do believe I'll have the fish.'

Vivian peered at the menu. 'In deference to my new-found patriotism, I will forgo the beef and settle for a mushroom soufflé and the *sole meunière*. What about wine: a nice dry Riesling?'

'Patriotism only stretches so far, I see.'

'We can pretend it's from Alsace,' said Vivian.

For the best part of four years Susan had been employed by Vivian Proudfoot to transcribe the controversial books that had earned Viv a degree of notoriety and quite a bit of money but in the spring of 1939, with the possibility of war looming, Vivian had urged Susan to apply for a 'safe' job with the BBC.

The interview had been conducted in one of the Corporation's poky little offices in Duchess Street.

'Where were you born, Miss Hooper?'

'Shadwell.'

'You don't sound like a person from the East End, if you don't mind me saying so.'

'My father felt it would be to my advantage to learn to speak properly.'

'And your mother?'

'She died when I was a child.'

'You were raised by a female relative, I take it?'

'No, I was raised by my father.'

'And what does he do? I mean, his profession?'

'He's a docker; a crane driver to be precise.'

'Really? How remarkable!'

The interviewer's air of superiority had galled her. He was nothing but a middle-aged, middle-rank staffer with a public school accent who clearly disapproved of the gender shift in BBC policy.

'I see from your application that you were an assistant to Vivian Proudfoot until very recently. Do you share Miss Proudfoot's political views?'

'I attended two or three rallies with Miss Proudfoot for the purposes of research. I'm certainly not a supporter of fascism and, may I point out, neither is Miss Proudfoot.'

'Forgive my caution, Miss Hooper. One can't be too careful these days. By the bye, I assume you're not married?'

'No,' she'd answered without a blush. 'No, I'm not married,' and three weeks later had received a contract of employment.

Unfit for army service and thoroughly unsettled, Danny had lost his job in Fleet Street and been coopted on to the staff of the BBC. From that point on their marriage had deteriorated into sharing a bed occasionally and nodding as they passed on the stairs.

Susan was well aware that the chap in the soiled fedora was interested in her. Hat notwithstanding, he was quite prepossessing in an unruly, un-English sort of way, not all stiff and haughty like so many of the young men she encountered in Broadcasting House. He held her gaze for four or five seconds, then, leaning forward, put a question to the

men at his table. They were journalists, foreign correspondents, men of the world and far too polite to look round at
her.

Vivian covered her mouth with the edge of the menu.

'Now see what you've done,' she whispered. 'He thinks
he's on to a good thing. Oh, God, he's coming over.'

He was broad-shouldered and heavy-set but walked with
a curiously light step, like a boxer or a dancer. He had the
decency to take off the fedora and hold it down by his side.
His hair needed trimming and the dark stubble on his chin
suggested that he hadn't shaved for days.

Fancifully, Susan imagined he might have stepped off a
freighter from Murmansk or, less fancifully, the boat-train
from Calais. He certainly had the air of a man who had
been places and done things.

She glanced up, gave him the wisp of a smile and waited,
a little breathlessly, for him to introduce himself.

'Miss Proudfoot? Vivian Proudfoot?'

'Yes,' Vivian said in her West End voice. 'I am she.'

'It's a real pleasure to meet you,' he said and, ignoring
Susan completely, offered Vivian his hand.

On the few occasions when Susan had persuaded her brother
Ronnie to take her up town after dark she'd been intrigued
by the massive cream-coloured edifice in Portland Place
that looked more like an ocean liner moored in a narrow
canal than a building in the heart of London.

She had wondered then at the magic that the wizards
cooked up within: dance bands and orchestras, singers,
comedians, plays, talks and interviews with famous people
all miraculously transmitted to the wireless in the Hoopers'

kitchen in Shadwell. After she'd gone to work in Broadcasting House, though, it hadn't taken her long to realise that the only magical thing about the organisation was that 'the voice of the nation' wasn't smothered by the avalanche of memos that poured down from the boardroom or drowned out by the bickering that went on between controllers and producers.

Now, with the walls painted drab green to fool German bombers, sandbags piled against the porticos and policemen on guard at every entrance, the seat of national conscience had the same down-at-heel appearance as most of London's other monumental institutions.

Vivian said, 'Why the long face? What's wrong?'

'Nothing.'

'It's not my fault Mr Gaines recognised me.'

'Gaines? Oh, is that his name?'

'Do stop sulking, Susan.'

'I'm not sulking. You'd hardly be full of beans if you were about to spend hours trailing some producer from pillar to post with a notebook in your hand.'

Vivian was a robust woman in her forties and in a military-style overcoat and fur hat had the imposing bearing of a Soviet commissar. She smoked a cigarette in a short amber holder and, with a certain panache, blew smoke skywards. 'I'm just as surprised as you are that an American newsman was more interested in hearing my opinions than flirting with you.'

'He was certainly impressed by your latest book.'

'Oh, that old thing,' said Vivian. 'Dashed it off in a couple of weeks when I'd nothing better to do.'

'Ha-ha,' said Susan.

'Ha-ha, indeed,' said Vivian. 'We sweated blood on *The Great Betrayal*, didn't we, my dear?'

'Is it selling well?'

'Better than I expected. Something to be said for cheap paper editions put out for the masses. Handy size for reading in air-raid shelters, apparently.'

'I'm sorry, Vivian, but I really must go,' Susan said.

'Of course.' Vivian tapped the cigarette from its holder. 'I must say, you've been a model of restraint.'

'I don't know what you mean?'

'Not one question about the rough-hewn Mr Gaines.'

'I was there. I heard how he flattered you. He seems to regard you as some sort of oracle.' Susan paused. 'He certainly had no time for me.'

'Ah!' said Viv. 'There you're wrong. Unless my old eyes deceive me our Mr Gaines is loitering by the staff entrance even as we speak.'

Susan, with difficulty, did not turn round.

'What's he doing there?' she said.

'He obviously expected you to have shaken off the boring old battleaxe and is seizing an opportunity to whisper a few sweet nothings in your shell-like without me around,' Vivian said. 'He's a nomad, Susan, a newsman, a stranger in a strange land. He's probably hoping you'll take pity on him and show him, shall we say, the sights. It's your own fault for flirting with him in the first place.'

'I did *not* flirt with him, Vivian.'

'Try telling him that,' Viv said, then, turning on her heel, headed for Oxford Street and left it to Susan to repair her tarnished reputation as best she could.

2

When the Welshman touched him Danny Cahill flinched and sat up. It was pitch dark in the bedroom, so dark that the hand that brushed his hair seemed disembodied.

There was nothing remotely sensual in Silwyn Griffiths's touch. He was merely being careful not to poke a finger into Danny's eye or up one frozen nostril. As soon as Danny sat up the hand floated away, swallowed by the all-encompassing darkness.

'What time is it?' Danny whispered.

'Ten to six.'

'What the hell're you doin' up so early?'

The stealthy creak of floorboards and a soft little 'ow' as Griff barked his shin on the dressing table were followed by the sound of the blackout shutter being raised.

'It's crisp out there,' Griff intoned in the sing-song baritone that Danny hadn't quite got used to yet. 'Deep and crisp and even, one might say.'

'You mean, it's snowin' again?'

'Heavily.'

Danny propped himself up on the pillow.

'Therefore, no bus,' he said.

'No bikes either,' said Griffiths. 'We're on the hoof this morning, boyo, by the look of it.'

He lowered the noisy blackout shutter and switched on a bedside lamp. He was clad in a roll-neck sweater that one of his innumerable girlfriends had knitted for him, and the sheepskin coat his father, a hill farmer in Brecon, had handed down.

Danny had been raised in a Catholic orphanage where cleanliness was next to godliness but the prolonged spell of wintry weather had undermined his principles too. He slept in his underwear and settled for a dab with a damp washcloth in Mrs Pell's kitchenette in preference to the icy cold of the bathroom on the landing.

Sucking in a breath, he flung aside the bedclothes, reached for his shirt and trousers and dressed quickly.

'What if we can't make it, Griff?'

'The boys on the night shift will stay on. We are, however, obliged to gird our sturdy loins and give it a go. You're a Scot, for heaven's sake,' said Griff. 'I thought you'd be used to weather like this.'

'I haven't set foot in Scotland in years,' Danny said. 'Anyroads, I was reared in Glasgow not a bloody Highland croft. Are you ready for breakfast?'

'I am. Indeed, I am,' Griff said, and led the way downstairs to the only warm room in the house: the kitchen.

They were billeted in a semi-detached council house in Deaconsfield, a tiny hamlet three miles from the monitoring unit in the grounds of the Wood Norton estate. They were more fortunate than some of their colleagues, for certain members of the rural community were suspicious of, not to say downright hostile towards, the eccentric foreigners that the BBC had dumped on their doorsteps.

The Pells were not of that ilk. Mr Pell was a lanky man with a laconic sense of humour and Mrs Pell, as small and chirpy as a sparrow, wasn't fazed by her lodgers' erratic hours and gave good value for her billeting fee when it came to dishing up the required two hot meals a day.

'My dear lady,' Griffiths purred, 'we'd no intention of dragging you from your beauty sleep at this unholy hour. I do hope we didn't wake you and, if we did, I can only offer my apologies. I say, is that French toast?'

The sight of thick slices of bread dipped in egg and fried to a golden brown made Danny's stomach rumble. He balanced his plate on the edge of the dresser and attacked the toast with a fork.

'Fifty-seven below in Finland, Mr Pell tells me,' Mrs Pell said. 'Heard it on the news. Even the Russians are dropping like flies, Mr Pell says. You'll know all about that, I suppose.'

The Pells were aware that Griffiths and Danny helped compile the daily Digest of Foreign Broadcasts, a thirty-thousand-word document dispatched to an ever-growing number of ministries and government departments, and were forever fishing for inside information on the state of the war in Europe, information that Griff and Danny mischievously refused to surrender.

'Fifty-seven below, eh?' said Griff. 'I wonder what sort of reading we have in Deaconsfield this morning. Whatever it is, we'd better get a move on before it gets any worse.'

He picked up the last piece of toast, stuffed it into his mouth and washed it down with tea. He wiped his fingers on the skirts of his coat, fished a knitted woollen cap from his pocket and fitted it snugly over his curly hair.

Danny settled for an old cloth cap.

'Got your gas masks, both of you?' Mrs Pell asked.

'Fully equipped, Mrs P,' Griff assured her.

'Will you be home for supper?'

'Lap of the gods, I'm afraid,' said Griff. 'Especially in this weather.' He unlatched the back door and stepped into the porch.

Drifting snow covered the steps and formed a steep bank against the side of the garden shed. There wasn't a warden within miles of Deaconsfield but Mrs Pell, taking no chances, swiftly closed the door behind them.

'God, what a mornin',' Danny said, shivering. 'Be no mail delivered today, I doubt.'

'And no letters from your lovely wife,' said Griff and yelped when Danny shoved him out into the snow.

Many of the women who worked in Broadcasting House would have been flattered by Robert Gaines's attentions, others would have been irritated by his inability to come to the point and one or two shy virgins, fresh up from the country and not yet wise in the ways of the world, would perhaps have viewed him as a serious threat to their maidenhood.

Susan, however, was neither impatient nor virginal and after four years consorting with Vivian's gang of right-wing toffs and sleazy intellectuals regarded herself as flatter-proof.

Her sister-in-law, Breda, would undoubtedly have forced the issue by throwing herself, bosom first, at Robert Gaines.

Breda had always been attracted to large, bear-like men.

In her halcyon days, before Ronnie had knocked her up and had gallantly agreed to marry her, Breda had run up an impressive tally of wrestlers and boxers, not to mention the odd Irish scallywag, all of whom, being the kind of men they were, had ridden off into the sunset as soon as they'd had their way with her. At least, Susan thought wistfully, Breda had had some fun before she'd settled down; *her* solitary affair had brought nothing but heartache in the end.

No more broken hearts now, she told herself, as she stood before the mirror in the ladies' cloakroom on the third floor of Broadcasting House and applied a light touch of natural lipstick and an even lighter dusting of face powder to disguise the fatigue that several hours of taking dictation from Mr Basil Willets had laid upon her.

She was no longer the uncultured young girl who'd crept out of Shadwell to work as a temporary secretary to lawyers, doctors and City gents but she was, she supposed, still pretty enough to attract the attention of sensible men now she'd learned to disguise her East End origins.

In fact, she'd left her roots and her family far behind even before she'd stumbled into marriage with kind, caring and utterly dependable Danny Cahill, a marriage that war, and her job with the BBC, threatened to undermine.

Now, with Danny out of sight if not entirely out of mind and every day tainted by uncertainty she was almost, if not quite, ready to throw caution to the winds and embrace the opportunity for a romantic adventure that chance, mere chance, had blown her way.

She put on her overcoat, hat, scarf and woollen gloves and made her way down by the stairs to the main reception area at the front of the building.

No light now, no gleam or glow was allowed to spill out into the street, for Broadcasting House was no longer a beacon to the world. 'The BBC must set an example,' the memo had read. 'It is the responsibility of all staff members to ensure that blackout restrictions are strictly observed.' Thick layers of dark green paint and metal shutters had taken care of the windows, all the windows on all floors, but the foyer and reception hall had caused problems.

She crossed the gloomy reception hall to the huge, heavily weighted drapes that covered the bronze doorway, curtains stolen, it was said, from the old Hoxton Empire; a rumour that, like so many rumours these days, had turned out to be false. The elderly commissionaire heaved aside the slip curtain and let her enter the muffled passage between the curtains and then, with much flapping, the duty policeman opened the doors and released her on to the pavement.

Half past six o'clock, the cold so keen that it scalded your skin: Susan turned up her coat collar and glanced towards the steps of All Souls Church where Robert Gaines might or might not be waiting.

There was no sign tonight of the American. If she'd been younger and less sure of herself she would have lingered on the pavement in the hope that he might show up but she was no wan little typist desperate for love and, like time and tide, would wait for no man. Besides, she had a gut feeling that Mr Gaines might be playing a game, not to tease but to test her; a novel kind of seduction that she found both irksome and exciting.

Of their three casual encounters in the past week none had led to dinner and dancing but only to coffee and cake in a café off Wigmore Street, surrounded by noisy young nurses and doctors in smart new uniforms, and a half-hour's guarded conversation in which neither Robert nor she seemed willing to give much away.

Squaring her shoulders, she walked on without breaking step. If he comes, he comes, she thought, and if he doesn't, well, that's up to him. He was, after all, a hard-pressed working journalist with deadlines to meet and for all she knew, for all he'd told her, might even now be on a boat heading for France or Italy or even off home to New York.

She had almost convinced herself that she didn't care when, waving his hat in the air, Robert Gaines appeared out of nowhere and, calling her name, hurried to join her.

'I thought I'd missed you,' he said.

'You almost did,' said Susan.

'Coffee,' he said, 'or would you rather have a drink?'

'Coffee,' she said, 'will be fine, particularly if you're pushed for time.'

'I'm always pushed for time. You know how it is.'

'Of course,' Susan said and, taking his arm, accompanied him through the darkened streets to the café just off Wigmore Street to play another cautious game of pussyfoot for the next half-hour or so.

Breda's mother, Nora Romano, thought that Ronnie in his fireman's uniform was the handsomest thing on two legs. Lots of women in Shadwell agreed with her. Even the old croakers, who should have known better, simpered a little when Ron strode up Fawley Street with the peak of his cap pulled down to hide the gimlet gaze he'd developed since trading a butcher's apron for a heavy wool tunic with a double row of chrome buttons.

It wasn't the old croakers that worried Breda as much as the young chicks who breezed about the East End at the wheel of ambulances or manned telephones in command posts and who, in Breda's jaundiced opinion, would have the trousers off any feller under the age of seventy who looked as if he might be up for a bit of hanky-panky now that conscription had thinned the ranks of available males, including husbands.

For that reason, among others, Breda had retreated from the school on the Commercial Road where, at the crack of dawn on the last day of August, half the mothers and children in the East End had assembled, complete with gas masks, rucksacks, suitcases and a mournful assortment of dolls and teddy bears, to be herded off to God knows where.

She'd taken one look at the doleful mob and, with Billy clinging to her hand, had turned tail and legged it back to the terraced house in Pitt Street where Ronnie, in vest and drawers, had been seated at the kitchen table bleakly toying with a poached egg.

'Changed your mind, 'ave you, love?' he'd said. 'Can't say I blame you,' and that, much to Breda's relief, had brought an end to all talk of leaving Shadwell.

As penance for remaining in London she was obliged to escort Billy to a school on the far side of Cable Street where in a half-empty classroom the handful of kiddies who'd stayed behind were taught the three Rs by a bad-tempered old spinster. The teacher did not like Billy, Billy did not care for the teacher, and Breda didn't like anything about the school, particularly the earth-filled sandbags that leaked filthy brown sludge across the playground, sludge that winter had turned to ice.

On that particular morning, she gave her son a kiss, made sure he had tuppence for his dinner and, with the usual twinge of anxiety, watched him join his chums on the slides that criss-crossed the playground. Then, flipping up her coat collar and sticking her hands in her pockets, she set off for Stratton's Dining Rooms where her mother continued to dish up grub to cabmen and dock workers and, increasingly, to men and women in unfamiliar uniforms who popped in off the street in search of a sandwich or a bowl of soup.

She had barely left the school gate when a long, black, bullet-nosed motorcar prowled up behind her and drew to a halt at the kerb. The nearside door swung open.

'Get in,' the driver said.

Clutching her coat to her throat, Breda stepped back.

'For God's sake, Breda, will you just get in.'

'Is 'e with you?' she asked.

'Nope. It's just me. Get in an' I'll drive you home.'

'I ain't goin' 'ome.'

'All right. I'll drop you wherever you wanna go.'

She had no fear of Steve Millar, her father's right-hand man. In fact, when Ronnie had been off fighting in Spain, she'd almost given her all to Steve in the back row of a local cinema. She hadn't clapped eyes on him for a couple of years, though, and was gratified to note that he was still smooth and fresh-faced and so fit you could almost see his muscles rippling under his alpaca overcoat.

She tucked a straggle of bleached blonde hair under her headscarf and then, sighing, climbed into the passenger seat. Steve reached across her lap and closed the door.

'That Billy?' he said.

'Who else would it be?' said Breda.

18

'He's grown since I saw him last.'

'Yeah,' Breda said. 'He's gonna be tall, like 'is dad.'

Steve took off his gloves, dug a packet of Player's from his overcoat pocket, knocked out two cigarettes, lit them and passed one to Breda.

'I got a kid too,' he said.

A faint sense of disappointment stirred in Breda, as if fathering a child had robbed Steve Millar of virility.

She said, 'Boy or girl?'

'Boy. Cyril.'

'Cyril?'

'Rita picked it, not me.'

'Don't tell me you married that redhead?'

'Who said anything about marriage?'

'Nah.' Breda blew smoke. 'You aren't that sort, Steve. You've given over to the old ball an' chain. Admit it.'

He grinned. 'Yeah, you're right. I'm spliced good an' proper.'

'Why'd you do it? To keep out of the army?'

'Havin' a kid ain't gonna keep nobody out of the army,' Steve said, 'leastways not for long. When things get really nasty we'll all be fair game for cannon fodder.'

'Where you living?'

'Got a flat not far from the club.'

As a child Breda had been unaware that her absent father earned his living on the shady side of the street. It had shocked her to discover that the Brooklyn Club, which her dad managed on behalf of some big-shot gangster, wasn't much more than a glorified knocking shop.

'Is he still runnin' that dump?' she said. 'I thought it might 'ave closed 'cause of the war.'

'One thing about a war,' Steve said, 'especially a phoney war, it brings all these young geezers with cash in their pockets pouring into London. All they want is to get a leg over before they ship out. It's like takin' candy off a baby.'

Breda hesitated then, unable to resist, asked, 'Your wife, Rita, she still work there?'

'Now an' then.'

'Doin' what?'

'She helps your old man with the books an' stuff.'

'What sorta stuff?'

Steve assumed the clamped-down expression that Danny Cahill described as deadpan, but Danny and Steve, as different as chalk from cheese, had never really got on.

'She looks after the girls, if you must know,' he said. 'You goin' to your ma's place?'

'Yeah, Stratton's,' said Breda.

He released the handbrake, fiddled with the gear-stick and eased the car into motion.

Breda said, 'How'd you know where to find me?'

'Leo always knows where to find you.'

'Is me dad in trouble?'

'Not him. He just don't want to get you involved in anything shifty, especially right now.'

They drove into Shannon Street at the top of Oxmoor Road where the fire station was. She resisted the temptation to point it out, for some folk regarded auxiliary firemen as little better than cowards.

She said, 'You coming in to see Ma?'

'Nope.'

'What *are* you doin' doggin' my footsteps?'

'Leo wants to know why you an' Billy ha'n't left London for a safe place in the country.'

'Does 'e?' Breda said. 'Well, you tell 'im to mind 'is own damned business.'

'He can get you out, you want out?'

'Out?' said Breda. 'Out where?'

'Canada.'

'Canada? What would I want to go there for?'

'Leo knows people in Canada who'll give you a new home an' a new life.'

'The three of us, you mean?'

Steve paused. 'He can't get a passport for Ronnie.'

'Well, I ain't leavin' without Ronnie.'

'When did you become so bloody loyal?' Steve said. 'If I was you I'd jump at the chance of gettin' out.'

'Why don'cha then?'

'I got responsibilities.'

'An' I haven't?' said Breda.

There wasn't much traffic in Shannon Street, even less in Thornton Street, just two blokes on bicycles and a taxi-cab with a big hand-printed sign pasted to the rear window announcing that the driver was engaged in Civil Defence.

The window of the pork butcher's shop where Ronnie had worked was boarded up. Herr Brauschmidt and his wife, having suffered discrimination during the last war, had thrown in the towel and gone off to live with one of their sons in Milwaukee. Gertler's Kosher Butchers remained open, though, for there were still plenty of Jews in Shadwell to keep the tills ringing.

'If you're not comin' in to see Ma, drop me 'ere.'

Steve shrugged and brought the car to a halt fifty yards short of the dining rooms.

Ronnie and his father, Matt, had boarded up Stratton's big window but had left a neat slot of glass, like a letterbox, at eye level so you could peep inside and see steam rising from the coffee urn and the rock cakes Nora had baked slanted towards you on a tray. The daily Bill of Fare, chalked on a blackboard, was propped against the wall below the window, though Matt and the local ARP warden argued heatedly whether or not it constituted a hazard to pedestrians and should be removed.

Canada, Breda thought: Canada was just trees and mountains, all wide-open spaces. If there was one thing she hated it was wide-open spaces.

She sighed and tapped Steve's arm.

'Listen,' she said, 'tell 'im thanks, but no thanks. I appreciate the offer, like, but I'm London born an' bred an' I'm not about to go runnin' off an' abandon the old homestead just 'cause some loony says I got to.'

'Your old man ain't no loony.'

'I didn't mean him; I meant Adolf.'

'Things is pretty quiet right now,' Steve said, 'but don't kid yourself. As soon as Hitler claws in Belgium, France and any place else he fancies England will be next. When that happens it'll be too late.'

'Too late for what?'

'To get out.'

'Told you once, tell you again, I don't want out.'

'Breda, Breda.' Steve Millar shook his head. 'You always was a stubborn cow. I just hope you know what you're lettin' yourself in for.'

''Course I do. I listen to the wireless.'

'Well, at least let me tell Leo you're thinkin' about it.'

'If it makes you feel any better, okay,' Breda said. 'But don't let 'im get 'is hopes up.'

She leaned back to let him open the door, slid from the car with as much poise as she could muster, closed the door with her knee then rapped on the window and watched it roll down.

'What?' Steve said.

'Give Cyril a kiss from me, will yah?'

He laughed. 'Sure I will,' he said and drove off down Thornton Street into Docklands Road, leaving Breda shivering on the pavement and more than a little confused.

3

Three days passed before Susan saw Robert again. He was waiting for her outside Broadcasting House and led her through the side streets to Oxford Circus. Blackout restrictions had eased in the past few weeks but the glimmer of light from reopened theatres and cinemas and the hooded headlamps of buses and taxis was still too dim to make the crossing anything but hazardous.

'I feel bad about this,' Robert Gaines said.

'Bad about what?' said Susan.

'Stealing you away from Viv at this ungodly hour.'

'Viv's only my friend, not my keeper,' Susan said, 'and she's had quite enough of my company lately. Is she still bending your ear with tales of Tom Mosley and his dastardly crew or has she finally run out of interesting things to say?'

'Hell, no. She has enough lowdown to keep me on my toes for months.'

'Lowdown?'

'Inside information.'

'I know what the word means,' Susan said. 'I'm just puzzled as to what sort of "lowdown" Vivian can provide. Did she tell you I was on late call tonight?'

'She didn't have to.'

'No, I did rather drop you a hint, didn't I?'

'That you did.'

'I was beginning to think you were wedded to your typewriter and wouldn't show up.'

'Aren't you pleased to see me?'

'Of course I am,' she said.

She had no idea where he was taking her. He'd been chatting to a policeman at the entrance in Portland Place when she'd come off shift and had invited her to join him for supper as nonchalantly as if they were intimate friends. She was wary, but she was also hungry, hungry and bored and the thought of returning to her empty flat in Rothwell Gardens to eat supper alone held no appeal.

He steered her across the Circus into Regent Street and, skirting the sandbags in front of Liberty's, turned into a narrow side street and abruptly drew up.

'Well,' he said, 'this is the place.'

'What place, exactly?'

'Down there,' he said, 'in the basement.'

She hesitated. 'What is it – an air-raid shelter?'

'It's a perfectly respectable nightclub, Miss Hooper. Nothing going on of which your mama would disapprove. What's wrong? Don't you trust me?'

'Not as far as I can throw you,' Susan said.

The door of the club opened and faint blue light lit up the well. She heard dance music. Leaning over her shoulder, Robert showed the doorman a card of some sort. A moment later, they were ushered into a narrow, wood-panelled passageway and the door was closed behind them.

The doorman, a gaunt middle-aged man in an old-fashioned dinner suit, relieved them of their overcoats.

'Many in tonight, Charlie?' Robert asked.

'The usual crowd,' Charlie answered. 'Some Canadian flyers we haven't seen before. High-rankers. Mr Slocum was asking after you.'

'He still here?'

'No, he left about an hour ago.'

'With a girl?'

'What do you think?' Charlie said.

Robert led her down the corridor into the supper room where tables were arranged round a dance floor and a six-piece band was playing. Off to the side was a bar which, in deference to the licensing laws, already seemed to be closed.

The tables were occupied mainly by men in uniform. Couples were dancing to an up-beat tune that Susan knew but couldn't name. To her relief, the girls were just like her, smart but not glamorous: secretaries, perhaps, or counter hands from better-class stores.

'Would you care to dance?' Robert asked.

It had been years since last she'd danced and she'd never danced with Danny, not even on their honeymoon.

'I think,' she said, 'I'd rather eat, if you don't mind.'

Robert pulled out a chair. 'I don't mind at all.'

The table was draped with a spotless linen cloth and lit by a tiny electrical lamp the cord of which seemed to be contained in one of the table legs.

Susan tucked in her skirt and seated herself.

'Does this place have a name?' she asked.

'The Blue Lagoon.'

'Is it a private club?'

'Anyone can join if they have the dough.'

'I see,' Susan said. 'This is a proper date then?'

'What sort of a date did you think it might be?'

'I thought you might be trying to have me on the cheap.'

'Have you?' he said, surprised. 'Aren't English girls supposed to be modest and unassuming?'

'Modest but not stupid.'

If his reaction was anything to go by, she had seriously misjudged Mr Gaines. Perhaps she'd spent too much time with Vivian's crowd where sexual allusion was a mainstay of conversation and almost every relationship was a subtle form of seduction.

'If you care to stand me a steak, a baked potato and a glass of wine,' she said, 'I think we might consider beginning this relationship again – on a somewhat different footing.'

'Would beginning again include dancing?' Robert said.

'I do believe it would,' said Susan.

It was peaceful in the Hoopers' kitchen that cold January night. Ron had tracked down a wavelength that supplied sweet music uninterrupted by news bulletins. He sprawled in the wooden-armed chair by the fireside, feet on the fender and a magazine on his lap.

'What you doin', love?' he asked.

'Writin' a letter,' Breda answered.

'You,' he said, 'writin' a letter. I don't believe it.'

Breda continued to scribble on the sheet of lined paper she'd extracted from one of Billy's school jotters.

'Danny,' she said. 'I'm writin' to Danny.'

'For why?'

''Cause he hasn't heard from Susan.'

'How do you know he hasn't heard from Susan?'

'He told me.'

'How?' said Ronnie.

'Sent me a letter.'

'You never said nothin' to me about a letter.'

'Wasn't addressed to you.'

Before he'd married Susan Hooper, Danny had lodged with the Romanos and had been like a big brother to Breda while she was growing up. Ronnie wasn't daft enough to suppose there might be anything lovey-dovey in Danny's letter, or in her reply; even so Breda was guarded.

'What's he sayin' then?' Ron asked.

'Wants to know if we've seen Susan.'

'We haven't, have we?'

''Course we 'aven't,' Breda said. 'Your sister's far too high-falutin' for the likes of us these days. She might at least 'ave the decency to send 'im some socks.'

'Socks?' said Ronnie. 'He's not a bleedin' Tommy.'

Breda sucked the end of her pencil. 'I wonder what she's really up to. I bet she's got a feller.'

'She's not up to anythin',' Ron said. 'I expect she's busy. Everyone's busy these days. There's a—'

'War on: yeah, I know.'

'We saw her an' Danny at Christmas, didn't we?'

'For half a bleedin' hour – an' we ain't heard a word from 'er since.' Breda nibbled the pencil end as if it were a breadstick. 'Maybe she's gone to Canada.'

'Canada!' Ronnie exclaimed. 'Why the heck would she go to Canada?'

'Dunno,' said Breda. 'More like, she's found some toff at the BBC to 'ave fun with.'

'Our Susan ain't like that,' said Ronnie.

'They're all like that, 'er kind.'

'Her kind? For God's sake, Breda, she's one of us.'

'No, she ain't. She was brought up to think she was special. Got your old man to thank for that.'

'Well, she hasn't done too bad, has she? Jobs at the BBC don't grow on trees.'

'She's only a typist.'

'She's a producer's assistant.'

'Whatever the 'ell that is,' said Breda. 'She should be a proper wife to Danny an' be with 'im in 'is hour of need.'

'His hour of need?' said Ron scornfully. 'He's sittin' on his arse somewhere in Worcestershire floggin' a typewriter. My guess, Susie's just up to her eyes in work.'

'She's wayward,' Breda said. 'She's always been wayward. Marrying Danny hasn't changed 'er.'

Ron hoisted himself from the armchair and came to the table. Breda took the pencil from her mouth and automatically covered the half-written page with her forearm. She shivered when he brushed the hair at the back of her neck.

'Jealous, are yah?' Ron said.

'Why would I be jealous of your sister?'

''Cause she got Danny an' all you got was me.'

'An' Billy,' Breda reminded him. 'Billy first.'

'What a bargain that was, eh?' Ron said.

'Huh!' said Breda. 'Some bleedin' bargain.'

Then, abandoning her letter, she let her husband kiss her and, ten minutes later, carry her, fireman's style, upstairs to bed.

Twelve guineas a week for a shared flat in Lansdowne House was a tad more than Bob Gaines could comfortably afford.

Pete Slocum, the *Union Post*'s number one reporter, had talked him into it.

The Lansdowne was the only residential club in London to admit women on equal terms with men and a bunch of the top guys, male and female, were holed up there. Anyhow, he felt he owed Pete something for steering him towards Vivian Proudfoot whose brother had been an active fascist in the 1930s and, according to the grapevine, remained at liberty on his farm near Hereford only because some bigwig had pulled strings to keep him out of prison.

Bob had made it plain from the outset what he wanted from Vivian. He liked the woman and had no wish to deceive her. He liked Susan Hooper too, but didn't quite know what to make of her. She was no traditional English rose, prim and self-contained; nor was she one of that breed of girl who could be, at one and the same time, both sexless and alluring and, according to Slocum, spelled trouble with a capital T.

When it came to judging women Pete was generally regarded as an expert. Rarely a night went by but some soft little form would be curled up in Slocum's bed or discovered, sleepy-eyed, at the breakfast table.

'Would you take umbrage if I told you I expected more of you?' Susan said.

'More?' Robert said. 'More of what?'

'I thought you were planning to sweep me off my feet.'

'Why? Because I'm an American?'

'Because you're a foreign correspondent.'

They had eaten in a Corner House and caught an early showing of Errol Flynn playing the hero in *Dodge City*.

Now, about nine, they were drinking coffee in a café on Charing Cross Road.

'Do you want me to sweep you off your feet?' he said.

'I'm not sure what I want. A little excitement in my life would not be unwelcome, I suppose.'

'What about this programme you're involved with? Won't that put fire in your belly?'

'Too early to say. My boss, Mr Willets, is struggling to come up with a format to attract an American audience.'

'Influence an American audience, you mean?'

'That is the general idea, yes.'

'Don't they say propaganda is a weapon fit only for bullies and gangsters?' Robert said. 'I guess that doesn't apply to the BBC?'

'You think we English are all wishy-washy, don't you? Smug, class-ridden and irresolute, isn't that what you called us in your article from Munich, which I just happen to have read? Why won't you take me seriously?' She hesitated. 'Is it because I have a husband?'

'I didn't even know you had a husband.'

'Didn't Viv tell you?'

'No, Viv didn't tell me,' Robert Gaines said. 'Why haven't you told me before now?'

'It didn't seem relevant.'

'Where is your husband?'

'He works for the BBC too. Out of town.'

'Are you saying you come with strings?'

'Does a husband count as strings?'

'In my book, yes,' Robert said.

'I'm just trying to be honest with you.'

'That isn't my idea of honesty. Correct me if I'm wrong but are you stating terms for an affair?'

'I suppose I am, rather.'

It was dark outside in the street. The window glass was painted green and passers-by moved across it like shadows from a nether world. Robert sat quite still, looking down at the grounds in his empty cup. He said nothing for eight or ten seconds, then pushed himself to his feet.

'Are you going home now?' he asked.

'No, back to Portland Place,' she answered. 'Mr Willets hasn't lost his penchant for convening late-night meetings.'

'I'll find you a cab.'

'I'm happy to walk. We've lots of time.'

'No, Susan,' Robert Gaines said. 'I'm afraid your time has just run out.' Placing a handful of coins on a saucer, he buttoned his overcoat, stuck on his hat and left her to settle the bill.

It wasn't until war came that Vivian realised what an idle life she'd led. In her forty-seven years, she'd published only four books and a handful of feature articles, a pace of production that certainly wouldn't challenge the average Fleet Street hack or, for that matter, any of the popular historians who cranked out weighty tomes on England's glorious past at, it seemed, the rate of one a fortnight.

Organisation had never been her strong suit and since Susan's departure she'd had no assistant. Books were piled in every corner of the office in her mews house in Salt Street, notes and newspaper cuttings scattered around the typewriter upon which Vivian, with two fingers, now did, as it were, her own dirty work.

She had laboured late into the night on her new book, *An Enemy in Our Midst*. It had started out as a study of political alienation during and after the Great War but had gradually become more open-ended, a fact that hadn't escaped Viv's agent who, well aware of his client's piecemeal approach to research and the snail's pace at which she worked, feared that the war might be over before she delivered a first draft.

Viv was still tired when Susan arrived at Salt Street shortly before noon and reprimanded her friend a little more forcefully than she'd intended.

'I don't see why you're making such a fuss,' Susan responded. 'And I certainly resent you sticking your nose into matters that don't concern you.'

'Matters that do concern Danny, however.'

'I know I've been remiss this past month but I've every intention of making up for it now.'

'Now?' said Vivian, scowling. 'Why now?'

'Mr Gaines and I have had a parting of the ways.'

'Surely you didn't reject his advances?'

'In fact, he made no advances. None at all.'

'So you didn't . . .'

'Of course I didn't. What do you take me for?'

'What were you doing with him then?'

Susan shrugged. 'Tempting fate, I suppose. As soon as I told him I was married he lost interest.'

'A man of principle; how unusual,' Vivian said. 'You shouldn't have encouraged him in the first place, you know.'

'Are we lunching, or are we not?' Susan said testily. 'Anywhere but L'Étoile suits me.'

'So you've given up flirting with foreign newsmen, have you?' Viv said.

'Only for the time being,' said Susan.

4

Whether it was luck or a degree of foresight unusual in the upper echelons of BBC administration no one could be sure, but some bright spark had seen fit to acquire the Greenhill Hotel, lock, stock and barrel, to serve as a non-residential social club for all the Evesham exiles. Here in the spacious lounge or the crowded bar one might rub shoulders – or ankles – with secretaries, typists and engineers as well as administrators, editors and over-worked translators.

The communal delights of the Greenhill almost made up for working conditions in the villa – Mrs Smith's house – in the grounds of Wood Norton Hall where listening, transcribing and editing staff were crammed together to process the foreign broadcasts that came down from the receiving station on top of the hill.

For reasons never explained, Susan's three letters were addressed to Danny care of the steward at the Greenhill.

Danny received them gratefully and retired to a quiet corner of the card room to read them in peace; three type-written letters filled with generalised BBC tittle-tattle and very little else, nothing about Breda or Nora, for instance, or what she, Susan, had been up to out of hours.

At the upright piano in the lounge, Griff whiled away the

time by playing a medley of popular tunes and displaying his noble profile to any young lady who happened to drift by in the hope that she might mistake him for Jack Buchanan which, oddly, no young lady ever did.

He had just embarked on a silly song about tulips when Danny, bearing two glasses, appeared at his side.

'Celebrating, are we?' Griffiths asked.

'After a fashion,' Danny answered. 'My wife's involved in puttin' together a new programme an' hasn't had a minute to spare to write to me until now.'

'Do you believe her?'

'Of course I believe her.'

Griff rolled whisky around in his mouth. 'I assume the new programme has some stuffing to it or it wouldn't be going out from London. Who's producing?'

'Willets.'

'Never heard of him,' said Griff. 'Which is hardly surprising since I did my training in Cardiff. Has he really chosen your wife to be his assistant?'

'It certainly looks like it,' Danny said. 'If we drink up, we might be able to catch the bus as far as the Cross. I'm starved for my supper.'

'Nothing like a letter from the wife to restore a man's appetite.' Griff knocked back the remains of his whisky. 'Precious little going on here tonight, anyway. I'm not tempted to hang around to listen to some learned gentleman lecturing us for the umpteenth time on the political situation in Albania. Are you sure the bus is running?'

'Aye, the army's cleared the road as far as the railway station. We can catch it outside if we hurry.'

★

The bus was an ancient charabanc with a square roof and a door at the rear like a Black Maria. According to Mr Pell it had been the first motorised vehicle on regular service in the Vale of Evesham and should have been pensioned off years ago.

There were no lights in the streets of the market town. Snow scalloped the eaves of the fine old buildings and moulded the pavements between the snow-carpeted gardens that flanked the road to the railway station. The station exit was lit by a single dim blue light. A solitary female figure was huddled under it, a suitcase by her side.

The bus ground to a halt. The conductor, a taciturn old fellow, fumbled with the door handle and put down a short wooden ladder to enable the female passenger to climb aboard. She pushed the suitcase into the aisle between the benches and, in a cloud of cold air, followed it.

The conductor retrieved the ladder, closed the door and from beneath the skirt of his coat fished out a machine like a mousetrap from which he extracted a ticket. The woman paid her fare and settled on the bench opposite the men. The bus shuddered, lurched round in a circle and prowled uphill past the deserted market square.

Half hidden by a hood, the woman's solemn features were just visible in the faint light. Her ungloved hands, slender and long-fingered, were clenched in the lap of her coat. She continued to look down at her hands until the bus stopped by the Cross where the road to Deaconsfield branched off into stark, silent orchards and icy fields.

'Is this as far as you go?' she asked, looking up.

In this weather, the conductor told her, it was.

Griff was fast off the mark.

'Are you getting off here, miss?'

'Yes, it seems I am.'

'Allow me to assist you with your suitcase.'

The conductor opened the door and dropped the ladder. Danny signalled Griff to exit first then courteously took the young woman's arm to help her alight.

She gave a little nod of gratitude and stepped down into the swirl of powdery snow that blew off the hedges.

They stood together, all three, and watched the bus swing back towards the High Street and disappear.

'At the risk of being inquisitive,' Griffiths said, 'might I ask who you are and what you're doing at Deaconsfield Cross all alone on a cold winter's night?'

'Katarina Cottrell. I expected to be met.'

'Met where? Here? No chance of that, I'm afraid.'

'No, at the station. I have papers.'

'Papers? What sort of papers?' Griff said.

They huddled close, facing each other. She had slipped the hood and Danny could make out dark hair and dark anxious eyes. She had the trace of an accent and might, he thought, be a Russian, a Pole or a refugee from some country in the Balkans.

'I've come to work at Wood Norton. I was told I'd be met by a welfare officer.'

'There's obviously been a cock-up somewhere,' Griff said. 'I think we should take a look at these papers of yours.'

The hooded garment was neither coat nor jacket but a light half-length thing. She had a scarf at her throat but no gloves and her shoes, Danny noticed, were quite inadequate for negotiating icy country roads.

She crouched by the suitcase, opened it and brought

37

out a large envelope. She closed the case and, rising again, handed the envelope to Griffiths. He switched on his pocket torch and scanned first the envelope and then the documents it contained: a typed letter on BBC notepaper, two khaki-coloured employment cards and a travel pass.

'Well,' Griff said, 'if you are a German spy they've done a damned good job of forging the stationery. What do you think, Danny?'

'Looks okay tae me.'

'I'm not a spy,' the woman said. 'I'm a British citizen. Do you wish to see my identity card too?'

'Where's your gas mask?'

'In my case.'

Griff brought up the letter, held it close to his nose and poked the torch beam almost into the paper.

'There's an address where I'm to be lodged; a house in Deaconsfield, wherever that is,' the woman said. 'I'll find my own way there if you'll point me in the right direction.'

Griff peered at the letter again and laughed. 'We can do better than that, Miss Cottrell. We can take you there.' He flapped the letter in Danny's direction. 'Guess what, old boy: she's landed a billet with the Pells.'

'You're kiddin'.'

'I'm not.'

'I wonder if Mrs Pell's been informed,' said Danny.

'If she hasn't,' Griff said, 'she's in for a big surprise.'

The previous August, with war inevitable, Broadcasting House had been scoured of more than half its personnel. Twenty-two variety artists and an orchestra had been packed off to the Bristol studio, others sent to Manchester or Bangor or as far afield as Glasgow. But the BBC governors had failed to foresee that imminent invasion would not be so imminent after all and that the great British public, egged on by irascible newspaper columnists, would swiftly become bored with a dreary diet of news bulletins and organ recitals and demand more and better entertainment from the wireless.

By the beginning of the year, the first full year of war, the balance of programming had been adjusted and the listening public largely appeased.

Appeasing a government reluctant to communicate was another, less public matter and a need to disseminate information while giving nothing away had become a thorn in the flesh of the BBC's policy-makers. High-level, closed-door arguments as to what constituted reasonable comment as opposed to flagrant propaganda came down as mere whispers to the rank and file, however, and even Basil Willets wasn't privy to all the issues at stake.

Mr Willets was small, sharp-featured and, though not yet fifty, almost, if not quite, bald. Appearances could be deceiving, however; he was not afraid to take the initiative when all around were dithering, an approach that served him well when it came to getting his own way.

Mr Willets's office was situated off the corridor that surrounded the studios on the third floor of the tower. As offices went it was fairly spacious and held not only Mr Willets's desk but, unusually, a small, almost child-sized desk for his assistant, Susan Hooper.

Carrying her shorthand notebooks, Susan followed Mr Willets into the room. A nervous young civil servant from an unspecified ministry trailed after them and, while Susan busied herself at her desk, exchanged a few words with the producer before he was shown the door.

'Fool!' Mr Willets said, sighing. 'If he supposes for one moment I'm going to take heed of anything that originates with his ministry he'd better think again.' He looked up. 'You didn't hear me say that, Miss Hooper, did you?'

'Say what, sir?' said Susan.

Mr Willets uttered a wry little snort that was his substitute for laughter and lowered himself on to the upright chair behind his desk.

'Do you wish me to type up the minutes, sir?'

'Lord, no. For all that's in them, tomorrow will do.'

'May I go?'

'By all means.' He rocked back on the chair, hands behind his head, like a captured prisoner. 'Just before you do, tell me, Miss Hooper, what do you make of them?'

'Make of what, Mr Willets?'

'The first crop of ideas,' he said. 'Please, be frank.'

Susan perched on the edge of her desk, folded her arms and pondered an answer.

'I think,' she said at length, 'you put them on the spot.'

'Really?'

'Which,' Susan went on, 'was rather unfair. You gave them no advance warning of what you expected from them, therefore they had nothing to say.'

'Go on.'

'I believe you have ideas enough of your own, Mr Willets, and you called another late-night meeting simply to forestall criticism that you're . . .' Susan hesitated.

'Yes?'

'Uncooperative.'

He snorted again. 'I see I'll have to keep an eye on you; you're too clever by half. Now, what do you make of *The Times* listing the wavelengths of German radio stations for the benefit of its readers? Why do you suppose German broadcasts in English are so popular here?'

'They have top-notch newscasters.'

Mr Willets brought the front legs of the chair to the floor and propped his elbows on the desk.

'Precisely,' he said. 'They have radio "stars" backed by excellent research. The Germans also have the advantage of uncertainty, of being able to trade on our doubts and fears. Something we – I mean this department – won't have when it comes to broadcasting to America. What we need first and foremost is a strong, convincing voice that people will trust.'

'Must it be someone from within the Corporation?'

'Not necessarily.'

'Perhaps an American might best fill the bill.'

'Hmm,' Mr Willets said. 'You know, I never thought of that. Trouble is, the best of the American journalists are already under contract to CBS.'

'Not all of them,' Susan said.

He cocked his head and studied her.

'Do you have a candidate in mind, Miss Hooper?'

'Actually,' Susan heard herself say, 'I do.'

The cable of the lamp wouldn't stretch as far as Danny's bedside and the room's only electrical socket was over by the window which was why the lamp had been placed on the floor and Danny, wrapped in quilt and blankets, was seated on the side of the mattress with Susan's letters scattered around him.

It would have been simpler to use a pocket torch but Griff claimed they were running low on batteries and must economise. With the sheepskin coat over his shoulders, a cigarette in his mouth and an ashtray balanced on his chest, he appeared content to sit up in bed and watch Danny pore over the letters from home.

Danny wasn't surprised when the Welshman said, 'Can you hear her, boyo? I swear I can. Breathing as gently as a summer breeze on her scented pillow next door.'

'She's snorin', that's all,' said Danny.

'Beauties like our Miss Cottrell do not snore.'

'She isn't our Miss Cottrell.'

'Not yet,' said Griff. 'But fate has been kind to us, Danny boy. Fate has been very kind, indeed.'

'Fate has nothin' to do with it. Some erk in admin cocked up,' Danny said. 'It's just as well Mrs Pell saw the funny side, an' had a bed to spare. I wonder what happened to the letter from Welfare. Lost in the post, like as not.'

'Now we have her, I trust we'll keep her.'

'Don't be so bloody daft. She's a clerical error. By tomorrow night she'll be settled somewhere else.'

'Mrs Pell is much taken with her.'

That much was true; precious few landladies would have greeted the unannounced arrival of a bedraggled stranger with such composure. Mrs Pell had taken it all in her stride. Dumplings had been added to the stew, more potatoes to the pot and a hot bath drawn to thaw out the poor lass. By the time supper had been served in the living room Katarina Cottrell – Kate – had been relaxed enough to answer the Pells' questions.

The only child of an Austrian mother and an English

father, she had been born in Linz, where her father had taught modern languages in the International Academy. She'd been educated at an English boarding school and had gone on to Oxford where she'd gained a First in Teutonic Studies, soon after which, on a tutor's recommendation, she'd been invited to join the BBC's monitoring unit.

'Are your parents still in Austria?' Danny asked.

'No, they left Linz in 1935. My father found a teaching post in a public school, St George's, near Coventry. He's still there, still teaching.'

'And we've got you?' Griff said. 'Only the best for old Hogsnorton. We pinched that name from one of Gillie Potter's pre-war monologues, by the way.'

He'd gone on to explain that work in the villa was not all sweat and tears and had mimed some of his colleagues' more outrageous eccentricities until Mrs Pell had reluctantly called a halt to the proceedings and shooed them off to bed.

It was late now, almost midnight, but Griff continued to wax lyrical on what joys the future might hold.

'It's obviously escaped someone's notice that two red-blooded males are already in residence chez Pell. We must be up with the lark tomorrow to see what strings we can pull to keep Miss Cottrell here,' Griff said. 'You wouldn't mind that, Danny, would you?'

'Nope,' said Danny, gathering up Susan's letters. 'I wouldn't mind that at all.'

5

Neither Breda nor her mother quite grasped the ins and outs of the war in Europe in spite of all the chat Stratton's customers exchanged over the tea mugs and coffee cups. Nora, in particular, couldn't understand what was going on between the Russians and the Finns up there in the frozen north, and, to the despair of her 'lodger', Matt, and her son-in-law, Ronnie, continued to refer to the General Secretary of the Communist Party of the Soviet Union as Herr Stalin.

The rationing of sugar, butter, bacon and ham worried Nora more than the rumours that Hitler had his sights on Belgium and Holland. Breda, however, was more able when it came to squaring up to possible shortages. She was fast out of the starting gate in currying favour with anyone who could help keep the larder filled and it wasn't long before extra stocks of sugar and salted butter piled up in the cupboards in the terraced house in Pitt Street, paid for by her wages, not Ronnie's.

It also crossed Breda's mind that if things got worse – and not everyone was sure they would – then she might call in her dues from her daddy who, she didn't doubt, would know people who knew people who would soon have the keys to a vast emporium of goods, lost, stolen and strayed, that might make wartime life more tolerable.

On nights when Ron was on duty she'd lie in bed and try to calculate just how many tins of peaches she might need to see the family through a war that had no end in sight.

In the room next door Billy was curled up in an army sleeping bag that his grandpa had bought from a shady market trader. Breda was warm enough in the double bed, provided she didn't roll too close to the outside wall, which was usually Ron's place anyway. She was still struggling with the problem of dividing days of the year into tins of fruit when she heard the stealthy creak of the bedroom door and saw a shadow pass across the wall above her head.

'Ron?' She sat up. 'Ron, is that you?'

No answer came from the shadowy figure.

'Ron,' she said, 'for God's sake stop muckin' about.'

The torch beam, as blinding as a searchlight, encompassed her. She opened her mouth to scream, then, remembering Billy asleep next door, clamped a hand to her mouth and drew her knees up to her chest.

Her first thought was that the Germans had invaded Shadwell in dead of night and that she was about to be raped. That was how they would do it, her father-in-law had told her. They'd come dropping down out of the skies on their parachutes when nobody expected it to round up all the men and rape all the women before they took over the country.

Breda peered, dazzled, into the light, and listened for sounds of other men, other Germans, crashing about in the kitchen or, worse, gleefully scrambling upstairs to pin her down and take her one after . . .

'Is he here?' said a voice, in English.

'Uh?' said Breda.

'Leo Romano, is he here?'

'Don't know what you're talkin' about.'

The beam slithered away, picking out objects in the room one by one then climbing up the far wall to illuminate the ceiling as if her daddy might be hanging there like a bat.

'Don't gimme that,' the voice said.

She peered at the figure at the foot of the bed: no webbing, no buckles, no swastikas, no gun. The intruder, she realised, wasn't a German invader but a plainclothes copper in the belted trench-coat and soft hat that was practically a uniform for the sneaky pigs from the Yard.

'Leo Romano, your father,' the copper said.

'Oh, that Leo Romano,' said Breda. 'Ha'n't seen 'im in years. What you want with 'im anyhow?'

'Never you mind what we want with 'im. Is he here?'

'Does it look like 'e's 'ere,' said Breda. 'Nobody in this 'ouse but me an' my kid. What you doin' breakin' in after dark without a warrant when my hubby ain't 'ome?'

'Don't need no warrant,' the copper said. 'Don't you read the papers, girly? No use you yowling about illegal entry. We've got a free 'and now. Where is he?'

'I told you, I ha'n't seen—'

'Your husband, I mean.'

'What you wanna know that for?'

'My report,' the copper said. But there was something in the way he said it, a slight patronising edge, that made Breda wonder if he really was a copper after all.

'My 'usband's a fireman. He's on watch up at the Oxmoor

46

Road station, you must know.' She sat forward. 'You ain't no copper, are yah?'

''Course, I am. Special Branch.'

'What's special about it?'

'Special powers. Now, who else is here?'

Doubt increased her caution. 'Only my kid.'

'I've searched 'is room already. He didn't even stir. I found all that stuff you got stashed away downstairs, though.'

'Bought an' paid for, all bought an' paid for.'

'Hoarding's illegal, case you didn't know,' the man said. 'I could have you up for that.'

He came closer to the bed and Breda saw his face above the torch beam for the first time: a youthful face, younger than the voice suggested, with an ugly scar meandering down from the corner of one eye to the point of the jaw.

'Look,' he said, 'I ain't got time to frig around. If you know where Romano's hiding, you'd better come clean.'

'I *don't* know,' Breda said. 'Honest to God, I don't.'

To Breda's relief he pulled back and, swinging the big torch like a drumstick, tapped the bed-end. 'Say nothing about my little visit, not to no one, not even your hubby. If Romano does turn up you let me know pronto.'

'How do I let you know?'

Her question brought him up short. It was on the tip of her tongue to suggest that if her old man did happen to appear on her doorstep she might telephone Scotland Yard but she was too scared to push the point.

At length, he said, 'You see your daddy, you tell him he better turn himself in. He don't, we'll make it hot for his nearest and dearest, you included. Got that?'

'He won't come 'ere, but if 'e does, I'll tell 'im.'

'And not one word to no one, girly.'

'No,' Breda promised. 'Me lips is sealed,' and when the man left the bedroom, swinging his torch, sank back against the pillows, sobbing with relief.

In the past few months CBS's European coverage had gathered steam. Even Mr Willets cast an envious eye at the American network's *European Roundup* which featured live conversations between a newscaster in New York and correspondents from London, Washington, Rome and Bucharest, linked by a complex intercontinental network of short-wave transmitters and land lines.

The BBC's new twice-weekly programme, tentatively and rather obviously called *Speaking Up for Britain*, would, of necessity, be less ambitious in scope and require the close cooperation of the Canadian Broadcasting Corporation who had studios in New York, Washington and Boston.

One could safely leave the technical aspects to the BBC's engineers, Mr Willets said. His concern was with content and tone and where to find an intelligent presenter who would bring more to the mike than a pleasant speaking voice; a problem his assistant, Susan Hooper, was doing her level best to solve.

'Bob, Bob Gaines?' Peter Slocum said. 'Where did he find a pretty little thing like you? Come in, come in, and welcome.'

Susan was not impressed by the Lansdowne's resident Lothario. He was tall, exceptionally so, with haggard, hawk-like features, though his voice was soft, almost beguiling, and his hands, which he waved about a lot, were hypnotically expressive.

'Is Robert here?' Susan said. 'May I speak to him?'

'Oh, so it's Robert, is it? Are you an intimate of my esteemed colleague and, if so, why haven't we met before?'

With a touch of hauteur that she instantly regretted, Susan said, 'I'm from the BBC.'

'That's what they all say,' Pete Slocum said. 'Step inside and tell me more.'

'No,' Susan said. 'I mean it: I am from the BBC.'

'Well, we won't hold that against you, Miss . . .'

'Hooper, Susan Hooper.'

There was quite a ruckus going on at the far end of the corridor. A stocky young woman burst from the door of one of the Lansdowne's suites and catapulted herself towards the elevator pursued by a skinny young man who seemed to have forgotten that he wasn't wearing trousers.

'It's only a month,' he shouted. 'It's not the end of the goddamned world, Phyllis.'

'He's now going to tell her he'll come back for her,' Mr Slocum predicted, *sotto voce*.

'I will come back, you know. I swear I will,' the young man cried as the woman hurled herself into the elevator, closed the gates and disappeared.

'And will he?' Susan said.

'Probably not,' Mr Slocum said. 'Bob's in Paris.'

'For how long?'

'It's not my habit to impart information to persons in passageways.' He extended a large hand and, without touching any part of her, ushered her into the apartment. 'And whatever you may have heard to the contrary, I don't bite strangers.'

Several doors opened off the hall, bedrooms and a bathroom, Susan guessed, and a small kitchen in which a very dignified man in a canvas apron was ironing shirts at a fold-down board.

'Our valet,' Peter Slocum told her. 'He comes with the apartment, whether we like it or not.' He shepherded her before him into a well-lighted, fully furnished living room at the end of the hall. 'Is it too early for martinis? No, it's never too early for martinis.' He moved to a Jacobean dresser that served as a bar. 'We have fresh lemons and the vermouth is guaranteed dry.'

'No, thank you,' Susan said politely.

'Something else then. Tea, maybe?'

'I'm fine, thank you.'

'Sure you are; very fine.' Cocktail shaker in hand, he glanced over his shoulder. 'But all business, I guess.'

'Yes, all business.'

'And what sort of business do you have with our Bob?'

'I prefer to discuss it with Mr Gaines personally.'

'Now, are you being coy or are you constrained by the BBC's policy of telling nobody nuttin'?' Pete Slocum opened the cocktail shaker and poured the mixture into a glass. 'You're not from the censor's department, are you?'

'Certainly not.' She yielded. 'News and Talks.'

'Then you must be Basil Willets's right-hand girl.'

'Robert told you, I suppose.'

'Bob didn't have to tell me. There are no secrets in the grill room of the Savoy. Old Baz is heading up an expansion of the North American service – what's it called? yeah: *Speaking Out for Britain*. Am I right?'

'Up,' Susan said. 'It's *Speaking Up for Britain*.'

'Time someone round here did,' Pete Slocum said. 'You can't leave it to Ed Murrow to make all the running for you.'

He sipped from the cocktail glass like a horse from a trough. 'If you want to influence American opinion you must fight your corner. Radio is one damned good way to do it.'

'Why is Bob in Paris?'

'He's covering the latest Allied War Council meeting in case the French decide to show Chamberlain the finger and sign a peace treaty with Germany.'

'Is that liable to happen?'

'No, no. The French have more grit than we give them credit for. If Hitler does invade France they won't surrender, at least not without a fight.'

'When will Robert be back?'

'Who knows? He can post from the Paris office and might hang on for a week or two if there's enough going on to make it worth his while.'

'Does Robert have a girl in Paris?'

'Hey, you don't beat around the bush, do you?'

'No,' said Susan. 'I don't.'

'Bob had a girl – but not in Paris. Back home.'

'Where is that?'

'Paterson, New Jersey.'

'What happened to her?'

'She ditched him for another guy.' Pete Slocum finished his martini, went to the bar and poured another from the shaker. 'Didn't he tell you?'

'We weren't – I mean, aren't close friends.'

'In that case,' Pete Slocum said, 'what harm in the whole truth? Pearl wasn't just any old girl. She was Bob's wife. Some sneaky Johnny-on-the-spot stole her while Bob was covering the Berlin Olympics back in '36. How come you know Bob, anyway?'

'We met through a mutual friend.'

'Vivian Proudfoot?'

'Yes.'

Susan had an uncomfortable feeling that Peter Slocum knew a lot more about her than he let on.

She glanced ostentatiously at her watch.

'Leaving so soon?' Pete Slocum said. 'I thought we were just warming up. Drag up a chair and have a drink.'

'Another time,' said Susan.

She didn't wait for him to put down his glass. He followed her into the hall with it in his hand.

The valet popped his head from the door of the little kitchen and said enquiringly, 'Mr Slocum?'

'Thank you, George,' Peter Slocum said. 'I have it.'

He came up behind her, so close that she could smell gin on his breath. She swung round to face him.

'When Robert returns from Paris . . .' she began.

'Ask him to call you.'

'Yes. Please.'

'At the BBC?'

'Yes.'

He juggled the glass and offered his hand. She hesitated, then took it. His fingers closed around her wrist.

'Maybe we'll meet at the Lagoon some time,' he said. 'If we don't – well, just make sure you don't break Bob's heart.'

'I don't know what you mean?' Susan said.

'Sure, you do, honey,' Pete Slocum said, and ushered her out of the apartment without another word.

6

Breda had been in the Brooklyn Club only once before. One afternoon, some three years ago, she'd brought Billy here to meet his grandfather. The club then had been empty of customers and, in the cold light of day, had seemed seedy and down-at-heel. How things had changed. Even at four in the afternoon the lane in which the club was situated was buzzing with young servicemen.

There was nothing furtive in the behaviour of the lads in the queue who, Breda guessed, were either on leave or, more likely, passing through London on their way to a posting. They were simply in search of a good time which, Steve Millar had indicated, meant a few beers and the chance to get off with a girl for a half hour or so, no questions asked.

Breda had left Billy with her mother, had filched a half-crown from the till and, to save time, had taken a cab to the club. The cabby had given her a queer look when she'd told him where she was going but only after he'd dropped her at the head of the lane did she realise that her wide-skirted camel coat and turban hat – her 'going out' rig – made her look more like a tart than a wife and mother.

She was not displeased, however, when the blokes in the queue whistled and exchanged suggestive remarks and when she gave them a wink and a wiggle they parted to allow her access to the big wooden door that was the Brooklyn's only entrance.

The door was already open. Two men in cheap lounge suits and gaudy ties were taking cash at a table on the landing at the top of the stairs; large men, much older than Steve Millar but just as well muscled.

'What you after?' one of the doormen asked. 'You lookin' for work, you come back later, talk to Terry.'

'I'm not lookin' for work,' Breda said. 'I'm lookin' for Mr Romano, Leo Romano. I'm his daughter.'

The doormen exchanged a glance.

One said to the other, 'Fetch Vince.'

'I don't want Vince,' Breda said. 'I want Mr Romano.'

For big men they moved with astonishing alacrity.

One grabbed Breda by the arm, yanked her over the threshold and, to howls of protest from the lads outside, slammed the door. The other man had already vanished downstairs. It dawned on Breda that she'd made a horrible mistake in coming here.

Snatching her arm from the doorman's grasp, she snapped, 'If you don't take your dirty paws off me, you'll be sorry when my daddy—'

'Your daddy!' the doorman snarled. 'Your daddy's as good as dead when Harry gets his hands on him.'

'Who's Harry?' Breda said.

At that moment two men came running up the staircase. She recognised the first one immediately by the ugly white scar that ran from his eye to the corner of his jaw.

'You,' she hissed. 'I knew you wasn't no bleedin' copper, you bastard.'

'Have you found him?' Vince said.

'Have I 'ell.'

He took her by the shoulders, pushed her against the wall and might have struck her if someone hadn't taken *him* by the shoulder and yanked him away. Something akin to a scuffle broke out – all Breda could see were flailing hands and arms – then she was staring up into a familiar, though not particularly friendly face.

'Breda,' Steve Millar said. 'What are you doin' here?'

'Come to talk to me daddy.'

'Stupid bitch,' Vince said. 'Ha'n't she got no sense?'

'Okay, okay,' Steve said. 'It's obvious she don't know nothing or she wouldn't be here. Jackie, get that bloody door open. We're losing custom.' Then, with an arm about Breda's waist, he escorted her downstairs.

The leaden cloud that had covered London for what seemed like months had broken up at last. It was still cold but pale mid-February sunlight caught the tops of the buildings around Portland Place and spirits within Broadcasting House had been high for most of the day.

Susan had seen precious little daylight, though, and the buoyant mood in which she and Mr Willets had started voice-testing candidates to take part in *Speaking Up for Britain* had gradually changed to one of gloom.

'Nothing abstract, Professor Schmautz. Every story must conjure up a picture. Imagine you're talking to an audience of blind persons. Mental vision is required. Imagery. Do you think you can manage that for me?'

The professor had nodded but had gone droning on in an impenetrable accent that, no matter how interesting his material, was an absolute stinker for radio. Susan had crossed the gentleman's name off the list even before Mr Willets drew a hand across his throat.

Eamon Riley, a 'People's Poet' from Liverpool, fared no better: 'Quieter, please, Mr Riley. You're booming.' But it was fiery old Sir Claude Endicott who really tested Mr Willets's patience to the limit.

'Thumping the table is not the same as thumping a tub, Sir Claude. I would be awfully obliged if you'd desist.' Sir Claude was unable to control his fist or his temper, however, and ranted on about how he had seen it all coming and how Roosevelt should be shot for not leaping to offer aid to Britain. Eventually Mr Willets slipped into the studio and, to the old boy's chagrin, wrested the microphone away from him.

It wasn't a live microphone, of course. It relayed the speaker's voice no further into the ether than the listening booth adjacent to the studio where only Basil Willets, Susan and Larry, the long-suffering sound controller, could hear it.

'A woman next,' Larry said apprehensively, for sound controllers were less than happy coping with female voices. 'It's not me doesn't like women, Mr Willets. It's the microphone, you understand.'

'Of course, Larry, of course. Just do the best you can.'

The 'Oxford' accent still dominated the airwaves but flattened vowels and clipped consonants had, of late, given ground to plain King's English with, now and then, traces of cosy regional accents that hinted if not at fish and chips at least at cocoa and carpet slippers.

In spite of intensive coaching, oiled by several gins, Susan was unsure which voice Vivian would bring to the studio, or, indeed, what she would choose to read.

She was more nervous than Vivian when she picked her friend up from the guest lounge.

'At least,' Susan said, 'you *look* very smart.'

'Oh, thank you,' Vivian said. 'Aren't you supposed to smarm all over me? Isn't that what assistants are for?'

'Now, remember, don't go all affected and, for heaven's sake, don't sound like a woman with a mission. My neck is on the block, Vivian, for recommending you.'

In fact, she'd encountered no resistance from Mr Willets when, with some trepidation, she'd put forward Vivian's name as a possible contributor.

They hastened along the corridor, Susan, trotting to keep up with Vivian's mannish stride, issuing all sorts of last-minute instructions. 'You must, absolutely must, lower the pitch of your voice to keep vibration to a minimum and do, please do, try to sound sympathetic.'

'Am I ever anything else?' said Vivian, then, when the door of the listening booth came in sight, quickened her pace and opened her arms wide.

'Basil,' she hooted. 'Dear old Basil, after all these years. You haven't changed a bit.'

And Mr Willets, waiting by the open door, said, 'No more have you, my dear. No more have you,' and, to Susan's utter astonishment, went up on tiptoe and kissed Vivian Proudfoot on the lips.

The band had an amplifying mike on stage and Tannoy speakers relayed the music to every corner of the room. The bar which had once been the Statue of Liberty had been renamed the Britannia but nobody seemed to care what it was called provided the beer taps worked which, in the glimpse Breda had of them, they seemed to be doing most effectively.

Steve steered her round the edge of the dance floor and shoved her into a room at the rear of the bandstand where, to her alarm, he left her to stew.

She seated herself on one of the chairs and looked nervously around. There was nothing much to see except a row of filing cabinets and a desk; nothing much on the desk save a telephone, a glass ashtray and something that looked like a black snake but that closer inspection revealed to be a torn silk stocking. She started when the door swung open and the raucous sound of jazz music swept over her. Steve put a glass into her hand and kicked the door shut to keep out the noise.

'Brandy,' he said. 'You look like you could use it.'

'Too bloody true,' said Breda.

She drank the contents of the glass in a swallow and accepted the cigarette that Steve offered with a nod of thanks. Steve hoisted himself on to the desk and, balanced there, looked down at her.

'What the hell possessed you to come here, Breda?'

'I really thought the guy was a copper.'

'What guy?'

'The geezer what broke into our 'ouse when Ron was on night shift. Scared the daylights out of me. Said 'e was some sort of copper. I believed 'im. Didn't you know Vince 'ad come to my place?'

'No,' Steve said, 'but it doesn't surprise me.'

'Where is 'e? Where's my daddy? What's 'e done?'

'He's scarpered,' Steve Millar said.

'Where's 'e gone?'

'My best guess, he's on a boat to Nova Scotia or some

other place in Canada. I reckon that's why he wanted you an' Billy over there. On the other hand,' Steve went on, 'he might be holed up waitin' for new papers. If he is hid, he better be hid good. Harry's got the word out.'

'Harry?' Breda said.

'Harry King.'

'Oh, God!' said Breda. 'Is that who's after 'im? No wonder 'e scarpered.'

'Unfortunately,' Steve said, 'a bag full of Mr King's money scarpered with 'im.'

'He stole from Harry King?' said Breda. 'Geeze!'

'He's probably been skimmin' off the top for years.'

'Your wife did the books for my dad, right?'

'Yeah, but Rita finally shopped 'im to Harry.'

'I thought you was Dad's friend.'

'I was,' Steve said, 'but I got a kid now. I can't afford to get on the wrong side of Harry King. I don't know who tipped Leo off but it wasn't me. Harry told me an' Vince to make sure Leo didn't do a runner until Harry got here with the boys. We were too late. Leo went out the back window of the girls' lavatory. Broke it down with a fire axe, blackout shutters an' all. He cleaned out two grand's worth of savings in cash from his bank plus whatever he had stashed in the office safe.'

'You was lucky Mr King didn't 'ave your neck.'

'Harry made Rita go through the books with an accountant an' the accountant gave her the benefit of the doubt.' Steve paused, then said wistfully, 'Used to be just jam on Harry King's bread, the old Brooklyn, but these past six months – a goldmine. You tell Ron about Vince's visit?'

'Nah, Ron's got enough on 'is plate without frettin' about

my old man.' She reached across the desk, stubbed out her cigarette in the ashtray and let her hand rest on Steve's knee. 'What you gonna do to me?'

'Nothin',' Steve told her. 'You ha'n't seen Leo and, my guess, you're not gonna. Fact is, if Harry lays his hands on Leo you might never see your old man again.'

'Harry wouldn't kill 'im, would he?'

'Maybe not,' Steve said, 'not if he gets his money back.'

Breda said, 'How much went over the wall exactly?'

Steve shrugged. 'Three grand, probably more.'

Breda whistled and removed her hand from Steve's knee. 'That *is* a lotta dough,' she said. 'Make quite an 'ole in anybody's pocket.'

'What's on your mind, Breda?' said Steve suspiciously. 'Come on, out with it.'

'Well, I'm thinkin', if someone got Mr King all 'is money back . . .'

'What?'

'Would there be a reward?'

'A reward?'

'Hmm,' Breda said. 'Ten per cent would do nicely.'

The restaurant below ground, shared by both staff and guest broadcasters, was a good deal less colourful now the entertainers had moved out. It maintained a certain modest elegance, however, and, thank heaven, continued to serve a decent afternoon tea. After her voice test Mr Willets had carried Miss Proudfoot off to the restaurant, an invitation that, rather pointedly, did not include Susan.

Squeezed behind her little desk Susan was typing up her notes when the producer, looking rather smug, returned.

'That went well, don't you think?' he said.

Susan was tempted to ask if he meant the test or the tiffin but prudently kept her mouth shut. She typed rapidly, noisily, taking out her irritation on the keys.

Mr Willets eased himself into the chair behind the desk and lit a cigarette. He folded an arm behind his head and blew a series of reflective, if imperfect, smoke rings.

Susan typed furiously.

'Now,' Mr Willets said, 'which of us is going to give in before that poor old Underwood catches fire?'

Susan ripped the paper from the platen.

'It's really none of my business, sir,' she said stiffly, 'but I do feel as if I've been used.'

'Used? Hardly, Miss Hooper, though there's nothing wrong with a bit of nepotism, is there? The BBC's not alone in favouring those who are in the know.'

'I didn't even know I *was* in the know,' said Susan. 'Was it Vivian's recommendation got me this job?'

'On the contrary,' Mr Willets said. 'Indeed, if we, the BBC, hadn't been in the midst of a frantic recruiting drive I question if your application would have been considered.'

'But *you* knew, didn't you?'

'Let's just say, I found out. Quite by chance I received your file from Personnel and found Vivian's letter of character.'

He attempted another smoke ring, gave up and dropped the cigarette into the ashtray.

'I'd kept track in a vague sort of way of Vivian's progress. Read a couple of her books and her articles in *The Times* and did, I confess, consider calling her. When you put her name forward for *Speaking Up*, it provided me with a perfect excuse for seeing her again. By the bye, that piece she read . . .'

'It's from her new book.'

'I thought it might be. Quite powerful, if somewhat . . .'

'Opinionated,' Susan suggested.

'She was always opinionated. I'm rather inclined to be opinionated myself which is why, I suspect, we hit it off so well.' He paused again. 'I'm surprised she never married. She does actually *like* men, I suppose?'

'Oh, yes,' said Susan. 'There's nothing ambiguous about Vivian.'

Susan had never really thought of Viv as young or of Mr Willets in the days when he had hair. She could not for the life of her imagine them together.

'I was at school with her brother, David,' Mr Willets went on. 'When war came I enlisted in the East Kent Regiment, the Buffs. Wounded in Salonika, not too seriously. But I fell so ill afterwards that I was sent back to Blighty. David invited me to convalesce on his farm. That's where I met Vivian.'

'Who nursed you back to health and strength.'

'No, Vivian isn't the nursing type. But it *was* summer and the apple orchards were heavy with fruit – and the rest, I fear, is a terrible cliché. Alas, after the war ended we went our separate ways. I joined the fledgling BBC – it was a company in those days, not a corporation – and broadcasting became my life.'

'And Vivian?'

'You would know more about that than I do.'

'I don't, really,' Susan said. 'Were you never tempted to take up with her again?'

'No. You see, by that time I had a wife.'

'I didn't know you had a wife.'

'I don't. We hadn't been married long when cancer took

her away,' Mr Willets said. 'After that experience, shall we say, I had little inclination to try again.' He glanced up at Susan. 'Well, Miss Hooper, now you know more about me than anyone in this building. I'm depending on you not to gossip. I prefer my private life, such as it is, to remain a closed book to my colleagues.'

'Of course,' Susan said. 'I do have one question I'd like you to answer, though.'

'Which is?'

'Are we taking Vivian on board?'

'Now what do you think?' Mr Willets said with a bashful little giggle that seemed totally at odds with his character.

7

After consultation with welfare staff the billeting officer who had been responsible for the gaffe in the first place reluctantly agreed that Miss Cottrell might remain lodged with the Pells until a place could be found in one of the 'all-girl' farmhouses or a room in town that didn't have two slavering males in close proximity. Mrs Pell's willingness to take on the role of moral watchdog had much to do with the decision, added to the fact that more and more 'foreigners' were arriving in Evesham every week and congenial accommodation, especially for females, was at a premium.

In the dog days of February, Griff and Danny saw less of Kate than they'd hoped. Indeed, as Griff glumly pointed out, during her training phase they saw more of Kate's knickers hanging on the washing line than they did of Kate herself.

She hadn't been drawn into any of the little cliques that formed among the foreign-language monitors, however, for the German-speaking group was less tight-knit than most and arguments over entries in the monitor's logbook and Teutonic debates about points of style proved heated and divisive.

Even in the relaxed atmosphere of the Greenhill subtle

tensions remained and Mrs Pell's lodgers tended to keep to themselves. On that evening, all together for once, Kate and Danny were seated on a couch in an alcove off the main lounge drinking beer while Griff hovered by the piano in the hope that the present incumbent of the stool, a female, would weary of butchering Rachmaninoff.

'How long have you been married?' Kate asked.

'Couple of years, give or take,' Danny answered.

'It must be hard for you being apart for so long.'

'You get used to it,' Danny said.

'What did you do, what job, before you came here?'

'Sub-editor on the *Star*.'

'Did you enjoy working on Fleet Street?'

'There are worse jobs,' Danny said. 'Are you wonderin' why I'm not in uniform?'

'The thought never entered my head,' said Kate.

Danny shrugged. 'I failed the medical.'

'On what grounds?'

'Flat feet an' poor eyesight. I'm off to an optician's for a proper eye test as soon as I can get myself up to London. Are you home tonight or are you on late shift?'

'Home,' she said. 'Lie in tomorrow. I start at noon on a twelve-hour stretch. They tell me February has been a quiet month but it hasn't seemed so to me.'

'Are you havin' trouble with the translations?'

'Sometimes,' Kate said. 'Frequently, if I'm honest.'

Back in the East End, when he'd lodged with Nora Romano, Danny had been an arbitrator, a problem solver, the dependable chap to whom everyone, including Susan, had turned for advice. All that had changed when Susan had gone to work for Vivian Proudfoot and had fallen for the agent, Mercer Hughes, after which he had been nothing more than a bridge between what Susan had been and what she was in process of becoming.

He watched Kate put down the beer mug and, stifling a yawn, stretch her arms above her head.

'I must admit I do find it exhausting sitting for hours listening to strange voices crackling through a pair of headphones,' she said.

'What you need,' Danny said, 'is a couple of days off.'

'We're not entitled to leave, are we?'

'You've heard what's comin' down the wires from Germany. Now Europe's thawin' out an invasion looks inevitable. Be no leave for any of us when that happens.'

'Have you been up in London recently?' Kate said.

'Not since Christmas.'

'Don't you want to see your wife?'

''Course I do,' said Danny, hiding his ambivalence.

'Then why not ask for a forty-eight-hour pass and go home for a day or two, have a proper eye test and spend some time with your wife?'

'I could certainly do with an eye test,' Danny said. 'I can barely read the transcripts these days.'

'Headaches?' Kate asked.

'Now an' then.'

'Time you did something about it, Danny.'

'Aye,' he said grudgingly. 'I suppose it is.'

If Billy had inherited an argumentative streak from his grandfather – a suggestion Matt vehemently denied – his appetite had surely come down from his dad. He happily devoured anything that was put before him and even opened his beak willingly to receive the daily dose of cod liver oil that Breda ladled into him.

'I wonder if he needs to be wormed,' Ron said.

'Don't be bleedin' stupid. He's a growin' boy who likes 'is vittles,' Breda said. 'Don't you, darlin'?'

'Yar,' Billy answered through a mouthful of sausage.

It was breakfast time in the Hoopers' kitchen. Since Ron had started shift work at the fire station, it always seemed to be breakfast time for someone and the frying pan was seldom off the stove for long.

Unusually, Billy's routine and Ron's had coincided on that brisk March morning and the whole family, all three of them, were eating together.

Breda scooped two slices of toast from under the grill and spread them with butter. She added marmalade to one and strawberry jam to the other and put the jammy slice on a plate where Billy could reach it without effort. The marmalade she ate herself, standing by the stove and puffing on a cigarette between mouthfuls.

'What would you do if we 'ad money?' she asked.

Ron, who was being very careful not to stain his uniform, looked up, a rasher of black-market bacon poised daintily on the end of his fork.

'How much money?'

'Say, three hundred quid.'

'Spend it all on drink.'

'I'm serious,' Breda told him.

'What? You won the pools, or somethin'?'

'It's two years' wages, close enough.'

'Oh, sure,' said Ron. 'We could retire to the country.'

'Wouldn't be bad, that.'

'I thought you didn't like the country.'

'I could get used to it, I suppose. Be good for Billy.'

'Billy's all right here. Ain't yah, son?'

'Yar,' said Billy obligingly.

Breda finished her toast and, with the cigarette dangling from her lip, said, 'Three hundred quid would make a nice nest egg for when the war's over.'

'What you talkin' about?' Ron said. 'Where's all this money comin' from?'

Breda dropped her cigarette into a tin ashtray at the sink and ran a washcloth under the tap.

Billy, still eating, stiffened.

'Nowhere: I'm just dreamin',' she said and, before he could bolt, snared her son by the scruff of the neck and vigorously applied the washcloth to his jammy face.

'He's making more of it than it deserves,' Vivian said. 'I wasn't much more than a child that summer.'

'By my calculation you were twenty-four,' said Susan.

'Three,' said Vivian. 'In those dear, dead days that was practically a child. You have no idea just how repressive society could be when I was young.'

'Hadn't you "come out" by then?'

'Come out?' Vivian said. 'What do you take me for? I was never a debutante. We were poor – relatively poor. In any case, Papa made his money from trade and the Old Bailey was the closest any of our lot was ever going to get to appearing at court. Basil Willets and I were thrown together for less than a month, and he wasn't very well for most of it.'

'What was wrong with him?'

'I don't know. Yes, actually I do. He had an infection of the blood, a condition that almost killed him. He also had a bit of a limp which I see has gone.'

'So,' said Susan, 'he was pale and interesting, was he?'

'More pale than interesting, unfortunately.'

'He says you were in love.'

'He may have been in love but I certainly wasn't.'

'I think he's still a little bit in love with you.'

'He's fast approaching middle age and, I suppose, tends to infuse the past with a rosy glow.'

'Why didn't you tell me you knew Basil Willets?'

'Because I thought you'd go all huffy and accuse me of securing you the BBC job which, I might add, you secured entirely on your own merits. Have you been in touch with your husband, by the way? The papers are full of rumours that Hitler is drawing up invasion plans again.'

'Don't change the subject,' Susan said. 'You're going out with him, aren't you? Basil, I mean, not Hitler.'

'We're meeting for a professional lunch,' Viv admitted.

'A "professional" lunch; what's that?'

'He's hinted – just hinted – that he wishes to use me on the programme. I can't think why.'

'Can't you?' Susan said. 'I can.'

'At least I wasn't foolish enough to marry a man I didn't love out of – out of – I don't know what. Pity, maybe.'

'Oh, that's below the belt, Vivian.'

'If you really are in love with Danny Cahill,' Vivian pressed on, 'why are you chasing after other men?'

'Other men? If you mean Robert Gaines, we want him for the programme and I was sent out to get him. Ask Mr Willets if you don't believe me. Besides, I do love Danny.'

'But,' said Vivian, 'not as much as Danny loves you?'

'I've no idea how much Danny loves me. How on earth do you measure it? I married him, didn't I? It certainly wasn't a marriage of convenience. It's not as if I was pregnant, or anything.'

'Might have been better if you had been.'

'Danny doesn't want children,' Susan said.

'How do you know? Have you asked him?'

'I don't have to ask him,' Susan said. 'We have a tacit understanding.'

'At least if you had a baby to look after he'd know where you were.'

'In some dismal council property in Shadwell, like as not, struggling to make ends meet.'

'God, what a snob you've become, Susan.'

'Snob? I'm no snob. I've worked bleedin' hard to get where I am and, for your information, woman or not, I earn just as much as Danny.'

'I'm not sure that's something to boast about.'

'What's wrong with taking advantage of changing circumstances?' Susan said.

'Oh,' said Vivian. 'Is that what you call it? Most people think of it as being in danger of losing their freedom, if not their lives. To you it's just another opportunity to haul yourself up the ladder.'

'Yes,' Susan said. 'I have a career now and I intend to hang on to it for as long as possible. How can you, of all people, grudge me a bit of independence?'

'I don't grudge you anything,' Vivian said, 'but I do hope you're aware what you may be giving up.'

'A home and children?' said Susan. 'A home that might

be shelled out of existence before the summer's over, and children who'll learn to salute the swastika before they can walk. No, Vivian, I *do* know what this damned war with Germany might lead to, but until it does I aim to make the most of what time I have and plan for a future that might never come to pass.'

'A future without Danny Cahill?'

Susan ignored the question. 'God knows, we might all be dead this time next year. Not you, of course. Oh, no, not a woman who took tea with Dr Goebbels and has a brother who'll be first on to the podium, grinning like an ape, when Hitler marches into Trafalgar Square.'

'I have work to do,' said Vivian curtly. 'I think it's time you left. I'll fetch your coat.'

'No need,' said Susan. 'I'll fetch it myself,' and, a moment later, stepped out into the darkness of Salt Street and set off, fizzing, for home.

They were eating at the dining table in the living room, all together for once. With the table pulled out from the wall to accommodate an extra chair the living room seemed more cramped than ever and a certain amount of conga-dancing and scraping of chairs was required before everyone was seated and Mrs Pell, with Kate's help, ferried dishes in from the kitchen.

The news that had crackled down the wires that forenoon suggested that Hitler and his cronies were up to something but so far no one could be sure which way the Jerries would jump.

'Crafty beggar,' Mr Pell said. 'Don't trust him as far as I could throw him. What else have you been hearing, Kate?'

Since Kate Cottrell's arrival Mr Pell had addressed all his questions to her as if, Griff grumbled, a pretty face and slim figure went hand in glove with intelligence and they, mere men, had suddenly become numbskulls.

'Babble, mostly,' Kate said. 'There's been rather a lot of stuff about Sumner Welles's visit to Berlin.'

'Now who's he when he's at home?' said Mr Pell.

'Under Secretary of State for Roosevelt,' Griff told him, through a mouthful of pudding.

'Is that who he is?' Mr Pell asked Kate who, with barely the flicker of an eyebrow, confirmed the information.

'There's an undercurrent of feeling in some of the broadcasts from Hamburg,' she went on, 'that Welles is trying to drive a wedge between Germany and Italy and that's why Roosevelt sent him on the tour of Europe.'

'He's in London right now,' said Griff.

'Got the chap now,' said Mr Pell. 'I'll swear I heard him on the wireless with that other American feller.'

'Ed Murrow,' said Griff with the resigned air of someone who expects to be ignored. 'On *Round Up.*'

'Is that one of your wife's programmes?' said Mrs Pell who had a habit of inflating Mrs Cahill's contribution to radio broadcasting.

''Fraid not, Mrs P,' Danny said.

'Oh!' Mrs Pell exclaimed, sitting up straight. 'I clean forgot. There be a letter for you from London. It's behind the vase on the mantel there.'

Mr Pell was tall enough to reach the shelf above the fireplace without leaving his seat. He steadied the painted vase, a fairground trophy, with one hand, removed the letter with the other and passed it across the table to Danny.

BBC stationery, the address not typed but printed in Susan's loopy handwriting: Danny put down his spoon, turned the envelope over and, to his embarrassment, saw that Susan had sealed it with a tiny red-ink heart.

He cleared his throat. 'Anyone mind if I . . .'

'Be my guest,' said Griffiths.

'It's from his wife,' Mrs Pell confided to Kate. 'It's got a kiss on the back.'

'It's not a . . .' Danny began, then, thinking better of it, wiped a knife on a serviette and slit open the envelope.

He was well aware that everyone was watching him while appearing not to. He held the letter below the level of the tablecloth and scanned it quickly.

'*My darling*,' it read, '*please come home soon, if you can. I miss you so much. I long to hear your voice again and to feel your arms about me. With all my love, Susan.*'

He folded the letter, returned it to the envelope and stuffed it hastily into his trouser pocket.

'Not bad news, I hope?' said Mr Pell.

'No,' Danny said. 'Nothin' of any consequence,' then, not meeting Kate Cottrell's eye, reached for the cider jug to refill his empty glass.

8

Tasty, Pete Slocum had called her, and ripe for the plucking, yet still the kind of girl who would climb all over you and, when it suited her, toss you in the trash like yesterday's newspaper. Pete was usually right about women. He could spot calculating females at a thousand yards and made it a rule to avoid them, but he, Bob Gaines, wasn't as cynical as old Slocum – at least not yet.

She looked so eager as she surveyed the people passing through the ground-floor reception area that he was tempted to believe that maybe she just wanted to see him again, to be his friend. She looked good, too, in a smart, slightly sassy way that reminded him of the Girl Fridays who worked in the newspaper offices back in New York.

Pleated skirt, plain white blouse, half-heeled shoes, hair cut short to fit under a gas mask; she bore no resemblance to Pearl, his wife – his ex-wife – who was full-breasted and broad-hipped and wore her hair in a thick, plaited pigtail that she unfurled only at bedtime.

The cop handed him back his press card and ushered him through the big glass door.

Susan came across the foyer to greet him, the shape of her breasts, modestly English, showing beneath her blouse.

74

She reached out and shook his hand.

'So glad you could come, Robert. How was Paris? Was it dreadful? We're upstairs, by the way. Mr Willets is dying to meet you. We'll take the elevator, shall we?'

At that moment, married or not, he wanted her.

And all he could think of to say was, 'Yes.'

Nora had been married to Leo Romano for the best part of thirty years but had barely exchanged a dozen civil words with him since he'd run off with the brassy blonde from the Fawley Street fish bar twenty years ago. Ancient history now for most folk in Shadwell, the gossip as cold as cod on a slab, but Leo's desertion had left a scar on Nora's heart that had never quite healed.

'You're bleedin' nuts not to apply for an annulment an' let Matt make an honest woman of yah,' Breda told her.

Nora saw sense in her daughter's argument and didn't doubt that her 'lodger', Matt Hooper, would lead her to the altar if she were free to marry again. But which altar? That, in Nora's book, was the rub.

Matt Hooper was a godless Protestant and she was a good Catholic girl who by letting Matt share her bed had become no better than a harlot and, as such, would burn in the fires of hell. She had given up going to confession but still drew comfort from hearing Mass in the fragile belief that, whatever God thought of her, Our Lady would manage to smuggle her into heaven by the back door.

She enjoyed Matt's kisses and cuddles and even the other thing but had a habit of confusing her few brief moments of post-coital guilt with a fear of eternal damnation and would roll away from Matt, sniffing tearfully.

'Do you love me, Matt?'

"Course I love you. Wouldn't be 'ere if I didn't.'

'If the German Menace comes, will you look after me?'

'The Germans won't come 'ere.'

'But if they do?'

'I won't let 'em take you alive, Nora, I promise.'

Nora's concept of the 'German Menace' was limited not by a paucity of information but by a lack of imagination.

Ron and Matt were forever ranting about the nasty Nazis but Nora contrived to hear only that which she wished to hear.

She refused to glance at the picture magazines Ron traded with his father that were filled with photographs of tanks and aeroplanes, marching men and queues of poor folk pushing handcarts. The closest she came to understanding the nature of combat was when she watched her grandson, Billy, play with his toy soldiers and heard him mimic the sounds of bullets and exploding bombs, and it didn't cross her mind that danger might be lurking on the doorstep.

'That guy in the soft 'at, Ma, you seen 'im before?'

'Can't say I have, dear. He comes in with Chalky.'

'Chalky?' Breda said.

'Mrs Greene's old man.'

'Did Dad know 'im?'

'Sure an' I expect he did. Chalky's been on the India Docks for years. Why you asking?'

'No reason, just curious.'

Nora's vagueness drove Breda to despair, especially now that every stranger might be packing a razor or a gun. Nipping between the tables and the steam-filled kitchen, she framed her questions carefully.

'Seen anythin' of Dad lately?'

'Leo never shows his face in Shadwell, you know that.'

'How long since we last seen 'im?'

'Not since Georgie's funeral, I suppose.'

Leo had paid for the funeral and a stone, a very hand-some stone, to mark the spot where his eldest lay but then he'd vanished into the shadows once more.

'Nobody round 'ere seems to remember Dad,' Breda said. 'I mean, nobody ever asks after 'im these days.'

'Some do.'

'Like who?'

'Them as used to fancy him.'

'Women, you mean?'

'Mrs Brighouse – Clara – she fancied him.'

'What about men?' said Breda.

'Leo was never like that, no.'

'I mean men askin' after 'im.'

'No,' said Nora, all unaware. 'No men.'

When March washed in with a mixture of sleet and warm rain and no further sign of Vince or Steve, Breda began to relax her vigilance. She was caught off guard therefore when two men in trench-coats and soft hats turned up in the dining rooms one morning and asked to speak to Nora.

There were three customers in the café, two charladies, just off work, nattering over a pot of tea, and one grey-haired cabman who, when the trench-coats entered, folded his *Racing Pink*, paid his tab and quietly took his leave.

Breda explained, truthfully, that her mother had gone to buy butcher meat and wouldn't be back for at least an hour. She asked if she could be of assistance.

'Could do with a coffee, love,' one of the men suggested.

She waited for them to be seated but when she went behind the counter to fill the cups from the coffee urn they followed her.

'Do you live here with your mother?' one man asked.

'No,' Breda said. 'I live with me 'usband in Pitt Street.'

'Your husband, what does he do?'

She put the cups on saucers and pushed them across the counter. 'I'd like to know who's askin' before I tell you anythin'. I mean, you might be Jerry spies, all I know.'

One of the hats, the elder, smiled. 'Quite right.'

He showed Breda a card that identified him as an officer of the Special Branch and left her in no doubt she was dealing with the genuine article this time.

'Okay,' she said. 'What you want from me?'

'Your husband . . .'

'Fireman. Oxmoor Road. We 'ave one kid.'

'Your mother, where does she live?'

Breda gestured with her thumb. 'Upstairs. My 'usband's father stays over most nights. Makes us feel safe case there's an air raid, know what I mean?'

'Your father-in-law, what's his name?'

'Matt Hooper, crane driver down the docks.'

The younger of the men heaped sugar into his coffee, lifted the cup and blew across the surface to cool it. 'What does *your* father have to say about that arrangement?'

'If 'e even knows – which I doubt – 'e wouldn't care.'

'So Mr Romano doesn't come round much?'

'Don't come round at all,' Breda said. 'We ha'n't clapped an eye on 'im since we buried my brother, Georgie, at the time of the Cable Street riots.'

'I remember that,' the younger man said to his companion. 'Kid got clobbered and died. Bad business. Home Office was involved.'

Breda leaned her forearms on the counter top. 'I know my daddy mixes with some bad company, but I don't know any more than that.'

'What about Steve Millar? Have you seen him lately?'

Half a lie, Breda decided, was the best way of covering the whole truth. 'Steve?' she said. 'Oh, sure. Saw 'im about a month ago. He dropped by my kid's school in 'is car an' picked me up for a chat.'

'A chat about what?'

'He was lookin' for me father, too.'

'Was he now?'

'Wouldn't tell me why, though,' Breda said. 'What's 'e done, my daddy? I mean, what you after 'im for?'

'Good coffee.' The older man drained his cup. 'You make good coffee. What do we owe you, Mrs Hooper?'

'Nothin',' said Breda. 'It's on the house. Ain't you gonna wait to speak to my mother?'

'That won't be necessary,' the older man said.

He reached across the counter, detached a leaf from Breda's check pad and removed the pencil from behind her ear. He printed a telephone number on the leaf and a name – Jessop – and slid the little oblong of paper towards her. He leaned further across the counter and looked her straight in the eye.

'You hear anything from Leo,' he said, 'you call this number. You ask for me, nobody else.'

Breda said, 'In other words, shop my old man?'

'Better us than others,' the officer told her.

79

Breda nodded. 'Yeah, I see what you mean,' she said, and carefully folding the leaf from the check pad, tucked it into her bra.

It had all gone swimmingly, much better than Susan had expected. For someone who had never broadcast before Robert had been quick to grasp what was required of him. He had taken to the mike like a veteran and, with his hat still on his head and a cigarette smouldering in the ashtray on the table, had read without faltering the script samples Mr Willets had laid out.

After the test Mr Willets had taken Robert off to lunch outside the building and Susan, on tenterhooks, had been left to twiddle her thumbs for the best part of three hours.

Mr Willets was smiling when he returned to the office.

'I,' he said, 'have h-had a drop too much to drink. I do believe I'll h-head off home. If anyone does happen to be looking for me . . .'

'Is he acceptable?' Susan blurted out. 'Will he do?'

Mr Willets had removed neither his hat nor his overcoat. Swaying slightly, he planted an elbow on his desk for support.

'Well,' he said, 'the question isn't if Mr Gaines will do for us but if we w-will do for Mr Gaines.'

'What do you mean?'

'He's employed by the *Post* and, understandably, he's reluctant to surrender his position with the paper.'

'Mr Willets, are you drunk?'

Basil Willets drew in a deep breath, pushed himself away from the desk and stood upright.

'Certainly not, not drunk. Perhaps a t-tiny bit tipsy. I will not, however, be matching glass with glass with Mr Gaines again. Dear G-God, can he put away the booze.'

'Mr Willets, sir, do we want him?'

'We do, we do, we do – I think.' Another deep breath to clear his head: 'Certain conditions will have to be met before we can claim Mr Gaines as one of our own. Will the powers that be upstairs agree to take on a foreign correspondent? Will the owners of the *Post* release him from his contract? Will we be able to afford him on our budget and what will the Controller have to say about employing a Yankee presenter?' He blew out his cheeks. 'And then there's the question of what we're going to do about you?'

'About me?'

'He doesn't like you.'

'What?'

'He's worried about working with you. I offered to have you replaced but he thought that was a bit harsh – which, actually, it is.'

Susan sank back against the edge of her desk.

'Replaced?' she said. 'What a bleedin' cheek!'

'I did point out,' Mr Willets said, 'that you'd recommended him in the first place – but that cut no ice.'

'*Are* you replacing me?'

'No, no,' said Mr Willets. 'No, no, no.'

'Did Mr Gaines tell you why he doesn't like me?'

'Actually,' Mr Willets said, 'I think he likes you too much. He never stopped talking about you. I believe our American cousin is a teeny bit afraid of you.'

'Oh,' said Susan. 'I can't think why.'

'Because,' Basil Willets said, 'you're married. Whatever it says on your employment record you do have a husband. Dennis, is it?'

'Danny,' Susan said. 'I don't see what my marriage has to do with Robert Gaines.'

'All things being equal – which they seldom are – I'd like to have Robert Gaines as our lead newscaster. We'll have Mr Gaines in again as soon as I've talked to the folk upstairs. Meanwhile, Susan, I'm depending on you to convince him that he has a future in Broadcasting House.'

'How am I supposed to do that?'

'Why don't you start by calling him,' Mr Willets said and meandered out of the office and left Susan alone with the telephone.

The property at the corner of Rothwell Gardens and Fenmore Street, a short walk from the King's Road, had once been part of David Proudfoot's portfolio but, three months before war began, ownership had changed hands and the rent was now paid to a reputable letting agency.

Danny had asked Vivian why her brother had shed his London holdings but Viv claimed to have no idea what David was up to in the wilds of Herefordshire, apart from growing cider apples. He rarely, if ever, came up to town, and his magnificent Mayfair town house had been requisitioned as part of a deal with some element in government and, with delicious irony, now housed an organisation dedicated to bringing Jews out of Europe.

The gardens hadn't changed much, though a public shelter replaced the flower beds and one or two of the stately oaks had been felled in the interests of safely. The apartment block, more concrete than brick, reared up out of the darkness, every window blacked out, the doorway outlined by one of the ubiquitous blue bulbs that only served to deepen the shadows.

Rolling stock carrying military machinery had precedence even on main lines and it had been a sluggish journey from Evesham to Paddington. Danny had no excuse for not letting Susan know he was coming and no reason to suppose she was cheating on him – apart from a niggling suspicion that her life outside Broadcasting House was a good deal more lively than her life within.

The night was shot through with whistles and shouts laid over the rumble of lorries and the clatter of trams, sounds that seemed almost threatening after the silence of the fields round Evesham. He peered up at the window of the second-floor flat but had no way of telling whether or not the room was occupied through the heavy blackout curtains.

Lugging his overnight bag, he crossed to the doorway, climbed the stairs to the second floor and, fishing his key from his pocket, let himself into the flat.

He put down the bag, switched on the standard lamp and looked round. He didn't know what he expected to find, what evidence of infidelity Susan might have left in view. The room was as it had always been, clean and tidy and cold. Kneeling, he lit the gas fire before he went into the bedroom.

The bed was strewn with tangled sheets and blankets. Susan's nightdress and dressing gown had been tossed across a chair and a garter belt and stockings lay on the floor by the dressing table.

He returned to the tiny kitchen behind the living room and found a half-pint of milk, a little piece of butter on a dish, some cheese wrapped in wax-proof paper, a couple of eggs and half a loaf fresh enough to cut.

He grilled cheese, made a pot of tea and ate at the table

in the living room. Then, at just after one o'clock, he washed the dishes, turned off the fire, made up the bed and fell into it and, within minutes, was fast asleep.

She blew softly into his ear. 'Why didn't you tell me you were coming?'

'Last minute,' he said, stirring. 'I tried callin' your office but the line was always busy.'

'Oh,' Susan said. 'Yes. It's been a madhouse all day.' She snuggled close to share his warmth. 'Still, I'm here now and you're here now and that's all that matters, isn't it?'

'What time is it?'

'I don't know – after four. How long do you have?'

'I'm due back day after tomorrow,' he said. 'Susan, where've you been?'

'Viv's. I partook of one gin too many and fell asleep on her couch. Aren't you wearing pyjamas?'

'No.'

'What are you wearing?'

'Underpants.'

'That,' she said, 'is disgusting.'

'I'll take them off if you like.'

'Please do.'

'What were you up to at Viv's?'

'Working on her intonation. Mr Willets wants her to contribute to *Speaking Up*. Didn't I tell you?'

'No,' Danny said. 'No, you didn't.' He rolled on to an elbow and peered at her. 'What else haven't you told me?'

'Lots,' she said. 'Everything's happening so quickly it's impossible to keep up. Tomorrow I'll tell you all about it.'

She pulled him to her and, seizing his hand, pressed it

between her legs. He wondered, vaguely, why she was naked and if this was how she slept when he wasn't here. He felt her nipples stiffening against his chest and her lips already moist under his hand. Tenting the bedclothes over her shoulders, she straddled him and lowered herself on to him, something she had never done before.

'Wait,' he said. 'I don't have a letter on.'

'I don't want to wait,' she said and, tilting her hips, brought him into her.

9

'Brown coffee, please,' he said, 'an' one o' your rock cakes.'

'Danneeee,' Breda squealed. 'You sneaky beggar!' She spun round and, to the alarm of Stratton's customers, yelled at the pitch of her voice, 'Ma, guess who's 'ere?'

Wrapping an arm round Danny's waist, she dragged him into the kitchen, chattering all the while. 'By gum, you're a sight for sore eyes. What they been feedin' you down there in the country? Never seen you look so 'ealthy. Ma, it's Danny. Danny's come 'ome.'

Ladle in one hand and a bowl in the other, Nora looked up from the cauldron that simmered on the stove.

'Danny,' she said. 'Mother o' God, it's our Danny.'

He kissed her cheek. 'Good tae see you again, Nora.'

Wagging the ladle, she said, 'Sure now and you'll be wanting fed. Are you staying for your supper?'

He laughed. 'Time enough to think of supper after I've had lunch. How are you?'

'All the better for seeing you,' said Nora.

'You up for the week?' Breda asked.

'Flyin' visit. Back to the grind tomorrow.'

'Have you seen 'er ladyship yet?'

'Seen who?'

86

'Your wife,' said Breda.

'Aye, I saw her last night.'

'That would be fun,' said Breda, then, when an angry male voice from the dining rooms demanded service, yelled, 'Keep yer bleedin' 'air on, 'Orace. I only got two 'ands.' She set about loading a tray with bowls of soup. 'Susie not come with you, then?'

'No, she had to work.'

'She should've called in sick,' said Breda. 'Here, make yourself useful.' She handed him the laden tray. 'Carry this out for me while I make the sarnies.'

'Oh,' said Danny, 'it's so good to be back.'

'Get out there, big boy, an' don't give me no lip.'

'Yes, dear,' Danny said, grinning, and carried the tray out into the dining rooms and served the startled customers with his own fair hands.

She took neither coat nor cardigan from the hook behind her desk and with Mr Willets engaged in conversation on the telephone, slipped out of the office as if she were heading for the cloakroom and not the public telephone box in the street behind All Souls.

Without her identity card or BBC pass she breezed past the doorman, calling cheerily, 'Back in a tick,' in the hope he wouldn't go all official on her return.

Fortunately, the phone box was unoccupied. She hauled open the door, plucked up the receiver, damp with some other person's breath, dialled the Lansdowne's number, fed pennies into the slot, pressed the button and, hopping like a schoolgirl, waited to be put through to Mr Gaines's suite.

The valet answered. In a voice stiff with disapproval, he

asked if she wished to speak with Mr Slocum. She informed him that, no, she wished to speak with Mr Gaines and added that she was calling on behalf of the BBC.

She waited, eyes closed, for the valet to tell her that Mr Gaines was not available but after a few tense moments heard Robert say, 'Hey, Susan, what's up? Has my contract of employment been approved already?'

'No, Robert, I'm not calling about the contract.'

'What is it, then?'

'It's about last night,' she said.

It seemed natural to take his arm as if he were her boyfriend or her husband. What with the war and half the men away – though you wouldn't think it given the crowd of touts and louts who were out in force that breezy weekday afternoon – Nora's neighbours had better things to gossip about than Breda Romano's scandalous behaviour.

She'd been pleased when Danny had said he'd walk her as far as Billy's school before he caught the Tube back to Charing Cross. It had irked her to have to share him not just with Nora, which was fair enough, but with a bunch of customers yapping for attention as if their time were more precious than Danny's.

It was a mild afternoon with fluffy cloud and fragments of blue sky showing above the river. After the murk and slush of winter Breda felt quite liberated to be stepping out with Danny again, even if it was just to hoof up Cannon Street to pick up her kid. It crossed her mind that she might tell Danny about the mess her old man was in and ask his advice but she was reluctant to share a secret that might yet turn out to be profitable.

She clung to his arm and matched his stride.

'What's she like, this floozy what got dumped on you?'

'She's hardly a floozy,' Danny said. 'First of all you don't cop a First from Oxford if you're the floozy type an', second, the BBC won't employ you.'

'They employed Susan, didn't they?'

'Come off it, Breda.'

'Okay, okay. This girl . . .'

'Kate.'

'Yeah, is she nice?'

'Very.'

'Oh, a spark there, is there?'

'My pal, Griffiths, would like to think so.'

'What 'e like then?'

'Welsh,' said Danny.

'Nuff said,' said Breda. 'Susie pleased to see yah?'

'Sure,' said Danny. 'Why wouldn't she be?'

'Well, we all know 'ow "busy" she is these days.'

'What're you drivin' at, Breda?'

'Nothin',' said Breda innocently. 'Anyhow, you got *your* chance now, ain't yah? Nice educated young thing sharin' your digs. Got a figure, has she?'

'Well, yeah, I suppose she has.'

'Flittin' about in 'er nightie, like.'

'In winter in Evesham? Hardly likely.'

They parted to give right of way to a young woman with a baby in a pushchair. When they came together again Breda said, 'Susie ain't the only one entitled to 'ave a bit of fun, Danny. This is wartime, right?'

'Are you havin' it off with somebody, Breda?'

'Me? Crikey, no! Ronnie's enough for me.'

'An' Susan's enough for me,' Danny said. 'Let it go.'

'Don't you wanna know if she . . .'

'Naw, Breda, I don't'.

'Never took you for a softy.'

'I'm no softy. I just happen to be in love with my wife. What the hell's wrong with you?'

'I just don't wanna see you get hurt.'

'You don't like me bein' hitched to Susan Hooper, do you, Breda?'

'Well,' said Breda, 'if you fancy a buttered bun, it's got nothin' to do with me.'

'Tae hell with your nonsense, Breda.' He unhooked his arm from hers. 'Tell Ron I'm sorry I missed him an' give Billy a hug from me.'

'Where you goin'?'

'Opticians for an eye test.'

'I didn't know you was blind.'

'Half blind,' Danny said. 'Only half blind,' then, kissing her perfunctorily on the cheek, turned off into Chater Street and headed for the Underground.

'Far be it from me to tell tales out of school, Daniel,' Vivian said, 'but I think you'd better keep an eye on your wife.'

'Really?' Danny said. 'Why's that?'

'She's becoming far too fond of the bottle. If she falls asleep on my davenport one more time I'm going to have to charge her room rent.'

'Two gins, just two,' Susan said. 'I was, I admit, tired.'

'I don't blame you for nodding off,' Vivian went on. 'It's all *your* fault, Basil, for convening meetings in the middle of the night.'

'If I'd known Susan's husband was in town,' Basil Willets

said, 'I'd have let her off early. Contrary to what you may think of me, Vivian, I'm no Simon Legree. Compared to the average producer—'

'No such animal exists,' Viv put in.

'Compared to some producers I'm a model of sweet reason.' He turned to Danny. 'What's it like at Wood Norton? Is it still "Yes, sir. No, sir. Three bags full, sir," or are you all chums together?'

'Might be a wee bit less formal than it used to be but the pecking order's still intact,' Danny said. 'It's tricky trying to explain BBC protocol to translators who've been top dogs in their own country. You've been a leading light in, say, Leipzig University an' speak five languages fluently, naturally you find it hard to kow-tow to a bloke who looks as if he should be sellin' insurance door-to-door.'

'Someone like you, Basil,' said Vivian, who, it seemed, had already gained the upper hand in that odd pairing.

They were dining in a fish restaurant off Baker Street, not far from Mr Willets's rooms in Gloucester Place. Susan would have preferred to spend the evening alone with Danny but could not, in conscience, refuse Mr Willets's invitation.

They had barely finished starters before, inevitably, the subject turned to *Speaking Up for Britain*.

Basil Willets was keenly interested in what Danny had to say concerning the skill of German broadcasters in opinion-shaping. Susan had downed two glasses of wine and devoured most of the turbot on her plate before the producer drew her into the conversation.

'Of course,' he said, 'we'll soon be doing a little opinion-shaping on our own account now we've found our newscaster – all thanks to Susan.'

'Susan?' Vivian chimed in at once. 'Susan had nothing to do with it. It was me who brought Robert Gaines into the fold. Credit where it's due, Basil. In your cavalier fashion, you assume that because Susan added his name to your list, Bob Gaines is her friend when, in fact, he's mine.'

'My error.' Basil Willets bowed graciously. 'I knew, of course, that Gaines was using you as a source.'

'A source of what?' said Danny.

'Information on home-grown fascist sympathisers,' said Vivian without hesitation. 'My crowd or, rather, my brother's crowd until everything went haywire. Are you shocked, Basil? You were quite close to David at one time.'

'A long time ago. I feel no loyalty to him now.'

'Very wise of you,' said Vivian. 'My brother, dare I say it, is not a jewel among men. Oh, he can be charming when it suits him but, basically, he's ruthless and has some exceedingly nasty habits. Isn't that right, Susan?'

'I don't know him well enough to pass judgement.'

'In that case,' Vivian said, 'you'll just have to take my word for it. David is a grade-A shit who should be locked up in jail.'

Basil Willets cleared his throat. 'Bit strong, Vivian. Blood's thicker than water, after all.'

'Not in my book,' Vivian said. 'Not in *any* of my books.'

'Speakin' of which,' Danny put in, 'how's the new book comin' along. Alienation, isn't it?'

'Aliens, really,' said Vivian. 'I'm interested in tracing the ideological diasporas of the twentieth century that began with the Bolshevik revolution and spread like wildfire throughout Europe.'

'Which by the twisted logic of history enabled Hitler and his henchmen to acquire power in Germany,' Basil Willets said.

And, to Susan's relief, they were off and running on a topic that would keep them occupied for the rest of the evening.

She'd known when she'd married him that Danny was no rugged Scotsman who would come charging out of the heather to take her willy-nilly. He didn't lack strength or stamina but, if anything, was too considerate of her feelings, as if he felt it necessary to respect her modesty, a modesty that most women – she, at any rate – discarded with their stockings.

She had restricted herself to two glasses of wine at dinner, had refused the liqueur that accompanied coffee and, soon after nine, had pleaded an early rise which, in the circum-stances, probably seemed like a double entendre, though neither Vivian nor Mr Willets had been crass enough to remark upon it.

Danny and she had left the couple at the table, not billing and cooing like would-be lovers but arguing with ever increasing heat about the ethics of government tribunals and the Acts that were currently being rushed through parliament.

'Think she'll spend the night with him?' Danny said.

'I doubt it,' Susan said. 'Mr Willets is too caught up in programming to waste time on sex. When it comes down to it Viv will have to make the running.'

They'd found a cab to ferry them home, had made tea and, seated by the fire, had listened to the latest news on the wireless. Closing in on eleven, they'd found the wave-length for a broadcast from Hilversum that Danny had listened to while Susan bathed and laid out her clothes for the morning.

Now he was seated on the side of the bed clad in vest and

93

underpants. She had fished out a clean pair of pyjamas and placed them, neatly folded, on his pillow. She flitted about the room in the new chiffon nightdress that had cost her more than a week's wages. The light of the little table lamp, reflected in the mirror of the dressing table, outlined her figure but Danny, lost in some dream of his own, seemed oblivious to it.

'Aren't you going to change?' she asked.

He glanced up, frowning. 'Change?'

'Into pyjamas,' she said.

'Oh, aye.'

He got to his feet, stripped off his vest, stepped out of his underpants and, rolling them into a ball, put them into the wicker basket by the dressing table with the rest of the dirty laundry. Susan had half a mind to hop into bed and haul the blankets over her head but the fact was that in spite of everything she needed him.

She watched him slip on the pyjama trousers and sit down on the side of the bed. He lifted the pyjama jacket, glanced at it as if he didn't quite know what to do with it and put it to one side. He had put on weight, she thought, not fat but muscle. His skin was smooth and tight and his hair, longer than she remembered it, formed a strange blond halo in the light from the table lamp.

He brought her to him, put his arms about her and dug his fingers into the small of her back. She pressed herself against him, shivering when he drew her closer and, trapping her between his knees, looked up.

'Susan,' he said softly, 'who's Robert Gaines?'

PART TWO

The Long Hot Summer

IO

Early in the morning of Friday, 10 May, Griff, Danny and Kate were dragged from their beds by a messenger from Wood Norton and, half dressed and *sans* breakfast, were bundled into a billeting officer's Morris Eight and driven at breakneck speed to the gates of Wood Norton estate where an armed sentry called out, 'Advance and be recognised' and, without awaiting a response, urgently waved them through.

The new huts had been erected in the nick of time, for every monitor, editor and supervisor on the roster had been called out, even those poor devils who had just finished night shift. Within minutes of their arrival Griff and Danny were hunched at the long table in the editing room and Kate was seated on a bench in M Unit's monitoring hut with a pair of earphones clamped to her head listening to a German announcer from Zeesen unleashing a torrent of justification for the Nazi attacks on Belgium and Holland.

There was no question now of a watching brief.

Every word of every bulletin from Germany was recorded, translated and transcribed, while French-speaking 'legionnaires' brought in the news from Paris, which, as Griff remarked to Danny, through a mouthful of cold coffee, was just this side of hysterical.

In the open yard at the back of the Oxmoor Road sub-station, amid trailer pumps and coiled hoses, a Divisional Officer, smart as paint even at that hour of the morning, assembled both night-and day-shift crews at the change and, in formal tones, announced that at five thirty that morning Wehrmacht troops, accompanied by armoured and motorised divisions, had entered Holland, Belgium and Luxembourg.

While there was every reason to suppose that the Allied forces would repulse the onslaught, he went on reassuringly, the nation must be on its guard, extra precautions taken and as a consequence – he cleared the gravel from his throat – all leave had been cancelled.

'Oh, bugger,' Fireman Clarence Knotts whispered into Ronnie's ear. 'That's my weekend in Monte up the spout.'

'It's no joke, Clary,' Ronnie told him.

'No,' Clary agreed, 'I don't suppose it is. Our turn next, do you think?'

'Yep,' Ronnie said. 'It's only a matter of time.'

Breda was in too much of a rush to get Billy off to school to pay attention to the news and the wireless was turned down to nothing much more than a murmur. She was vaguely aware that the announcer's voice sounded marginally less monotonous than usual but, running late, shrugged off an impulse to tune in properly.

She was halfway to school, Billy trailing behind her, before the raucous shouts of a newsvendor touting the latest editions alerted her to the fact that something big had happened across the Channel.

At the school gate half a dozen anxious wives had gathered, aprons and headscarves fluttering in the breeze.

'Heard the news, Mrs 'Ooper?'

'What news?' said Breda, as Billy scampered off to join his chums. 'Is it bad?'

'He's done it again.'

'Done what again?' said Breda.

'Adolf – 'e's gone for 'Olland now.'

'Like Denmark wasn't enough for 'im.'

'Won't be no room for dodgers now, Mrs 'Ooper. They'll be weeded out an' sent to fight proper, you'll see.'

'If,' said Breda, 'you're referrin' to my husband, he ain't no dodger. He's an auxiliary fireman.'

'White feather, that's what 'e is.'

Breda had suffered taunts before but never so directly.

Most of the women had husbands in the army and one, Mrs Baskin, had lost a brother when his ship had been torpedoed by a U-boat. None of Breda's nearest and dearest was anywhere near the front line, on land or sea, a fact that obviously rankled with the other wives.

'You won't be sayin' that, Mrs Collins, when your 'ouse burns to the ground,' Breda snapped.

'Never 'appen. Not 'ere.'

'Yeah,' said Breda. 'Tell that to the Dutch.'

Then, with a last glance at Billy playing happily with the other kiddies in the mud-caked yard, she walked away before she said something she might later regret.

★

'But what does it mean, dear?' said Nora. 'What does it mean for the likes of us?'

'Didn't Matt tell you?' Breda said.

'He was gone before the news came on.'

'Well, don't ask me,' said Breda. 'I'm as much in the dark as you are. Ronnie'll tell us, he gets 'ome.'

'How will Ronnie know?'

'Ronnie knows everythin'',' said Breda confidently. 'Maybe we should turn on the wireless since there'll be more news comin' in by this time.'

'No,' Nora said. 'You just leave the wireless alone.'

'You can't keep your head in the sand for ever, Ma.'

'I've got cakes to make.'

'Cakes ain't gonna be enough to satisfy 'em today.'

'I'll put the pan on for doughnuts then.'

'Oh, God!' Breda sighed and, tying on her apron, went out into the dining room to serve the paying customers who, that particular forenoon, were few and far between.

Richard Dimbleby, the BBC's sole foreign correspondent, was somewhere in France with the BEF when Hitler's great offensive began. While Dimbleby recorded reports for later transmission, little Basil Willets went one better and pulled off a coup with the first broadcast of *Speaking Up for Britain* which aired on the Home Service at 8 p.m. and at two in the afternoon across the eastern seaboard of America.

Thanks to Bob Gaines's connections, and a transmitter in Rotterdam, the first edition of *Speaking Up* began with a live eye-witness account of the Luftwaffe's attack on an Allied airfield in Holland by an excitable young English-speaking Dutchman who, by sheer ill luck, happened to be in the wrong place at the wrong time. BBC sound engineers succeeded in capturing the thud-thump of explosions and the whine of dive-bombers behind the Dutchman's commentary until, abruptly, transmission ceased.

Even on a day crammed with news, Robert Gaines's silence – two beats, three beats, then four – and his softly uttered response to the breakdown, '*He's gone,*' was enough to make the most casual listener sit up and po-faced journalists on both sides of the Atlantic reach for their typewriters.

A stranger to British reticence and the art of turning a blind eye to the obvious, Bob paused once more and, in that same level tone, said, 'I fear we may not hear from Pieter again,' then, putting the script to one side, delivered an unsentimental prayer for his colleagues in the Low Countries.

'Oh, Jesus!' Mr Willets, a man not given to profanity, murmured. 'Now we're in for it,' as the telephone on the wall of the control booth rang and rang again.

'I believe we may have a link with Washington, DC,' Bob Gaines continued, 'where Mr Burton Wheeler, Senator for Montana and spokesman for the America First campaign, is waiting to tell us what *he* makes of today's developments.'

By which time Susan was already sprinting down the hall to fetch anyone in the guest lounge who might be willing to cross swords with America's most vociferous isolationist.

Billy, worn out with play and stuffed with corned beef hash and suet pudding, had fallen asleep curled up on the carpet in front of the fire. He made no protest when Breda undressed him and Ronnie carried him upstairs to bed.

By five to eight Ronnie and Breda, also fed and watered, were seated close to the wireless set which, for some reason, was acting up. Studio voices kept fading in and out as if there were lightning in the air and even Ronnie's expert twiddling of the tuning knob couldn't quite find the wavelength and make the dashed thing settle down.

It was more by accident than design that the American announcer's voice came through loud and clear, followed by an interview from 'an Allied airfield somewhere in Holland' delivered in staccato English by a young Dutchman against a background of thumps and thuds that Ronnie instantly identified as an aerial bombardment.

'Susie's not there, is she?' Breda said.

'No, no, 'course not. She's in London.'

'What's that?' Breda hissed. 'It's fadin' again.'

She reached for the tuning knob but Ronnie grabbed her wrist and held her off and they were caught, frozen in the moment, brow to brow, when the American announcer uttered the words, 'He's gone.'

Shaking his head, Ronnie said, 'Poor bastard.'

Breda, bewildered, whispered, 'Ronnie, Ronnie, what's happenin'?' Then, a few minutes later: 'Is that Susie's friend, Vivian, talkin'?'

'Yeah,' Ron said. 'It is.'

'What's she doin' with an American in Washington?'

'Tearin' him to pieces, by the sound of it,' said Ron.

The office phone was ringing off the hook. Basil Willets told Susan not to answer since he'd had enough excitement for one night. He would come in early on Saturday morning to deal with the protests that would inevitably descend from on high for, as he put it, 'too much reality is one thing our lords and masters cannot stand.'

A complimentary decanter of sherry had been supplemented by whisky, gin and a dozen brown ales that Basil had purchased at his own expense and hidden in the office. Three guests, including Vivian, Larry the sound controller, Susan and, of course, the 'star' of the show, Robert Gaines, were gathered in the guest lounge to celebrate the achievement of pulling off a programme that had threatened to become a disaster.

Basil was supping ale from the bottle and whisky from a glass, turn and turn about, when an envoy arrived from Whitehall, accompanied by the Assistant Director General in full evening dress to lead Baz away to face the music in the Controller's office.

'What,' said Mr Stanhope, a well-known authority on international affairs, 'are they going to do to him?'

'Either offer him a knighthood or execute him on the spot,' said Vivian. 'Almost certainly the latter.'

'I didn't think it went too badly after that rocky start,' said the other guest contributor, novelist Angus Bowman.

'Losing our friend Pieter to the Luftwaffe was rather more than a rocky start,' Vivian said. 'How well did you know the young man, Robert?'

'Fact is, I never met the guy,' Bob said. 'I fixed him up through a contact in our Paris office.'

'I still don't see what the fuss is about,' Angus Bowman said. 'Basil couldn't possibly have known the Germans would stage a raid in the middle of his broadcast.'

'Death by radio,' Bob Gaines said. 'I guess it's not the done thing. I wonder what the British press will make of it?'

'The columnists will love it,' Angus Bowman predicted. 'Beaverbrook's boys will have a field day.'

Mr Stanhope said, 'I'm still not clear if we were meant to be speaking up for Britain or speaking out against Germany.'

'Which,' Susan put in, 'is something we're not really supposed to do – speak out against Germany.'

'When's your next broadcast?' Mr Stanhope asked.

'Tuesday,' Susan told him.

'Will it be cancelled?'

'I doubt it,' Susan said, 'but our scripts are bound to be censored, every last nut and bolt tightened to ensure we give no offence to anyone.'

'I shouldn't have gone for Senator Wheeler with quite so much venom,' Vivian said. 'I probably sounded like a shrieking harridan.'

'You sounded just grand, Miss Proudfoot,' Larry assured her. 'Not like a woman at all.'

'That's comforting,' Vivian said drily as the lounge door opened and Basil returned.

'On the carpet, Mr Willets?' Larry asked.

'Actually,' Basil said, 'no.'

'Well, what did the big cheese want with you?' said Vivian. 'Was it a pat on the head or a smack on the bum?'

'Someone in the Ministry of Information wants to have a word with me,' Basil said. 'That's all.'

'The fellow must have some clout if he can drag the Assistant DG away from the dinner table to deliver a message to a humble producer,' said Vivian.

'You do realise,' Mr Stanhope said, 'that you've given the ministry an ideal opportunity to meddle in programme content.'

'That' – Basil wiggled his eyebrows – 'is what concerns the DG most of all: government intervention. I've just been reminded in no uncertain terms that the BBC, while loyal to King and country, is *not* Whitehall's plaything.'

'My God!' said Mr Stanhope. 'Half of Europe's being trodden under the jackboot and the BBC is still concerned with keeping up its reputation for impartiality.'

'Whatever the fuss is about it seems we're full steam ahead for Tuesday,' Basil said. 'All hands to the pump first thing. Meanwhile, drink up, gentlemen. I'm off home.' He offered Viv his hand. 'Are you coming with me?'

'For what purpose?' Vivian asked suspiciously.

'To cook my supper, of course,' Basil answered, then, with a bow, added, 'Ta-ta for now,' and, ushering Vivian before him, toddled off into the night.

II

Reading a newspaper while riding a bicycle was an art Danny had never mastered. It seemed to come naturally to Silwyn Griffiths, though. He pegged the paper against the junction of the handlebars, steered with his elbows and pedalled the old Raleigh effortlessly while scanning the day-old copy of the *Daily Mirror* he'd plucked from Mr Pell's paper rack.

'I see they're still going on about it,' he said, while Danny wobbled along beside him. 'True, it's on page five but there's also an editorial comment. Public interest is obviously keen. Do you want to know what it says?'

'Not particularly.'

'You've heard it all from the Pells anyway,' Griff said. 'High drama on the airwaves. Pity we missed it. Are we stopping off for a pint?'

'Probably not a good idea,' said Danny, 'not with a long shift ahead of us.'

'I bow to your sagacity,' Griff said. 'I'm barely conscious as it is.' He sat back in the saddle and yawned. 'Incidentally, he isn't dead.'

'Who isn't dead?'

'The Dutchman.'

'What Dutchman?' said Danny, who knew perfectly well what Dutchman.

'Pieter: the fellow who was being interviewed when the bombs started falling. Oh, come on now, Cahill, you can't fool me. I know you're interested,' Griffiths said. 'In any case, Pieter, the hero of the hour, is slightly less of a hero now the *Standard* has tracked him down. Singed eyebrows doth not a martyr make. That's the fickleness of fame for you. Nary a word about eighteen dead airmen or the destruction of an operational Allied airfield which, by this time, has probably been overrun by Nazi tanks.'

'Try the front page, Griff,' Danny suggested.

'No point.' Griff let the newspaper float away behind him. 'No point in keeping yesterday's news when it's out of date before it hits the streets. Lord knows what fresh disasters have occurred since this morning. Doubtless Fritz what's-his-name will be shouting the odds about the cowardly French fleeing across the Meuse and trying to convince us that the peasants in Picardy are lining up with open arms to welcome their German liberators. Are you sure you don't want to drop in at the Greenhill for a slurp? Kate might be there.'

'Kate won't,' said Danny. 'She's on until midnight.'

Griff and Danny had ridden home from Wood Norton at eight that lovely Whit Sunday morning and were riding back in the hazy sunshine of Sunday afternoon for another long stint with pencils, scissors and paste.

Stooped over the handlebars, sweating in the heat, they swooped down, shoulder to shoulder, into the town.

Shops were closed but soldiers and local girls, pretty in their Sunday best, were strolling the streets. Folk were gathered at the gates of churches too, for morning and evening services had been bolstered by special Whitsun prayer meetings as if, Griff said, the God of our fathers had come into His own again.

They were still a half-mile shy of their destination when a camouflaged lorry roared past, almost knocking them down. The lorry was followed by two unmarked motorcars, long and lean and black, then by a van with blacked-out windows, all the vehicles travelling at top speed.

Griff steadied the Raleigh and wiped dust from his eyes. 'Someone's in a hurry,' he said. 'The army on the move?'

'Nah, it's not an army exercise,' Danny said. 'I've seen enough of those black cars in my time: coppers.'

'Couldn't possibly be heading our way, could they?'

'Aye,' Danny said, pedalling faster. 'They could.'

He entered the yard from the lane at the back of the terrace and sidled past the brick-built lavatory that the council had been promising to replace with an indoor facility since Ronnie had been in pantaloons.

Ronnie had taken Billy to the park and wouldn't be home before five. Breda was washing shirts in a tub at the sink when she spotted the intruder through the lattice of paper strips Ronnie had glued to the kitchen window to protect the glass from bomb blast.

Craning her neck, she scowled at the man whose arrival was observed only by next door's cat perched on top of the dividing wall. His beard was grizzled-grey and bushy. His beret and heavy half-length black coat reminded her of Rabbi Abrahams who'd run a mission for the poor out of the synagogue in Fletcher Street and had had a kind word for everyone, Jew, Christian or Hindu, until he'd passed away last year.

The stranger carried a brown paper package under one arm but, as far she could tell, no gun. He certainly didn't look like one of Harry King's henchmen. Even so, she dug the coal hammer from the bucket by the hearth and, hiding it in a fold of her apron, opened the back door a couple of inches and growled, 'What you after, then?'

He glanced left, right and behind him before answering: 'Breda, darlin', for God's sake let me in.'

'Daddy?' Breda said. 'Is it really you?'

''Course it's really me,' Leo Romano said and Breda, grabbing his arm, yanked him indoors.

The ornate gates of Wood Hall estate lay open, entry barred not by a couple of squaddies but by what appeared to be half a battalion of military policemen armed to the teeth with rifles and batons. Fortunately Griff and Danny were lightly clad in open-necked shirts and flannel trousers, otherwise the inspection might have been embarrassing. As it was, the fact that they had bicycles and knew how to ride them was reason enough for suspicion.

'What the devil's going on?' Griffiths was injudicious enough to enquire and, before he knew it, had the point of a bayonet resting against his chest.

Danny kept the bike between himself and the MP in charge. He handed over his pass, his identity card and, as a hasty afterthought, his gas mask case.

'Kaa-ill? What sort of a name's that?'

'Cay-hill,' said Danny apologetically. 'It's Scottish.'

'Never heard of it.'

'Oh, it's common enough,' Griff began. 'Irish in orig—What? Yes, of course, sir. Sorry.'

They could make out the Hall bathed in tranquil light, Mrs Smith's villa and, partly screened by shrubs, the long-bonneted motorcars drawn up on the grass in front of the huts. Men were being led from the huts and herded into a van and Mr Gregory, M Unit's supervisor, was waving his arms and shouting.

The MP handed them back their passes and signalled to the guards to let them through the gates. Danny and Griff, not daring to speak, wheeled their bicycles up the driveway towards the huts outside of which the entire Wood Norton staff was assembled, including engineers brought down from the hill.

'How, pray tell,' Mr Gregory was shouting, 'am I supposed to supply over forty government departments with essential information when you're purloining my best men?'

The officer in charge, a uniformed copper with gold braid on his hat, ignored the supervisor's furious protests and the cries of the prisoners who, Danny noted, were clad in shirt-sleeves and braces as if they'd been dragged bodily from the benches.

'That's old Friedelmann. What the devil are they doing with him? Christ, is he in handcuffs? Don't tell me he's in handcuffs?' Griffiths said. 'Look, they've got Greiner and Olbrich too. Have we made a deal with Adolf to hand over all our Jews, or what?'

A struggle in the doorway of M Unit's hut revealed little Thomas Heckroth, a jovial imp of a man and one of the unit's best translators. He was arm-locked by two burly policemen and backed by an MP with a baton which, even as Griff and Danny watched, was placed across Thomas's neck with enough force to bring him to his knees.

'Three years in a Nazi labour camp,' Griff said. 'How can they possibly mistake Heckroth for a fascist?'

'My wife, please find my wife,' Thomas Heckroth pleaded as he was bundled into the back of the van.

Mr Gregory had been joined by Mr Harrison and three other supervisors, all clamouring to be shown warrants of arrest which, it appeared, were not forthcoming.

Hanging on to their bicycles, Griff and Danny stopped some way short of the crowd.

Kate appeared from behind the editing hut, accompanied by four or five young women who gathered about Griffiths and Danny. Griff lowered his bicycle to the grass then put his arm around one of the typists, Ursula, while Femi, a good-looking Finnish girl, rested her head on his shoulder.

'What's goin' on?' Danny said.

'They're arresting all the Germans and Austrians,' Kate informed him. 'The police have already pounced on those in the village, Jews, non-Jews and anti-fascists all bundled in with Nazis, semi-Nazis and any other poor soul who might be considered a threat.'

'What will they do with them?' Ursula asked.

'Stick them in internment camps for the duration, I imagine,' Griff answered. 'Guilty until proven innocent, that's what war does to natural justice. No surprise, really. Thank God, I can trace my ancestry back to Gwyn ap Nudd or they'd have me in handcuffs just for riding a bicycle.'

'Mr Gregory will sort it out, won't he?' said Ursula. Neither Griff nor Danny had the gall to inform her that Mr Gregory was just as helpless as the prisoners in the face of emergency orders. 'What about their wives? Who'll tell their wives? Or will they take the women too?'

'Not you, Ursula,' Griff said and, giving the beautiful Finn a squeeze, added, 'Nor you, Femi. Danny's right: Germans and Austrians only.'

'Until Mussolini throws in with Hitler,' Danny said, 'after which there won't be an ice-cream seller or spaghetti house waiter left in London an' we'll lose our four Italians.'

Doors at the rear of the van slammed. On a signal from the policeman in the braided hat, the van reversed across the grass and, gathering speed, vanished down the driveway. The coppers scrambled into the motorcars and clambered into the back of the lorry and, within minutes, were gone too, leaving nothing behind but dust.

Mr Gregory called out, 'Translators whose second language is German please report to my office immediately. I know. I know. We've all had a shock and we've all lost friends, at least temporarily, but, please, people, remember why we're here and how important our job is.' He paused and then, gathering breath, shouted, 'All of you, back to your desks.'

Monitors, editors and typists, Kate, Griff and Danny among them, trailed obediently back into the huts which, without the presence of Friedelmann, Greiner and cheerful little Tommy Heckroth, seemed less like home than ever.

Seated at the table in the kitchen, wolfing down a second ham sandwich, Leo Romano said, 'So who told you I was on the run?'

'Steve.'

'He tell you why?'

Breda poured boiling water into a teapot, swirled it around and tipped it into the sink. For a moment a cloud of steam hid her face from her daddy's enquiring glance. He wiped mustard from his beard with his sleeve and crammed the rest of the sandwich into his mouth.

Breda measured tea from a caddy and filled the teapot with hot water. She paused to squint from the window but the back yard was deserted; even the cat had gone.

'You 'ad your 'and in Harry King's till,' she said, 'an' Harry wants his money back.'

'Well, he ain't gonna get it,' Leo said.

Breda put the teapot on the hob, washed a mug and dried it carefully on her apron. 'How long you been wearin' the face-fuzz?'

Leo grinned and stroked his beard. 'Like it?'

'Not much.'

'I needed a new look to fit my new identity. Thought I'd be long gone by now but the papers didn't come through an' I missed the boat.'

Breda decided to say nothing about Vince's midnight call or her visit to the Brooklyn or the geezers from Special Branch sniffing around Stratton's. She trusted her father even less than she trusted herself.

'What papers?' she said. 'What boat?'

'Identity card an' passport,' Leo told her. 'I thought it'd be easy but turns out half the crooks in England had the same idea so I had to join the queue at the forgers an' wait for the right boat to turn up.'

'The boat to Canada?' Breda said. 'You've been plannin' this for months, you crafty old sod. That's why you wanted me an' Billy over there.'

He picked crumbs from the plate with the ball of his thumb. 'You're all I got now, Breda, you an' Billy.'

Breda poured tea into the mug and put it on the table together with a milk jug and sugar bowl. She lit a cigarette and, leaning on the edge of the sink, sized him up.

He didn't look like her old man, not a shadow of the man she remembered from childhood, all brash and natty, never a hair out of place. Only his eyes were the same, those sexy dark eyes that told you he was all Italian, eyes that the ladies of Shadwell had found irresistible.

She blew smoke. 'So where you stayin'?'

'A safe place.' He sipped tea. 'Safe as it can be. I've got my papers an' a berth all bought an' paid for on a cargo boat due to sail on the 27th.'

'You can't 'ave much dough left, Dad,' Breda said. 'I can lend you a few quid if you need it.'

To her astonishment she saw his eyes fill with tears. He sniffed and tried to smile, sniffed again, then buried his face in the tea mug to hide his distress.

'You're a good girl, Breda. You was always a good girl. I couldn't ask for a better daughter,' he mumbled. 'Breaks my heart to think how I treated you an' your brother. Poor Georgie, gone now, poor kid. There's only one person in this whole wide world I can depend on an' that's you, darlin'.'

Breda crossed to the table and placed a reassuring hand on the crown of his shoulder.

'Yeah, Dad, you can always depend on me.'

He fished the heavy paper-wrapped package from beneath his chair and placed it solemnly on the table.

'What,' Breda said, 'is that?'

'Money,' Leo told her. 'Cash money.'

'Cash?' said Breda. 'For me?'

'Not exactly.'

'What is it for then?'

'It's my life savings. I need you to keep it for me till the war's over and I'm ready to start up again. I've taken what I need to see me through. The rest is gravy.'

'How much gravy?'

'Three grand, give or take.'

'That's an awful lot of give or take,' Breda said. 'What you want me to do with it?'

'I told you, keep it till I come back.'

'You got a bleedin' nerve expectin' me to stash money you stole from Harry King. Geeze, Dad, if he ever finds out there's no sayin' what 'e'll do to me.'

'He won't find out. Who's gonna tell him?'

'You might when he tickles your feet with a blow torch.'

Leo laid a pale hand on top of the package. 'I can't put it in a bank, Breda. Too many funny folk asking too many funny questions about where money comes from these days. No, you gotta keep it for me, someplace safe.'

'Where? In my knickers?'

'Don't be dirty.'

'You're a fine one to talk.' Breda pressed her belly against the edge of the table. 'In a shoebox, is it?'

'Cashbox.' He reached for her hand and, sensing her hesitation, squeezed her fingers and applied a dollop of the old Romano charm which, given his sorry state, was a lot more resistible than it used to be. 'War's over, I come back, I'll see you right – you and Billy – see you both right.'

'Unless Harry King sees me right before then.'

'Steve won't let that happen.'

'Does Steve know you're 'ere?'

''Course not.'

'Where exactly are you 'oled up?'

It was her father's turn to hesitate.

Breda said, 'Bleedin' hell, Dad, you don't think *I'm* gonna shop you to Harry King, do yah? Come on!'

'Brighton,' Leo said. 'I'm rooming in Brighton with a woman I know. She's my go-between.'

'What's 'er name?'

'You don't need to know her name,' Leo said.

'Okay, but why Brighton?'

'Brighton's the one town on the coast where Harry's boys ain't welcome. Ada's lot might not be as tough as they once was but they're still tough enough to keep Harry's boys from showing their faces in Brighton. Anyhow, Ada's got all the necessary contacts at her fingertips.'

'How much you payin' this woman?'

'An arm and a leg,' Leo admitted. 'I cashed in my retirement fund.' He squeezed her hand again. 'Say you'll do it. Say you'll look after my nest egg till the war's over.'

''Course I will. Your secret's safe with me.'

'And my money?'

'An' your money,' Breda said.

'Good, good,' her father said. 'Now all I gotta do's say goodbye to Billy. Where is my little darlin' by the way?'

'Out with 'is dad – an', believe me, you don't wanna be 'ere when Ronnie gets back. Since 'e put on that uniform 'e's gone all righteous an' might even turn you in. I'll say goodbye to Billy for yah. Okay?'

'Okay,' Leo agreed and, rising, took her in his arms and hugged her. 'You're a good kid to do this for your old man, Breda, you really are a damned good kid.'

'I know I am,' said Breda.

Ronnie would disapprove; that wasn't guesswork, inspired or otherwise, but a fact as plain as the nose on your face.

It was as if his fireman's uniform had come complete with a whole new set of values that added up to Patriotism with a capital P. One thing Breda was glad of was that Ronnie was now far too principled to go chasing after skirt and far too conscious of his role as a public servant to go out of a night for a skinful.

He hadn't lost his sense of humour or his fondness for rolling his wife in the hay, thank goodness, but when it came to stashing stolen cash, let alone spending it, you didn't have to be a genius to predict how Ronnie would react. She and Leo's cashbox would be down the local nick before you could say Tommy Trinder.

She hated deceiving Ron but her conscience was salved somewhat by the two thousand, eight hundred and fifty quid that her father had managed to stuff into the dented metal cashbox.

At first she thought of taking the box up to Stratton's and hiding it in the back of the larder. But Matt and Ron had converted the larder into an air-raid shelter that Matt visited from time to time to ensure that the bottled beer stored there for emergencies hadn't gone off.

In any case, she wanted to keep as close to the money as possible. She roved frantically about the house in search of a safe hiding place and, just minutes before Ron and Billy arrived home, while seated on the throne in the lavatory at the end of the yard, she found it.

In the angle of the roof behind the cistern she prised out a loose plank and, balanced precariously on the pedestal, slid the cashbox into the cavity and carefully replaced the board. She had barely finished her task when Billy barged through the gate from the lane.

'Mum,' Billy shouted. 'Mummy. You in there?'

'Yeah. Won't be a tick.'

She smoothed her skirt, adjusted her bra and, smiling, opened the door to allow her son to bulldoze past her and, with no inhibitions, tinkle into the pan.

'Flush,' Ron called out.

Billy obediently pulled at the ball on the end of the chain and, still fiddling with his trousers, emerged to the sound of rushing water. Breda crouched and helped him with his buttons then, patting his tail, sent him shooting off into the kitchen in search, no doubt, of something to eat.

She linked arms with her husband.

'Nice time?' she asked.

'Billy enjoyed it. You?'

'Nice enough.'

'Dad didn't drop round then?'

'Dad? Whose dad?'

'My dad, of course,' Ron said.

'No,' Breda said, 'no one dropped round. All very quiet an' peaceful, really,' then, gripping his arm a little more tightly, steered him away from the water closet and safely into the house.

★

Susan's father had always been a modest man and had made sure that she hadn't been subjected to a casual education in male anatomy. She'd seen him bare-chested, of course, when he'd washed off the grime of the docks at the sink and once, though only once, she'd caught a glimpse of her brother in the altogether and had been less than impressed by the twiddly little bit of flesh he'd tried to hide with his hand before, yelling, he'd chased her from the room.

There had been statues and the unabashed nudity of males in paintings on show in the Tate, plus the distasteful drawings that the girls at school had passed about, giggling, and the sight now and then of a boy baby scampering about bare-bummed. But the first adult male Susan had ever seen naked had been her lover, Mercer Hughes, who, for better or worse, had become the yardstick, as it were, for the men who came after whom, to date, numbered only two.

Bob Gaines might have scruples about bedding another man's wife but when it came to lovemaking he had no inhibitions at all. Susan couldn't shake the feeling that he was evaluating her in the light not of a small table lamp but of ten or twenty women who had gone before; women with unblemished complexions and perfect shapes to whom she, narrow-hipped and small-breasted, would never match up.

He had kissed her in the taxi on the way back from the Blue Lagoon where they'd danced up close in the hour after midnight, so close that she could feel his need of her pressing against her stomach and, gratified, had rubbed against him in the half-dark in the centre of the dance floor where the rotating beam from the crystal ball did not fall and where all around in slow, swaying circles, young men and girls clung to each other as if there would be no partings, no regrets come morning.

'Time to go,' Bob had whispered.

'Go where?'

'My place.'

There were ten or a dozen people in the shared suite in the Lansdowne, all drunk or getting there. Pete Slocum was sprawled on the couch, two girls half lying on top of him, one of whom was already asleep.

Bob took Susan's hand and led her along the corridor to the bedroom. No one cocked an eyebrow or stirred themselves. Only Slocum's hooded glance brought Susan a moment of guilt. Then she was safe in the bedroom, alone with Bob; fearful that she wouldn't be good enough or bad enough or woman enough and that by shedding her clothes she would be revealed as a skinny little East End girl to whom Bob would make love only out of pity or because she was handy.

He propped a wooden chair under the door handle to keep out unwanted guests and then, to Susan's dismay, stripped off all his clothes.

The pink-painted wickerwork chair seemed more suited to a Camden Town boudoir or a bijou nursery in Chelsea than an elegant room in Lansdowne House.

It creaked under Bob's weight when, naked now, he seated himself upon it and, leaning forward, invited her to undress. She had no nightgown, no pyjamas, no excuse to escape into the bathroom. He rested his elbows on his knees, head cocked, watching her. He looked huge in the slant of light from the lamp, more naked than nude, if such a thing was possible. He was heavy but not fat, his chest and belly sprinkled with dark hair, the shadow between his thighs dark too.

'Don't you want to?' he said.

'Yes,' she said. 'It's just . . .'

'You don't want me to look, is that it?'

She nodded and, when he beckoned, went to him and stood meekly before him like a child awaiting a reprimand.

Resting his brow against her, he buried his face in her skirt. She looked down at his broad shoulders and the curve of his back. He slipped his hands under her skirt, stroked her thighs and softly, almost teasingly, opened her with his fingertips.

She sagged against him and closed her eyes.

The first helpless rush rose and broke and immediately rose again. She kicked off her shoes and hoisting up her skirt showed him that she was ready.

He rose from the chair, lifted her on to him and, locking her legs about his hips, rode her across the room until they fell, still locked, on to the big broad bed.

12

While much of Europe was falling to German advances and British soldiers were piling up on the beaches of Dunkirk, a number of 'heap big pow-wows', as Basil called them, took place in the smoke-filled offices of Broadcasting House in the course of which BBC administrators and representatives from the Ministry of Information sought to protect their personal agendas. Basil, of course, would have none of it. The subject of *his* programme, he said, was Britain on the brink and if that wasn't dynamic enough for his overlords then he would gladly turn in his stopwatch and let someone else take the strain.

Favourable comments in the press and reports from the CBC that several regional stations in North America had picked up the programme for re-broadcast indicated that *Speaking Up*'s blend of reportage, comment and discussion was having the desired effect and Basil vowed that, within the parameters required by military censorship, he would continue to deliver what the public wanted without treating listeners on either side of the Atlantic like dolts.

Susan barely had time to bathe, change her clothes and snatch a few hours' sleep as crises piled on crises and the production staff struggled to keep on top of the news.

She saw little of Bob outside the studio save for an occasional snatched 'lunch' in the flat in Rothwell Gardens and heard nothing at all from Danny who was probably as busy as she was and not, she told herself, sulking.

'Not a word?' Vivian said.

'Not so much as a postcard.'

'You have written to him, haven't you?'

'A couple of letters. I haven't had much time.'

'Didn't he reply?'

'No.'

'Why haven't you telephoned him?'

'He isn't allowed personal calls.'

'Doesn't his silence concern you?' said Vivian.

Susan hesitated. 'I suspect he's playing tit-for-tat and he'll come round in his own good time.'

'For God's sake, girl, he's your husband. You can't just prance about as if you were footloose and fancy-free.'

'You're a fine one to talk.'

'That's the second time you've told me that,' Vivian said. 'May I point out that I'm an old maid and Basil's a widower and that anything we choose to do hurts no one. Let me ask you one question and beg the favour of a straight answer: do you think Danny would do this to you?'

'Do what to me?'

'Take a lover,' Vivian said.

'He wouldn't dare.'

'I see,' said Vivian. 'What's sauce for the goose is not – repeat not – sauce for the gander?'

'Be all right if I were a chap, wouldn't it?' Susan said. 'Give me one good reason why a girl shouldn't have a little bit of fun too.'

'Is that all it is, a little bit of fun?'

'Not so little, if you must know.'

'Don't tell me you're in love with Robert Gaines?'

'Of course not. I'm not in love with anyone.'

'What about Bob Gaines, what if he's in love with you?'

'He's not that much of a fool,' Susan said. 'It's a fling, that's all, a nice little fling for both of us.'

'Well, I just hope you're right,' said Vivian. 'And I just hope that Danny doesn't catch on.'

'Fat chance of that happening,' Susan said, 'given that he's chained hand and foot to a desk in Evesham.'

Monday, mid-afternoon: they lay together in sweltering heat in a few hours stolen from their hectic schedules.

'Don't fall asleep,' Bob said.

'If I do, I'll never waken up,' Susan said.

'Have you anything round here to eat?'

'Not much,' Susan said. 'Eggs, I think.'

'Fresh?'

'Probably not.'

He moved against her, cupped her breast and touched her nipple lightly with his thumb. The window was open an inch or two but there was no breeze and the air in the flat was stale and lifeless. Something was going on in Rothwell Gardens, some vaguely military thing, but neither Bob nor she had the energy to look out to see what the shouting was about.

'Are you working this evening?' Susan asked.

'No option. I've promised the *Post* a piece on the paddle-wheelers that made the run to Dunkirk. It's a gift of a subject and I have all the notes I made in Ramsgate so it shouldn't take more than a couple of hours to knock off.'

'We also need your material for Tuesday, remember.'

'You never let up on a guy, do you?'

The sheet that had covered them had been discarded and she could see all of him, no part hidden. He was flaccid now and had carefully removed the rubber and, like a true blue gentleman, had wrapped it in a handkerchief and hidden it in his shoe to dispose of later.

She said, 'Why did you never have children?'

'Beg pardon?'

'With your wife: children?'

'What the hell sort of a question's that?'

'I'm just curious.'

'What sort of a father do you think I'd make,' he said, 'when I spend nine-tenths of my life out in the field?'

'Like a farmer.'

'Foraging for news; yeah, right.'

'Wouldn't you like to have a son?' Susan said.

'You're not trying to tell me you're pregnant, are you?'

'Not even in jest, darling; not even in jest.'

The sound of gunfire from the gardens was startlingly loud in the cloying afternoon heat.

'Shooting traitors, I expect,' said Susan.

'Blanks,' Bob told her. 'Home Guard drill, maybe.'

'You didn't answer my question.'

'Pearl didn't – let's be polite about it and say she just wasn't ready for motherhood.'

'You mean she didn't like sex.'

'Oh, yeah, she liked sex well enough. She just didn't like doing it with me.'

Susan sat up. 'Why ever not?'

'She thought I was too demanding.'

'You are, you know, far too demanding.'

'Is that a complaint?'

'Far from it.'

'Look,' he said, not moving, 'I really must shove off.'

She lay back on the pillow. 'Me, too. Baz will have fits if I'm not back by four. The running order for Tuesday's gone to pot. Major Cazalet's been called away, apparently, and left us rather stranded.'

'Who's doing the piece on the Emergency Powers Act?'

'At the moment, no one. The ministry are griping at the very idea. We're trying to persuade Walpole to do it but he isn't at all keen.'

'Viv?'

'Basil thinks it should be a man.'

'That won't please her highness,' Bob said.

'Wouldn't know. She's not speaking to me these days.'

'Because of us?'

'I think she's worried about her brother.'

'Have they arrested him yet?' Bob said.

'No, but they should have. He's a black-hearted villain through and through.'

'How well *did* you know him?'

'Not as well as he'd have liked.'

Another round of rifle fire peppered the air, followed, anomalously, by the blast of a whistle as if the drill were a football match governed by the rules of fair play.

'Proudfoot wasn't one of them then?' Bob said.

'One of them?'

'One of your paramours.'

'Just how many "paramours" do you think I've had?'

'Dozens for all I know,' Bob said.

'One,' Susan said. 'Just one.'

'And a husband?'

'Husbands don't count.'

'Well, who am I to disagree?'

'I'm sorry. I didn't mean to be insensitive.' She tangled her legs with his and rested her head against his shoulder. 'Forgive me?'

'Nothing to forgive.'

'Did you love her – your wife, I mean?'

'She was the only girl in Paterson, the only girl for me.'

'As it turned out she wasn't, was she?'

'No, she wasn't,' Bob said. 'It was my mistake, not Pearl's. Hey, enough with the Freudian stuff. I really do have to go home and do some work.' He kissed her on the nose and swung his feet to the floor. 'Who's first for the bathroom?'

'I am,' Susan said.

The building and its plumbing had baked in hot sunshine for weeks and the water from the taps was cool but not cold. She stood upright in the bath in the cramped half-tiled bathroom and, squeezing a sponge with both hands, trickled water over her breasts and belly.

Danny had nailed plyboard across the pebble glass window and the room, even in daylight, was dark. She had left the door to the kitchen open an inch to let in light but the flow of water from the taps and the gurgle of the cistern above the lavatory drowned out sounds from the living room.

Crouching, she splashed water into her lap, then, refreshed, stepped out of the bath and dried herself with the big bath towel that Danny had given her last Christmas.

She was relaxed after lovemaking but aware that time was pressing. If she couldn't find a cab it would take her all her time to make it back to Broadcasting House by four o'clock. She had eaten nothing since breakfast. She would pick up a sandwich from the snack bar at Green Park or, if the worst came to the worst, scrounge something from Larry who always had food to spare. She pulled out the bath plug, wrapped the towel around her and padded through the kitchen into the living room.

Danny, motionless as a statue, stood in front of the empty hearth, arms folded across his chest.

'What do you think?' he said.

'The glasses?' Susan said. 'They suit you. How long have you been here?'

'Couple of minutes.'

'Who told you? Was it Vivian?'

'No one told me. I came up to town to collect my spectacles an' dropped in on the off-chance you'd be here. I didn't mean to intrude.'

The bedroom door opened. Barefoot and struggling into his pants, Bob came into the living room.

'Susan, I thought I heard . . .' he began.

'Robert,' she said, 'I'd like you to meet my husband.'

'Oh, peachy,' Bob Gaines said, 'just peachy,' and, not knowing what else to do, stepped forward to shake Danny's hand.

13

The tinkle of breaking glass in the front shop wakened Nora instantly. She dug Matt in the ribs and, reaching for her dressing gown, had just put one foot on the floor when the door of the bedroom burst open and a uniformed constable switched on the ceiling light.

Matt sat up, blinking. 'What the . . .'

'Mrs Leo Romano?' the copper growled.

Nora, mouth hanging open, nodded.

'Got her, sir. In here,' said the copper and a man in a double-breasted lounge suit and snap-brim hat stepped past the constable into the room.

Matt reached for the alarm clock on the bedside table and squinted at the dial. Twenty minutes past five. For a moment he was convinced that the alarm would go off, his dream would end and he'd get up and make ready to go to work.

'Put that down, please,' the lounge suit said.

'It's just a clock,' said Matt.

'It's a weapon,' said the lounge suit and directed the constable to remove the object from Matt's hand which, swiftly, the constable proceeded to do.

Matt knew then that it was no dream and, with a roar,

pitched himself out of bed. One copper, then two, threw themselves upon him, locked his arms behind his back and jammed his face into the wallpaper.

'This 'im, sir?'

'No, it's the woman we're after, just the woman.'

Clad only in her nightdress and dressing gown, Nora was taken by the arm and hustled towards the door. Past the peeler's broad shoulder Matt caught a glimpse of her terrified face and, enraged, kicked at the constable's shins.

'Now, now, you dirty old sod, you've 'ad your fun for one night,' one said and, jerking Matt by the arm, forced him down into a praying position by the bed. 'Stay there like a good lad, an' be thankful your name ain't Romano.'

'Bastards,' Matt shouted. 'Nazi bastards.'

A gloved hand shoved his face into the mattress and a gloved hand whacked his ear.

And then they left.

Matt clambered to his feet, crept on to the landing and looked down the stairs into the corridor that led into the kitchen.

He crouched at the top of the stairs until the shop door slammed, then, clutching his pyjamas to his belly, leaped down into the corridor, ran through the kitchen into the shop and out through the open door into the street.

The motorcar was already halfway to the corner, a van with blacked-out windows hard on its tail. Matt pursued the van for a hundred yards, cursing at the top of his voice, then, badly winded, gave up the hopeless chase and limped back to Stratton's to find help.

*

'How the hell do I know where they've taken 'er, Dad?' Ronnie said. 'I'm a fireman, not a bloody copper.'

'You want some more of this?' Breda shook the bottle of brandy that she kept for emergencies.

'Yer.' Matt held up his tea mug. 'I mean, what they want with Nora? She's Irish, for God's sake. She never done no 'arm to no one.'

'Didn't they tell you anythin'?' said Ron.

'Not a bleedin' thing,' Matt said. 'Near tore me arm off, they did, when I tried to stop them.' He raised his left arm to shoulder height and winced. 'Lucky it ain't broke. Didn't even let 'er dress. I mean, nightie an' dressing gown; what sort of a way's that for a woman to go out in public? Where's Billy?'

'Still asleep,' said Breda.

'Not even a warnin',' Matt went on. 'They broke the front door an' just barged in. Can they do that, Ron?'

'They can now,' Ronnie said. 'Musso declared war yesterday so it's woe betide anyone Italian.'

'Nora ain't an Eye-tie,' Matt said

'No, but she's married to one,' Breda reminded him.

'If she'd only married me, she'd be safe as 'ouses.' Matt ran a gnarled hand over his face and scrubbed at his thick grey hair. 'What they gonna do to 'er, Ron?'

'First we got to find out where they've taken her, an' that might not be so easy.'

'It's the law,' said Matt. 'Ain't it? Habus Corpsus; they can't keep 'er without a charge. We need a lawyer. You know any good lawyers, son?'

'Not me,' Ronnie said.

'Susan might,' Matt said. 'Susan would.'

'Forget about Susan,' Breda said. 'I can 'andle it.'

'You?' Matt Hooper said.

'Yeah, me,' said Breda.

She unfolded the scrap of paper that she'd kept hidden in the drawer with her rosary beads, the lace handkerchief that had once belonged to her Irish grandmother and the bone and silver teething-ring, a christening gift from Danny, that Billy had chewed through before he was a year old.

She dialled the number carefully, pressed pennies into the slot, pressed the button and in a clear, calm voice asked to be put through to Mr Jessop's office.

'Tell him,' she said. 'It's Leo Romano's daughter.'

The box was on the corner by the Co-op bank at the head of Docklands Road. The road was already bustling with drays, motor vans and the big tarpaulin-covered flat-bed lorries that always looked as if they were just about to shed their tottering loads. Even with the door of the box closed Breda could hear the traffic sounds vibrating in the summer morning air.

She was nervous, too nervous even to smoke. She didn't really expect Jessop to be there so early. She was already planning what she might do next when a soft, soothing voice spoke into her ear.

'Mrs Hooper, what a pleasant surprise.'

'Yeah, I'll bet it is,' said Breda.

'What can I do for you?'

'Where is she? What've you done with my ma?'

'Your ma?'

'Come off it, Mr Jessop. I know you got her.'

'I don't have her here, lass. In fact, I'm not entirely sure who has her. I know my friends in the CID are interested but . . .'

'It's my dad you're after, ain't it?'

'Of course, it is,' Jessop admitted.

'How much tug you got, Mr Jessop?'

'Beg pardon?'

'I mean,' Breda said, 'are you in a position to get my mother released?'

'I am.'

'Can I count on you to deal fair?'

'Absolutely.'

'Okay, tell me where an' when we can meet.'

'I take it you know where your father is?'

'Yeah,' Breda said. 'I do.'

'He's not with you right now, by any chance?'

'He's not that stupid.'

'Tell me where he is and—'

'You think I'm fallin' for that one, think again, Mr Jessop,' Breda said. 'I'll tell you what you wanna know when I see my mother face to face.'

He uttered a strange little sound, like a cat purring, as if her caution pleased him.

'All right,' he said. 'Holloway prison at ten o'clock.'

'Inside or out?'

'I'll be at the gates at ten.'

'See you there then,' said Breda and hung up.

It took her all her time to persuade her father-in-law that he would be better off at work. Ronnie took no persuading; only serious illness or injury were accepted as excuses for ducking a watch.

'Holloway?' he said. 'Nora's no crook. What's she doin' in prison?'

'She won't be there long. I've been in touch with the Irish embassy,' Breda said in a moment of inspiration and, rather to her surprise, saw her father-in-law nod as he swallowed the lie.

'The Irish embassy?' said Ronnie. 'Really?'

'Ma's a – what-they-call-em?'

'Alien national,' Ronnie suggested, giving her a long look. 'I suppose you're gonna tell us the Irish ambassador's taking up the case personally?'

'That's it,' said Breda. 'The Irish ambassador.'

'He'll do 'is stuff, won't 'e, Ron? They'll listen to the Irish ambassador, won't they?' Matt said.

'You bet they will,' Ron said, then, drawing Breda to one side, whispered, 'What the hell're you up to?'

'Got a copper on our side.'

'Copper? What copper?'

'Used to be a friend of mine long time ago.'

Ronnie grunted. 'Like that?'

'Yeah, like that,' Breda said. 'Gone up in the world, he 'as since them days. He remembers me, though, remembers me fondly enough to say he'll 'elp.'

'What's he gonna get in return?'

'Not what you think, darlin',' Breda assured him. 'Not what you think at all. How long you got?'

'Short of an hour.'

'Make sure the old man eats somethin' then pack 'im off to work. Get Billy up an' dressed an' give 'im 'is breakfast. I'll be back in time to take 'im to school.'

'*Now* where you goin'?' said Matt anxiously.

'Up to Stratton's to collect Ma's clothes. Don't want 'er paradin' through the streets like Lady Godiva, do yah? Did you patch up the front door?'

'Best I could, state I was in,' said Matt.

'I'll stick up the "Closed" sign. That'll 'ave to do for now.' Breda planted her hands on her hips, thrust out her chest and, like the harridan she yearned to be, said, 'You got that, both of you? You know what you gotta do?' and, without waiting for an answer, rushed upstairs to dress.

Many of the trees that had screened the towers and turrets of the old Holloway Castle had been removed but those that remained were in full, dusty leaf and the arched doorway still had the menacing appearance of a keep.

Breda experienced a flutter of panic when the door opened and a warder, sweating in his serge uniform, sourly inspected Mr Jessop's pass.

'We're expected,' Mr Jessop said.

Brooking no argument, he stepped over the threshold and led his little party of three men and Breda into a communal hallway and, obviously familiar with the building, swung left into a vaulted corridor floored with worn brown linoleum.

Sunlight stole through high unbarred windows that reminded Breda of churches she'd visited with her mother, churches with histories as long as your arm. At the first corner, she caught a glimpse of a vast tunnel-like room with tiers of cells rising up to a glass roof and a spider's web of iron bars and railings. She had no opportunity to gawp. Mr Jessop cracked on at a fair pace and it was all she, in the middle of the group, could do to keep up.

She had no idea who the other men were but one very

tall man with a neat moustache seemed too well dressed to be a copper. Even Mr Jessop called him 'sir'.

Ronnie had unearthed an old rucksack brought home from Spain that, stuffed with Nora's clothes, Breda carried in her arms. Mr Jessop wheeled round another corner and there, at the corridor's end, was a varnished wooden door guarded by a male warder who snapped to attention as soon as Mr Jessop's party appeared.

'How many?' the tall man with the moustache asked.

'Eleven, sir,' the warder answered.

'All women, I take it?'

'Aye, sir.'

'Have they been fed?'

'Tea, sir, an' bread.'

'How long ago?'

''Bout an hour, sir.'

'All right,' the tall man said. 'Open up.'

The long room was more like a civic hall than a jail cell. Small square windows admitted scant light. In the centre of the room was a trestle table with two chipped enamel pails upon it, three or four empty milk bottles and an array of tin mugs. There were no chairs, only benches upon which women crouched or lay in uncomfortable positions.

A pair of female warders in black skirts and stiff white shirts stood guard, one on the door, the other by an open recess at the far end of the room within which were two lavatories, side by side. A woman in a velvet ball gown squatted on one of the pedestals, skirts drawn up to her waist.

When the tall man with the moustache appeared in the room, she stretched out her neck and screeched, 'Richard, you toad. It's about time you got here,' then, fairly obviously, sat back and relieved herself.

'*Noblesse oblige?*' Mr Jessop murmured.

'I've seen her piddle in worse places than this,' the tall man said. 'Leave her ladyship to me. Do what you have to do with the girl.'

Rising from the benches, all chattering at once, the women converged on the tall man. Unlike her mother, Breda realised, they were toffs. Some were in evening dress – one even had an ermine stole about her shoulders – others wore cashmeres or long elegant summer frocks. Never before, Breda thought, had her ma been in such exalted company.

The women harried the tall gentleman mercilessly. They were furious that they had been swept up like common criminals and insisted on reminding him who they were, what influence their husbands exercised and that if they weren't released at once they would see to it that his career in government was over and his position in society doomed.

'Breda,' Nora said, 'you come for me?'

''Course I did, Ma,' said Breda.

Barefoot and barelegged, nightdress and dressing gown hanging on her like rags, her mother looked so wretched that Breda's grit dissolved and, dropping the rucksack and clasping Nora to her breast, she burst into tears.

One of the policemen moved to separate them but Mr Jessop said, 'Wait.' He signalled to the wardress by the door and, while Breda and Nora sobbed in each other's arms, gave the woman instructions. Then he laid a hand on Breda's shoulder. 'Time to go now,' he said.

'Where you takin' her?' Breda spun round. 'You said – you promised . . .'

'Calm yourself, lass,' Mr Jessop said. 'She'll have a wash and a brush up and a place to change into her street clothes. You'll see her again shortly. Meanwhile, we'll step outside, away from this bedlam, and have a little chat. All right?'

'Right,' Breda sniffed. 'All right,' and watched her mother being led away.

The office wasn't really an office, more of a storeroom. Sewing machines were stacked on a table and an ancient spinning wheel, covered in dust, stood in one corner. There were mops, brushes and pails, two big tubs of wax polish and a huge tin of disinfectant that made the room smell like a public lavatory.

'Close the door, Syd, please,' Mr Jessop said.

The plainclothes officer, saying not a word, obliged.

Mr Jessop reached into his coat pocket and brought out a cheap silver-plated cigarette case, opened it and offered it to Breda who, still sniffing, picked a cigarette from under the band and allowed Mr Jessop to light it.

She gulped in smoke and tried to stop trembling.

'Who's the bigwig?' she said at length.

'Oh, he needn't concern you,' Mr Jessop said. 'We only brought him along to sign a few papers.' Syd laughed, and Mr Jessop went on, 'Well, Mrs Hooper, we've kept our side of the bargain. Now it's your turn. Where is he?'

'I got one question first,' Breda began.

'Oh, dear, I hope you're not going to renege on—'

'No, just one question: my dad, what'll you do to 'im?'

'That's not up to us,' Mr Jessop informed her.

'You won't top him, will yah?'

'Of course we won't top him,' Mr Jessop said. 'Your daddy

138

might be a bad lad but he's no traitor. As it stands, he's wanted on minor criminal charges. If he gives us certain information, information useful to us, we can have him re-classed as an alien national. Do you know what that means?'

'He goes into a camp for the duration without a trial,' Breda said. 'It's Harry King you're really after, ain't it?'

'No flies on you, Mrs Hooper,' Mr Jessop said. 'What happens to your father now is solely up to him. There's nothing you can do to help him, one way or t'other. So where is he?'

'Brighton,' Breda said. 'Can't give you an exact address, 'cause I don't 'ave it. He's lodged with a woman called Ada.'

'Ada!' Syd slapped his brow. 'I might have known it. Bloomin' Ada Levinson!'

'Do you know her, Sydney?' Mr Jessop asked.

'Oh, sure, I know her. Born in the East End but decamped to Brighton about fifteen years ago. Queen of the rackets on the south coast and a slippery piece of work if ever was. We've been after her for years.' He rubbed his hands glee-fully. 'Oh, I like this. I do like this. Hold the girl and her mother for a quarter of an hour to give me time to make a few phone calls, then release them.' He pulled open the door. 'Can't thank you enough for your cooperation, Alf, you and your department.'

'Only glad we could help, Inspector,' Mr Jessop said.

'What about me?' said Breda. 'Don't I get thanked?'

'You get your mother back,' said Mr Jessop. 'Isn't that enough?' and ushered her out of the store.

14

There were few more beautiful places in England than the Vale of Evesham in the height of summer. The air was no longer scented by sage and gillie flowers but by orchards in full bloom. The fragrance of plums, cherries and other fruits was intoxicating and if that wasn't enough for you there were plenty of waterside pubs and quaint little inns along the Avon's banks where a jug or two of cider would complete the job.

There were certainly more peaceful spots to spend your off-duty hours than the meadow at the top of Common Road. The open-air swimming pool had become a magnet for BBC types and, in the past week, for survivors of the Dunkirk evacuations who were convalescing in the hospital nearby.

By noon the joint, as Griff put it, straining his lyric gift to the limit, was jumping.

Bicycles were piled against the changing sheds and the grass around the pool was littered with sun-soaked bodies munching sandwiches, drinking bottled ale or ginger pop. Girls frolicked in the water, shrieking. Men ploughed doggedly up and down, heads bobbing, and one portly continental gentleman floated idly on his back, a panama hat tipped over his nose, a lighted cigar in his mouth.

The soldiers were more circumspect, easing themselves into the green-brown water to test their injured limbs while a little group of four or five, too damaged to risk immersion, sat in a circle, and reminded themselves how lucky they were to be alive – and the sight of Femi, the long-legged Finn, rising from the water in a white sharkskin bathing suit was enough to make any man glad to be alive.

Neither Danny nor Griff had ever learned to swim and were too embarrassed to cling to the ropes and thrash about like little kids. They lolled, shirtless, on a carpet of towels while Kate, slim and athletic in a black woollen swimming costume, her dark hair tucked under a pale blue bathing cap, swam in the deepest part of the pool.

Griff would have preferred to camp close to the pool to watch the bathers but Danny said that was too much like ogling. Besides, he, Danny, had something to get off his chest and now was as good a time as any.

'Why didn't you tell me this before?' Griff said as soon as Danny had finished speaking.

'The time didn't seem right,' Danny said.

'Then why are you telling me now?'

'I've kept it bottled up for too long,' Danny said. 'I have to tell someone an' you just happen to be handy.'

'Does Kate know?'

'Naw, of course Kate doesn't know.'

'So what did you do? Punch the blighter on the nose?'

'I shook his hand,' Danny said. 'I mean, can you believe it? I actually shook his hand?'

'Congratulations, sir, you've just had the pleasure of bedding my wife,' Griff said. 'Oh, boy! Oh, boy! Is this the American broadcaster, the voice on the wireless?'

'Aye, that's him.'

'Did you know they were at it?'

'I had my suspicions,' Danny said. 'But I certainly didn't expect to bump into them in my flat in the middle of the afternoon.'

'Why, in God's name, did you shake his hand?'

'I felt sorry for him,' Danny said.

'Sorry for him? Are you crazy?'

'He looked about as shaken as I was.'

'And her? The missus, what about her?'

'Cool as a bloody cucumber.'

'Have you heard from her since you got back?'

'A couple of letters, yeah.'

'Saying what?'

'Not much.'

'No apology, no contrition, no going down on her benders and promising never to do it again?'

'Nope, nothin' like that.'

'She wants a divorce,' Griff stated. 'Plain as the nose on your face, she wants out of the marriage.' He laid a hand on Danny's shoulder. 'I'm sorry, boyo. I really am dreadfully sorry. Just bear in mind that it's not your fault.'

'I'm not so sure about that,' Danny said. 'I caught Susan on the rebound.'

'The rebound from what?'

'A love affair, her first love affair.'

'Who was the bloke?'

'Mercer Hughes, a literary agent,' Danny said. 'My wife moved in some fairly arty circles after she left Shadwell.'

'What happened to Hughes? Did he ditch her?'

'He took off for America an' didn't come back.'

'This one,' Griff said, 'this current American, he's not going to stay in England for long, is he?'

'Probably not,' Danny said. 'He's a reporter first an' a newscaster second so he's under no obligation to hang around if an' when Hitler invades.'

'A fact of which your wife is well aware.'

'I suppose she must be.'

'It may be a fling, nothing more,' Griffiths said. 'The question you're now asking yourself, Daniel, is whether or not you'll take her back after it blows over. Your wife may simply be testing you.'

'Testing me?'

'To see if you love her enough to forgive her. Do you, old son? Do you love her enough to forgive her?'

'That's what I don't know.'

'Naturally, you don't know,' Griff went on. 'In this world, at this time, nobody can be certain of anything. It does occur to me, though, that perhaps the lady wants you to fight for her. Punching the Yank on the nose would have been a good start. What did you do, by the way?'

'I apologised for intrudin',' Danny said, 'picked up a couple of shirts an' left.'

'You did yourself no favours there, unless . . .'

'Unless what?' said Danny.

'You're the one who wants out of it.'

'Why the hell would I want out of it?' Danny said.

'Search me, Danny boy,' Griff said as Kate, carrying her bathing suit and towel, came up the grassy slope to join them. 'Search me.'

★

The woman had let herself go too long ago for anyone to remember what she looked like when she first arrived in Brighton. Much water or, to be accurate, gin had flowed over the dam since then. Only a few of the old gang were still around to remember the glory days, though in some less than salubrious pubs, far from the piers, esplanades and coastal defences, the story still went the rounds how Norris Levinson had married Ada on his deathbed only because she'd threatened to rip out his breathing tube if he didn't.

To look at her now you'd never suspect that she'd once been the shapely tart in the Fawley Street fish bar who'd lured Leo Romano from the relatively straight and narrow and, a mere six weeks later, on a jolly trip to the seaside, had dumped him for Norris Levinson.

A huge, quiet, sullen woman, utterly devoid of sentiment, she'd taken Leo in not for old times' sake but only because he'd done the dirty on Harry King and, of course, had money.

She provided Leo with a refuge in a top-floor room of her shabby little boarding house on the strict understanding that he wouldn't show his face out of doors while she pulled strings to get him a new identity and a berth on a ship to Canada. She'd been none too pleased when Leo had slipped up to London to say goodbye to his daughter and now she'd squeezed him for every last penny she was just as anxious to be rid of him as he was to leave.

She gave no impression of haste as she climbed the stairs from the hall to bring him a plate of fried fish and chips, some bread and scrape and a mug of hot tea which, she warned him, might be the last decent meal he'd have for some time.

She assured him that the bus that meandered along the

south coast to Southampton would be liable to checks by local coppers on the lookout for deserters but that no copper would ever spot his papers as counterfeit. Then, in a pub in Southampton he'd be met by a crewman from the *Carolina* who would give him a forged dock pass.

Once he was on board the merchant ship, however, her work was done and he was on his own. The bus left the station at a quarter after three. Without wishing him luck or even saying goodbye, Ada lumbered downstairs and left Leo alone to eat his fish and chips.

It was very quiet in the terrace house in the heat of the summer afternoon. He could just make out the throb of the strange machine in the dust-destructor's yard a quarter of a mile off, smell smoke from the railway and cattle stink from the abattoir across the backs.

Discarding the beret and long overcoat, he settled for an old donkey jacket and a cloth cap he'd found on the hall stand downstairs and tried to convince himself that he looked like a seaman. He went to the window and studied the road below: a cat on a wall, an old man with a dog on a lead, two women, not young, looking up at the blue sky as if they were counting clouds; no loud noises, not even the yelping of seagulls who, he guessed, had followed the ebbing tide to escape the sizzling onshore heat.

Ten minutes to three: he put on his jacket, patted his pockets to make sure his papers were secure, lifted his canvas kitbag and his gas-mask case and took one last look at the room in which he'd been imprisoned for the past month.

He opened the door and went downstairs to the hall.

He wasn't surprised when Ada didn't appear from her lair in the kitchen. He slipped the latch and opened the front door.

Blinking in the strong sunlight, he stepped from the house.

And a hand grabbed him by the arm and another by the neck and a jovial voice cried in his ear, "Allo, Leo. Surprise! Surprise!'

Breda put his supper on the table in the kitchen behind the dining rooms and, exhausted, slumped into a chair and lit a cigarette. She had been on her feet for the best part of sixteen hours and was too tired to eat.

Her father-in-law peered at the mound of mashed potato floating in a puddle of tinned stew. He opened his mouth to complain, then, glancing at Breda, prudently decided not to.

He reached for the sauce bottle. 'She down?'

'Yeah. Gave her a couple of Aspro with her cocoa an' she's sleepin' like a baby.'

'What about Billy?'

'Tucked up in Danny's old room.'

'You leavin' him 'ere with me?'

'Nope, I'm stayin' over.'

'You don't have to,' Matt said. 'You've done enough.' He spooned up stew and shoved the spoon into his mouth. 'Don't know how you done it neither.'

No, and you never will, Breda thought. She drew in smoke, coughed and said, 'Ronnie's on day watch so he can 'ave the bed to himself tonight. I'll see you off in the mornin' before I open the shop.'

'Why don't you close for a day or two?' Matt suggested. 'Can't see the harm in that.'

'The harm in that,' said Breda, 'is we lose business.'

'She should've got rid of Romano years ago.'

'Water under the bridge,' said Breda warily. "Sides, we don't know where he is right now.'

'I'll bet our Susan could find out.'

'Susan? What the heck can she do that I can't?'

'She's got friends in high places.'

Breda exhaled a mouthful of smoke. 'You want bread?'

'What?'

'For your gravy?'

'Yer,' Matt said.

'Then fetch it. It's in the bread tin.'

She watched him shuffle to the long shelf of the dresser, lift the lid of the bread tin and dig out a day-old loaf.

'Knife,' Breda said. 'Top drawer.'

Sometimes she had to remind herself that this old codger had raised two kiddies on his own and had been regarded by all and sundry as a bit of a freak for doing it.

She stubbed out her cigarette and watched him saw three thick slices from the loaf with the breadknife. He left knife and loaf on the dresser shelf and returned to the table. He mopped gravy with a heel of bread and said, 'Never comes round no more, does she?'

'If you mean Susie, why should she?' Breda said. 'There's nothin' here for 'er now.'

'There's us,' Matt said.

'She don't give a toss about us, Dad. Sooner you get that into your noodle the better.' Breda paused, then, to soften the blow a little, added, 'Can't say I blame her. If I'd had her chances in life I'd be off too.'

'What? Leave Ronnie?' Matt said, frowning.

'I don't mean now, I mean then. If my dad 'ad done for me what you done for Susie . . .'.

'All I did I done to make 'er mother proud.'

'Her mother was dead.'

'That don't matter.'

'Don't tell me you think your missus is lookin' down from heaven with a smile on 'er face?'

'Might be, for all we know.'

'Geeze!' Breda said. 'You'll be lighting candles next.'

Matt wiped the plate clean with a last pinch of bread. 'You wouldn't leave Ron, would you?'

'Nah,' Breda said. 'I'm stuck with him – an' you.'

'An' Billy,' Matt reminded her.

'Yeah,' she said, smiling. 'An' Billy.'

'Breda, how'd you do it? How'd you get Nora out?'

'Friends in high places, Dad,' Breda said, then, relenting, shoved herself away from the table to open a tin of peaches for his pud.

15

The official representative of French Radio in London, Jean Masson, had been interviewed several times on *Speaking Up* but when communications from France broke down after the Germans swept into Paris he was immediately recalled to Bordeaux. He left soon after General de Gaulle's first stirring broadcast from London in which the general called upon all free Frenchmen to continue the fight against Nazi oppression.

Susan had been eager to nab de Gaulle and his translator for an interview but Basil was less than enthusiastic.

The general was known to be touchy and Basil guessed – correctly, as it happened – that he wouldn't be amenable to wasting his breath addressing the people of North America when the people of France had urgent need of him. In any case the general had a ready-made platform on *Ici la France* where, without supervision, he could ignore foreign advice and say what the devil he liked.

Speaking Up had to make do with two smart young French journalists, Yves and Pierre, on occasional loan from CBS. Their English was impeccable and their breezy style of reporting provided an ideal counter to hectoring German propaganda, an arrangement that seemed to satisfy everyone except Bob Gaines.

'What's wrong with him these days?' Basil asked. 'He's going about like a bear with a sore head. I can hardly get a civil word out of him.'

'He's suffering,' Susan answered.

'Damn it, we're all suffering,' Basil said. 'What is it? Doesn't he like our tame Frenchmen?'

'It's not that.'

'Well, what is it then?' Basil said. 'Aren't you keeping him happy out of hours?'

'That,' Susan said, 'is none of your business.'

'Probably not,' Basil conceded. 'But I don't want him upping sticks right now. You know how listeners are. They love a familiar voice, a voice they feel they can trust. Why is he suffering?'

'He thinks he should be in France.'

'Well, we can't send him to France.'

'He knows that,' Susan said. 'He hates not being there, though. His colleague, Slocum, is on the ground covering momentous events for the *Post*. Bob feels he's missing out.'

'Slocum, I assume, has neutral status.'

'An American Press Association card, yes,' Susan said. 'Even if Robert did manage to sneak across the Channel, chances are he'd be rumbled and thrown out on his ear.'

'Rumbled?'

'Denounced as an agent of the BBC.'

'If he keeps referring to Marshall Pétain as Hitler's lick-spittle and taking sideswipes at the new government in Vichy he'd be lucky if he wasn't shot,' Basil said. 'I'm giving him all the rope I can without the ministry jumping on me.'

'I'm sure Bob understands that,' Susan said. 'But it really makes his blood boil to think of German tanks driving up the Champs-Élysées and Nazi officers lounging at café tables sipping Pernod while the French dance meekly to the Führer's tune.'

'I wouldn't go so far as to call it meekly,' Basil said. 'There are those in our government who regard it as a necessary capitulation. If Robert is eager to be on the ground floor when momentous events take place I suggest he stays put in London.'

'Do you think we're next?'

'Of course, we're next,' Basil said. 'Who else is left?'

Susan was well aware that there was more to Bob's dark moods than the absence of a free pass to the Continent.

He hadn't forgiven her for her coolness when Danny had barged in on them. Lunch-hour lovemaking might have ceased but at least he hadn't broken off with her. Late-night, after-work suppers at the Lansdowne invariably wound up in Bob's bed where he took her so forcefully that she couldn't be sure if he was pleasuring or punishing her.

The Lansdowne was buzzing at all hours of the day and night. Foreign journalists expelled from France, Canadian flyers, soldier boys and assorted camp followers packed every room. Raucous parties went on into the wee small hours and the only peaceful spot in the building at present was Pete Slocum's suite, for, with Pete out of town, Bob had the apartment to himself. When any of Pete's cronies turned up looking for booze or a place to sleep Bob gave them short shrift and even friends and colleagues whom he'd known for years were turned away.

Bob was already at work when Susan wakened.

The bedroom door was open and she could make out the clacking of typewriter keys from the living room. She groped for the travelling alarm and peered at the dial in the scant light that escaped the blackout curtains.

It was not yet seven.

The valet wouldn't appear for another hour.

She knew without opening the curtains that it would be another hot day. She was weary of glaring sunlight and enamelled blue skies, of dusty streets and suffocating rooms, of restless nights and sticky sheets; weary too of her husband's silence and her lover's hostility. She climbed from the bed, peeled off her nightdress, put on her dressing gown and headed for the bathroom. She had all the symptoms of an approaching period but it was five or six days late.

Bob was still going at it hammer and tongs when she came out of the bathroom. The curtains were open and a carpet of sunlight stretched down the length of the hall. She wrapped the dressing gown about her, stepped into the kitchen, filled a kettle and put it on the gas ring then went purposefully into the living room.

Bob was crouched over a typewriter balanced on a side table close to the open window. He wore flannels and an under-vest, no socks or shoes. His hair was rumpled and a cigarette hung, shedding ash, from the corner of his mouth. A packet of paper was tucked under the rungs of his chair. A whisky glass, doubling as a paperweight, held down finished sheets and carbons.

'How goes it?' Susan said.

He took his fingers from the keys but did not look up.

'It goes well.'

'Is it something for the *Post*, or for us?'

He ground the cigarette into an ashtray, picked a fleck of tobacco from his tongue then sat back and stretched his arms above his head. 'I doubt if it's Basil's cup of tea,' he said, 'and it's way too long for radio. I'll probably trim it for the *Post*.'

'What's the subject?'

'It doesn't really have a subject.' He paused. 'Well, I guess it does. It's Paris, Paris the way I remember it, the way it used to be, the way it was last time I saw it.'

'That sounds – romantic.'

He looked up. 'Romantic? Paris was never romantic. It was lovely, yeah, a beautiful city but it was always a tough place to make your mark or, worse, fail to make your mark. I'm not sentimental about it.'

'Will you look back on your time in London and write about it too some day?'

'I'm not quitting,' Bob said, 'if that's what you mean, if that's what Basil's worried about.'

'Why are you mad at me?' Susan said. 'It's not my fault you can't go back to Paris.'

'Paris has nothing to do with it. Fact is, I don't like being used. If you want out of your marriage, Susan, all you have to do is say so. You didn't have to subject me to that humiliating charade.'

She seated herself on the ledge below the window and felt a little draught of cool air tickle her spine.

'I had no idea Danny would walk in on us,' she said. 'I didn't enjoy it any more than you did.'

'You sure knew how to handle it, though.'

'What's that supposed to mean?'

'Look, it's too early to argue. Besides, I'm beat.'

'I'll make coffee as soon as the kettle boils.'

'When are you due?'

'What?' she said, startled. 'How did . . .'

'At Portland Place?'

'Oh!' she said. 'That! Eight thirty.'

He tilted the chair round to face her, an arm slung across the chair back. 'What did you think I meant?'

'Nothing.'

'Are you late?'

'No, but I'd better keep moving.'

'Susan, are you late?'

'Only a little. Nothing to worry about.'

'How little is a little? A week, a month?'

'Four or five days. It's happened before.'

The kettle had no whistle on the spout but when it boiled it rattled on the ring. She could hear it rattling now. He caught her arm before she could make for the door.

'Is this another of your goddamned games?' He mimicked her voice. '"Oh, darling, I'd like you to meet my husband."'

'I didn't call you "darling".'

'You sure as all hell wanted your poor schmuck of a husband to know we were screwing.'

'He'll get over it.'

'Is that what you're counting on? If you can't have me, you'll settle for him. Is that how it goes? Now this, this maybe-I-am, maybe-I'm-not crap. If there is a kid in your belly you know and I know and your poor schmuck of a husband knows whose kid it has to be. I've been down this route before. My duplicitous wife taught me exactly what it means to be the guy on the losing end. Your husband and I aren't competing with each other, Susan; we're competing with you.'

'Robert, I'm sorry.'

'For me? Don't be.' He pulled the chair against the table, ratcheted up the paper to read what he'd written, and began typing again. 'Go make coffee. Go on, make coffee.'

She hesitated for a moment then headed for the hall.

On the day of the French surrender 'the legionnaires', male and female, had wept. Since then there had been hardly a moment of respite for Wood Norton's monitors as they struggled to keep up with the pandemonium from the Occupied Zone.

Extra staff had not materialised and at a Monitors' Meeting, supervised by Mr Gregory, there had been a heated discussion of the need for a firm division between day and night shifts now that so many foreign stations were being watched continuously. So far, no improvements had come into effect. Russian and Spanish speakers with a smattering of German did their best to plug the gap but the burden fell on Kate and her cohorts who, deprived of fresh air as well as sleep, had the haggard, hollow-eyed look of front-line troops.

Mid afternoon and as hot as a baker's oven in the listening hut: Kate had eaten nothing since 5 a.m. Mrs Pell had insisted on cooking breakfast, though Kate was too groggy to do it justice. Griff had donated her use of a bicycle while Danny and he shared the other. Luck had been on her side that morning. An early service bus had come by and, bike and all, she'd bundled in with Hogsnorton's other bleary-eyed civilians to begin another interminable stint on the headphones.

The pencils in Kate's tray were bitten at the ends, a habit

less detrimental to health than chewing on an unlit pipe, sucking boiled sweets or puffing one cigarette after another. She knew she was fraying at the edges, though, when she stumbled over several easy phrases and mistook a quotation from Goethe for a report on the weather in Hamburg.

She was on the point of declaring herself too tired to go on when a friendly hand closed on her shoulder and a mug of tea and a plate of tinned salmon sandwiches appeared at her elbow.

'Chin up, my little chickadee,' said Griff. 'It'll soon be Christmas.' Then he planted a kiss on top of her head and hastened back to the editing hut.

16

The best fires, Ronnie had learned, were not necessarily the biggest. The one he'd enjoyed most had been a small but smoky affair in the attic room of a spindly tenement at the far end of Dockside Road. Mercifully there had been no loss of life unless you counted the two budgerigars who'd died of fright when Clary Knotts, brandishing an axe, had snatched up their cage and carried it down one of the ladders that were supposed to be off-limits to auxiliary firemen.

Ronnie had been first into the building. He'd charged up four flights of stairs and, following procedure to the letter, had got down on his belly and opened the garret door an inch or two in case the draught created a searing blast of heat.

At this point in the proceedings an old lady, clad only in a big pair of floral bloomers and obviously deficient in any knowledge of the chemistry of combustion, had yanked open the door and, using Ron's head as a stepping stone, had gone leaping down the stairs, wailing like a banshee.

Somewhat dazed, Ron had groped his way into the acrid smoke that the old lady's husband had managed to generate using nothing but a frying pan, a blanket and a bolster. First he'd dived for the stove and switched off the gas, then, aware that saving life was his priority, he'd smacked the frying pan from the old boy's grasp and, grabbing the smouldering blanket, had smothered the burning fat with it.

Unfortunately, this action had released another cloud of thick smoke that had poured through the half-open window and prompted Mr Reilly, the Station Officer, to order the building cleared; an order that, unfortunately, came too late for Clary Knotts, who had already hooked his ladder to the window ledge and clambered into the garret to rescue the hysterical budgerigars.

It had all been a huge joke to the rank and file, not so funny for the Station Officer who'd been on the carpet before the Divisional Commander and had, in turn, read the riot act to the ill-disciplined Oxmoor Road auxiliaries and put Ron and Clary on extra duties as a punishment for insubordination.

At first telling Breda thought the story hilarious. When Ron repeated the tale she found it less amusing and by the third or fourth recounting saw nothing in it to laugh about, for it had finally dawned on her that Ron's job was dangerous.

She was beginning to realise that there was more to this war than evacuations and rationing, gas masks, identity cards and stupid laws that could see an innocent woman imprisoned. Therefore, she wasn't entirely surprised when Steve Millar, minus motorcar, appeared at the school gate one morning in early July dressed in a pair of old grey flannels and an open-neck shirt.

'Spare me a minute, Breda?' he said.

'Sure,' she said. 'What's up now?'

He put an arm about her, a big, muscular arm and, while the other wives watched askance, gave her a cuddle.

'It's your old man,' he said. 'They grabbed your old man.'

Breda's mouth went dry. 'Where?'

'Brighton.'

'What was he doin' in Brighton?'

'Hidin' out while he waited for papers.'

'Oh!' Breda said. 'Is he in jail?'

Steve still had an arm about her and, slipping it to her waist, steered her away from the nosey women to a quiet corner by an ARP hut. He stopped by a pile of spilled sandbags that no one had seen fit to remove and gave her a cigarette. Breda shakily guided the ciggie to her mouth and let Steve light it.

'Look,' he said, 'nobody knows where Leo is. All we can say for sure is the coppers scooped him up in Brighton along with a gang of fakers. They nailed Harry King too, nailed him good an' proper.'

'In Brighton?'

'No, in London,' Steve informed her. 'Best guess is your old man handed the coppers Harry on a plate. They'll have Harry up on criminal charges, which means a jury trial with sworn witnesses, including me an' Vince. The boys in blue don't want no fuss right now so they've given me an' Vince a choice: enlist or be arrested. They reckon Vince an' me will look more convincing front of a jury if we're in uniform. Better a soldier than a convict, right?'

'What about my daddy? Where's he?'

'Chances are they've interned him or maybe deported him to somewhere like Quebec.'

'At least he'll be safe till the war's over.'

'Wouldn't be too sure of that, love,' Steve said.

He pulled a rolled-up copy of the *Daily Express* from his

waistband, unfurled it and gave it to Breda to read the banner headline: *Germans Torpedo Germans.*

'My dad ain't German,' Breda said.

'It wasn't just POWs went down with the ship,' Steve said. 'It was mostly Italian internees. Hundreds of them.'

Breda tried to make sense of the text but her eyes had gone funny. She lifted the paper closer to her nose and peered at the photograph below the headline.

'Says here, they're safe in a Scottish port.'

'A few,' Steve told her, 'not many.'

'What's the boat called?'

'The *Arandora Star.* Used to be a liner before the war but there wouldn't be much luxury for anyone on this trip.' Breda continued to stare blankly at the newspaper. Steve went on, 'She got plugged off the Irish coast by a U-boat, Monday, an' most of the Italians were drowned.'

'We don't know my daddy was on board, do we?'

'Nope, an' it might be months until we find out one way or the other. The government will have to publish a list, I suppose,' Steve said, 'eventually.'

'What am I gonna tell Ma?'

'You don't have to tell her anything.'

'If he is dead then she's legally a widow.'

'There won't be no money, Breda.'

'Money? Wha'cha mean – money?'

'From the government: compensation.'

'I wasn't thinkin' of money,' Breda said. 'I was thinkin' if Leo's dead Ma could get married again.'

'That's none of my business,' Steve said. 'I just thought I should be the one to bring you the bad news.'

'Yeah. Yeah, thanks,' Breda said. 'Now the coppers 'ave

Harry King under lock an' key, 'ow long before they fetch 'im up for trial?'

Steven shrugged. 'Three months, maybe four. They'll need time to build a watertight case against him.'

'Will they 'ave enough evidence to hang 'im?'

'They might,' Steve said. 'He's been up to some big money deals tradin' arms to foreign governments, so I've heard. Now we're at war an' they've rewritten the rule book they might nail him for treason unless he gives them some real big fish in exchange for his neck. They already pulled in most of the small fry, here an' in Brighton.'

'But not you, Stevie?'

'Nope, not me,' Steve said; he paused. 'An' not Vince neither. We're just a couple of ordinary Tommies, far as the army's concerned.' He paused again. 'Funny thing is nobody seems to know what 'appened to the loot.'

'The loot?'

'The dough your old man stole.'

'You mean the three grand?' Breda said.

She saw him smile, or, rather, almost smile, for the little dimple at the corner of his mouth was anything but endearing. 'Yeah,' he said. 'The three grand.'

'Maybe the cops got it,' Breda said.

'Then again maybe they didn't.'

Breda drew in a stiff little breath. 'Hey, don't look at me, chum. Think I'd be standin' 'ere chattin' with you I had three grand stowed away?'

'You might,' Steve said, 'if you was keepin' it safe for Leo.'

'Fat lotta good it'll do 'im if he's dead.'

'That's what we reckoned, me an' Vince.'

161

'Well, if you do find it,' Breda said, making light, 'don't forget to share it with Leo's nearest an' dearest.'

An' who might that be?'

'Me, of course,' said Breda.

'Yeah, that's what we figured too.'

Breda wasn't sure if she was being threatened but it gave her the shivers just to think what a beast like Vince might do to her to lay his hands on three thousand quid. She kept her voice as even as possible and casually changed the subject. 'When do you leave for your training camp?'

'This afternoon.'

'What about Rita an' your kid?'

'Goin' off to stay with her folks in Croydon.'

'Is it safe in Croydon?'

'Safe as anywhere,' Steve said. 'It's not likely I'll hear anything about Leo, not in an army camp. But if I do, I'll certainly tip you the wink. The paper, keep it if you like.'

'You do think he's dead, Stevie, don'cha?'

'I think he might be, love. I really think he might be,' Steve said and, for old times' sakes, gave her another cuddle which, oddly, made her shiver too.

Whatever patriotic urge had moved Vivian to volunteer for fire watch duties had died long ago. She regretted her impetuosity all the more now that Basil had taken to spending the night in her house in Salt Street.

Crawling into bed beside him at four o'clock in the morning, she was not entirely consoled by a drowsy kiss and a mumbled, 'Goodnight, Chucks,' before he rolled over and went back to sleep.

'I do wish you'd stop calling me Chucks,' she said.

'My mother used to call me Chucks whenever I'd been a good, brave boy,' Basil explained.

'Well, I'm not your good brave anything,' Vivian said. 'God knows, fire watching was bad enough in winter but these summer nights are worse. The sheer boredom of standing on a rooftop and scanning a clear sky for hours on end could drive a person cuckoo.'

'More coffee – Chucks?'

She opened her mouth to chide him again but he looked so impish in pyjamas, dressing gown and slippers that she hadn't the heart to pursue an argument over something as trivial as an endearment.

She watched him pour coffee from the Georgian pot he'd unearthed from the back of a cupboard, had rinsed and polished and brought into service at the breakfast table. He had also cleaned her house from top to bottom and seemed as much at ease with a carpet sweeper in his hand as a stopwatch or a rehearsal script. Vivian's only constraint on his fastidiousness was to warn him, on pain of death, not to lay a finger on her desk in the office, a stricture that Basil wisely took to heart.

As a reward for his consideration she stopped leaving cigarette butts burning on the edge of the dining table, wet towels strewn on the bathroom floor and her corset draped on a chair in the living room.

She also purchased a new silk dressing gown, new night-dresses and even some lingerie suited to the fuller figure and had been gratified when Basil, modest as he was, had remarked upon it by wiggling his eyebrows and whistling softly through his teeth. As a lover Basil was no better than he should be but as a house guest he was absolutely perfect and, in her mellower moments, Vivian wondered how she'd ever managed without him.

'Toast?'

'Thank you.'

'Now, eat your boiled egg like a good girl.'

A girl she was not, and never would be again. Love had come late, but, she told herself, better late than never. Obediently, she topped her egg while Basil gazed adoringly over the rim of his coffee cup.

'I see,' he said at length, 'that the US Senate has accused the Allied Purchasing Committee of haggling over prices for warships.'

'Really?' Vivian said, through a mouthful of toast. 'Is there anything you can do with that for the programme?'

'I doubt it,' Basil said. 'Too political. There are probably faults on both sides. I'll pursue the piece on Woolton's latest round of restrictions on the serving of food in posh restaurants. That'll be popular with folks in the Midwest. We'll bring in someone from the ministry on the pretext of explaining the thing and ambush him with an ordinary housewife struggling to make ends meet.'

'I thought Bob Gaines was doing a report on the "Ready for Anything" speech in the House. He was down there for it, wasn't he?'

'Indeed, he was,' Basil said.

Vivian dabbed her lips politely with a napkin before she put a shot across her lover's bows. 'Have you heard anything from the Home Office in respect of my request for access to an internment camp?'

'On that score the Home Secretary is intractable.'

'Adamant, or just in need of persuasion?' When Basil did

not answer, she went on, 'This ship going down off the coast of Ireland . . .'

'I knew you'd bring that up. We might interview a widow, I suppose, if only we knew who the widows were.'

'Basil, you know how much getting into one of these internment camps means to me. I need material for my book.'

'Yes, dear, I know. However, even if I did manage to get you into one you'd only get to see what they wanted you to see.'

'This country is becoming more like Nazi Germany every day,' Vivian said. 'Whatever happened to a free press, let alone civil liberties? We have a right, a positive right, to know what's happening to all the Italians who've been spirited away without a word to anyone.'

'Have they arrested David yet?' Basil asked innocently.

'Apparently not,' Vivian said. 'Stop trying to distract me. I want to see inside one of these camps for myself.'

Basil put down his cup and, reaching across the table, took her hand. 'What would you do in exchange for, say, a Home Office *carte blanche*?'

'Practically anything.'

'Would you marry me, for instance?'

'Beg pardon?'

'It's simple. If I succeed in getting you a *carte blanche*, will you marry me?'

'Hah!' Vivian said. 'You're daring me to take you on, aren't you? Well, my dear Mr Willets, given what you've told me about the Home Secretary's intractability, never mind all the brouhaha with the War Department—'

'Yes, or no, Vivian?'

'Well, let's see just how desperate you are to make an honest woman of me. My bet is that it's just a ruse to soften me up because you know you'll never pull it off.'

'But if, somehow, I do?'

'All right, damn it, if you do, I will.'

'Scout's honour?'

'Scout's honour.'

Basil dipped a hand into the pocket of his dressing gown, brought out a long manila envelope and a small leather-bound box and placed them neatly side by side on the tablecloth.

Cagily, Vivian said, 'What's that?'

'It's a letter to the commandant of an internment camp at Congleton Grove, which is up near Nottingham, I believe. It grants limited permission for you and one other to visit the camp and talk with the internees.'

'Good God, Basil, how did you do it?'

'Bribery, corruption and a deal of special pleading.'

'And the box? What's in the little box?'

'Your engagement ring, of course.'

'What a devious swine you are, Basil Willets.'

'Aren't I just,' said Basil, and giggled.

'Isn't this a bit early even for you?' Bob Gaines said.

'Look who's talking,' Pete Slocum said. 'You guzzled that gin like it was branch water. Will I send our man downstairs for another bottle?'

'Not unless you're planning on getting pie-eyed before lunch,' Bob said.

'I have every excuse.' Pete Slocum sank back in the sofa, crossed one long leg over another and stirred the air with the toe of his shoe. 'Tossed out of Berlin, barred from the Ruhr and now we neutrals aren't even welcome in Paris. Is your girl still sleeping?'

'Hell, no,' Bob said. 'She's been gone for hours.'

'Will she be here for the party tonight?'

'What party?'

'My welcome home party,' Pete Slocum said. 'You don't think I'm passing up the chance of a boozy do just because you knocked up some tart.'

'She isn't a tart,' Bob said, 'and she isn't knocked up.'

'Just pretending, was she?'

'She panicked a little, that's all. She was late by a week and jumped to the wrong conclusion.'

'London's a far cry from Passaic Falls, chum. Big city girls will always make you pay for your folly. Didn't wise old Uncle Pete warn you that this one was dangerous?'

'It was a genuine mistake,' Bob said. 'A miscalculation.'

'Was her husband walking in on you also a miscalculation?' Pete Slocum asked.

'It certainly wasn't intentional,' Bob answered. 'Susan was pretty damned cool about it, though.'

'She's a pretty damn cool lady.' Pete paused to remove the olive from his glass and pop it into his mouth. 'Has she asked you for dough yet?'

'Susan's not like that.'

'Well, if it ain't your dough she's after it must be you, body and soul,' Pete Slocum said. 'Jesus, Bob, I can't leave you alone for five minutes 'fore you get yourself in trouble.'

'She's not in trouble. *I'm* not in trouble.'

'You shake hands with your lover's husband and you think you're not in trouble?' Pete reached for the cocktail shaker and poured more of the mixture into his glass. 'Don't you get it yet, you dope? She's got you on the ropes. She's your girl now, your responsibility. Next thing, you'll be invited to meet her folks.'

'Not if Susan has anything to do with it.'

'Ditched her family too, has she?' Pete Slocum said. 'Ditched the family, ditched the husband. Now it's just you and her against the world. Gaines, you're cooked.'

'Maybe,' Bob said, 'but it's me that's cooked, not you. Keep your big nose out of it.'

'Sure, I will, just make sure you bring her along to the party tonight.'

'Why?'

'So that I can look Medusa in the eye.'

'Do you want me to bring her sister, too?'

'She has a sister? I thought you said—'

'Kidding, Pete, just kidding,' Bob said and, putting down his glass, went into the bedroom to sleep.

The little scrap of paper that Breda had preserved was soiled and crumpled but the numbers Mr Jessop had printed upon it were still legible. Tongue between teeth, she dialled the number and pressed the receiver against her ear as if she expected to be answered in a whisper.

On the third ring a brusque female voice with an upper-crust accent shouted down the line, 'Which department do you require?'

'I'd like to talk to Mr Jessop.'

'There is no Mr Jessop here.'

'Oh, but—'

'Thank you. Good day.'

Breda fiddled with the coin return button but six unsat-
isfactory seconds of conversation had swallowed up her
pennies. She dug into her purse and, muttering under her
breath, fished out more coins and dialled the number again.

'Which department do you require?'

'Listen,' Breda said, 'I gotta talk to Mr Jess—'

Once more her request was cut off.

Chucking her purse on the shelf, she shook out the last
of her loose change, dialled the number for the third time
and steeled herself to cope with that glacial voice. But there
was no voice, no ringing tone, just a prolonged, high-pitched
whine that set Breda's teeth on edge.

Throwing the receiver back into the cradle, she stepped out
of the telephone box and, pacing up and down, lit and smoked
a cigarette before she went back into the box and, after several
deep breaths, rang an operator.

'Can you get me a number?' she asked.

'Local or national?'

'Local – I think.'

'Have you tried to dial it?'

'Yeah,' Breda said. 'I've tried to dial it.'

'What is the problem?'

'I keep gettin' cut off.'

A sigh: 'What's the number?'

Breda gave the operator the number and, hopping from
one foot to the other, waited for a connection – waited and
waited, while the receiver hummed in her ear.

At last: 'Caller, are you still there?'

'Yes, I am.'

'I'm afraid that number has been discontinued.'

'Discontin—'

'Sorry. Please try again.'

'Try again? How am I supposed to bleedin' '

'Sorry. Please try again.'

'Piss off, you cow,' Breda yelled into the mouthpiece and, leaving the receiver dangling, gathered up her purse and stomped out of the phone box, not one whit wiser as to her father's fate.

17

They left St Pancras at 6.45 a.m. on a train crowded with servicemen. Many were in khaki, several in air-force blue and a few were weather-beaten naval ratings heading for heaven knows where. There were women in uniform, too, and a clutch of nurses, undaunted by the early hour, flirting with the RAF chaps. There had been thunder overnight and a rain front moving across the country had left the air fresh and clean. The train's crowded corridors were anything but fresh and clean, though, and before the train was an hour out of St Pancras the compartment stank of sweat and smoke.

Vivian or, rather, Basil had thoughtfully filled a Thermos flask and put some cheese biscuits in a little tin that Vivian unearthed from her bag. Crammed into a corner seat, she managed to pour coffee without spilling a drop. She passed the cup and biscuits to Susan and advised her to stoke up as it might be some time before they ate again.

'Is Congleton Grove in Nottingham?' Susan asked.

'I haven't a clue,' Vivian answered. 'I suspect it may be a half-built council estate that the War Office has requisitioned. The fact that we've been "offered" – for want of a better word – access to a camp three hours out of London suggests it's not exactly Devil's Island.'

'We are expected, aren't we?'

'Oh, you can bet your bottom dollar we're expected,' Vivian said, 'and that our welcome will not be warm.'

On that score Vivian's prediction was correct.

Three men in civilian suits and a junior army officer formed a posse on the platform. Their disapproval was palpable. No introductions were forthcoming. Vivian and Susan were marched out of the railway station and across a yard to a Post Office sorting bay where two motorcars were parked.

The drivers, army privates, snapped to attention and one, rather ungraciously, Susan thought, opened the rear door on the larger car and allowed Vivian and her to slide inside. One of the civilians took his seat in front by the driver while the others piled into the car behind.

The private started the engine. 'Sir?'

'Yes, we're ready. You may go.'

The private released the handbrake and steered the car smoothly through an unguarded gate on to a road that Susan took to be a high street. The second car followed close behind.

'You haven't asked for our credentials,' Vivian said. 'I have a letter signed by Lord Hobhouse, if you wish to see it.'

The man swung round and planted an elbow on the back of the seat. He was about thirty-four or -five, sallow-skinned and tired-looking. 'I know all about the letter,' he said.

'And you're not happy about it,' said Vivian.

He smiled, showing a row of small, stained teeth.

'I do as I'm told, Miss Proudfoot. I follow orders. I trust you will do the same. By the way, my name is Rudd.'

'Hobhouse's man on the spot, I take it,' Vivian said.

A pause: 'Eden's man, actually.'

'One of the glamour brigade,' said Vivian.

'Hardly that.' Mr Rudd's smile blinked on and off. 'There are certain rules we must ask you to obey and, need I add, any article intended for publication must be approved.'

'To prevent Mr Eden getting egg on his face now the Home Office has taken over responsibility for the internment situation,' Vivian said. 'Please, continue.'

'There are no German prisoners of war at Congleton Grove which is basically only a transit camp for B- and C-class prisoners. You will be permitted to talk to a selected number of internees and interview the commandant, Major Hargreaves.'

'Tell me, Mr Rudd,' Vivian said, 'will I be permitted to quote the prisoners' views verbatim?'

'That,' said Mr Rudd, 'hasn't been decided yet.'

'How many men and women, guilty or innocent, are currently under War Office jurisdiction?'

'In the region of thirty thousand, I believe.'

'And you clearly don't know what the devil to do with them now you've rounded them up,' said Vivian. 'I find it astonishing that the government was able to evacuate a million children in less than a week but can't cope with thirty thousand men and women arrested on suspicion of – of what?'

'Oh, you're one of those, are you?' Mr Rudd said.

'One of what, pray?'

'A bloody Communist,' he blurted out.

Vivian laughed. 'First time I've ever been mistaken for a Communist. No, Mr Rudd, I belong to a faction the government fears more than the Communists.'

'What faction might that be?"

'The fourth estate.'

'You reporters—'

'I'm a journalist not a reporter.'

'Whatever you are, you've no right to jeopardise the security of the nation in the name of free speech.'

'The right to free speech is about the only thing that separates us from the Nazis right now,' said Vivian.

'That's an outrageous thing to say.'

'I'm an outrageous person, Mr Rudd, which is why I've been sent to see what you're up to.'

'Mr Rudd, sir,' the driver interrupted. 'We've arrived,' and braked the car to a halt in front of a huge, decaying building that smelled, Susan thought, like a brewery.

There had been several 'false alarms' during the early summer months but as July wore on the alerts became more frequent and urgent. If Breda happened to be serving at Stratton's when the siren sounded she led her mother and any customers who were on the premises to shelter in the larder and, soon after the all-clear, returned to dishing out soup and sausages again as if nothing had happened.

What concerned her more than the prospect of being blown to bits was how to keep her son in clothes. Billy seemed to grow out of shirts and trousers as soon as she'd purchased them and his shoes pinched long before they required repair. Her own wardrobe was adequate. A bit of letting out made her old frocks and coats fit for purpose and, as Ron kept reminding her, no one ever got to see the patches on her knickers.

The Romano family had never been rock-bottom,

spare-us-a-crust-mister poor and Breda had never known real hardship. But the responsibility of having a fortune in cash hanging above her head every time she went to the lavatory wasn't lost on her. The veiled threat that Steve Millar had made hung over her head too, no matter how often she tried to reassure herself that Steve knew nothing for certain and that he would surely not allow any harm to come to her.

Uncertainty sharpened her temper, though. She was snappish with Ron, with Billy and especially with her father-in-law, and woe betide any customer in Stratton's who dared complain that the tea was weak or the soup too salty.

When school closed for the holidays, Breda had no option but to take Billy with her to Stratton's where, against her better judgement, she allowed him to play in the street with the other children; play that seemed to consist of yelling, screaming and rolling in the gutter or, huddled in furtive little groups, in devising original ways of getting up to mischief. The sole benefit of allowing her son to run wild all day was that, come supper time, he was so tired out he went to bed without protest which gave Breda some extra time to herself.

The stars were out and the shadows in the yard as soft as caramel when Breda, clutching cigarettes, matches and a wad of toilet paper, made her way to the outhouse to check on Leo's cashbox and speculate just how much it might cost to turn Billy into a gentleman.

Fortunately she had completed her business and had almost finished her cigarette when the air-raid warning sounded.

She stuffed the cashbox into the space behind the cistern, jumped down from the seat, pulled the chain and came out of the water closet at the double.

Far off, she heard the pounding of guns from the battery downriver at Deptford. Fearing that Billy might be roused by the racket, she made a beeline for the back door and almost ran into the man leaning against the doorpost.

'Dad?' she whispered. 'Is that you?'

'Me, it's me, Breda.'

'Danny.' She let out her breath. 'Thank God!'

'Where's the wee chap?'

'Upstairs asleep.'

'Best dig him out an' get to a shelter.'

'It's probably another false alarm.'

'Can't be sure of that.' Danny took her arm and led her into the house. 'Better safe than sorry.'

'What you doin' here anyway?'

'Twenty-four-hour pass. By the way, you were right.'

'About what?'

'Susan. She is havin' it off with another guy.'

Breda counted to five then said, 'You really suit those glasses, Danny. They make you look real posh.'

'I'm not sure that's a compliment,' Danny said. 'Where is your shelter?'

'Under the stairs.'

18

It was after eight that evening when Vivian, with Susan on her heels, barged into Basil's office and started shouting the odds. Basil got up and closed the door, Robert poured a shot of whisky and Susan, travel-stained and weary, slumped into a chair behind her desk.

'As for bloody Major Hargreaves,' Vivian plunged on, 'he should have been pensioned off years ago. Miserable old beggar is completely out of his depth, although, to give him his due, he did apply for five hundred beds, and the War Office sent him ten. Ten beds for seven hundred men. Ye Gods! The young lads don't mind sleeping in tents, all a bit of an adventure, but half the prisoners are frail old men.'

When Vivian paused to catch her breath, Basil said, 'I gather it was not a fruitful excursion, my dear?'

'Fruitful?' Vivian cried. 'Of course it was bloody fruitful. Good God, Basil, I'm about to deliver you a piece for broadcast that will bring the government to its knees.'

'I'm not sure that's such a good idea,' Basil said. 'Tell me about Congleton Grove.'

'Congleton Grove is an abandoned brewery, a rotting, rat-infested shell filled with bewildered old men coughing their guts out. Outside, four or five hundred prisoners are sleeping in tents with little or no sanitation beyond a cold water tap and a couple of shallow trenches dug in the ground.'

'Mr Rudd did say it's only a transit camp,' Susan said.

Vivian rounded on her. 'Don't tell me you were fooled by that little weasel's lies. You're not on their side, surely? I mean, you *can't* be on their side, not after what we saw today.'

'You're right, Vivian, absolutely right,' Susan hastily agreed. 'Conditions are appalling, but the Home Office—'

'Will do nothing. Do you hear me – *nothing*.'

'Interviews?' Bob Gaines asked. 'Quotable stuff from the prisoners? How did that go?'

'I was only permitted to talk to a few hand-picked chaps who were as uncritical as it's possible to be when you've spent six weeks cut off from any word of what's happening in the world. News, that's what they wanted most of all, news and cigarettes.'

'Are they being properly fed?' Basil asked.

'Bread and porridge, vegetable stew, mostly potato, a cube of cheese for supper,' Vivian answered. 'Oh, they gave *us* a lovely lunch in the barracks; all those grinning jackanapes in army uniform scoffing mutton chops and treacle pudding and congratulating themselves on how well their prisoners are treated compared with other camps.'

'Oh, now,' said Basil, putting an arm around her. 'We can't have this, dearest. I've never seen you so upset.'

'I'm not upset. I'm furious that such things are allowed to take place in Britain. What's more I'm not going to let the government get away with it.'

Basil said, 'There isn't much you can do, I'm afraid. If

we do try to put together a radio piece we'll have to tread very, very carefully.'

'Damn it, Basil, you're as bad as the rest. You've seen the stuff the newspapers are publishing; tissues of lies spread on blankets of silence. Aliens. Traitors. Fifth columnists – a few, perhaps, but the vast majority of those arrested are entirely innocent. I don't really expect you to use my material. I'm not without influence in publishing circles, if you recall. First I need to find out who convenes these damned tribunals, who sits on them, where they meet, and how often.'

'Be careful you don't wind up behind bars, Vivian,' Bob Gaines said. 'All you'll be doing is adding a few extra feathers to Hitler's cloak of righteousness and that won't get you anywhere.'

'I'm afraid that's true,' Basil told her. 'Why don't I take you home and—'

'Tuck me into bed? What do you think I am: a child?' Vivian reached for her overcoat and, rejecting Basil's offer of help, shucked it over her shoulders. 'Enough damned mollycoddling. You're not my husband yet.' She pecked Basil's cheek. 'Call me tomorrow,' then, yanking open the door, she flounced out of the office.

'Are you really going to marry her, Basil?' Bob asked.

'Yes,' Basil answered. 'We'll slip off to a registry office for a special licence some time soon.'

'Rather you than me, pal,' said Bob. 'I wouldn't marry Vivian Proudfoot if she was the last woman on earth.'

'Fortunately for you,' said Basil stiffly, 'she's not. Susan, fetch your pad and pencil. We've a schedule to revise.'

★

'Ron's done a good job on this place,' Danny said. 'Did he put in that baulk all by himself?'

'Matt helped,' Breda said. 'They shored up the larder in Ma's place too. It's bigger than this an' can take ten people, easy. Is his majesty asleep?'

'Out like a light. He's quite happy on my lap.'

'You was always Billy's favourite. Remember when Ron was off in Spain an' you came with us to the park?'

'Aye, I remember,' Danny said. 'Good times.'

'They were, they were,' said Breda. 'We got sandbags the other side of that wall. Ron bought them from a builder's yard. The whole of that back wall – blast-proof. This used to be the coal 'ole, though you'd never think it. We 'ave our Primus, a storm lamp an' two electric torches with spare batteries.'

'Ron's thought of everything.'

'Bein' a fireman he knows all about this stuff,' Breda said. 'See that thing up there? That's a vent to let the air in.'

'How often have you been in here?'

'Four, five times: all false alarms.' She tilted her face towards the ceiling. 'Hear anythin'?'

'Nope, not a thing.'

'Stray plane goin' over, most like. Our boys'll make short work of it.' She leaned on Danny's shoulder, paused, and said, 'Danny, are you sure about Susie?'

The bench seat was broad enough to serve as a bed but with Billy asleep in his arms Danny had settled for the floor, Breda on the blanket next to him.

'I walked in on them,' he said. 'Red-handed.'

'What about the bloke?'

'Journalist. American.'

'The one on the wireless?' Breda said. 'Oh, yeah, too good

an opportunity for our Miss Fancy-pants to let slip. You're not still in love with 'er, are yah?'

'That's the problem. I don't know if I am, or not.'

'I never liked Susie Hooper but I never reckoned she'd do this to you. Wait till Ron hears about it. He'll be livid. Matt, too. Not,' Breda added hastily, 'that *I'm* gonna tell them. It's bound to come out sooner or later, though, unless you want to pretend it never happened.' She paused again. 'What about this girl who shares your digs?'

'Kate. What about her?'

'Somethin' goin' on there?'

'Nah,' Danny said a little too quickly.

'Ooo,' Breda said. 'You can't fool me, Danny Cahill. You like her, don'cha? Come on, admit it. What does she do?'

'She translates German radio broadcasts.'

'A clever clogs,' said Breda approvingly. 'Have you kissed 'er yet?'

'Naw.' Danny laughed. 'Not yet.'

Breda reached over and tapped a fingertip to the bridge of his glasses. 'Not even one liddle peck?'

'Not even one.'

'I'll bet she's dyin' for you to kiss 'er.'

'Kate's not that sort of a girl.'

'We're all that sort of a girl when it comes to havin' a feller fancy us. Go on, Cahill, tell me you don't wanna clasp 'er to your manly bosom an' smother 'er with kisses.'

'Cut it out, Breda,' Danny said, grinning. 'I'm not some joker out o' one of your soppy novels.'

'Oh, but you are, Danny Cahill, you are. You're not gonna ride off on a camel an' leave a girl in the lurch. That counts for a lot these days.'

Billy stirred. Danny drew the blanket over his knees and stroked his hair while Breda watched, soft-eyed.

'The thing is,' Danny said, 'I've got a free pass to do what the hell I like now. Susan can't say a bloody word.'

'Yeah, but a leg-over's never gonna be enough for you, is it? What about marriage?'

'Marriage?'

'To this Kate.'

'I'm still married to Susan in case you hadn't noticed.'

'But if you get 'alf a chance with this Kate . . .' Breda sat up. 'Hey, she's not married too, is she?'

'Not as far as I know.'

'Well, then, there you are. Off you go.'

The sound of the all-clear drifted into the bunker.

Cradling Billy to his chest, Danny got up. 'The only place I'm goin', sweetheart, is up the road to your ma's house for a good night's kip.'

'You don't 'ave to go, you know,' Breda said. 'You can stay 'ere with me an' Billy.'

'What's Ronnie gonna say about that?'

'He won't mind.'

'I wouldn't bet on it.' Danny tugged open the door. 'Anyhow, Nora's expectin' me.'

Breda let Danny precede her into the darkened kitchen, then, taking her sleepy son from his arms, kissed him.

'Yeah, maybe you'd better go,' she said, 'before I forget I'm a happily married woman.'

'See you soon, kid,' said Danny.

'Not so much of the kid,' said Breda.

★

The party in the Lansdowne had barely got under way but the living room and corridor were already crowded with Pete Slocum's friends and acquaintances.

The valet had gone for the night and a small, feisty woman, *Time* magazine's London correspondent, was cooking spaghetti on the stove in the kitchen while swigging from a straw-wrapped bottle of Chianti and puffing on a cigarette.

Four or five men were hanging about in the kitchen but whether in pursuit of supper or the feisty little blonde Susan neither knew nor cared.

She'd had a long, stressful day and would have preferred a quiet dinner alone with Bob before slipping off home to catch up on sleep. Bob had insisted that she tag along to Slocum's party, though, and had assured her that what she needed to take her mind off the 'horrors' of Congleton Grove was a few drinks in the company of men and women whose experiences in the hell-holes of occupied Europe made a British internment camp look like a picnic.

It was, she gathered, a floating party that had drifted from Madrid to Munich, from Stockholm to Marseilles and, in happier times, had dropped anchor in Paris; always the same sort of people, newshounds, photographers and hard-drinking, front-line reporters who had no fear of anything save censorship.

'Well, that's it for tonight, I guess,' said a voice in her ear.

'What is?' Susan said.

'Didn't you hear the all-clear?' Pete Slocum offered her a martini. 'You're too sober for your own good, Mrs Cahill. Here, drink this and give thanks with a smile.'

'I don't feel much like smiling.'

'You're very beautiful when you do,' Pete said. 'I can see why you've stolen Bob's heart away.'

'I've done nothing of the kind.' She sipped from the glass and felt the gin sting her throat. 'Where is he, by the way?'

'Queuing up to grab a dish of Mary's special spaghetti,' Pete said. 'Rough day at the office?'

'How did you know?'

Pete Slocum tapped the side of his nose. 'It's my business to know everything.' He grinned. 'And I do mean everything. Another of those?'

Susan had drunk the martini without thinking. She held out the glass and watched Slocum refill it.

'We've got onions but no olives,' he said. 'I'd sack that goddamned valet if only I knew how to do it. You don't want to be too hard on the old boy. He's running scared, you know.'

'Who, your valet?'

'Churchill,' Pete Slocum said. 'He's afraid a fifth column will spring up like it did in Holland. He's flying blind right now and has no ready spur to victory, no plan for a bright tomorrow. Not that tomorrow will count for much if your fly boys can't keep Goering from bombing the bejasus out of your factories. If they fail then it's all up with Merry England and bye-bye to a thousand years of history.'

'And you Americans will retire behind your high walls and let us stew in our own juices.'

'Our walls aren't that high, Mrs Cahill,' Pete Slocum said.

'Why have you taken to calling me Mrs Cahill?'

He changed gear without a hitch. 'Because you're a married lady and it behoves me to remind you of it.'

'That's rich coming from someone who sleeps with a different girl every night.'

'Sure, but I don't trade in commitment. With you – well, I guess you're every woman's ideal: footloose, fancy-free and able to pick and choose who you sleep with. You've got it all, Mrs Cahill, haven't you?' Pete Slocum said. 'A responsible job, a devoted husband and an ardent lover. You're covered every way.' He raised his glass. 'Good luck to you, Mrs Cahill.'

'Why, thank you, Mr Slocum,' Susan said just as Bob appeared at her side carrying two plates of spaghetti smothered in tomato sauce.

'What are you two talking about?' he asked.

'Politics,' Susan answered. 'Just politics,' then, relieving him of one of the plates, headed for the living room to find somewhere to sit.

She left him sprawled on the bed in his room in the Lansdowne. She washed and dressed quickly, picked her way through the glasses and plates that littered the hallway and, ignoring the early-risers nursing coffee and hangovers in the kitchen, made her way out of the building and set a course for Portland Place in the hope that a brisk walk would clear her head.

In addition to the usual office workers and shop girls, Oxford Street was peppered with policemen and soldiers. She glanced at the headlines on newsvendors' stalls but could make no sense of them and, drawn by the prospect of breakfast in the canteen, concentrated on dodging the traffic.

She crossed the open corner of Langham Place where

BBC staff hurrying towards the grey-green building rubbed shoulders with worshippers emerging from communion in All Souls' soot-stained church. She would have walked straight past him if he hadn't called her name.

He was seated cross-legged on the steps of the church where the last of the morning's communicants picked their way, disapprovingly, around him. He wore a donkey jacket and collarless shirt and had a greasy haversack tucked between his knees. He didn't rise when she approached but, looking up, patted the stone step beside him.

'Grab a pew,' he said.

'I'll do nothing of the kind,' Susan said. 'What the devil are you doing here, Danny?'

'God,' he said, 'you look like death warmed up.'

'I'm fine, I'm perfectly fine. What do you want?'

He leaned on an elbow and peered up at her. 'A few quiet words, that's all.'

'Well,' Susan said, 'if you insist on ambushing me at this hour of the morning the least you can do is stand me breakfast. I assume you have your BBC pass with you?'

'Never travel without it,' Danny said.

'Come along then.'

'Rather not, actually,' he said, rising. 'Frightfully busy, darling, awfully pressed for time. You didn't come home last night. By home I mean the flat we share in Rothwell Gardens.'

'The air raid—'

'One stray plane an' a nuisance bomb in the City.'

'Did you wait up for me all night?'

'Don't be bloody daft,' Danny said. 'I stayed at Nora's.'

'Oh, how – how is she?'

'Kind of you to ask,' Danny said. 'She's recoverin'.'

'Recovering from what?'

'Susan,' he spoke without heat, 'you really are a stuck-up bitch. You can treat me like dirt if you like but your folks deserve better. Where were you last night? Were you with him?'

She hesitated. 'Yes, at a party.'

'Where?'

'Lansdowne House. It's a residential club.'

'I know what it is. Did you sleep with him?'

'That's all I did: sleep,' she said. 'What about us? What do you want to do about us?'

'Tell me the truth, Susan: does Gaines make you happy?'

'I do believe he does.'

'Well, if you want to be with him, I won't stand in your way.' Danny consulted his watch. 'Look, I really do have to get back to Evesham.'

'When will you be in town again?'

'God knows!' Danny said.

'Next time, call me and we'll talk properly.'

He made no attempt to kiss her and was on the point of turning away when, on impulse, she said, 'Danny, do you have a girl in Evesham?'

'What if I have?' Danny said. 'It's none o' your business, Susan.' Then, shouldering the haversack, he set off to catch a bus to Paddington.

PART THREE

Blitz

19

It came as a great surprise when Basil's brother turned up at the wedding breakfast. It wasn't, strictly speaking, a breakfast at all but an intimate lunch in a side room in L'Étoile which – the restaurant not the side room – was conveniently situated for a quick sprint back to Broadcasting House where groom and bride would kiss and go their separate ways, Basil back to the office and Vivian off to the House of Commons to catch what promised to be a heated debate on the legality of the Home Secretary's unlimited powers of preventative detention.

In the past few weeks Vivian had spent much time in the gallery of the Commons and in meeting members of various bodies concerned with funding Czech and Slovak refugees, so much time, in fact, it was all Susan could do to drag her to a fitting for the suit that would substitute for a bridal gown and to the milliner's to pick a matching hat.

Vivian had never met anyone from Basil's family. His widowed mother lived in the wilds of Scotland – Troon, was it? – and his sister, her husband and children were ensconced somewhere near Penzance. Basil had informed them of his impending nuptials but had politely discouraged them from coming up to London for the event. Naturally, Vivian had dropped no hint to her black sheep brother and Susan's suggestion that she might invite one of her nieces to be a bridesmaid had been greeted with a snort of derision.

Susan had trimmed one of her old dresses for the occasion and Bob had stuffed himself into a rumpled three-piece suit. In old-fashioned morning dress, complete with topper, Basil looked decidedly out of place and the registrar's temporary confusion as to just which couple he was expected to unite in wedlock didn't help matters.

After the deed was done, bride and groom, accompanied by Bob and Susan, trudged round to L'Étoile in Charlotte Street. Here, rather to Basil's chagrin, a number of CBS correspondents were lunching and, swiftly putting two and two together, stood up and applauded the happy couple before the wedding party was shown into the side room where Commander Derek Willets, in full naval uniform, waited to greet them.

'Good Lord!' Basil exclaimed. 'I thought you were somewhere in the middle of the Atlantic. How did you know where to find us?'

'Intuition,' Derek Willets said. 'Besides, you mentioned it in dispatches to Mother who mentioned it in dispatches to me. Now, please, introduce me to my brand-new sister-in-law.' He bowed to Vivian. 'Mrs Willets, I assume? I'm the dreaded brother, in case you hadn't guessed. Welcome to the family.'

To Susan's surprise, Vivian blushed and the air of melancholy that had marked the proceedings vanished.

Commander Willets signalled an elderly waiter to wheel in the champagne, bride and groom were duly toasted and everyone sat down to tuck into mock turtle soup and whitebait and dispose of the two bottles of Chablis that the *maître d'* had been persuaded to produce from his dwindling stock.

'By the bye,' Derek Willets said, 'there's an account in your name in Heal's to which we all contributed. We'd no idea where you'd be setting up house so an open account seemed like the best solution.'

'That's very kind of you, Commander,' Vivian said.

'Derek, please.'

'Very kind of you, Derek. In fact, we'll be living in my house in Salt Street and Basil will give up his flat. But, tell me, how did you contrive to be here today?'

'Pure chance. My ship was damaged during an enemy raid and we put into Portsmouth for repairs. I wangled a day's leave on compassionate grounds.'

'Compassionate grounds,' Basil said. 'Very funny.'

'Your ship, sir?' Bob asked.

'A battered old rust bucket employed on convoy duty.'

'Is it bad out there, Derek?' Basil asked.

'Well, shall we say it's not too jolly.'

'Invasion or blockade?' Bob Gaines said. 'What's Adolf's game, do you think?'

'Naval officers aren't really paid to think,' Derek Willets said. 'But it's obvious that nuisance raids on London are a means of lowering morale and blitzkrieg bombing a way of testing the Luftwaffe's superiority.'

'A battle upstairs you seem to be winning,' Bob said.

Derek Willets raised an eyebrow. '*You* seem to be winning? I rather thought you might have aligned yourself with our cause by now.'

'He has,' Basil said. 'He's only pretending to be neutral.'

'Point taken, sir,' Bob said. 'We're all in it together.'

Derek Willets was a model naval officer, Susan thought. Eight or ten years younger than his brother, he was tall, lean, tanned and had the most piercing blue eyes she had ever seen. How easy it would be to fall for him. And how foolish. Even so, she couldn't help but wonder if he had a wife tucked away somewhere. The thought had apparently crossed Viv's mind too.

She put the question bluntly. 'And you, Derek, have you never been tempted to marry?'

He laughed, not at all offended. 'I'm biding my time and waiting for the right girl to come along.'

'Best not bide too long,' Basil said. 'You're not getting any younger, you know. Whatever happened to that Wren you were so keen on last summer?'

'Grace? I haven't seen her in ages.'

'Where is she these days?' Basil persisted.

'Gibraltar, last I heard.'

'The Rock?' Bob said. 'God help her!'

'Have you been there?' Susan asked.

'On my way back from Spain, yeah,' Bob answered. 'Your friend, what's she doing in Gib?'

'I really couldn't say,' said Derek Willets and promptly changed the subject.

At a little after 10 p.m. Deutschlandsender, Germany's main radio station, abruptly went off air. Medium-wave stations soon followed suit and even talks in English from Hamburg and Bremen petered out.

Kate and the other German monitors were quick to summon the supervisor, Mr Gregory, who put through a telephone call to London and returned, smiling slyly, to inform them that RAF bombers were out in force and, choosing his words with care, that the raids were not entirely confined to military targets.

'In other words,' Griff said over the breakfast table next morning, 'deniability is a two-way street. If Hitler wants the gloves off then he can't expect Churchill to fight by the Queensberry Rules.'

'Kate,' Mr Pell said, 'what do you have to say? Is your boyfriend right?'

Danny, more asleep than awake, cocked an ear and waited for Kate to deny that Silwyn Griffiths was her boyfriend.

She said, 'I think the stations went off early last night because the German Ministry of Propaganda got caught out. There was one bulletin only and it concerned itself with changes to the type of siren to be used in air-raid warnings. After that – dead air.'

It was only just light outside. Summer was fading into autumn and quite soon no one in the Pell household would see much daylight. Mr Pell was used to early rising. He worked in a factory that had once produced parts for industrial washing machines but now turned out something – Mr P wasn't saying what – more appropriate to the war effort.

'It won't be in the papers yet, will it?' Mr Pell said. 'I mean, they won't give us the gory details. They seldom do.'

'Oh, they might,' Griff said. 'You can bet the wires are humming in the Press Association offices. The Americans will have it well covered. If there was a big raid on Berlin we'll hear about it one way or another.'

Griff was in a jaunty mood which, Danny thought, was odd for someone who'd just finished a twelve-hour shift.

No one seemed in any hurry to rush off, Mr Pell to work,

Griff, Kate and he to bed. He dripped marmalade on to a piece of toast and nibbled it. He was so tired he could barely chew, so tired that he missed all the subtle signals that might have warned him what was in the wind.

Mrs Pell appeared from the kitchen bearing a fresh pot of tea. Griff cleared his throat and said, 'Oh, by the way, Mrs P, we'll be away for a couple of days, Saturday through to Monday.'

'Taking some leave?' said Mr Pell.

'While the going's good,' said Griff.

'Going somewhere nice?' said Mrs Pell.

'Home to Brecon,' Griff said, 'to see my folks.'

'We?' Danny sat up. 'Who's we?'

'Kate's coming with me,' Griff said. 'Dad can always use an extra hand dipping sheep.'

'Dipping sheep,' said Mr Pell, frowning. 'Bit late in the year for that. Bit smelly too.'

'I don't think Silwyn meant it literally,' Kate said.

'Don't be too sure,' Griff said. 'Anyhow, it's high time you had a taste of farming given that I might inherit the blasted place some day.'

'You?' Mr Pell said. 'A farmer?'

'A true son of the soil, that's me,' Griff said.

'I can't see you as a farmer's wife, Kate,' Mr Pell said, 'not with your education.'

'She can call in the cows in German,' said Mrs Pell.

And everyone laughed, everyone except Danny.

There was really no need, Basil said, to go diving downstairs to the underground shelter every time a warning sounded. Most alarms were precautionary and only lasted ten or fifteen minutes. You wouldn't, he claimed, find a CBS or NBC broadcaster cowering in the basement of Broadcasting House. The American corporations' mistrust of recorded material had their reporters chasing round bomb-sites and holding mikes up to the sky when, that is, they weren't flying sorties with Bomber Command or clinging to the deck of a minesweeper.

The *Union Post*'s London office, which had once been not much more than a guy, a gal and a telephone, was now home to an assortment of footloose European correspondents that Slocum had pulled together to supply New York with news.

From this source Bob Gaines, with Basil's encouragement, poached writers and reporters to enliven the output of *Speaking Up* which, in Bob's opinion, was in danger of becoming too stuffy for a show whose purpose was to sell the war to uncommitted Americans.

On that late August night the lion's share of the programme was given over to Morley Richards, the *Daily Express* military correspondent, who Basil had personally buttonholed at lunch in the London Press Club.

At Basil's request Mr Richards had agreed to address the question of how Britain would turn defence into attack and just when this reversal might take place.

A consummate professional, Mr Richards had timed his essay to the second and was in process of delivering it in a voice crisp enough to suggest not optimism but inevitability when the first warning siren sounded.

At first no one in the control booth turned a hair.

Mr Richards, at the mike, raised the volume but not the tempo of his delivery.

Sharing the studio table, Bob lit a cigarette. He had before him a sheaf of questions culled from listeners' letters from home and abroad but when a blast of high explosive shook the building it seemed that Joe Soap of Glen Falls and 'Outraged' of Tunbridge Wells might have to wait for answers.

The 'On Air' light flickered, Larry, the sound controller, uttered a colourful oath, and Basil Willets, in a voice that would have done his brother proud, growled, 'Steady, lads, steady.'

'For all these coming campaigns,' Mr Richards went on smoothly, 'we need newer weapons, new methods. We must have troop-carrying planes, paratroopers to man them and . . .'

From just outside the door of the booth came the sound of running feet and faint and far off the fairy-music of a fire bell.

Basil ticked off the final seconds of Mr Richards's talk.

Bob put the first of the listeners' questions.

The clock's silent second hand swiftly counted the programme down. Bob thanked Mr Richards, delivered his closing and as soon as the wall light changed from red to green switched off the studio microphones.

And, as Elgar played them out, Basil blew out his cheeks and said, 'Christ, do I need a drink.'

Although it was well after three the tearoom at the rear of the Greenhill was crowded with BBC wallahs partaking of late lunch. The lid of the piano in the lounge was closed, the stool unoccupied but Griffiths was not in a musical mood, it seemed, particularly as his colleagues were either stuffing themselves with salad or hovering in the vicinity of the wireless set in the billiard room to catch the latest bulletins.

It was a hot, humid afternoon. Blinds had been raised and windows thrown open and a faint breeze sifted through the empty lounge and ruffled the pages of the newspaper that Griff was reading. He was seated alone on a wicker chair in an alcove with a pint of beer and a half-eaten ham sandwich on the glass-topped table before him.

As soon as Danny appeared, he tossed the newspaper aside and got to his feet.

'What'll it be?' he said.

'I don't need you tae buy me drink,' Danny said.

'Oh, dear,' Griff said. 'We're about to have a showdown, are we? I can't say I'm surprised.'

'Why didn't you tell me?'

'Tell you what?'

'About you an' Kate.'

'Kate asked me not to.'

'You bloody liar.'

'Where is Kate, by the way?'

'Shoppin' with Mrs Pell, I think.'

'You think?' said Griffiths.

'*I'm* not her bloody fiancé.'

'All right, all right,' Griff said. 'No need to fly off the handle. Park your bum, sup a pint and we'll talk about it like—'

'Gentlemen?' Danny said. 'You're no bloody gentleman, Griffiths, takin' advantage of an innocent girl.'

'Oh, is that what you think?' Griff jumped in. 'You think I lured Katie off the straight and narrow to have my wicked way with her.' He paused. 'For God's sake, Danny, sit down.'

Danny dragged a chair from against the wall and swung it into position at the little table. Two men from the monitoring unit, one puffing a huge meerschaum pipe, strolled past and nodded, rather patronisingly, to Griffiths before going on into the tearoom, leaving a trail of smoke behind them.

'Who's that?' Danny asked.

'Petrovitch.'

'Russian?'

'Ukrainian, I think. Ukrainian via Manchester.'

'How do you know him?'

'I don't, really,' Griffiths said. 'The other one's Dutch. Martin something. Kate introduced us.'

'Why you an' not me?' said Danny.

Griff sighed and reached for his glass.

'That,' he said, 'is the question.'

'So what's the answer?'

'I don't know.' Griff swallowed a mouthful of beer, placed the glass on the table and leaned forward. 'I've absolutely no idea why Kate prefers me to you.'

'You've slept with her, haven't you?'

'No, in fact, I haven't.'

'But you will this weekend?'

'Not,' Griff said, 'a snowball's chance in hell, not with my parents hanging over us like vultures. I'll be damned lucky if they don't lock me in the barn when the sun goes down. Anyhow, just because you stumbled into a bad marriage is no reason to take it out on me.'

'Don't tell me you're in love?'

'Yes.' Griff shrugged. 'I am. What's more, there being no let or impediment, I hope to marry Kate some day.'

'You want her, don't you?'

'What's wrong with you, Cahill? Of course, I want her. Do you think it's wrong to desire a woman who you also happen to admire and – well, love.'

'Does Kate feel the same way about you?'

'Why don't you ask her?'

'Naw, naw,' Danny said. 'I'm not that much of an idiot.'

'At least it's out in the open now,' Griff said.

'What about the Pells?' Danny said.

'Mrs Pell's no fool. She saw it coming before we did,' Griff said. 'I'm not going to sit here and make apologies for stealing your girl, Danny. Kate was never going to be your girl. Besides, you already have a wife.'

'You're right, of course. I do have a wife an' that puts me out of the runnin' as far as Kate's concerned.' Danny reached across the table and shook the Welshman's hand. 'I wish you luck, Griffiths, even if you don't think you need it. Now, are you still buyin'?'

'I am,' Griff said. 'What'll you have?'

'Cider, I think,' said Danny.

20

In his time in Spain Ronnie had seen many dismembered corpses, some headless, some limbless and some so charred by high explosives that the remains did not seem human at all. It was something he never talked about and on those nights when he wakened from sleep with images of the mutilated dead dancing in his mind's eye he told Breda nothing of what tormented him but clung to her warm, substantial frame until the horror faded and he could breathe again.

Clarence Knotts had never seen a corpse before, not counting his maternal grandmother whose body had been dressed and powdered and laid out in a coffin and looked, Clary said, more contented in death than she'd ever done in life.

There was nothing contented about the body of the child, a small boy of eight or nine, that the firemen discovered in the ruins of a tenement in a Wapping cul-de-sac in the dusty light of an Indian summer afternoon.

At just after four o'clock Observer Corps spotters had picked up a massive formation of German bombers flying on a twenty-mile front at two miles high and heading for the Thames estuary. By twenty past four British fighter squadrons had been scrambled and were on course to engage the enemy. Shortly before five, a red alert sounded in the peaceful precincts of Oxmoor Road substation and the call came down from the watch room to muster all appliances.

Before the Oxmoor Road's trailer pumps were halfway to Wapping the sky to the south was filled with cauliflowers of black smoke and, thinned by sunlight, a strange vermilion glaze that reminded Ron of fresh varnish. The Highway was cluttered with ambulances, police vans and heavy units from other fire stations all heading for the docks while the mass of German raiders droned overhead and incendiaries, screamers and high-explosive bombs showered down on the terraced houses packed between the warehouses and the quays.

A District Officer in a motorcar was barking orders and two trailer pumps were already at work in the cul-de-sac when the Oxmoor Road crew arrived.

There was no evidence of an uncontrolled fire in the box-shaped street but the end building had been raked open to show tables set for supper, a bed with a chamber pot beneath it, a chair upturned by an empty fireplace and a sideboard with all its little ornaments scattered.

First and ground floors had slipped sideways, beams and floorboards funnelling the avalanche of rubble from above and spewing it into the street where, drenched by the fire hoses, it looked weirdly clean and neat.

The tenants of the cul-de-sac had trooped to the shelters when the alarm had sounded but a handful of young men and women remained, gawping, behind a rope that the wardens had slung up. The fat worm-like hoses that connected the trailer pumps to the hydrants were stretched to the limit and the water jets curved feebly over the mound of brick and timber, wallpaper, plaster and glass.

Ronnie and Clary set about uncoupling their trailer pump and connecting hoses to the breechings. They were stopped by the Station Officer who had been told by the District Officer that two light pumps were enough for this job and all spare crews must deploy to St Katharine Docks. Ron and Clary had just begun to unhook the hose brackets and make the appliance ready for the road again when a deafening explosion shook the cul-de-sac.

The jets from the operating pumps wavered, spray billowed back into the faces of the fire crews and a cloud of granular dust swarmed over the roof of the tenement which, shaken like a doll's house, disgorged a further assortment of domestic furnishings to add to the litter below.

'By God, that was close,' Clary shouted, then, grabbing Ron's arm, said, 'Hey, what's that?'

It looked like a length of rope lying uncoiled on the debris and rolled a little when the hoses played over it.

'Cat?' Clary asked.

'No,' Ron answered and signalled to Mr Reilly, the Station Officer, who, fortunately, had seen the thing too.

The line of spectators strained at the barrier. A young woman screamed, 'Jackie, Jackie,' and might have jumped over the rope if a policeman hadn't caught her by the waist.

'Where's the rescue squad?' Ron called out.

Mr Reilly shook his head and, with a sweeping motion, like a man throwing a carpet bowl, urged Ron and Clary to go forward. Ron struggled to put what might be happening in Shadwell out of mind and, with Clary behind him, picked his way cautiously over the unstable debris.

He said, 'Where is it, Clary?'

'There,' Clary said. 'Can you see it? What the 'ell is it?'

They crouched and inspected the mysterious object.

Clary said, 'Is that an arm?'

'No,' Ron said. 'It's a leg.'

'Can't be a leg. There's no foot on the end.'

'It's a piece of a leg,' Ron said. 'Go back, Clary.'

'A leg?' Clary said. 'Do you think it's a boy?'

'I think it might be,' Ronnie said. 'Yeah, it probably is.'

'Where's the rest of 'im?'

'Under the timbers, I think,' Ron said. 'Why don't you—'

'If we get 'im out they'll patch 'im up an' he'll be okay, right?' Clary inched closer. 'What's that, Ron? Oh, Jesus God, what is that?'

'Clary,' Ron said, 'get out of here.'

'Is that a – a head?'

What blood there had been had washed down into the trough in which the body lay. The head, partly severed, cocked up coyly, mouth and eyes open, a fringe of soft fair hair defining what was left of the scalp.

'Oh, God, Ron, we're too late. He's dead, the poor kid's dead,' Clary said, and dropped to all fours and was sick.

Whether it was conscience or plain ill luck that brought Susan into the East End of London that gorgeous Saturday afternoon remained a mystery.

She carried with her a box of Dairy Milk chocolates for Nora and a packet of fruit gums to keep her nephew happy but the closer she got to Stratton's Dining Rooms the more inadequate the peace offerings seemed.

She began to wish she'd gone with Bob on his trip to Dover to observe first hand the barrage of shells the Germans were lobbing over from Cap Gris Nez and the aerial dog-fights that were taking place over the Kentish coast.

Bob's frustration with *Speaking Up* had grown in the past week or two. He'd nagged Basil to let him take to the streets with an Outside Broadcasting unit and not just fool around Broadcasting House vetting pre-scripted interviews and writing linkage. He should have been out on the steps of Trafalgar Square, he said, shoulder to shoulder with Ed Murrow when the CBS reporter, brilliantly mixing sound and commentary, had broadcast an air raid 'live' to shake up the audiences in North America.

'Don't you think I have the guts for it, Baz?'

'It's not your guts I hired you for,' Basil had answered. 'I hired you to write intelligent commentary and deliver it in your own inimical style, which is something you do very well,' a compliment that had placated Bob not at all.

What was worse, from Susan's point of view, was that Bob appeared to blame her for his predicament and had been giving her short shrift both in and out of the bedroom. It was, she'd told herself, no bad idea to have a weekend apart, to allow Bob to let off steam with fellow pressmen who revelled in being close to the actions of war and, no doubt, would get royally drunk in some seaside hotel afterwards.

By all the laws of common sense, she should have gone home to Rothwell Gardens that Saturday afternoon, had a bath and a good long nap. Instead, she'd had a bite to eat in the canteen, stopped off only to buy sweets and had caught a bus for the crowded streets of the East End.

An old woman and a little girl were seated on the pavement outside Stratton's guarding a hand-printed placard and an old biscuit tin into which they hoped, rather optimistically, passers-by might drop a coin or two to aid the Shadwell Spitfire Fund. The door to the shop was wedged open and, even as she paused to fumble in her purse, Susan heard the hiss of the coffee urn and Breda calling out an order for sausages.

She dropped a sixpence into the biscuit tin, took a deep breath, and stepped into the shop.

There were two customers present, a young woman in Civil Defence uniform and a scruffy-looking man in soiled overalls who, between mouthfuls of sausage and egg, glanced with furtive longing not at Breda but at the pretty volunteer who, alone at a table by the boarded-up window, sipped coffee and smoked a cigarette with all the élan of a Dietrich or a Garbo.

Breda turned from the counter and, seeing Susan, reared up and snapped, 'He ain't 'ere.'

'Who isn't?' said Susan.

'Ronnie.'

'I didn't come especially to see Ronnie. I thought my father might be—'

'He isn't 'ere neither. He works Saturdays,' said Breda. 'Sorry you wasted a journey. Ta-ta.'

'Where's Nora?' Susan said.

'Never you mind where Nora is,' Breda said. 'I ain't havin' you badgerin' my ma.'

The young woman was listening while pretending not to and the chap in overalls was eyeing up Susan with the same wistful longing with which, a moment ago, he'd appraised the uniformed volunteer.

'I brought her chocolates,' Susan said.

'Did yah now?' Breda said. 'How's Danny?'

'Danny?'

'Your 'usband – remember?'

'Danny is – he's fine.'

Revelling in her role as inquisitor, Breda leaned against the serving counter and folded her arms.

'Come off it,' she said. 'You don't know nothin' about how Danny is. Too busy with your fancy man to give 'im – or us – the time of day. Where is 'e then?'

'He's still in Evesham.'

'I mean your fancy man, your feller? Got 'im tied up outside on a leash, 'ave yah?' Breda drawled.

'If you mean Mr Gaines, he's working,' Susan said. 'And, whatever you may have heard to the contrary, Mr Gaines is a colleague, no more and no less.'

She experienced a pang of guilt at denying Bob his rightful place in her life but the alternative was to let Breda bully her.

'That's not what Danny tells me,' said Breda. 'Danny tells me you're shaggin' this Yankee bloke every bleedin' chance you get.'

The CD volunteer coughed and the chap in overalls so far forgot himself as to utter an astonished little 'coo' under his breath, though neither showed any sign of leaving.

'Danny,' Susan said, 'doesn't know what he's talking about.'

'He caught you on the job, didn't 'e?'

'It's none of your damned business, Breda. I wouldn't expect you, of all people, to understand.'

'Me, of all people?' Breda's voice rose. 'At least me, of all people, can tell right from wrong. If Danny was my 'usband, I wouldn't go cheatin' on 'im.'

Situated on a pole at the near end of Thornton Street, the air-raid siren released an urgent wail.

The CD volunteer shot to her feet. 'My check, please.'

Whipping a pencil from behind her ear and snatching a pad from the counter, Breda scribbled two bills. She handed one to the CD volunteer, took payment, then tossed the other on to the table before the chap in overalls, his mouth full of sausage, could make a break for it. He glanced at the check, dropped a shilling on to the table and, still chewing, hastily followed the young woman out into the street.

Drying her hands on her apron, Nora appeared from the kitchen. 'Susan?' she said. 'What a nice surprise!'

'Ma, where's Billy?'

'In the lane, playing with his pals.'

The wail of the siren was overlaid by other sounds: a strange, low-pitched humming and, like a firework going off, a ripping swish followed by a soft explosion.

Mugs and cups on the shelves behind the counter rattled and the drawer of the till on the counter top popped open of its own accord.

'Oh, God! It's a real one.' Breda caught Susan's arm. 'You, turn off the gas under the urns. Ma, make sure the ovens are closed. I gotta find Billy,' then, tearing off her cap and apron, she vanished into the kitchen.

'What's happenin', Susan?' Nora asked.

'An air raid, Nora, a bad one by the sound of it.'

'Have you come to help us? Is that why you're here?'

'Yes,' Susan said. 'That's why I'm here. Do what Breda says and then get into the shelter.'

Crockery rattled once more and the steady, menacing drone grew louder. Susan found the cock of the gas pipe that fed the urns and, with some difficulty, turned it off.

Crouching behind the counter she felt the weight of the planes press down on her, the air compressed by the noise of their engines. She crawled out from under the counter and, driven by curiosity, ran out into the street.

There was movement everywhere, people running from the market stalls in Cherry Street; men helping women, women pushing prams, carrying infants or dragging young children along by the hand, small boys staring up at the German aircraft, a plane-spotter's dream.

Shading her eyes, Susan peered up at the sky. They were high, the bombers, so high that in the golden afternoon light they appeared almost transparent.

An ambulance came whizzing down Thornton Street, horn blaring, followed by two fire tenders. The old folk and children that the ARP wardens were herding towards the public shelter cheered as the tenders roared past as if the appearance of firefighters in their street signalled victory.

Clouds of black smoke were visible above the rooftops. Millwall, Limehouse and the Surrey Commercial are taking a pasting, Susan thought, and the basins of the Upper Pool, quays, warehouses and cargo ships must be sitting ducks too.

An incendiary struck the roof of a house three down from Stratton's and tumbled, splashing flame, into the street.

Old folk and children scattered. The woman who had been sipping coffee a few moments ago appeared with a stirrup-pump and extinguished the fiery puddle just as another incendiary fell close by and, bursting like a vegetable marrow, spilled flames across the pavement.

On the corner, where Thornton Street folded into Docklands Road, the front of the Co-op Bank exploded.

Susan watched the building shudder and lean out, folk running, then a plane appeared through the eruption of smoke and she heard the chatter of machine guns and, transfixed, saw the plane dip and, close enough to touch, zoom away over her head.

'What the 'ell do you think you're doin'?' Breda shouted.

'I have to get back to London,' Susan said.

'This *is* London, you silly cow,' said Breda and hauled her off the street and into the larder where Nora, Billy and three frightened neighbours were already taking shelter.

21

Falling in love had conferred a degree of reticence upon the garrulous Griffiths. Even Mrs Pell, an expert in wheedling, had been unable to tease the truth from her lodgers. Kate was just as unforthcoming as Griff on what exactly had happened on the Brecon weekend and what plans, if any, the couple had made for the future.

'Oh, come on, Danny,' Kate said. 'Don't be so grumpy. Dance with me.'

'I can't dance.'

'Anyone can do a quickstep,' Kate said. 'I'll show you.'

'I tell you I don't dance.'

'Silwyn doesn't mind.'

'Of course, I don't mind. I could do with a breather.'

The tea dance had been arranged at the last minute, the band made up of musicians of varying degrees of talent. The floor of the Greenhill lounge shone like a skating rink in the glare from the open windows and girls in frocks or slacks and men sweating in suits and collared shirts might have tumbled out of a gala at the Hammersmith Palais.

The afternoon dance was intended to appease those on late shift who would miss the Saturday night free-for-all which, in the scented dusk of the harvest month, ran serious risk of becoming an unbridled orgy of booze and petting.

The band was playing 'What Is This Thing Called Love?'. Danny had often heard it on the wireless. He had watched Griff dance, elegant and assured, and had taken grisly pleasure in noting how Griff's hand rode on the swell of Kate's hip and how her long legs flashed in the turns and runs.

He no longer resented Griff stealing Kate away. Griff had so much more to offer her than an orphaned Glaswegian with a failing marriage on his hands.

'You don't know what you're missing,' Griff said.

'He just wants to be coaxed.'

'No, Kate, I do not want tae be coaxed.'

'Sit there feeling sorry for yourself if you must. If you won't dance with this lovely lady then I will,' Griff told him.

Kate arched her back and gave a little shiver of pleasure as Griff took her by the hand and, catching the beat, swirled her away from the table by the wall.

Danny followed their progress among the dancers.

How happy and carefree they looked, he thought, how ideally suited. He wondered what Susan was doing right now, who she might be with and regretted that he had never learned to dance, had never danced with his wife.

In an hour or so, the band would strike up a goodnight waltz, the drinkers would leave the bar and the dancers the floor and head out into the early evening light to catch a bus to Wood Norton or, arm-in-arm, walk through the quaint streets and tree-lined lanes to relieve their colleagues who, even with a long shift behind them, would shake off fatigue and head for the Greenhill, and, Danny thought, nothing much would change except that by then it would be dark.

Then, abruptly, the music stopped.

The bewildered dancers gathered round the bar where, standing on a stool, Mr Gregory prepared to address them.

'I'm sorry to be the bearer of distressing news,' he began, 'but, as you will no doubt hear soon enough, the Luftwaffe has just launched a massive air raid on London.'

'Nothing new in that,' said a voice from the floor.

'Unfortunately,' Mr Gregory went on, 'it appears the blitzkrieg Hitler has been promising us in recent weeks has begun in earnest.' He held up a hand to silence the mutter from the floor. 'The news tonight will be bad. I want you to prepare yourselves for it. It's important – nay, essential – that we aren't distracted by exaggerated German claims of casualties but stick to our tasks with our usual objectivity and' – he paused – 'do not dwell too much on what might be happening' – he paused again – 'elsewhere.'

'Are we finished here?' someone asked.

'Pardon?' Mr Gregory said.

'The dance?'

'For God's sake, man,' Mr Gregory exploded, 'what sort of a fatalist are you? The Nazis are bombing London to bits and you want to go on dancing.' He closed his eyes, sniffed and got control of himself. 'The bar will remain open and food will continue to be served but, no, ladies and gentlemen, I'm afraid the party's over for tonight.'

Kate and Griffiths, hand in hand, returned to the table. Danny got to his feet.

'What do you want to do?' Griff said. 'Is there someone you can telephone?'

Danny shook his head.

'What about your wife?' Kate said. 'Will she be at work?'

'I doubt it,' Danny said. 'In any case, the chances of gettin' through are slim.'

'What then?' Griff said.

'Head for Hogsnorton, I suppose,' said Danny.

Kate touched his arm. 'Danny, are you all right?'

'Aye,' Danny said. 'I'm fine.'

The larder still smelled of cheese but when the electric light bulb flickered and suddenly went out the odour of the paraffin lamp that Breda lit soon chased the friendly smell away.

The lamp stood on a small, knee-high table that Nora used as a step to reach the high shelves. The faces of the occupants of the shelter were lit from below as they leaned forward to converse in whispers, like conspirators.

There were two bench-bunks, each piled with blankets. Four quart bottles of water and an assortment of fizzy drinks had been placed in a corner which, Matt said, was safer than putting them up on shelves where they might fall on someone's head. Tucked under the table were a small camping stove, a kettle and a cardboard box containing mugs, a canister of sugar and a tin of Fry's cocoa, but at that hour of the afternoon no one was interested in sampling the home comforts.

Nora had Billy on her knee. He seemed quite unperturbed by the thunderous explosions that shook plaster dust from the overhead beams and made the glassware in the corner chatter. He had filled his mouth with fruit gums from the packet his Aunt Susan had brought and, cheeks bulging, was content to suck and slaver noisily, unaware that his mum, his grandma, his aunt and the three elderly neighbours to whom Nora had offered shelter were putting on brave faces for his benefit.

'Nora tells me you were in the trenches in the last war, Mr Brennan?' Susan said. 'You must have experienced a great deal worse than this.'

'Never gassed,' the man said. 'Never feared nuhfink but the gas. Bloody Huns. We 'ad 'em on the run then all right.'

'What regiment were you with?'

'Artillery. Big guns. By God, they was noisy.'

The timing, Susan thought, was broadcast perfect: no sooner had Mr Brennan uttered the word 'noisy' than a huge explosion somewhere close by shook the building and brought down more plaster dust.

One of the women let out a shriek.

Billy, still sucking, turned and looked up at Nora who, with more savvy than Susan might have expected, just raised her eyebrows and said casually, 'Ooow, that's a big one.'

'Where's Dad?' said Billy.

'Out with the fire brigade,' said Breda.

'Hmm,' said Billy and, apparently mollified, settled into Nora's lap and dug into the sweet packet for another gum.

It was close to six o'clock before the raid ended.

By then both female neighbours were shaking and tearful, Billy was bouncing around from one bunk to the next and Breda had smoked so many cigarettes that her throat was raw.

Susan pulled open the larder door.

Shafts of sunlight from the yard were defined by a thick white clogging dust. The door to the yard had been blown in but, Susan noted, there wasn't much debris on the stairs.

She stepped cautiously along the corridor.

The kitchen was littered with broken glass. The blackout curtains had been torn to shreds but the ceiling was still in place, the big dresser, the table and the oven too, though some of Nora's ornamental plates had toppled from the high shelf and were ornamental no more.

There was almost no damage to the front shop. The tiny window was intact and also the door, though the upper panel bulged ominously inward. The tables were coated with a layer of fine grit but there was no smell of gas.

'Could be worse,' Breda said. 'I'll fetch them out, okay?'

'No,' Susan said. 'Wait.'

Scraping open the front door, she went out into the street.

On the corner where the Co-op Bank had been was a ragged-edged void. The sky was smeared with smoke as far as the eye could see. Vehicles were jammed into the far end of Thornton Street where pipes and cables crawled from a gaping crater and wardens, policemen and CD volunteers were frantically trying to organise a clear way for the rescue teams.

Susan surveyed the rubble-strewn street and wondered just how far she would have to walk to find a bus to carry her back to Portland Place.

Breda came out of the shop with Billy on her back. The hustle-bustle, din and smoke had excited him. If she put him down even for a second he'd be off like a shot for sure.

'I'd better be going,' Susan said.

'Goin'? Goin' where?' said Breda.

'Home,' said Susan. 'I mean, to work.'

'How're you gonna get there?'

'Walk, if I have to.'

'You just want to get back to your fancy man, don'cha?'

'What?' said Susan. 'Bob? No, he's in Dover.'

'Bully for 'im,' said Breda.

Billy twisted from side to side, taking in the carnage. Breda clamped her arms over his knees.

'Tell Dad . . .' Susan began.

'Tell 'im what?' said Breda.

'Tell him I'll see him soon,' Susan said and, before Breda could stop her, stepped over the rubble and started out for home.

The ground-floor concert hall had been stripped of seats and turned into a dormitory complete with mattresses where newsreaders, typists and supervisors rubbed shoulders with producers from the Empire Service and reporters from America.

For news staff three days on and three days off was the general rule but producers of topical programmes like *Speaking Up* did not have the luxury of punching a clock and it came as no surprise to Susan to bump into Larry heading through the entrance hall with a blanket over his arm and, floating on a wire hanger, a spare shirt.

'What are you doing here?' she asked.

'I'm not risking a trip out to Kennington tonight,' Larry answered. 'My sister can look after herself for once. This place might not be the Ritz but it's better than a stinky Anderson shelter. Where you been?'

'Shadwell.'

'How'd you get back?'

'Hoofed for a bit then found a taxi.'

'Word is it's bad down that way.'

'It is,' Susan said. 'Very bad.'

It had been less difficult than she'd imagined it might be to put the East End behind her. She'd avoided the worst areas of devastation and when she'd reached the top end of Fleet Street a cabby had taken pity on her.

She said, 'Is Basil in his office?'

'Doubt it,' Larry said. 'I think he went home.'

'Mr Gaines?'

'Haven't seen him all day,' Larry said. 'What you need right now, if you don't mind me saying so, is a wash and brush up and a nice cup of tea. Canteen's not closed but they're using the annexe. Even if you don't have a ticket I'm sure someone will find you a berth in the concert hall. Ladies are at the back behind the curtains if you're worried about decency.'

'Decency is the last thing on my mind,' Susan said. 'Have you been here all afternoon, Larry?'

'Yer, on loan to the Canadians. They're very excited 'cause the war has finally arrived on our doorstep. They've been firing off bulletins all evening. Half of them, along with the Yanks, are watching the fireworks from the roof.'

'If it's damage they're after,' Susan said, 'they should be downriver. Lots of casualties.'

'Bully-boy tactics,' Larry said. 'If Churchill hadn't bombed Berlin . . .' He shrugged. 'Well, heck, we can't just sit back and let the beggars do as they like. You're not going upstairs, are you?'

'I do have work to do, you know.'

'Only the news studios are in use. The offices are deserted,'

Larry said. 'By the sound of it, it's going to be a heavy night. I'd keep my head down, if I were you.'

'Talking of heads, you wouldn't happen have a spare hairbrush on you, by any chance?'

Larry laughed. 'No, nor a spare pair of knickers either,' then, still chuckling, headed across the foyer to the door of the concert hall and left Susan to make her own way to the ladies'.

22

The acoustics in the concert hall had been designed to enhance sound but the chorus of snores, sighs, moans and other unsavoury noises that rose from the bodies huddled on the floor was a far cry from a nocturne by Debussy or a Brahms lullaby. Even muffled by the curtains that screened the tiers at the rear of the auditorium the snores of a couple of hundred men trying to snatch some shut-eye was enough to keep Susan awake.

There was also much coming and going along the dimly lighted aisles. Duty Officer, House Supervisor and various other officials, including wardens, matrons and a nosy copper or two, kept popping in not just to ensure that everyone was comfortable but to check that there was no hanky-panky going on which, given the circumstances, there most certainly was not.

Susan removed her stockings and dress but kept on her slip, unlike some of the younger girls who, defiantly throwing modesty to the wind, had peeled down to bra and pants before snuggling down to sleep.

Sleep, though, was hard to come by. Susan dozed fitfully on and off, waking every time the door above her squeaked or the light of a warden's torch flickered and, of course, every time a bomb went off in the vicinity of Portland Place.

At four, or shortly after, an all-clear sounded.

The dishevelled pack stirred, yawned, groped for trousers or skirts and set about buttoning, fastening and lighting cigarettes or, draped in blankets, stumbled off to find the nearest lavatory. By five, the canteen was in full swing serving breakfast to those whose day was about to begin and supper to those who had been on watch all night.

By six, washed, dressed and fed, Susan was at her desk in the third-floor office peering blearily at her memo pad when the door flew open and Bob Gaines pranced into the room.

His tie was loose, his jacket unbuttoned. The sweat-stained fedora, pushed back from his brow, added a raffish touch to his appearance that seemed at odds with the early hour and the fact that it was Sunday.

'I thought you were in Dover,' Susan said.

He looped an arm about her neck and kissed her mouth.

'I was,' he said, 'and I'm damned glad to be back. For a while there I thought we might not make it. The bastards were machine-gunning the trains. Can you believe it? Coming in low and shooting the daylights out of passenger trains. More than half the lines are closed and Waterloo station is belching smoke like a goddamned volcano.'

'How did you get here?'

'Come on,' he said, tugging her arm. 'Come and I'll show you how I got here. Bring your coat, honey. We won't be coming back any time soon.'

'Robert, I'm on duty.'

'Not any more, you're not. This,' he said, 'you've got to

see,' and waltzed her out into the corridor and along it to the lift.

The van was one of two damaged Outside Broadcast vehicles that had been dumped in a yard behind the plant room. Its side panels were pocked by shrapnel and the cab door hung half off its hinge. A mechanic in a tin hat and blue overalls was poking about in the rear where turntables and cables had been wrenched from their fittings.

'This?' Susan said. 'You came all the way from Dover in this wreck? How in heaven's name did you all fit in?'

'There were only four of us, plus a couple of your guys. The unit was useless anyway. Took a blast from a shell that ruined all the recording equipment. We persuaded the OB crew that sitting in the open on Dover harbour in a busted truck wasn't the safest place to be and we'd be better off heading for London.'

'In the dark, in middle of the biggest air raid we've had so far?' Susan said. 'You're mad, you're completely mad.'

'Call it resourceful,' Bob said. 'Heck of a ride, though. Heck of a ride. We scrounged a couple of gallons of gas from an army truck at a checkpoint somewhere near Ashford. It's great what you can pull off if you work for the BBC.'

'You saw it then? You saw the fires?'

'Are you kidding? The whole goddamned sky was ablaze. The closer we got to London the more detours we had to make.' He leaned against the sagging door. 'God, what a ride that was.'

The mechanic emerged from the rear of the van, shaking his head. 'Buggered up proper,' he said, then, to Susan, 'Sorry, miss – but it's not my job to fix it. We'll need to wait for the electrical chaps.'

'Of course, you will,' Bob said. 'Where are they?'

'Haven't a clue,' the mechanic said.

'Busy elsewhere, I guess,' Bob said. 'I could run her down to the depot for you, if you like.'

'The depot?' the mechanic said.

'Our place at King's Cross.'

'Your place?'

'The depot, yeah. Surely you've heard of the depot?'

''Course I've heard o' the depot.'

'There you are then. Bob's your uncle.'

'I ha'n't got the keys,' the mechanic said.

'I have.' Bob dug into his jacket pocket and produced a ring with three keys on it. 'All bona fide, see.'

Clearly at a disadvantage, the mechanic capitulated. 'You takin' the lady with you?'

'She's my navigator.'

'Well, if you're sure, like?'

'Sure, I'm sure,' Bob said.

He helped Susan into the cab and followed her on to the bench behind the wheel. He closed the door as best he could, fitted a key into the ignition and fired the engine.

'Where is this depot?' Susan said.

'What depot?' Bob said, grinning.

'Dear God,' Susan said, 'you really are—'

'Resourceful?' Bob suggested.

'Incorrigible,' said Susan.

Salt Street Mews, like much of central London, had escaped the overnight raid unscathed. Vivian had spent most of the night on the roof fire-spotting. The spectacle of flames and smoke, flares, searchlights and the incredible din of ack-ack guns banging away had been exhausting. As soon as she stepped into the house, however, her resolve took over and, pausing only to change her clothes, she headed straight for the typewriter to put in an hour or two on her new book.

She was pecking furiously at the keys when Basil, bathed, shaved and dressed in his Sunday best, appeared at her side with a breakfast tray.

She glanced up at him and scowled.

'I must say, Chucks,' Basil told her, 'you've never looked as lovely as you do now.'

'Hah!' said Vivian.

'No, truly. There's something incredibly stimulating about a woman wearing only a dressing gown and a steel helmet.'

'Sarcasm does not become you.' Viv paused long enough to take off the tin hat. 'Why are you all done up?'

'I am not done up,' Basil said. 'I have merely made myself presentable.'

'You're not going to the office, are you?'

'Of course, I am.'

With the forefinger of her left hand Vivian added a semi-colon to the text on the page in the typewriter, then, picking up a fork, pierced the surface of the egg that Basil had poached for her and dipped a piece of toast into the yolk.

'It's Sunday,' she said. 'Isn't it?'

'Indeed, it is,' Basil said. 'But it's also wartime and war, as we are learning all too quickly, is hell. I may not be home for a day or two, possibly not until the weekend.'

'Why?'

'I've a strong suspicion yesterday's raids might signal the beginning of the Luftwaffe's attempt to soften us up for an end of the month invasion.'

Vivian ate a mouthful of toast and washed it down with coffee. 'Hitler won't invade.'

'You may be right,' Basil said. 'He probably won't risk a landing until he's absolutely sure our airfields are out of action. We're a long way from that happening. Hence the increased number of raids to weaken our morale.'

'He's just mad at Churchill for bombing Berlin.'

'Actually, he's just mad,' said Basil. 'Eat your breakfast, Viv, and assure me – word of honour – that you'll take care of yourself until we meet again.'

'For God's sake, Basil, you're not going off to join the army.' She paused and sat up. 'Are you?' She dropped the fork, pushed her chair back from the desk and scrambled to her feet. 'Oh, my God! Don't tell me you've enlisted.'

'No, no, dearest. My goodness, I didn't mean to alarm you. I'll be no further away than Portland Place if you need me.'

'I do, Basil. Oh, I do need you,' said Vivian.

'If it's anything urgent pop round to Broadcasting House and flash your guest pass. If that doesn't work have them call me.' He drew her to him and peered into her tear-stained face. 'What is it? Vivian, what's wrong?'

'I love you, you idiot,' Vivian said, snuffling.

'Oh!' said Basil, nonplussed. 'I don't think I've ever heard you say that before.'

'Well, damn it, I'm saying it now. I love you and I'd rather not lose you. So be careful, Basil. Please, please, be careful.'

'I will,' Basil said. 'I promise you, I will.'

He kissed her and, picking up his overnight bag, left her to pull herself together, finish her breakfast and presumably get on with her book.

*

It was close to nine on Sunday morning before Breda returned to Pitt Street. She was surprised to find her house still standing. The night raid had reduced many buildings to smouldering ruins and the sight of people picking over the rubble in search of some small thing around which they could begin to rebuild their lives was chastening.

Carrying their belongings on their backs or pushing prams and handcarts laden with salvaged goods, the homeless of Shadwell headed for schools, rest centres and any temporary accommodations they could find. Vans and lorries came and went. Fire tenders, exhausted firemen clinging to the rail, rattled along the bottom of Docklands Road and in one side street an isolated group of soldiers was cautiously probing the debris for an unexploded parachute bomb.

Billy was very quiet. He walked by Breda's side carrying a bundle of comics that his grandfather had saved for him and a brown paper bag of chocolates that Nora had tipped from the box that Susie had brought her.

What Billy made of it and what he would remember in later life Breda couldn't begin to imagine. Then, suddenly, there was her house, roof in place, walls upright, windows still in their frames. Mrs McNair, three down, was sweeping debris from the pavement while old Mr Johnston, who'd never done a hand's turn in his life, beat dust from a coconut mat that had once said 'Welcome'.

Breda had spent the night in the larder in Stratton's.

Her father-in-law had staggered in just after the siren announced the second wave. He'd told them that the quays, warehouses and some of the ships in St Katharine Docks were on fire, that he, high up in the cabin of a crane, had watched incendiaries dropping and dive-bombers strafing the barges and that the glass of the cabin had blown in and he'd only just managed to shin down the ladder before the coaster at the quay below had been blown to smithereens.

Billy, all agog, had swallowed his grandfather's lurid tale without question, but Breda was not so sure. Ronnie's old man was prone to exaggeration. She doubted, for instance, if a union representative had ordered him to find shelter and, when the all-clear sounded, to scuttle off home.

Nora's neighbours had been carried off by their grown-up children who apparently thought there were safer places to shelter than Stratton's Dining Rooms. By 2 a.m., when the raid was at its worst, Breda had been inclined to agree with them. The larder had been shaken by explosion after explosion. Nora had prayed and fingered her rosary and Matt had been too scared to deliver his usual speech about pagan superstition.

Prompted by Breda, he'd fiddled with a water bottle, the kettle and the little paraffin stove and had made them all cocoa which he'd laced with rum from a bottle hidden under one of the mattresses, a potion that had blunted their fears somewhat and had helped get them through the night. Billy had slept through most of it. He'd wakened only when one ear-splitting crash signalled the loss of a chimney or part of the roof.

When morning had finally arrived and Breda had crept out to see what damage had been done, however, she found that it wasn't a chimney-head that had been blown down but the whole front wall of the shop.

She'd expected her mother to throw a fit at the extent of the damage but Nora had been unusually sanguine. 'Sure and this will take a bit of clearing up,' was all she'd said, had sent Matt upstairs to check the bedrooms and, picking about in the kitchen, had managed to salvage enough unspoiled food to make them all a breakfast of sorts.

Breda unlocked the front door of her terraced house and, with Billy close behind, stepped into the little hall.

The place reeked of smoke. There were fragments of glass on the torn lino, a broken mirror on the hallstand and the stairs were covered in dust. Soot had fallen from the flue and piled up in the grate in the kitchen. There was no electricity, no gas and only a thin trickle of water from the taps at the sink. The window above the sink was cracked and the frame so loosened that when she touched it, it almost fell out.

She hurried to the back door, yanked it open and, heart in mouth, looked across the yard to the outhouse which, thank God, was all in one piece. Mightily relieved, she returned then to the kitchen to clean out the fireplace, sweep up the glass and make the place tidy for Ronnie coming home.

For many years Nora had attended Mass at the Church of St Mary and St Michael up on Commercial Road. On that particular Sunday, however, with half the streets in the borough closed off and rubble everywhere, she chose to go no further than the little Church of St Veronica tucked away in Pound Lane at the far end of Fawley Street.

At one time, long before Nora had arrived in Shadwell, the church had been a Carmelite monastery, a small, shrug-shouldered building that you would pass without a second glance, but on that Saturday night its crypt had proved a godsend to those in search of shelter.

The church itself hadn't escaped unmarked. Roach's Motor Garage at the blunt end of Pound Lane had suffered a direct hit and the back side of St Vee's had caught some of the blast. Nora rather expected Mass to be cancelled but, shortly after nine, a young priest appeared on the steps to explain that Father McFall had been injured, not, thanks be to God, too seriously but for that reason, among others, confessions would now be heard in a temporary cubicle in the side chapel followed by Mass in the church as soon as the area had been cleared of debris.

Nora trailed the other communicants indoors. Looking up, she saw that part of the roof had been holed and some windows smashed. The crucifix from behind the altar had been removed and lay at an angle against the wall close to the statue of Mary, untouched in all her glory.

She watched the curtain of the temporary confessional open and close. A chap not much older than her son-in-law emerged, then a young woman in the uniform of the ARP rescue service who was so overcome by emotion that she had to be helped away by one of the Boy Scouts who were clearing fragments of glass from the pews.

On the way to church Nora had seen the corpses that the rescue squads were pulling from the rubble and grieving women clinging to the selfish hope that the corpse would be somebody else's husband, someone else's child. Now more than ever she needed penance and forgiveness if only to lend her prayers validity and ease her fear of dying or, worse, of losing Matt or Breda or, worst of all, her grandson, Billy.

She watched the curtain sway and a woman come out and, looking round, realised that she was the last person on the bench. No help for it now, no turning back. She rose, brushed the skirts of her coat, adjusted her headscarf and slipped through the curtain into the vestibule where an old wooden draught-screen had been set up in lieu of a grille, a chair, a single, solitary chair, placed before it.

She drew the chair as close as she dared to the blank wooden surface and, clearing her throat, asked, 'Are you there?'

'Yes,' came the answer, clear and curt.

'Father, forgive me for I have sinned,' Nora said, though, at that particular moment she was no longer sure what sin meant or who was paying the price for what.

At first it seemed like the height of folly to appropriate a BBC OB vehicle to tour the blitzed streets of the East End. Once they'd entered the worst hit areas of the docklands, however, it hadn't taken Susan long to realise just how enterprising Bob had been. Many roads were closed to all but rescue workers. Repair men struggled with broken mains, sewage pipes and torn cables, while small groups of soldiers ferreted in the rubble in search of body parts. WVS stalls had been set up to serve the workers and mobile canteens provided a measure of comfort – hot sweet tea and jammy buns – to homeless citizens.

Bob had seen it all before. He knew what to do to make the best of the situation. He drew up the van to the edge of a crowd, leaped from the cab and, before a copper or officious warden could chase him away, called out, 'BBC, we're from the BBC,' and pointed towards the van to confirm his credentials.

Seated in the cabin Susan saw what a seasoned reporter

Bob Gaines really was, a practitioner of good, old-fashioned pad-and-pencil journalism who relied on anecdote not observation. She watched him tease quotes from anxious mothers, weary wardens, cocky corner boys and one poor old woman who had lost absolutely everything, including – and here she began to cry – Timmy, her cat.

'Timmy,' Bob said as he climbed back into the cab. 'Who ever heard of a cat called Timmy?'

'You'll use it, though, won't you?'

'Sure, I will,' he said. 'Won't be a dry eye this side of Memphis before I get through with Timmy.'

'And the old woman?'

'You don't get it, Susan, do you?' He started the engine. 'There are thousands of old women like her out there but only one Timmy. When it comes to war no one can truly latch on to the big picture. One old woman with a lost cat named Timmy, that much they *can* handle.'

A St John's nurse and a middle-aged man in gumboots shepherded a string of six children across the street; young children, half-clad, carrying not dolls and teddy bears but a cup or a bowl or a crumpled scrap of cloth that might once have been a blanket.

Bob leaned on the steering wheel and squinted through the windscreen. 'Now I wonder where they're headed? Is there a school around here?'

'I don't know,' Susan said.

'I thought the East End was your home turf?'

'Not this part,' she lied. 'In any case, it all looks different.'

'Not that different,' said Bob. 'Where are we?'

'Fawley Street – I think.'

She resisted an urge to direct him down the next street

on the right so that she could look into Thornton Street and see if Stratton's had survived a second night's bombing. She watched the children pass by the van and then, to her relief, felt the van jolt and inch down Fawley Street towards the canopy of smoke that hung over the transit sheds of the Western Dock.

And then it stopped.

'Hey,' Bob said, nodding. 'How about that?'

She leaned across his lap and looked from the window.

'Geeze!' Bob said. 'He's kissing her? Why's he kissing her?'

The couple was standing outside the shell of Brauschmidt's butcher's shop where Ronnie had served his apprenticeship. The shop had been boarded up for months and there was precious little left of it now, only the façade reaching up into burned-out rooms where Herr Brauschmidt and his wife had lived for forty years before decamping to America.

The man, no youngster, pointed out to the woman a pretty little cluster of flowering weeds that clung tenaciously to the ledge that separated the shop from the flat above and, while Bob and Susan watched, the couple kissed once more.

'Now there's a story if ever was.' Bob groped for the door handle. 'One old guy and one old dame spooning on the pavement. What the hell is that all about?'

'No.' Susan caught at his sleeve. 'No, Bob, don't interfere.'

'What's gotten into you, Susie?' Bob said. 'Don't you know a good story when you see one?'

'Leave them alone. Please, just leave them alone.'

Reluctantly, Bob removed his hand from the door.

'I never figured you for a romantic, Susan,' he said. 'Do you know them, is that it?'

'No,' Susan said. 'I've never seen them before in my life,' then, in the nearside mirror, watched her father and Nora Romano grow smaller and smaller until they vanished from sight.

23

She remembered how bad he'd looked when he'd limped off the train that had brought him back from the war in Spain. He looked like that again, she thought, only worse. The mandarin collar of the heavy wool serge tunic had chafed his neck so badly that blood oozed from his Adam's apple and the uniform was so thoroughly soaked that she had to peel it off him practically strip by strip.

He stood naked before her, too exhausted to be embarrassed, and let her sponge him with warm water from the kettle and rub him down with her own special bath towel. He looked bad, Breda thought, really bad but also rather magnificent, with his pale skin and long stringy muscles and the haggard face that hinted what he'd look like in ten or twenty years' time.

'How long've you got?' she asked.

'Four hours.'

'Do you want to eat first, or sleep?'

'Sleep.' He winced when she massaged his shoulders. 'Had some Bovril at the station; that'll do me.'

'Bend over.'

Stooping, he let her draw his head down into her lap to dry his hair. He groaned and closed his eyes.

ore?' said Breda.

'Stiff.'

In other circumstances she might have teased him with a suggestive remark but she had too much respect for what he'd been through, whatever it was, to do so now.

She gave him the towel to finish himself off, lifted his boots, spread the tongues and placed them carefully in the hearth. She picked up his trousers and, stepping to the sink, tried to wring them out, but the serge was too heavy to release much water. She would hang them, and the tunic, out on the line to dry in the sunlight as soon as he went upstairs.

He wrapped the towel about his waist and stood quite still while she dabbed Germolene on to his Adam's apple and tied one of Billy's old baby bibs around his neck to keep the ointment from soiling the bed sheets.

'There!' she said. 'You niff a bit but you do look better.'

'Is Billy okay?'

'He's out in the yard shootin' down Germans.'

'Tonight,' Ronnie said.

'What about tonight?'

'You can't go back to your ma's place.'

'Why not?'

Ron shook his head. 'The building isn't safe.'

'How do you know?'

'Came round that way.'

'Did you talk to the old man?'

'He wasn't there. Nobody was there except coppers.' He clutched the towel with one hand and, frowning, said, 'Listen to me, darlin'. I mean what I say. I saw what happened to Stratton's an' I'm tellin' you, the building isn't safe. It may look okay but it's shook to the foundations an' one big blast will bring it down on you.'

'What do you want us to do?'

'Stay 'ere.'

'You think the Jerries are comin' again?' Breda said.

'I'm sure they are.'

'Right.' Breda nodded firmly. 'Here we stay.'

'Fetch your mother an' my old man,' Ron went on. 'Bring them down here too. It'll be a tight squeeze but our shelter's well protected an' the vent'll keep the air sweet.'

'You won't be 'ome tonight,' Breda stated.

'No,' Ron said. 'I don't know when I'll be back. Wake me at three. I'll have to shave before I go out.' He looked around the kitchen. 'Be careful with that loose window, Breda. Keep Billy away from it. I'll fix it when I—'

'Stop frettin' about the window an' go to bed,' Breda said. 'You do what you gotta do. I'll take charge of things 'ere.'

'Yeah,' he said. 'Yeah, I know you will.' He drew her to him and kissed her. 'Three o'clock, love?'

'Three o'clock, it is,' said Breda.

'Calm down, Basil,' Robert Gaines said. 'It wasn't her fault. I dragged her away.'

'You can't simply go haring off without a word to anyone. Where were you?' Basil said, then added, 'No, don't tell me.'

'It's not what you think,' Susan said. 'We were working.'

'Working? Where? Not here, that's for sure.' He leaned forward on his chair, planted his fists on the desk and glowered up at Bob. 'I thought you'd gone to Dover for the weekend.'

'That,' Bob said, 'is one story.' Digging into his jacket

pocket he brought out his notebook and flapped it in Basil's direction. 'And this is another. Gold, my man, solid gold. We've been down in the East End collecting hot copy from the horse's mouth. Give me fifteen minutes air time and I'll deliver you a programme that'll really make our listeners sit up.'

'Trust you, in other words?'

'Why not?' said Bob. 'I've never let you down before.'

'That's true,' Basil conceded. 'I must have the script first thing tomorrow. Do you need a desk and a shorthand typist?'

'Nope,' Bob said. 'I'll hole up in my apartment, catch a few hours' sleep then get down to it. You'll have the material by nine Monday, I promise.'

'I trust you're not planning on taking Susan with you.'

'She's your girl, Baz, not mine,' Bob said. 'Anyhow, I prefer not to be distracted.'

'Quite!' Basil said. 'Well, don't let me keep you. You're not the only one with a lot to do. Susan, do you have every-thing you need for a long stay?'

'I could do with an hour off to pick up some clean clothes.'

Ostentatiously, Basil consulted his wristlet watch.

'Four,' he said. 'I need you back here by four. All right?'

'What if there's another raid?'

'Do the best you can,' Basil said.

Bob opened the office door and ushered Susan into the corridor just as Basil called out. 'By the by, how did you get into the East End?'

The van was back safe and sound in the yard, and no one seemed to have missed it.

'Taxi,' Susan said. 'We hired a taxi.'

'I hope you're not going to charge it to expenses?'

'Wouldn't dream of it,' Bob Gaines said and chased Susan towards the lift before Mr Willets could ask any more awkward questions.

It took Breda all her time to persuade her mother that Stratton's was unsafe. Only a declaration by an inspection officer that the building needed shoring before it would be habitable again finally convinced Nora that, with Matt at work on the dock, spending a night in Pitt Street with Breda and Billy was preferable to going alone to a public shelter.

She packed a canvas shopping bag with food scoured from the ruins of her kitchen, including a piece of boiled ham that, when washed, would do nicely for supper, and collected clothes and sheets from the bedrooms in spite of Breda's warning about the shaky state of the stairs.

There was still no gas or electricity in Pitt Street but men were digging under the macadam at the street's end and water from the taps in the sink had been restored. Breda built up the fire in the grate, filled a kettle and, using an old piece of wire mesh as a grid, set the kettle on the coals to boil, then, seizing her chance, nipped out to the lavatory to make sure that the cashbox was still safe behind the cistern.

On returning to the kitchen she found Nora setting out plates for an early supper. Billy, hungry as usual, had been given a slice of bread and marmalade to keep him going and, seated cross-legged on the carpet, contentedly watched the kettle come to the boil. Breda lit a cigarette and, perched on an arm of the fireside chair, said, 'Ma, do you ever think about Dad?'

Nora polished a fork with a dishcloth before she placed it on the table. 'Not after what he done to me, no.'

'It wasn't 'is fault.'

'Sure an' who's fault was it then?'

'Oh,' Breda said. 'You mean what 'appened years ago. I was thinkin' of what happened more recent, like.' She paused. 'Ever wonder what 'e's up to these days?'

'Don't know. Don't care.'

'What if 'e was to walk in that door right now?'

'I'd send him packing.'

'What if I was to tell you 'e might be dead?'

'More likely he's in the jail. Serve him right.'

'If 'e was dead, though,' Breda pressed on, 'I mean, if we knew for sure 'e was dead . . .'

'Would I marry Matt Hooper, is that what you're asking?'

'Uh-huh.'

'Sure an' I would.' Nora placed the fork on the table and squared it precisely. 'You wouldn't mind, would you, dear?'

'Not a bit,' said Breda. 'I'm all for it.'

'What about Ronnie?'

'Ronnie'll do what 'e's told,' Breda said, then, laying it on a little thicker, added, 'Anyway, Ron's always looked on you like you was 'is mother.'

'Does he?' said Nora, pleased. 'He's a good man, Breda. You're lucky to have him.'

'Yeah,' Breda said. 'I reckon I am.'

She went to the window and tucked the blackout curtain around the shaky frame, then, by candlelight, they sat down to eat. A half-hour later the big Sunday night raid began.

There had been some damage to a railway bridge that crossed the King's Road and a gang of workers in brown overalls were noisily unloading scaffolding from a lorry parked at a corner of the Gardens. There was activity around the mouth of the ground shelter too but, thankfully, no sign of fire engines or ambulances. Aware that Basil had done her a favour by turning a blind eye to her absence that morning she'd summoned a taxi to bring her home and, with the meter ticking away like a time bomb, had asked the cabby to wait outside to return her to Broadcasting House.

To her surprise no windows in her flat were broken and the lights still worked. The bed tempted her, the bath more so, but with Basil waiting and the taxi meter eating up her salary, she settled for a cold-water splash and a change of clothes then packed a suitcase with everything she might need for a long stay in the stuffy corridors of Broadcasting House.

She grabbed Maugham's *The Painted Veil* and Compton Mackenzie's latest, which Vivian had insisted she read, and stuffed them into her case. Looking round, she suddenly became aware how empty the flat seemed in the afternoon light and, yielding to impulse, fished a fountain pen and notepad from her bag and dashed off a brief letter to Danny.

She signed it, hastily added a kiss, found an envelope and addressed it and then, with the suitcase in her hand and the letter in her pocket, left the flat in Rothwell Gardens for what, as it happened, was the very last time.

Three was bearable, Breda thought, but with Ron and his old man in here too, vent or no vent, the atmosphere would be suffocating. She'd purchased a box of batteries from the same shifty source as she'd purchased the tinned fruit but half of them turned out to be duds. Wary of running out, she extinguished the pocket torch and lit a candle instead, a candle that stank the place out and, in Breda's imagination, sucked up air like a vacuum cleaner sucks up dust.

Nora was propped up on the bunk, Billy by her side. She had started out with a blanket over her legs but the heat in the shelter under the stairs didn't take long to build up and she'd soon discarded it. Even Billy was sweating. Nora peeled off his pullover and shirt and fanned him with one of his comics while crooning her version of a South Sea Island ditty that still managed to sound like 'The Rose of Tralee'.

Such diversions did not distract Billy for long. When the bombs began falling in earnest he too became agitated. He kneeled on the bunk, braced like a runner in the starting blocks, and neither Nora nor Breda could persuade him to lie down.

Breda was never sure at what point in the course of the raid it dawned on her that the outhouse might be a target and that if it went up in smoke her father's cash and her son's future would go up in smoke with it.

'Ma,' she said shrilly, 'I hafta pee.'

'Hold it in, dear. It can't last much longer.'

'I hafta pee. I hafta.'

'Use the pail. That's what it's for. We'll close our eyes.'

'No, I gotter go to the toilet,' Breda cried, petulant as a child, and wrenched open the shelter door before her mother could stop her.

Cool air rushed in. The window above the sink had been

blown halfway across the kitchen, the tattered shreds of the blackout curtain plastered against the guard that Breda had hooked over the grate. The wireless set, Ron's pride and joy, had toppled from the dresser to the floor where it lay in a tangle of valves, wires and splintered wood.

Crouched in the doorway, Breda hesitated.

She found her pocket torch, switched it on and played the beam on the carpet of debris in the corridor. She could hear guns barking in the distance and the strange, soft, sifting sound of the breeze billowing through the hole above the sink but, at that moment, no planes and no explosions.

'Two minutes, Ma. I'll only be two minutes,' Breda called and, stepping over the junk, stumbled through the kitchen and ran across the yard. She tugged open the outhouse door, clambered on to the pedestal and, with the torch between her teeth, fumbled for the cashbox and brought it down.

She felt better at once. With the box under her arm, she stepped down from the pedestal and backed out into the yard.

She didn't really hear the bomb.

First thing she knew of it, the lavatory door was bowling over and over, like the page of an old newspaper, her skirts whipped up around her waist, her mouth was pulled open and her hair felt as if it were being ripped out by the roots. Then, punched square-on by the blast wave, she was hurled backwards into the sludge that poured from the roots of the outhouse.

She lay spread-eagled on the ground, blinded, deafened and unable to breathe for several seconds, with only the stink of drains and the shrivelling stench of high explosive to tell her that she was still alive. Then, hoisting herself up, she saw that where her house had been there was nothing but a vast heap of debris illuminated by a roaring gas jet that flared up like a beacon into the smoke-filled sky.

24

The announcer's voice was all too familiar to the monitors of late-night Radio Bremen. His tone was, as a rule, smug and scoffing, which no doubt added credibility to the script if you happened to be German. Tonight, however, there was an added element in the mixture of rant, cant and threat that the Nazi propaganda machine churned out.

Shaking off fatigue, Kate made careful note of it and, for the benefit of editorial, underlined one tell-tale statement: '*It is a question of time – a few short weeks, then this conflagration will have reached its natural conclusion.*'

Danny didn't miss the trick. He passed the transcription down the table to Mr Harrison, his supervisor, who scanned the notes and looked up, frowning.

'And the natural conclusion is?' he asked.

'Invasion,' Danny answered.

'Who marked it, Danny, you, or Miss . . .'

'Cottrell,' Danny said. 'She marked it.'

'Well, it isn't much.' Mr Harrison stroked his nose with the stem of his pipe. 'But it is something. I take it you have the entire Bremen transcription?'

'I do, sir,' said Danny. 'Kate – Miss Cottrell – was right tae mark it up. Somehow it doesn't fit the context, an' there might have been somethin' in the way Fritz said it. She's done Bremen every night for weeks an' understands the inflexions.'

'Point taken,' Mr Harrison interrupted. 'Does anyone have anything that might back it up?'

Heads rose from the papers that littered the editorial table but no one had anything to contribute. They were all aware that every scrap of information that might hint at Hitler's plans to invade before winter was vital and not even the most casual-seeming comment could be discounted.

'How far behind are we?' Mr Harrison said.

'Forty minutes at most,' Griff said. He was seated directly across the long table from Danny and, at the mention of Kate's name, had looked up. 'Fritz goes off air at ten thirty.'

'Have we heard anything from the fat Field Marshall this evening?' said Mr Harrison. 'Goering, I mean.'

A general shaking of heads.

Mr Harrison puffed on his pipe for ten or fifteen seconds then said, 'All right. We'll headline it. But first, Danny, pop over to M Unit and ask Miss Cottrell for her interpretation.'

'Kate's our best translator,' Griff reminded him.

'Spoken without prejudice, of course, Mr Griffiths,' said Mr Harrison with a smile, and signalled Danny to be on his way.

Danny darted between the huts, identified himself to the soldier on duty and, careful to show no light, slipped into the monitoring unit. After checking in with Mr Gregory, he tiptoed down the aisle between the cubicles, each one lit by a little cup-shaped lamp. He drew up short of Kate's desk. Even with a pair of earphones clamped on her head, she looked lovely. At that moment, for only a moment, he felt as if his life were drifting away from him.

He dropped the slip of paper on to her desk and asked, 'What does it mean?'

'Just what it says,' Kate answered.

'How did Fritz sound when he said it? Did he sound as if he knew something he couldn't let dab about?'

'Let dab?'

'Divulge.'

She angled her chair to face him. He could make out the shape of her breasts under the white blouse and regret was suddenly tinged with longing.

'Yes,' Kate said, after a pause. 'There was definitely something fishy in his delivery. Something I can't quite put my finger on. He sounded – what? – sly when he talked about a natural conclusion.'

'Natural, not inevitable? You're sure?'

'Oh, yes, there's no confusion in German.'

'A few short weeks?'

'Exactly what Fritz said, word for word.'

'Harrison wants to know if we should headline it?'

'That's not for me to say,' Kate said. 'If you don't trust my translation why don't you give the wax to someone else and see what they make of it?'

'We don't have time,' Danny said. 'Make a snap judgement, Kate. You're pretty damned good at that.'

'What's that supposed to mean?'

'Do we go with it, or not?'

'Yes, go with it.'

'You sure?'

'Danny, what do you want from me?'

'A straight answer.'

'I've given you my answer.'

'An' you're not going to change your mind?'

'No, Danny,' she said. 'I'm not going to change my mind.'

Crafty Basil Willets had secured himself a berth in the lovely old studio dedicated to religious broadcasts. He looked rested, well groomed and smelled of after-shave. He obviously hadn't had to fight for space at a sink or keep a wary eye open for Matron who was stalking the ladies' cloakrooms to ensure that the latest memo prohibiting the washing of hair in hand basins was strictly obeyed.

There had been precious little 'Dunkirk spirit' in evidence in the canteen early that Monday morning. Even chirpy young typists had had the pith knocked out of them by the second night-long raid. There had been angry spats over the breakfast tables, tearful apologies and, here and there, smothered fits of near hysterics that even the appearance of Leslie Howard, the film actor, looking slightly less than heart-throb material in a borrowed greatcoat and carpet slippers, had failed to quell.

It was after eight o'clock before Basil showed up.

Susan had been at her desk for almost an hour trying to make sense of a schedule that had been revised to death and cope with telephone exchanges that had been bombed to blazes. Basil's trim appearance made her feel all the more grubby and that, added to lack of sleep, rendered her irritable.

'Ah, there you are,' Basil said breezily.

'Where else did you think I'd be,' Susan snapped. 'And where the bleedin' hell have you been?'

'Now, now, Susan,' Basil admonished, 'please remember who you're talking to.'

Susan tried to sound contrite. 'I'm sorry. It's been an awful morning. For one thing, I can't get through to the Air Ministry, not for love nor money.'

Basil took his place behind his desk and lit a cigarette.

'Lines down, I expect,' he said. 'You may not have heard but the City took a pasting last night.' He paused, then went on, 'Are you worried about your people?'

'My people?'

'Your relatives.'

'Oh!' she said. 'Of course. Of course, I am.'

Basil pulled a wire tray to the centre of his desk and began leafing through his correspondence.

'At least,' he said, 'you don't have to worry about your husband. He'll be safe enough in Evesham.'

'I'm sure he will,' said Susan.

'After all, the BBC knows how to take care of its own.' Basil balanced his cigarette carefully in the ashtray. 'I've just been speaking with Rupert Talbot. He tells me the News Department is suffering problems of under-staffing. Lots of their young tigers have gone off and enlisted, it seems. If I planted a word in the right ear—'

'Danny isn't the type.'

'The type? He's an experienced editor, isn't he?' Basil said. 'You might at least have the decency to let me finish.'

'Yes, sorry. It's just I know he wouldn't fit in here.'

'You mean you don't want him back in London to queer your pitch.'

'My pitch?'

'Your – ah – friendship with Robert Gaines.'

'Danny's happy where he is,' Susan said. 'He has a girlfriend in Evesham.'

'Does he, indeed? Well,' Basil said, 'one can hardly blame him for that. Nevertheless, there's a vacancy for an editor in News and, in spite of your reservations, perhaps it might be better to let your husband decide for himself.'

'Is this an offer,' Susan said, 'or is he being seconded?'

'Contrary to popular perception,' Basil said, 'the BBC is not the Gestapo. He will have a choice.'

'He won't come.'

'Wishful thinking, Mrs Cahill?'

'Call it what you like,' Susan said desperately. 'I know he won't come. He won't leave this – this person in the lurch.'

'It's a serious affair, is it?'

'Absolutely.'

'And your affair with Robert Gaines,' Basil said, 'is that absolutely serious too?'

She couldn't give him an answer because she didn't know the answer. Biting her lip, she sat motionless behind her desk.

'No matter.' Basil lifted his cigarette and inhaled. 'You're right, of course,' he said, as if he had read her mind. 'It is none of my business.'

'What,' Susan said, 'about my husband?'

'Yes,' Basil said, 'what about your husband?'

'Will you . . .' Susan began, then, startled, glanced up as Bob Gaines loped into the office waving a script and grinning all over his stupid face.

'Well, speak of the devil,' Basil said and, stubbing out his cigarette, hastily cleared space on his desk to receive the result of Bob's labours.

25

It was fortunate that the high-explosive bomb that ripped apart the terrace houses in Pitt Street did not wipe out the Wardens' Post in nearby Grover Road.

Ignoring the risks, the wardens came running out to investigate. Peering through a thick pall of dust, they swiftly assessed the extent of the damage, dispatched a messenger to the Control Centre to summon ambulances, stretcher parties and rescue equipment then headed into the wreckage to aid the injured and search for survivors.

It took two wardens and a strapping young policeman to drag Breda away from her frenzied digging but they were unable to persuade her to accompany them to a first-aid post and didn't have the heart to insist.

Supported by a WVS volunteer, she waited for news while rescue workers, a dozen or more, moved in with picks and crowbars to tunnel into the shifting mass of broken brick and splintered woodwork on the off-chance that the cry Breda claimed to have heard was not just wishful thinking.

Phantom figures clambered over the wreckage lit at first by the spouting gas flare and, after it had been capped, by shaded torches. Medical and rescue squads removed the injured and the dead while Breda, shivering, watched, until her legs finally gave way and the WVS woman lowered her into a sitting position on the ground.

Shortly thereafter, a warden arrived to question her. He squatted before her, notebook in hand.

'Are your ears okay? Can you hear me?' he asked.

'Have you found them?' Breda said.

'Not just yet, Mrs . . .'

'Hooper.'

The warden made a note of her name. 'How many were in the house with you?'

'Two. My mother an' Billy.'

'Billy's your son?'

'Yes.'

'How old is he?'

'Six.'

'Your husband, Mrs Hooper? Where is he?'

'He's a fireman.'

'Which station?'

'Oxmoor Road.'

'Now, think carefully, Mrs Hooper; where were you when the explosion occurred? What part of the house?'

They had given her water from a bottle but her mouth was dry again, her tongue as thick as old leather.

'Shelter,' she said. 'Shelter under the stairs.'

The woman said, 'Good, that's good.'

'How did you get out?' the warden asked.

'I wasn't – I wasn't with them.' Breda tried to turn her head but her neck was so stiff that she couldn't. 'I was in the outhouse. In the toilet.'

'The toilet!' The warden glanced up at the woman. 'You're a lucky girl, I'd say, a lucky, lucky girl.'

Only then did it dawn on Breda that she was in her own back yard, that walls as well as houses had been blown down which was why everything seemed so unfamiliar.

'I 'ad to pee,' she said. 'I really 'ad to.'

The warden inched closer. 'When you came out of the lavatory and saw what had happened, what did you do?'

'I heard 'im,' Breda said. 'Heard 'im cryin' through the 'ole.'

'What hole? The hole you dug?'

'The hole Ronnie dug,' Breda said. 'The hole – a pipe, a vent for air. Got it off an old car. Bashed it into shape. I heard Billy cryin' through the pipe.'

'Are the men digging in the right place?'

'I – I think so.'

She watched a man in oilskin leggings and a white-painted helmet pick his way over the debris. For an instant she thought it might be Ron, but he was too small to be Ron and when he spoke, spoke posh. The warden scrambled to his feet.

'Anything, sir?' he said. 'Any sign?'

'There is someone alive down there,' the officer said. 'No doubt about it. Is this the woman?'

'Mrs Hooper, sir. Two in the shelter. Woman and child,' the warden reported. 'The shelter's under the stairs. There's an air vent – the husband put it in – where the lady heard the noise.'

'Have you found them?' Breda said again.

'Rest assured we won't give up until we do,' the officer said. 'Now, if you're up to it, Mrs Hooper, I'd like you to come with me and point out the exact position of this air vent. Can you do that for me?'

'Yes,' Breda said, 'I can.'

★

The Princess Hospital in Glamis Road, north of the Highway, smelled of cooking, disinfectant and smoke from the smouldering warehouses that flanked the Shadwell basins. The building, which had so far escaped damage, had recently been brought into service as an emergency clinic, a way-station for children with serious injuries and a place of safety for one or two poor little beggars who had been found wandering amid the wreckage with no one to lay claim to them.

Superficial flesh wounds were dealt with by trained first-aiders, broken limbs by doctors and experienced nurses. Burns, head injuries, punctured eardrums, collapsed lungs, damaged organs and mute trauma required specialist attention and temporary wards on the first and second floors were crowded with beds filled with children who, as soon as transport could be found, would be whisked away to other hospitals.

The ground-floor receiving hall was awash with social workers, council officers and women from the voluntary agencies all endeavouring to wring names from children too young, too sick or too shocked to speak coherently and with distraught relatives ready to pounce on anyone who looked as if they might know what had become of Johnny, or Ernie or little Violet-Rose.

In the wards upstairs mothers, sisters and aunts squeezed into the narrow spaces between the beds, to the dismay of the nurses, and wept at the sight of their offspring wrapped in bandages or lying there, a tiny head on a huge pillow, unresponsive to everyone or anything.

On her release from the emergency room Breda had no difficulty in locating her son. During the short drive to

Glamis Road in the WVS woman's motorcar she had cradled him in her arms, a salvaged towel pressed to the wound on his head, and, on arrival at the Princess, had had enough sense to ensure that he had a nurse to take care of him before she'd allowed herself to be led away to have her hands dressed.

'Gloves?' Billy said as soon as he saw her. 'You got gloves on, Mummy.'

The fiery pain had yielded to the cream with which the doctor had coated her torn fingers, aided by the tablets he'd given her before he began his examination. She felt woozy, as if she might fall asleep, but nagging anxiety about Billy had kept her alert. She was overwhelmingly relieved to find him sitting up in bed, dressed in a clean nightshirt three sizes too big for him and with a turban of bandages on his head.

The child in the next bed, a girl, had a huge pad of gauze plastered over one eye and whimpered incessantly while her mother, a broad-hipped woman much older than Breda, tried to distract her with a Pontefract cake. There was no visible sign of the occupant of the bed on the other side save a lump in the blankets and a sinister-looking tube attached to a rubber bag that hung between the cots like a polyp.

Breda edged carefully past the rubber bag and balanced an elbow against the metal bed head. She didn't dare sit down in case she dozed off and didn't dare take Billy in her arms for fear that the pain in her hands would flare up again.

'Sore hands,' she said. 'What 'appened to you?'

'I got stitches.'

'How many?'

'Lots. They cut all my 'air off.'

'Never mind,' said Breda. 'It'll soon grow in again.'

He too looked sleepy, more sleepy than surly. She was sure he had been crying but there was no sign of tears now. She had no intention of quizzing him about his ordeal, wedged under his grandma in the dark for several hours until the rescue squad broke through the muck and fished them both out.

She said, 'Have you 'ad somethin' to eat?'

'Soup.'

'Was it good?'

'Yus. Rice an' prunes for afters.'

'You'd enjoy that,' Breda said.

'Yar, I did.'

'Are you thirsty?'

'Nah.'

Clinging to her broad-hipped mother, the little girl in the adjacent bed was wailing now. Billy did not look at her: Breda rather wished he would. He stared straight ahead at the commotion on the other side of the ward where two doctors in bloodstained coats were hauling a screen around the bed of a young boy whose mother, weeping, was being escorted towards the stairs.

'It's all right, darlin'. It's all right,' said Breda softly.

'Where's Daddy? I want Daddy.'

'He's at the fire station. He'll be 'ere soon as 'e can.'

'Where's Grandma?'

'Grandma's fine. She's gone 'ome.'

'I want to go 'ome,' Billy said.

Which, Breda realised, might be easier said than done.

With No. 12 Pitt Street destroyed and Stratton's declared unsafe she had no notion where she would take Billy when he was released. Everything was gone, clothes, shoes, furniture, ration books – everything. Ronnie would sort it out, she told herself: Ronnie would find a place where they could all be together and sort it all out.

She had no idea where her ma was right now.

Last she'd seen of Nora she'd been drinking tea on the step of a first-aid post, scratched and bruised but all in one piece, which, a warden had told her, was a small miracle in itself. Where her father-in-law had spent the night didn't concern her. Matt Hooper was an expert at taking caring of himself and would turn up when it suited him.

'Mrs Hooper, is it?'

The doctor was a small, moon-faced chap in his sixties. He wore a soiled three-piece suit and looked, Breda thought, as if he hadn't slept in a week.

'Yes,' Breda said 'Can I take 'im home?'

'Not just yet,' the doctor said. 'How are you – Billy?'

'Fine,' Billy answered, scowling.

The doctor slipped into the slot by the bed and, dipping a hand into his coat pocket, produced a little pencil torch. He placed a hand lightly on Billy's chest and shone the beam of the torch into Billy's eyes.

'Do you like sweets, Billy?' the doctor said.

'Yus.'

'Have one on me, then,' the doctor said and, fishing in his pocket again, brought out a large paper bag. 'Just one now. No, make that two.'

Billy plucked two wine gums, one red and one black, from

the bag. He put them both into his mouth. Breda was on the point of reminding him that manners make the man, or words to that effect, when Billy, a gum in each cheek, said, very clearly, 'Fank you.'

'Polish those off,' the doctor said. 'Then, if I were you, young man, I'd catch forty winks before supper time.'

Billy dipped the turban obediently. 'Forty winks.'

The doctor slid out from the bedside and, motioning Breda to join him, stood facing her at the bed end. He spoke in a quiet, unhurried voice, as if he had all the time in the world to devote to her concerns.

'He has a deep scalp wound, as you probably know, Mrs Hooper. Sixteen stitches. But the skull is intact; no fractures. He's sedated right now but he's going to have a whale of a headache for a day or two. We can give you something to ease the pain. However . . .'

'However – what?'

'He may have a touch of concussion.'

'What's that?'

'A little bit of brain swelling. We've some patients waiting to transfer to our place in Sussex for recuperation. I can arrange for Billy to go with them, if you like.'

'No,' Breda said. 'He stays with me.'

'Do you have a place to stay?' the doctor asked.

'Yeah,' Breda said without hesitation. 'We can stay with my mother. Is Billy going to recover?'

'Of course, he is,' the doctor said. 'We'll keep him here overnight and, assuming his condition doesn't deteriorate, you can collect him tomorrow morning.'

'What if there's another air raid?'

'We have a basement shelter here.'

Still sucking on the wine gums, Billy closed his eyes and appeared to be drifting off to sleep.

'All right,' Breda said. 'I'll leave 'im with you but you gotta promise me you won't take 'im to Sussex.'

The doctor smiled. 'No, Mrs Hooper. I promise.'

'An' if there's another air raid . . .'

'Yes, yes,' said the doctor, suddenly losing patience, 'if there's an air raid we'll see he's safe. Now, if you've no other questions, may I suggest you say goodbye to your son and make way for the nurses get on with their jobs.'

She barely had time to thank him before he stepped across the aisle to the next bed and, stooping, peeped in under the blankets at the invisible patient.

Breda kissed Billy on the cheek and wiped a dribble of sticky saliva from his mouth with her bandaged hand.

He opened his eyes and scowled, drowsily.

'See you tomorrow,' Breda said. 'Be a good boy now.'

'Yus,' Billy murmured, and closed his eyes again.

He had survived a German bomb and several hours buried underground and she would have him back with her tomorrow. She should have felt better than she did. Before she'd reached the head of the stairs, though, a million other things she had to do crowded in on her: find Nora, find Matt, find Ronnie and, first and foremost, rummage through the wreckage of No. 12 to see if she could find the cashbox.

She picked her way down the staircase, bandaged hands tucked into her armpits.

Light spilled across the floor of the reception hall like a great pool of milk. The front doors opened and closed. The shapes of the folk who milled about in the hall were like shadows against the light.

'Breda,' said a small voice in her ear. 'Breda, dear.'

There, standing to one side of the door, was her mother, or some remnant of her mother, stooped and shrivelled, her face drawn into a thousand folds and creases, her eyes sunk back into her head.

Behind Nora, looming, was a man in uniform, a warden, Breda thought, or a copper who, stepping forward and taking off his helmet said, 'Mrs Hooper? Mrs Ronald Hooper?'

'Yeah,' said Breda warily.

'I'm afraid I have some very bad news.'

26

In less harried times the London Fire Service would have done a better job of honouring the three auxiliaries who were killed in the line of duty on the night of 9 September. There would have been a parade in dress uniform, a laying out of flag-draped coffins in one of the local churches and a watch, however brief, kept by four colleagues while friends, relatives and off-duty firemen filed past to pay their last respects.

Helmets, webbing and axes would have graced the tops of the coffins and wreaths the base and someone as high up as a Divisional Commander would have delivered a eulogy praising the firemen's courage and dedication before the coffins were taken off in government-subsidised vehicles for committal.

Five sporadic daylight raids followed by another savage 'all-nighter' had wreaked too much havoc to permit the luxury of official mourning but it was lack of foresight, rather than indifference, that really put the kibosh on any sort of ceremony. No one in the Home Office or the Ministry of Defence, let alone the London Fire Service, quite knew what to do when there was nothing left to fill a coffin but a few shards of bone and scraps of flesh, not enough to gather up and carry to the mortuary for a coroner's assistant to piece together like a jigsaw puzzle.

If there had been no eye-witnesses cynical anti-war protesters might have put it about that the three auxiliaries weren't dead at all but had simply done a bunk and would pop up again, all smiles, when the war was over. Breda wasn't daft enough to subscribe to that calumny and if anyone had dared suggest it within earshot of Matt, never mind Danny, they'd have wound up on the floor with two black eyes and a bloody nose.

It was left to Clary Knotts to seek Breda out, several days later, and answer her question: 'Did 'e suffer?'

'Over in a flash, Mrs Hooper,' Clary told her. 'They never knew what 'it them. We thought it was a landmine at first. Twelve, fifteen feet long, a black tube with a fin on the end. Torpedo, they tell me, naval torpedo, first one we'd seen. If it hadn't fallen right outside the school where folk were sheltered we'd 'ave left it for the bomb squad. Ronnie wouldn't wear it, though. He sent me inside to keep folk away from the doors and windows while Jim, Eric and 'im dragged the thing away. Got it clear out the gate before it went up. Big, big explosion. Knocked over a fire tender an' two motorcars an' left a crater a mile deep. Broke all the glass in the school, every single pane, but nobody inside was killed. Ron was a hero. You should be proud of 'im, Mrs Hooper. Real proud of 'im.'

'Oh, but I am,' said Breda. 'Believe me, I am.'

Susan's first thought when she received the call from Breda was not that she would never see her brother again but that she didn't have a black dress to wear to the funeral.

Making the call from a public phone box, and presumably short of change, Breda had been curt to the point of rudeness. She hadn't said a word about how Ron had died or when he would be buried and seemed more concerned with extracting a promise that she would let Danny know as soon as possible.

Susan replaced the receiver of the telephone on Basil's desk and, with a little *tut* of annoyance, said, 'I'm afraid I'm going to have to ask for time off.'

'What?' Basil said. 'Now?'

'Yes,' said Susan. 'My brother's been killed, apparently.'

'Apparently?' Basil said. 'Has he or hasn't he?'

'No,' Susan said, 'I don't think there's any doubt.'

'Good God!' said Basil, rising. 'You poor girl.'

He came around the desk and took her, unresisting, into his arms. 'Bomb, was it?'

'What?' said Susan. 'I've no idea. I think I've something at home that might do at a pinch.'

Basil pulled away. 'Susan, take hold of yourself.'

'What?' Susan said again. 'You don't know what it's like with us, do you? It's important to keep up appearances. I really should have my hair done too. I don't want to turn up looking like a scarecrow.'

He moved her as if she were a puppet, jerking her towards the chair behind his desk and easing her into it. He leaned into the desk and spoke softly.

'Who called you?'

'Breda, Ron's wife. Why she called *me* I really can't imagine. What does she expect *me* to do? I can't bring Ronnie back. Call Danny, call Danny, that's all she could say. Does she think I'm operating a switchboard here? Still,

I suppose I'd better show my face or I'll never hear the end of it.' She looked up at Basil, frowning. '*Can* you spare me for a couple of hours?'

'I suspect it might take longer than a couple of hours, Susan. In any case, I can't let you go in this state.' Basil paused. 'Will I send for Vivian to accompany you?'

'Vivian has better things to do with her time, I'm sure.'

'Bob, then? I'll call the Lansdowne, shall I?'

'You're right, of course.' Susan said. 'A couple of hours isn't going to do it. There'll be things to do, arrangements to make. They'll be running around like headless chickens without Ronnie. Ronnie always took care of things.' She looked up. 'Bob? No, no, not Bob. That wouldn't be fair to anyone.'

'Tell you what,' Basil said gently, 'why don't I try to contact your husband? I'm sure our operator will have a number where, with a bit of prodding, I can reach him.'

'Danny? Yes,' said Susan, sitting up a little, 'why don't you phone Danny? He'll know what to do for the best.'

She arrived in Pitt Street by taxi-cab during a lull in the late afternoon sorties. All down the road people were queuing for shelters, arms full of food, rugs, babies and blankets. The mouths of the Tube stations were mobbed not with passengers coming home from work but with families seeking a safe place in which to spend the night.

There were no signs of fresh damage east of Aldgate but the cabby, a garrulous type made more talkative by nerves, informed her that a single raider had zoomed over London and dropped a few incendiaries before vanishing off to the west but that the guns had been flashing all afternoon south of the river and another big night attack was on the cards sure as eggs.

'Got somewhere safe to go, miss?' he asked.

'Oh, yes,' said Susan brightly, and tipped him well.

The fact was that she didn't have anywhere to go, safe or otherwise. It didn't take her long to discover that No. 12 Pitt Street was no more than a pile of rubble and Stratton's Dining Rooms a shell. In an hour or so dusk would settle over London, blackout restrictions would come into force and the only people left in the streets would be fire-spotters, wardens, Civil Defence volunteers and policemen.

Loitering by the ruined front of Stratton's, she wondered not only where she might find her family but just how many of her family were left alive. Not knowing what else to do, she set off in the direction of Oxmoor Road driven by a notion that even if Ronnie wasn't there at least his body might be.

A number of men, mostly dockers, had gathered outside the Crown which, at one time, had been Ronnie's favourite pub. It was after five o'clock and habit as much as thirst had drawn them there, though the Crown's snug interior was snug no more. Evan Hobbs, the publican, was passing out bottled beer from a trestle table in the doorway while his lad washed glasses in a tub on the pavement.

Susan had been gone from Shadwell for so long that she barely recognised her old schoolmates and the brothers of girls that Ronnie had courted. She was on the point of enquiring if any of them knew what had happened to Ronnie when someone called out, 'By gum, it's Susie 'Ooper. You're in trouble now, Matt,' and her father, clutching a stick in one hand and a beer glass in the other, hobbled out of the throng.

His trousers, jacket and shirt were filthy and he wore only one shoe. The binding on the other foot, the left, was, by contrast, brilliantly clean; a stubby, white boot that he swung inexpertly before him while trying to balance his weight on the stick and, at the same time, preserve the beer in his glass.

'Susie,' he said, 'what you doing 'ere?'

He doesn't know, she thought: Oh, God, he doesn't know and now I have to tell him. Then she noticed the men sidling away and heard Evan Hobbs call out, 'Stow it, Jackie,' and someone else called out, 'Sorry, kid. Real sorry.' She took her father's arm to steady him and at last began to cry.

It was typical of her father to finish his beer and place the glass neatly on the trestle before he gave himself up and, leaning into her, wept too. At length, she fished in her handbag, found a hanky and gave it to him. He wiped his mouth with it and then, loudly, blew his nose.

'Best get 'im home, love,' Evan Hobbs advised.

'Yes, thank you, I will,' she said and to save further embarrassment all round, led her father some way down the street before she put the question. 'Where are we going, Dad?'

'St Vee's,' he told her. 'She said she'd be at St Vee's.'

'Who? Breda?'

'Nora. Breda's with 'er, I expect.'

'What about Billy?'

'Hospital.'

'Hospital?'

'He's all right. Stitches in 'is head. Gets out tomorrow.'

'What about you?'

'Tripped on the dock. Broke my foot.'

'I'm surprised you managed to get this far,' Susan said.

'Somebody 'ad to do it.'

'Had to do what?'

'Fetch Ron's body.'

'Oh, Daddy,' Susan said, 'you should have waited for me.'

'Don't matter. There is no body. Blown to bits, our Ron. We'll need to register it, o' course, soon as the Fire Service cough up a certificate. Might be some money comin' Breda's way. You never know with them things. Nora'll say prayers for 'is soul an' light candles but that ain't the same as a decent burial, is it?' her father said and began, once more, to cry.

He had always worked best at night, pumping out his copy for the *Union Post* into the wee small hours. But Susan, the BBC and now, it seemed, the blasted Luftwaffe had so messed up his routine that he found himself cheating on the thing he did best, which was, basically, writing good, tight, punchy prose.

He hadn't realised just how sloppy his style had become until he sat down to do justice to the account of his wild ride from Dover for the *Post* and his foray into the blitzed areas of the East End for *Speaking Up*. He was, thank God, still enough of a craftsman to make the switch from print to broadcast script without too much sweat but had, none the less, been relieved when Basil had given him not one but two thumbs up and cleared fifteen minutes of the Tuesday schedule for his version, with quotes, of London under the cosh.

To celebrate he had slept all afternoon and, with Susan stuck in Portland Place, had allowed Pete Slocum to lure him out to dine at the Mayfair.

There, raid or no raid, some of the old Paris gang had gathered, dinner continued to be served and Jack Jackson's band played 'These Foolish Things' so slow and sentimental that it should have been banned by the Lord Chamberlain.

Tina, the girl he was dancing with – one of Slocum's young honeys – had whispered things in his ear that no decent young woman should know let alone suggest to an able-bodied stranger. Suddenly it was fun again and as they dashed back to the Lansdowne through London's dark streets the tedium of waiting for war to come lifted and they were no longer bored spectators but excited participants, ducking bombs and shrapnel right here in old London town.

Tina, the blonde honey, young, slim-hipped and as sinuous as a snake, would have gone to bed with him at the drop of a hat.

God knows, he was so high he was almost tempted to take her up on it. But he owed Susan something, he supposed, and went off to his room with nothing hotter than a jug of black coffee and, locking the door, pulled up the typewriter, lit a cigarette, and went to work on a tailpiece for Tuesday's programme.

'So she lost a brother,' Pete Slocum said. 'In a shooting war everyone loses someone sooner or later. You never met the guy, did you?'

'Never did,' Bob said. 'Kind of wish I had now.'

'Surely you aren't thinking of gatecrashing the funeral?' Slocum said. 'Though you could probably cobble up a moist thousand words out of it, given that the guy was a fireman.'

'Susan doesn't want me there. She made that clear.'

'Of course she don't want you there,' Slocum said. 'It'll be a big family do with buckets of tears and fond memories.

You're not part of it. If anyone climbs into bed with your sweetheart tonight, it'll be her husband. Anyhow, you don't care for her enough to give it up, do you?'

'Give what up?'

'Your career.'

'What's Susan got to do with my career?' Bob said.

'London will be burned out soon and there'll be nothing left to write about and we'll all move on.'

'Do you really think we'll be pulled out?'

'Sure of it. It's the way of all wars, the beauty of all wars,' Slocum said. 'Your Miss Hooper isn't like you and me. She's no vagrant, no pilgrim on life's highway taking it all as it comes. She's enjoyed a wartime fling but reality has bitten her on the butt and she's no longer interested in some he-man who makes her feel like Gloria Swanson every time he rips her panties off.'

'Baloney!' Bob said. 'You don't know what you're—'

'Right now,' Slocum went on relentlessly, 'she needs – let's call it, in quote marks, sympathy and understanding. You might deliver good sex, Gaines, but with her brother lying dead on a slab in the morgue the woman isn't interested in counting orgasms. She'll probably convince herself she's to blame for whatever happened and when she gets tired of blaming herself she'll get around to blaming you. Believe me, man, the last thing you want in your bed is a guilt-ridden dame.'

'Hasn't it occurred to you yet that I might love her?'

'Do you?'

Bob did not answer.

'What's up? Cat got your tongue?' Pete Slocum said. 'Or have you just figured your sweetheart has got you by the short hairs. She's free to choose between you and the husband My guess is it won't be you. You've done your bit, served your purpose, but now she's scared and hurting and wants it back the way it was before. And that means bye-bye Bob.'

'I owe her—'

'You owe her nothing,' Pete Slocum said. 'She's the one who led you on. She didn't even tell you she had a husband until she had you hooked. She was a lay, Bob, an easy lay, that's all.'

'Hell, Pete, she's just lost her brother.'

'And you feel sorry for her?'

'Of course, I do.' Bob hesitated. 'But . . .'

'But what?' Pete Slocum said.

'I'm beginning to think you're right.'

27

Father Joseph O'Mara, known to all and sundry as Father Joe, not only came from Limerick but before he'd joined the priesthood had been ten years a Boy Scout. He was thus able to engage Nora in conversation about the beauty of the Shannon estuary, which he regarded as just next door to heaven, while at the same time building a fire out of scrap wood and rigging up a grid on which to balance not one but three frying-pans, two kettles and a little saucepan to warm milk for babies.

With the sleeves of his surplice rolled up and fastened by what looked suspiciously like a pair of lady's garters, Father Joe cheerfully cooked sausages, bacon and, speciality of the house, savoury potato cakes that melted in your hand before they even reached your mouth. Meanwhile his team of youthful helpers, who didn't have to try too hard to look pitiful, scuttled round the markets and purchased such comestibles as they couldn't scrounge for free.

While the feeding of the not quite five thousand was taking place on the steps of St Veronica's, the Borough Council ferried in a load of timber and a couple of carpenters to line the ancient walls with bunks to provide rest as well as shelter for upward of seventy souls; all of which activity made it plain that the crypt of St Veronica's was destined to become a home for the homeless, Breda, Billy, Nora and Matt among them, for some time to come.

Father Joe was not alone in dispensing succour to a flock that included Jews as well as Catholics and a few diehard Protestant agnostics like Matt Hooper. Four nuns had popped up out of nowhere accompanied by a venerable priest, Father Grogan, who, name notwithstanding, was frightfully English and frightfully posh. It was he who heard confessions, he who, at Nora Romano's request, held a special Mass for the soul of her son-in-law and who, kneeling on the flagstones by her side, offered Breda comfort when a great storm of grief overwhelmed her.

Utterly exhausted, Breda had slept through Monday night's air raid curled up on a mattress in a corner of the crypt with Nora on one side, Matt on the other and her sister-in-law, Susan, stretched out beside her.

Now, seated on the steps of St Vee's in hazy morning sunlight, a mug of tea clamped in her bandaged hands, she was waiting impatiently for Danny to show up and her life as a widow to begin.

Fifteen hours it had taken him to travel from Evesham to London; fifteen hours of what, under other circumstances, he would have regarded as hell.

Three trains, two short bus rides, several interminable hours in a temporary shelter under a railway bridge not more than ten miles from Paddington while drivers, guards, repair workers and one harassed station master waited for instructions from some mysterious source up-line and what seemed like half a battalion of Scots Guards, on the move from somewhere to somewhere else, had foamed and snorted and threatened mutiny if something wasn't done to sort things out.

Huddled up in a raincoat that Griff had loaned him, Danny had kept himself to himself. He had four pounds and fifteen shillings in his pocket; four pounds and fifteen shillings that Mr Harrison had grudgingly doled out when it became obvious that, short of clapping him in irons, Mr Cahill would not be deterred from abandoning his post and taking three days' leave to travel up to London to comfort his wife.

London had been badly hit in Monday night's raid. Even the soldiers had been subdued when the train had limped alongside the one and only platform in Paddington station that hadn't been damaged.

Danny had tried not to look at the twisted girders and buried carriages piled up beside the train, at fires still burning by the main entrance and the bodies of travellers, whose journeys had come to an abrupt end, laid out on a stretch of platform by the postal clearing offices like so many damaged parcels.

He ran for the one exit that showed daylight, and, darting among the ambulances and fire tenders that cluttered the side street, headed for the Edgware Road in the hope of finding a bus to carry him east into Shadwell.

'You took your bleedin' time,' Breda said. 'You'd think there was a war on or somethin'.' She rested her head on his chest and let the tears flow, while Danny, looking over her shoulder, scanned the steps for Susan.

'She's down below,' Breda said, at length, 'helpin' sort out blankets. Billy's in the Princess an' somebody's got to collect 'im an' bring 'im back 'ere. That's you, Danny. That's your job.'

'Whoa!' Danny said. 'That's not something I should be doin', Breda. The wee guy'll expect you to be there.'

'I got other things to do.'

'Funeral arrangements, you mean?'

She thumped his chest with the back of a bandaged fist and told him why there would be no funeral for Ronnie Hooper, why they were all here in Pound Lane and why he was the one she'd chosen to break the bad news to her son. ''Cause I can't do it without cryin' an' I don't want Billy to see me cry.'

'What about Nora?'

'Nora's not up to it an' the old man's got a busted foot. He can't walk ten yards without sittin' down.'

'What happened to your hands?'

'Never mind my bleedin' 'ands. I'm askin' you to do this for me, Danny. If you won't do it for me,' she paused and, with a stifled sob, added, 'do it for Ronnie.'

'That's blackmail, Breda,' Danny said.

'It certainly is,' said Breda.

Susan hated the airless crypt, the smell of unwashed bodies, the chatter of unruly children, snivelling women and screaming infants and, most of all, the priests and nuns whose optimism was so patently forced.

Fatigue had much to do with her foul mood. She had slept badly, waking with every muffled thud, every rattle, every exaggerated cry with which the women around her dramatised their fear and drew attention to themselves.

She was better dressed than most of them and better spoken too but, leery of seeming haughty, smiled and nodded and, when required, pitched in by conducting some wretched child to the lavatory, or collecting greasy plates and carrying them into the vestibule where a nun and a young boy were washing them in a tin bath, all the while seething with impatience to be back in Portland Place or Rothwell Gardens or in bed with Robert in his room in the Lansdowne.

She climbed the steep stone staircase that led up from the crypt, the damp-wool smell of blankets clinging to her clothes.

The sky was free of aircraft, though a barrage balloon, soggy in the soft morning light, drifted like a cloud over the rooftops. She stared up at the balloon for a moment, then, stepping into Pound Lane, found herself face to face with her husband.

He was seated on the steps with her father, Nora and Breda calmly sipping tea and eating a potato cake. He didn't rise to greet her and she resented his lack of response. After all, she was his wife and had just lost her brother and he had no right to ignore the conventions of mourning.

She stood before him, looking down.

'I take it,' she said, 'you know what happened to Ron?'

'Aye, Breda told me.'

'It seems we're to be denied a proper funeral.'

'That's how it looks.'

'Obviously you got my message. I wasn't sure you'd be able to leave Wood Norton but I thought you ought to be informed. I mean, I thought you'd want to know.'

''Course 'e wanted to know,' Breda said. 'He's come up to 'elp us through it. Ha'n't you, Danny?'

Susan ignored her. 'Are you staying at the flat?'

'I haven't thought about it. I've only just got here.'

'If you do go to the flat,' Susan said, 'will you pick up some things for me and leave them at the House?'

'What 'ouse?' her father said. 'You got a 'ouse now?'

'She means the BBC, Matt,' Danny said, then, to Susan, 'Even if we don't have any more raids, I doubt if I'll be able to make it to Rothwell Gardens. I've too many things to do here.'

'What things?' said Susan.

Danny got up slowly, wearily. Only then did she realise that what she had taken to be hostility was probably nothing more than exhaustion. She felt a wave of pity rise up in her, though whether it was pity for Danny or for herself she could not at that moment be sure.

He took her arm and walked her away from the steps.

'For God's sake, Susan, go easy,' he said. 'Aye, you've lost a brother but Breda's lost everythin'. No house, no husband, her boy lyin' sick in the Princess; a kid without a father. Nora's in a state of shock an' your father's useless. Who else do you think Breda's goin' tae turn to? I'm about all she's got, poor bitch.'

'What about—' Susan began.

'You?' Danny said. 'Losing Ronnie hurts – I'm damned sure it does – but you've got as much as anybody to hang on to an' a damned sight more than most.'

'And you, what about you?'

'I've still got a job an' a place to—'

'No. I mean, do I still have you?'

She saw his eyes widen and he did not answer at once. 'No, Susan,' he said at length, 'you don't have me.'

'Didn't you get my letter?'

'What letter?'

'I sent you a letter.'

'Sayin' what?'

'Just that I loved you and always will.'

'I don't have time for this right now,' Danny said. 'Breda needs me to fetch Billy from the hospital.'

'Why doesn't she do it herself?'

'Because she's scared he'll ask her where Ron is. Besides, she'll have to get down to Pitt Street to see if she can find anything worth salvaging. Clothes, shoes, any food that hasn't been eaten by the rats. Wee bits of stuff she might want to keep.'

'Mementoes, you mean?'

'Aye, that's what I mean,' Danny said. 'Look, there's no point in you hangin' round here, Susan. They'll have shelter in the church for as long as they need it. I'll see them settled before I go back to Evesham. Go on, you've an important job to do.'

'Actually,' she said, 'I have.'

'If you've any spare cash in your purse,' Danny said, 'you might want to slip your old man a few bob. With that foot he won't be workin' again for a while an' God knows when they'll dole out compensation.'

'You think of everything, Danny, don't you?'

'Go on,' he said. 'Do it, an' scarper.'

It wasn't habit or an echo of the affection she had once felt for him but rather a gesture of gratitude for being the sort of man he was. She tweaked the belt of his raincoat, brought him to her and kissed him on the lips.

'If you do happen to drop by the flat . . .' she began.

'No chance, Susan,' he said. 'Not a hope in hell. Now make your excuses, say your goodbyes an' get out of here,' which, rather promptly, she did.

★

277

It was one of those weird things but her back hurt worse than her hands. Every time she stepped over rubble or picked her way through broken glass she felt as if her spine would snap. She'd read somewhere – probably in the *Daily Mail* – that pain in the body could be a defence against painful thoughts but she reckoned her backache had more to do with sleeping on a stone floor than her brain playing tricks on her.

As soon as Danny had appeared in Pound Lane she'd begun to feel a bit like her old self again. After all, she'd known Danny longer than she'd known Ron and Danny had never let her down. Ron had never let her down either, come to think of it, though she'd been mad at him for trotting off to Spain and hadn't been too kindly disposed towards him for knocking her up, though, to be fair, he had agreed to marry her without anyone putting a gun to his head.

Pitt Street didn't look like Pitt Street any more. There were new views, new vistas and when she clambered, wincing, on to the mountain of rubble, all that was left of her home, the first thing she noticed was that you could see the tops of the trees in the park that you'd never been able to see before.

She watched a troop of small boys leaping about like goats on the remains of a house on the far side of the street, an old woman hauling a battered pram laden with bits and pieces of furniture down a cleared stretch of pavement and two men, one young and one not, digging with spades in a tiny patch of garden and, even as she watched, triumphantly uprooting a couple of onions and the ragged remnant of a leek.

She looked down at broken bricks and cracked timbers, shredded wallpaper and chunks of plaster. Beneath it, buried deep, were her stove, her sink, her chairs and carpets, her precious tins of fruit and crushed, no doubt, into matchwood the dresser in which she'd kept her rent book, ration books, identity cards and a few trinkets that Ron had given her over the years.

The corner of a quilt stuck out of the rubbish like a rabbit's ear but she wasn't tempted to unearth it. She had an irrational fear of disturbing the heap, as if Billy and her mother were still down there cowering under the big creaking beam and sucking air from the pipe that Ron had installed.

She shaded her eyes and looked out over the debris that spilled across the back yard to the stump of the wall that bordered the lane.

Brown sludge, disgorged from the sewer, marked the patch on which the outhouse had stood. It was coated with black flies that rose in a cloud as Breda approached. She had a queasy feeling that the cashbox might have been blown to pieces, then, to her relief, she spotted it up-ended on a ramp of crushed bricks.

Gritting her teeth, she hunkered down and drew the box towards her. She knew as soon as she turned it over that she had arrived too late.

'Bastards!' she screamed. 'Bleedin' thieving bastards!' and hurled the empty cashbox into the lane.

The boy was dressed in short trousers, short stockings and what looked like a borrowed pullover. He slumped on a bench in a cloakroom just off the main hall where he and three other youngsters had been put to await collection like, Danny thought, the corpses on Paddington railway station, except that this lot were mercifully live.

'Billy?' he said quietly.

Billy lifted his chin from his chest as if his bandaged head weighed a ton. Clutching a bedraggled doll, a little girl on the bench by his side sat bolt upright and enquired, 'Are you my Uncle Johnny?'

'Sorry,' Danny said. 'I'm not. He'll be here soon, I'm sure.'

'I wish he'd come. Oh, I do wish he'd come,' the little girl said anxiously and went back to cuddling her doll.

Danny gave Billy his hand and helped him slide down from the bench just as a nurse in a dark blue uniform called out, 'Hooper, William Hooper.' Billy squinted up at Danny as if he wasn't quite sure if that was still his name.

Danny said, 'Aye, we're here. Is he ready to go?'

'Are you his father?'

'No, his uncle,' Danny said, to keep things simple.

The nurse peered down at Billy.

'William, do you know this man?'

'Yus.'

'*Is* he your uncle?'

'Yus.'

'Tell me his name?'

'Danny.'

Still holding Billy by the hand, Danny dug out his wallet and showed the nurse both his identity card and his BBC pass.

'Cahill?' she said.

'I'm his mother's brother.'

Billy did not contradict him.

'Very well,' the nurse said. She produced a small bottle of tablets from her pocket and dropped it into Danny's hand. 'Two per day, no more. He'll need to have his stitches removed in a week or ten days. When the wound begins to draw it may well be painful. Bring him here, or to your own doctor if you prefer it, or' – she paused – 'if necessary to a First Aid post with a qualified nurse in attendance. Do you understand?'

'I do,' said Danny. 'Thank you.'

They went through the hall and out of the big door and through a tunnel of sandbags on to the steps and down the steps into the sunlight.

Billy held on to his hand and said nothing until they passed out of the shadow of the hospital building.

Then he asked, 'Where's Mummy?'

'She's got a lot to do,' Danny said. 'She sent me instead.'

'Is she gettin' supper ready?'

'No,' Danny said. 'The bomb – I'm sure you haven't forgotten the bomb.'

'It blew the house up.'

'It did, so we're all stayin' in St Veronica's Church till we can find somewhere else to live.'

Danny held his breath. He knew what was coming next. 'Where's Daddy?'

'Dad's had to go away for a while.'

'Overseas?' Billy said, though Danny doubted if he knew what the word meant. 'To fight the Germans?'

'That's it, Billy, to fight the Germans.'

'With a rifle?'

'With a rifle,' Danny confirmed. 'Hey, you look a wee bit wobbly on those pins. Would a piggyback be out of order?'

He put his hands on his knees, let the boy climb on to his back and secured Billy's arms about his neck.

'Okay up there?'

'Okay,' Billy said and, resting his bandaged head against Danny's ear, appeared happy enough to ride on Danny's shoulders for the long walk back to Pound Lane.

She salved her conscience by giving her father two pounds which left her with just three shillings in her purse. She had an emergency fiver hidden in a box on top of the wardrobe in the bedroom of the flat and an urgent need to wash away all trace of Shadwell and change her clothes before she hurried back to Portland Place to help Basil put the finishing touches to the evening's broadcast.

There had been no daylight raids so far.

Even so, Susan scanned the sky anxiously as she made her way, more in hope than expectation, to the Tube. To her surprise, the trains were running fairly normally and carried her as far as Sloane Square, not too far from Rothwell Gardens.

Slender columns of smoke rising above the rooftops confirmed rumours of damage to the West End but Susan had too much on her mind to pay heed to them. Still absorbed in her thoughts, she rounded the corner at the bottom end of the Gardens and, as if autumn had arrived overnight, suddenly found herself walking through a shoal of fallen leaves.

Looking up, she saw that many of the garden's old oaks had been scalped. Huge branches flattened the palings and a massive crater spewed chunks of pavement and sods of earth across the grass. Two vans and a lorry were parked at the end of the road and a bollard, guarded by a police constable, barred entry.

'No access, miss,' the policeman told her. 'Best go round the other way.'

'I live here,' Susan said.

'Where?'

'There. In the flats.'

'Not now you don't,' the policeman said.

He pointed up at the block of flats, the gable of which had been ripped open from top to bottom.

'Relatives, miss? Any family or friends in there?'

'No. None. How many – I mean . . .'

'Nine,' the policeman said. 'They've been took off.'

'Taken off where?'

'The mortuary.'

'Oh, you mean they're dead.'

'Yes,' said the policeman patiently. 'The injured have gone to hospital. Happened about ten last night. Lucky you wasn't in residence.'

'Are you telling me I can't get in?' Susan said.

'In?'

'To my flat. I've a few oddments I'd like to pick up.'

The policeman blew out his cheeks and shook his head. 'Even the rescue and repair chaps won't risk going in there right now. It took the firemen all their time to get the injured out.' He paused. 'Are you feeling all right, miss?'

'I'm perfectly fine, thank you,' Susan said. 'I just want my things. I work for the BBC.'

'I don't care if you work for Mr Churchill. The salvage boys will decide what's to be done then you might 'ave a chance of collecting what's yours. Right now it's more than my job's worth to let you near the place.'

'Yes,' Susan said. 'Yes, I understand.'

The galling thing was that she could see into the living room and beyond it the bedroom, could even make out the bed sloping away into shadow, as if the tangled wreckage of the home she'd shared with Danny was a mirror of her marriage.

'Come back a bit later,' the policeman told her. 'We might know what's going on by then.'

'Yes, later. I'll come back later,' Susan said and, turning on her heel, walked away swiftly.

28

The Prime Minister had broadcast to the nation at six o'clock. His grim warning that an invasion might be imminent within the week had overshadowed Bob Gaines's lengthy contribution to *Speaking Up*, and Bob was not pleased about it.

'Did you expect the phones to ring off the hook and crowds to gather outside chanting "author, author"?' Basil said. 'Come along, Robert, you know better than that. I have no doubt whatsoever that your excellent piece – excellent it was too – will be noted in quarters and we'll have quite a postbag to cope with in a day or two.'

'Stop buttering me up, Baz,' Bob said. 'I don't need you to tell me how good I am.'

'Given that we finished in the middle of an air raid,' Basil went on, 'I think we were fortunate to get the blessed programme out at all. By the by, chaps, thank you for standing by your posts. Many a midshipman would have fled the quarterdeck.'

'Oh, for God's sake!' Bob said. 'If you're going to start quoting Kipling . . .'

'Nelson, I believe,' Basil said. 'Loosely paraphrased.'

'. . . I'm getting out of here.'

'You can't,' Susan said.

'What's stopping me?' Bob said.

'Nothing really,' Basil said, 'if, that is, you discount three or four hundred German bombers flying overhead.'

'I've been in worse raids than this, believe me,' Bob said.

'Quite!' Basil said curtly. 'May I have my bottle back, please. I can't stop you risking your neck by making a run for it but I'd rather you didn't do it sozzled.'

'Call this sozzled?' Bob said. 'Heck, you don't know what sozzled is. Do you think Churchill's serious? Does he really believe Hitler will order an invasion within the week?'

'He's merely preparing us for the worst,' Basil said. 'I doubt if barges being lined up on the French coast signifies any new development. Hitler's not entirely a fool. He won't embark on a full-scale invasion until he's exhausted every possible means of bringing us to our knees. Indeed, I wouldn't be surprised if he asks the Turks or some other intermediary to approach us with yet another peace offer.'

'Churchill won't wear it,' Bob said.

'Of course he won't. Winston knows only too well what a treacherous little bugger Herr Hitler is. But,' Basil went on, 'another couple of months of indiscriminate bombard-ment and intensive German propaganda might bring the public round to thinking that peace is worth any price. Speaking of indiscriminate bombardment, I believe the time has come for us to wend our way downstairs to the base-ment. I'm beginning to feel a shade vulnerable up here.'

Larry and the rest of the programme staff had quit the third floor as soon as the broadcast was over. By that time only the boys in the news departments remained at their desks. Studios, corridors and staircases in the upper levels were almost deserted and the dormitories below the tower were filling up with folk resigned to spending another night in the House.

Basil gathered his notes and packed them into a briefcase.

Balanced on a chair with his feet on the edge of Basil's desk, Bob sipped whisky from the bottle. He had been at Basil's elbow pretty well all day, Susan gathered, editing his script with neurotic thoroughness, as if he were no longer sure of his ability to deliver under pressure.

He had greeted her appearance with a hug and a few casual questions but had kept her, she thought, at a distance.

She'd said nothing about the bombed-out flat or the loss of her possessions. She had enough savings to buy under-wear and make-up and, when the weekend came, would decide whether to move into the Lansdowne with Bob or, if that arrangement didn't suit, impose herself on Basil and Vivian until she could find an affordable place of her own. Meantime, she would eat, sleep and work here in Broadcasting House and try to put thoughts of Ronnie out of mind.

The explosion was so violent that every stick of furniture in Basil's office leaped inches off the floor.

The telephone lost its receiver which lay vibrating on the desk. Susan's typewriter was too heavy to shift but the carriage-turn bell *tinged* twice and several keys on the keyboard bobbed down as if invisible fingers were trying to tap out a message. Bob's chair tipped backwards and clattered to the floor. Only an acrobatic reaction prevented Bob from going with it, an involuntary half-somersault that shot him upright, the whisky bottle still pressed to his chest.

'Bloody hell!' said Basil. 'It *is* time to go.'

'What the hell was that?' Bob said, then answered his own

question. 'Five-hundred-pounder by the sound of it, too damned close for comfort. Wonder what took the hit? The Round Church or the Langham Hotel maybe?'

'We don't have anyone staying in the Langham, do we, Susan?' Basil asked. 'I mean, we don't have any guest speakers lodged there? Susan? Are you all right, Susan?'

Basil's voice was filtered through thick flannel. She could still make out the *pop-pop-pop* of ack-ack guns in the distance, though, and a soft, slow rumble, like distant thunder and yelling in the corridors close at hand.

'Susan? Susan? Are you all right?'

She felt remarkably calm, a brittle sort of calm. Only when Bob touched her did she realise that she was trembling: hands, arms, legs all trembling.

Bob held the bottle to her lips. 'Here, take a sip of this.'

She felt her teeth click against the glass. Her mouth was full of whisky. She was choking. She couldn't breathe. Bob slapped her, one cheek then the other, quite hard. She felt her head snap back and whisky trickle out of her mouth and air rush back into her lungs.

Shaking uncontrollably, she said, 'I want my brother. I want our Ronnie,' and, with a huge, tearing sigh, stared up at the American as if she had never seen him before. 'What's happening? Tell me what's happening?'

'You're in shock,' Bob told her, 'which isn't surprising,' then, leaving Basil to look after her, dashed off to find a nurse.

There were worse places to endure another night of bombing than the crypt of the Church of St Veronica, a fact that hadn't escaped the attention of what seemed like half the inhabitants of Shadwell's battered slums.

Father Joseph, two nuns, three wardens, four WVS ladies and a one-legged crane driver, as Matt Hooper now styled himself, provided a welcoming committee for any man, woman or child who came running out of the half-dark to be ushered down the steps into the crypt where a less than merry throng was already fighting for possession of the bunks.

Some idiot with a harmonica tried to strike up a round of community singing by playing the opening bars of 'Knees Up, Mother Brown' over and over again until old Father Grogan, with great dignity, sailed through the unruly crowd, plucked the harmonica from the would-be entertainer's lips and secreted it in the folds of his cassock.

'Not now, Ernest,' he said. 'Later, perhaps, but not now.'

Seated on a bunk bed with Billy on her knee and Nora by her side, Breda listlessly watched the little charade without cracking so much as a smile.

One of the voluntary organisations had ferried in several big pots of soup that Danny and other strong lads had carried downstairs and set out on a long oak table that Father Joe told them had once belonged to Henry VIII, a fact that no one had the energy to dispute.

There were jugs of cocoa, too, and a baker's tray with bread cut into slices and a crate of milk for the children. In the interests of safety, however, no fires or stoves had been lighted and the soup and cocoa were lukewarm, much to the disgust of some of Shadwell's less stoical strays who muttered darkly about Catholic conspiracies while selfishly stuffing their faces.

Breda had fed Billy pinches of bread soaked in cocoa and had given him one of the tablets that Danny had brought back from the Princess which was the least she could do for her poor, sick son now his future had been stolen from him by some black-hearted looter who hadn't even had the decency to leave a thank you note.

It crossed Breda's mind that the cash might have been handed into a police station and was at this moment lying in a safe waiting for her to claim it. Even if that was the case – a pretty far-fetched case – how could she possibly prove the money was hers and explain where such a vast sum had come from without shopping her dad who, of course, she'd shopped once already and who was most probably dead because of it.

Salvage crews were made up of rough, tough men, dockers, miners and labourers, brave men doing a nasty job but without a scruple among the lot of them when it came to finding a large sum of money which they'd probably divvied up on the spot, which, Breda reckoned, was why the box had been left behind. She looked out on the milling crowd of folk who with food in their bellies and a roof over their heads were already settling down for the night, as if having their houses smashed to smithereens and losing everything was nothing but another of the minor inconveniences that society had piled upon them throughout the years.

The four low-wattage light bulbs that one of Father Joe's more talented parishioners had strung out on cord cables between the arches of the roof flickered and dimmed. Apart from the mewing of a few infants, a sudden silence descended on the unruly flock.

Slumped on Breda's lap, Billy opened his eyes and looked up at the roof. There was fear in his eyes now, a fear that had not been there before, as if the terrible experience of being buried underground had made him aware of his own mortality.

Bombs were thumping somewhere not far off but the sound was smothered by the thick stone walls and here, deep in the crypt of St Vee's, bombs seemed less threatening than the darkness that might descend at any moment.

The bulbs flickered once more, swayed a little on their trailing cords and then, miraculously, flared brightly and steadied.

Cheers went up. Some wag shouted, 'Need another shillin' for the meter, Father?' and there was laughter, nervy laughter. Breda saw Matt over by the staircase, laughing too, and Danny, a grin on his face, picking his way carefully through a minefield of babies, baskets and blankets with a mug of soup in each hand.

'Here.' He handed her one of the mugs and gave the other to Nora. 'You'd better eat somethin', Breda.'

She held the mug in both hands and looked up.

You could never say he was handsome, not as handsome as Ronnie, but the new glasses gave him a professorial air and added a kind of gravity that hadn't been there when he first came to lodge in her mother's house all those years ago.

'What is it?' she said.

'Leek an' potato, I think.'

'Ooo, lovely,' said Breda, and smiled.

Danny seated himself on the bed beside her and watched her sup soup from the mug while Billy, eyes wide open, lay back against her breast, saying nothing.

Danny said, 'It's goin' tae be a tight squeeze, Breda.'

'What is?'

'The three of you in that wee bed.'

'We'll manage,' Nora said. 'Won't we, dear?'

'No bleedin' option, 'ave we?' Breda said. 'Have you an' the old man found a place to lie down?'

'His foot's hurting,' Nora said. 'He won't sleep much.'

'Well, 'e won't be on the dock tomorrow, that's for sure,' said Breda. 'He won't be on the dock for a long time.' She supped another mouthful of soup. 'What are we gonna do, Danny? Where are we gonna go?'

'Limerick,' Nora said.

Danny, Breda and even Billy stared at her.

'Pardon?'

'Sure an' we could all go to Limerick where there's no war,' Nora said. 'I was a girl there an' me aunts would take us in.'

'Your aunts are about a hundred years old,' said Breda. 'Anyhow, what would we do for money?'

'There's always work on the harbour.'

'Yeah, guttin' fish,' said Breda. 'No, Ma, you're not draggin' me over to Ireland.'

'I could take Billy then.'

'Over my dead—' Breda began, then bit her lip.

Danny said, 'Do you really have relatives in Ireland, Nora?'

'Sure an' I do.'

Danny said, 'There's not much left for you here, Breda. It would certainly be better for Billy if you got him out of London for a while.'

She finished the soup, put the mug on the floor and wrapped an arm possessively about her son. 'Nobody's takin' Billy anywhere. Where 'e goes, I go. An' I ain't goin' to no Limerick, not even for you, Ma.'

'Is Daddy fightin' the Germans in Limerick?' Billy asked.

'I told you, Danny,' Breda said. 'Told you it was a mistake.'

'No, dear, there's no Germans in Ireland. You'd go with Gran on a big boat,' said Nora. 'It's lovely there. There's horses an' cows an'—'

'I want to stay 'ere,' said Billy, 'where Dad can find us.'

'See,' said Breda. 'See what you've done.'

'We could take Granddad with us,' Nora said a little desperately. 'You could play in the sand an' ride on a donkey.'

'No,' Billy said and buried his face in Breda's bosom.

'It's the best thing, Breda,' said Danny quietly. 'I don't mean Ireland, I mean puttin' off the evil day until he's old enough to understand.'

'The evil day?' said Breda. 'They're all evil days.'

'Not in Ireland,' said Nora.

'Oh, for God's sake, Ma, shut up.'

'You're just being selfish,' said Nora. 'You know I can't go an' leave you here without anyone to look out for you.'

'I can look out for myself,' Breda said 'Fact is, I been lookin' out for *you* for years, though you're too stupid to notice.' She opened her mouth to continue then closed it again and said very softly, 'Oh, Ma, I'm sorry. After what you done for Billy, after what you been through, I don't know what I'm sayin'.'

Danny put an arm round her. Billy, a good little soldier, sat up and patted her cheek just as Matt, swinging the grey-white boot before him, appeared out of the gloom.

'What's wrong with 'er?' he asked.

'What do you think's wrong with her?' Danny answered.

'You was talkin' about Ronnie, wasn't you?' said Matt.

'No, we was talking about Ireland,' said Nora.

'Ireland? What's Ireland got to do with us?'

'Ma wants us to go there till the war's over.'

'All of us? Me included?'

'Yes,' Nora said. 'You an' your gammy leg included.'

'Here,' Matt Hooper said, 'that's no bad idea, no bad idea at all. We could stay with your aunties, couldn't we?'

'How would we get there, tell me that?' said Breda.

'There's boats,' Matt said.

'Yeah, an' submarines,' said Breda.

'Liverpool,' said Matt. 'The boats leave from Liverpool. If it came to it, I could probably fix us up on a coaster. Once my foot's healed up I'll get work on the docks. They got docks in Limerick, don't they?'

'You're English born an' bleedin' bred,' Breda said. 'How can you think of leavin' England in the lurch?'

'I give England enough,' Matt Hooper said bitterly. 'I give England my boy's life. What more does England want from me? My life? Susie's life? Nah, if there's a way out for me an' Nora then I'll take it. It's what Ron would 'ave wanted.' He tapped Nora lightly on the knee with his stick. 'You write your auntie, see if she'll take us. I'll find out about boat times an' ticket prices.'

'What about us? What about Billy?' said Breda.

'You can come, or you can stay,' Matt Hooper told her. 'If you was sensible, you'd at least let us take Billy with us.'

'Never,' Breda said. 'Never.'

Matt leaned closer, his face twisted with rage. 'I suppose you won't be 'appy till you see 'im dead too,' he hissed, 'till you see us all dead for the sake of bloody England.'

Shocked by his callousness, Breda let out a yelp of anger and frustration and, dumping Billy on to Nora's lap and leaping to her feet, stalked off into the depths of the crypt to find a quiet corner in which to have a real good cry.

'Now see what you've done,' said Nora as Billy, baffled by the argument, began to whimper and squirm in her arms.

'Here, give him here,' Danny said and, detaching Billy from Nora's grasp, hoisted the boy into his arms and carried him out of earshot of his grandparents' sour squabbling.

He took him to the trestle and put him down.

'Does your head hurt, Billy?'

'Yus, a bit.'

'Are you hungry?'

'Yus.'

'Would a piece of bread an' jam help?'

Billy nodded and watched while Danny negotiated with Father Joe for a thick slice of bread spread, quite liberally, with blackcurrant jelly. He gave Billy the bread and poured a cup of milk which he held in readiness.

The noise in the crypt was so loud now that it all but drowned out the sounds from upstairs.

'Limerick,' Billy said, through a mouthful of bread and jelly. He tried the word again, experimentally. 'Limerick,' then added, 'Gran comes from Limerick, don't she?'

'She does.'

'If we go to Limerick will you come with us?'

'Nope,' Danny said. 'I have to get back to work.'

'Where's that?'

'Evesham.'

'Are you a soldier, Danny?'

'No, I work in an office.'

'Are there Germans in Evesham?'

'No, no Germans.'

'Bombs?'

'A few,' said Danny. 'Not many.'

'Does Daddy know where Evesham is?'

'Daddy will always know where you are, Billy, no matter where you go,' Danny said.

'That's all right then,' Billy said and, with a little sigh, handed him back the cup.

29

There were fresh flowers in the vase on the table and a cleaner in an overall and beret was quietly dusting the grand piano just above her head. The pillow beneath her head was soft and the blanket that tickled her nose smelled pleasantly of soap flakes. She had a strange floating feeling in her limbs and would not have been surprised if a choir had started singing softly into one of the microphones that stood out like inkblots in the pale blue and pink-tinted studio.

No choir, though; just Basil dressed in a brown woollen dressing gown that made him look, she thought, like Friar Tuck.

She stretched her arms above her head, then, realising that she was wearing nothing on the upper half of her body but a brassiere, pulled the blanket up to her chin again.

Basil, looking down, said, 'Sleep well?'

'Like a log.'

'Feeling better?'

'Much better, thank you.'

'Lord knows what was in that syringe the nurse shot into you but it fairly did the trick. You went out like a light.'

'What time is it?'

'Half past seven.'

'I'd better rouse myself, I suppose.'

'Are you sure you're up to it, Susan? You can have some time off, if you want.'

'I'd rather work than – well, brood.'

'Good girl,' Basil said. 'Viv will fix you up with some clothes and, of course, you'll stay with us – unless you have other plans.'

'My flat,' Susan said. 'How did you know it had been hit?'

'You told me.'

'Did I?'

'Just before you sailed off to the land of Nod,' Basil said. 'Don't you remember?'

'Actually, no. I was in rather a state, wasn't I?'

'Indeed, you were,' Basil said. 'I think things caught up with you all of a sudden. Not surprised you had a fit of the vapours. Nothing to be ashamed of.'

'What else did I tell you?'

'Nothing of any consequence,' Basil said.

She raised herself on an elbow and looked around the studio. There were half a dozen men in the room and two women, fully dressed, whom she didn't recognise and who paid her no attention at all.

'Are they broadcasting from here?'

'Morning service at ten fifteen,' said Basil.

'I'd better get up.'

'We've loads of time,' said Basil. 'Your clothes are just behind you. Matron would have had you in the first-aid room overnight but I thought you'd be safer here.'

'Was the building hit?'

'Some external damage, nothing too serious,' Basil told her. 'The Langham Hotel copped it, though. We won't be boarding guests there for quite some time, I fear.'

'Many injured?'

'I really don't know.' Basil stooped and lifted a blanket from the mattress beside her, shook it out and folded it neatly. 'There's a cloakroom reserved for ladies just across the gangway; you can wash and dress there.'

'Where's Robert?'

'Bob decided to make a run for it as soon as he saw that you were all right.'

'Make a run for where?' said Susan.

'The Lansdowne, I suppose. He said he had work to do.'

'Another piece for us?'

'He's already delivered a tail-end for Friday.'

'Is it good?'

'Very good,' said Basil. 'Very relevant.'

Holding the blanket in front of her, Susan sat up. She had a slight headache and just for an instant the room swam. She drew in a few deep breaths, got to her feet and wrapped the blanket around her.

'I don't suppose you've heard from my husband?' she said.

Basil did his best to look surprised. 'Oh, is he in town?'

'I told you that, too, didn't I?'

'Yes, I believe you did mention it. And, no, Susan, I haven't heard from him, though it's early yet and last night's raids were very intense.'

'You don't have to make excuses for him, Basil,' Susan said. 'What you can do, if you don't mind, is stand me breakfast.'

299

'Delighted to do so,' Basil said. 'Are you hungry?'

'Starved,' said Susan.

By ten o'clock there was a bit of a breeze and it was cooler than it had been of late but there was no sign of cloud cover and 'softening-up' raids before nightfall seemed inevitable.

Council officials and billeting officers had arrived early at St Vee's to record details of families' needs and attend on the spot to cases of extreme hardship. Some items of essential clothing, mainly underwear and shoes, had been brought down from a Salvation Army depot but dealers in second-hand clothes had been quick off the mark and a tidy little market had sprung up in the side street that bordered Pound Lane.

There were only two lavatories in St Vee's and no washing facilities apart from a couple of hand basins, but a functioning tap had been unearthed in the wreckage of Roach's Garage and a hose run out to provide clean water to fill buckets and tubs.

Not a man to dawdle when his mind was set on something, Matt had hobbled off for the union offices to find out how the land might lie in respect of compensation and, Danny suspected, enquire about steamer services to Ireland.

Billy was fractious and clingy. Even a slice of fried bread dipped in egg yolk and a cup of weak tea didn't settle him. He hung on to Breda's skirt, cried when it dawned on him that Danny was leaving and was not consoled by Danny's promise that he wasn't going off to fight the Germans and would be back in no time at all.

The Tube turned out to be impossible. Lines were closed on many of the routes. It took Danny the best part of two hours to wend his way by bus as far as Victoria, hoof along the King's Road and cut over to Rothwell Gardens.

It had been in his mind that if Susan had moved in with the American, he might billet Breda and company in the flat; a tight squeeze for four but a lot more comfortable than camping out in the church crypt. As soon as he rounded the corner into the Gardens, however, that half-baked scheme went up in smoke.

The area around the block was cordoned off by policemen who were watching two men on a turntable ladder outlined against the sky.

'What are they doin'?' Danny asked.

'None o' your business. Move along.'

Danny handed over his identity card and BBC pass. The policeman carried them off to show to two men who had replaced their helmets with bowler hats and who, after checking Danny's name against the tenants' register, gave the copper the nod to let Danny through.

His first reaction to the sight of the torn building was fear, fear that Susan and her lover had been together in bed when the bomb had fallen.

As he approached the crowd of builders, salvage men and tenants who flanked the crater on the park side of the street the ladder swung away and a huge slab of concrete crashed down through three floors and buried itself in the debris by what had once been the doorway.

Everyone stepped hastily back, turning their heads away and covering their eyes as a cloud of dust billowed across the street. An elderly woman clad in a fur coat, who Danny recognised as a neighbour, let out a shriek. Two rather effete young men who lived in the flat above hugged each other and sobbed as the ladder swayed and a slice of polished wood flooring slipped from its moorings and followed the slab to the ground, bringing with it an antique chiffonier, three tapestry chairs and a beautiful swan-neck standard lamp.

'Oh, my God! Oh, my God, Dickie! We're losing the lot,' one of the young men cried.

Wiping dust from his eyes, Danny sought out one of the bowler hats from the letting agency.

Danny said, 'When did this happen?'

'Monday night,' the agent told him.

Danny let out his breath: he no longer had to worry about Susan. 'What's happenin' now?' he said.

'The building's being inspected to make sure it's safe.'

'Safe?' Danny said. 'Safe for what?'

'Salvage work. If you have possessions you wish to reclaim I suggest you wait with the others on the off-chance the crew will be able to fetch stuff out.'

'What about the lease?'

The agent was in his fifties. He had a small dark moustache, probably dyed. His eyes were pouched with fatigue.

'Too early to say. The building may not be redeemable, in which case you should apply in writing for reimbursement of rent paid in advance. Contents, of course, are not our responsibility.'

'How long will all this take?'

'For ever,' the other bowler hat put in. 'For bloody ever.'

The ladder moved closer to the third floor where a corner of the gable wall remained in place. The man on top of the ladder stretched across the gap and shook what appeared to be the end of a joist which instantly released another heavy shower of debris. The man on top of the ladder stooped and spoke to the chap three or four rungs below him who, in turn, swung out one-handed and shouted, 'No go this side. I ain't no expert but it looks ter me like a demo job.'

The man in the bowler hat swore loudly.

'What does that mean?' Danny said.

'It means we'll have to pay a specialist to take the building down,' the agent told him, 'and nobody's going to get anything out of it.' He stroked his moustache with his fore-finger. 'Have you got anything in there you really can't live without?'

'Only my Sunday best suit.'

'You what?'

'No,' Danny said. 'Nothin' I can't live without.'

She expected Bob to turn up full of concern for her welfare. When he hadn't appeared by noon she was tempted to telephone the Lansdowne to make sure he was all right.

She was more in control of herself now than she'd been in quite a while and applied herself to typing up the letters that Basil dictated and – a monthly chore – compiling a budget to send round to the Accounts Department in the building in Duchess Street; a building that had not escaped unscathed and within which, according to Basil, a certain amount of papery chaos currently reigned.

There had also been damage to the west wing of the House and part of Portland Place had been closed off to traffic but Susan hadn't been outside to see for herself, and had no desire to do so. Whether it was the lingering effects of the sedative or a sign that she was adjusting to life under nightly bombardment she couldn't be sure, but she felt safe within the walls of Broadcasting House and protected by the anything-but-humdrum routine of putting together another edition of *Speaking Up for Britain*. It occurred to her in a rueful moment that if she could persuade someone to collect her laundry she might pass the duration of the war here quite peacefully.

Basil was solicitude personified. He had a page-boy – sixty if he was a day – fetch coffee and sandwiches from the canteen and when he saw that Susan was having difficulty with some dolt in the Censors' Department discreetly took over the call.

It was a little after noon. Susan had just popped out to the cloakroom when the message came up from the reception desk. Basil had barely replaced the telephone receiver when she came back into the office.

He looked up, frowned and said, 'There's someone waiting to see you in the front hall.'

Robert, she thought, first Ronnie and now Robert, and experienced a fleeting moment of dread.

'Who is it?' she heard herself say.

'Your husband.'

'Danny? Why doesn't he come up?'

'I've no idea,' said Basil. 'He wants you to go down.'

'He's been to see Rupert Talbot, hasn't he? He's been interviewed for a posting in the News Department and now he wants to tell me—'

'Susan, calm down,' Basil said.

'What? Yes, of course, of course.'

'Go and see what he wants,' Basil said. 'If he's looking for a place to lay his head he is, of course, perfectly entitled to stay here overnight. He is staff, after all.'

'Yes,' said Susan. 'I do tend to forget that. May I . . . ?'

'Go, go. For God's sake, go.'

The hall was even more crowded than usual and had lost all semblance of orderliness. Workmen on ladders were repairing the wiring that fed the lifts and some of the big square lights that topped the columns of English marble were flickering frantically. By the doorway four char-women, tails in the air, were scrubbing at a huge black stain that had mysteriously appeared on the floor, while refugees from outlying offices stepped cautiously over and around them. To the left of the reception desk, in one of the nooks between the columns, Danny and Bob Gaines were chatting.

Bob was smartly dressed in a plaid jacket and dark blue flannels and had exchanged the grubby fedora for a soft felt hat with a feather in the band. He carried a scuffed pigskin briefcase plastered with luggage labels and, Susan noticed, had neglected yet again to burden himself with a gas mask.

'Susan,' he called out. 'Come and join us.'

Danny turned and watched her approach. He seemed, she thought, rather annoyed at her intrusion. He looked skinny, almost waif-like in a raincoat that was miles too long for him. He wore no hat, his hair needed washed and his shoes were filthy. At his feet were two plump brown paper parcels neatly tied with department store string.

He said, 'I know you're busy. I won't keep you long.'

She waited for one or other man to kiss her but neither of them did. She said, 'What are you doing down here, Danny? Why didn't you come upstairs?'

'Same question I asked,' said Bob. 'Look, I'll leave you to it. You obviously have things to talk about. I'll be up in the office when you're through, Susan.'

No matter how urbane she pretended to be, she could not meet her lover's eye while her husband stood by. She nodded, saw the men shake hands and Bob give Danny's shoulder a little slap, the way men do, before he hefted up the briefcase and headed for the stairs.

Danny watched him go.

'Nice guy,' he said. 'You could do worse, Susie.'

It occurred to her that whatever had brought her husband to Broadcasting House it wasn't a meeting with Rupert Talbot or anyone else from the News Department. Even Danny wouldn't turn up for a crucial interview looking like a ragamuffin.

Danny said, 'I wasn't sure I'd find you here.'

'Where else would I be?' Susan said.

'I thought maybe you'd taken shelter with Mr Gaines.'

'No,' she said. 'I've been here all night.'

'Then you don't know about the flat?'

'Oh, that!' she said. 'Yes, in fact I do know about the flat. Have you been down there this morning?'

'Aye,' Danny told her. 'About an hour ago.'

'How soon can we move back in?'

'Are you kiddin'? The block's been declared unsafe, same as Stratton's. Chances are it'll be demolished.'

'What about my stuff?'

'The salvage crews won't risk their necks for your stuff,

or mine, or anybody's else. Anyroads, there could be another raid tonight – probably will be – and who's to say another bomb won't finish the job. The flat's still in your name so you better do the paperwork if you want some money back on the rent. There's insurance on the contents, too, isn't there?'

'Why must you always be so bloody practical, Danny?'

'Badly brought up, I suppose,' Danny said. 'Are you gonna lodge with Gaines?'

'I don't know. Perhaps.'

'There's always Vivian to fall back on if you have to.'

'What about you, Danny? Do you have somewhere to go?'

'Back to Wood Norton.'

'I mean tonight,' Susan said.

'I'll stay at St Vee's,' Danny said.

'You can stay here if you wish. You're staff, after all.'

He shook his head, stooped and brought up one of the brown paper parcels. 'I brought you a few things I thought you might need. Knickers, stockings an' the like.'

She took the parcel and hugged it to her chest.

'Don't tell me you walked into Marshall and Snelgrove's ladies' department and—'

'Crossland's: you know what a cheapskate I am.'

'No, never that. Whatever else, never that,' Susan said. 'Thank you. I mean it. Thank you very, very much.' She looked down at the parcel at his feet. 'Is that one for your girl?'

'My girl?'

'Your girl in Evesham.'

'I don't have a girl in Evesham.'

'I thought you said . . .'

'I didn't say it; you did.' He bent down, picked up the parcel from the floor and tucked it under his arm. 'Look, I've done what I came here to do so I'd better push off.'

'Who's the other parcel for, Danny?'

He seemed surprised that she even had to ask.

'Breda,' he said. 'Who else?'

30

It was only after Danny went back to Evesham that Breda began to accept that Ron was dead. There were too many loose ends, nothing but loose ends, and the biggest loose end of all was that she would never see Ronnie again, never hear his voice or see his face or feel him inside her and that her bed, wherever her bed might be, was empty without him.

She tried not to feel sorry for herself and she certainly wasn't idle. Her hands, fortunately, were almost healed and she'd had the bandages taken off. She had plenty to do – too much, in fact – but there was no pattern to her life, no centre now that Stratton's, her house in Pitt Street and, of course, Ron were gone.

She was interviewed by council officers. She filled in forms. She took Billy to a First Aid post to have his dressing changed and helped Nora compose a letter to the aunts in Limerick. She gritted her teeth and ventured up to Oxmoor Road to set in motion the process of obtaining a certificate from the Fire Service that would allow her to register Ron's death and claim a little bit of money from the government.

What troubled her more than lack of income, though, was the effect the nightly bombings were having on Billy.

When the siren sounded, as it did every evening, he would

throw himself upon her, drag her to the bunk and cower under the blankets, fists clenched and face pressed into her breast. He could not be persuaded to join in the boisterous games Father Joe organised to amuse the children, or sit cross-legged in a circle while one of the nuns told the story of Moses or Noah, how Daniel survived the lions in King Darius's den or how Jesus made a crippled man walk again.

He shunned Nora, avoided Matt, and refused to be bribed with sweets, comics or even an ice cream that his grandfather had limped half a mile to fetch for him.

When his head ached, which it did quite often, he stuck his fists in his mouth and closed his eyes so tightly that it was all the tears could do to squeeze out from under the lids. And when Breda finally took him back to the First Aid post to have his stitches removed, he screamed and struggled and had to be held down until the deed was done and, afterwards, kicked Breda's shins as if the pain were her fault.

All Breda had to hang on to in that dismal week was the postcard Danny had hidden in the parcel of clothes he'd brought back from town. The postcard had a pretty picture on one side: a thatched cottage with apple trees in the sunny garden and a creature that was either a dog or a lamb peeping out from under a rose bush.

On the back of the card Danny had printed two words: *Stay Put*. Nothing more: no promise to return to London or send money or that he had any plans to involve himself in her future.

Just: *Stay Put*.

She showed the postcard to no one, not even Nora and certainly not to Matt. She kept it hidden under the blanket she used as a pillow. When the lights were switched off and the bombardment raged upstairs, she would fish out the postcard and a pocket torch and, hidden beneath the blanket, study the pretty picture and Danny's enigmatic instruction and puzzle over what, if anything, it signified.

She knew that Danny had her interests at heart and she was determined to sit tight in Shadwell and scratch along as best she could until the situation improved.

Sooner or later the council would have to start repairing the damaged houses, though whether they'd do so while the skies were filled with German bombers was doubtful. Ronnie would probably have told her that borough councillors don't think like ordinary men and women and were quite capable of ordering Shadwell's broken houses and warehouses razed to the ground and starting all over again after the war.

After the war, after the war: Breda was already sick of hearing about after the war. Now her daddy's legacy had been stolen from her the future had lost its gilt. It offered only the same sort of drudgery that had gone on before Britain had entered the war – except that she wouldn't have a husband. With her breasts sagging, her face turned to mince and a kid to contend with she'd be unlikely to find anyone to take her on.

The prospect of escaping to neutral Ireland with her mother and Matt Hooper held no appeal. She regarded Ireland in somewhat the same sort of way as she regarded Canada, somewhere distant and inhospitable. And the very idea of lodging in a stranger's house filled her with horror.

No, she thought, tucking her head beneath the blanket, here we are, Billy and me, and here we'll stay.

But the next afternoon, at approximately half past four o'clock, she suddenly changed her mind.

*

The bulldog spirit had finally taken hold and, to mix one of Basil's favourite metaphors, the stiff upper lip was much in evidence within the confines of Broadcasting House. No more weeping over the porridge plates, no hysteria, no signs of panic, just a general air of determination to make the best of it, whatever 'it' might be.

Filling up the schedule for Basil's twice-weekly programme had become more difficult as September wore on and the nightly blitzkrieg continued without let or halt. Rail and road links suffered. The West End was slapped, theatres closed and visiting celebrities were few and far between. Fortunately there were still a few brave souls willing to risk their necks trekking to Portland Place to venture an opinion on the progress of the war or, prodded by Robert Gaines, predict if Adolf would attack before winter set in or hold off until spring.

Figures from CBC and cables from the BBC's New York office indicated that *Speaking Up* was gathering an audience across much of North America. The postbag, too, increased in size and a fair portion of Basil's mornings were taken up dictating replies that Susan, aided by a couple of secretaries, typed up and dispatched.

Late one week night, just as Baz was brushing his teeth before hitting the mattress, a call came through from no less a person than the Prime Minister and Basil was hastily summoned back to his office to listen to Churchill's barking voice thanking him for his efforts on behalf of the nation. Though he was by no means the first producer to receive a personal call from the PM, Basil was very pleased and tottered off to bed in the shade of the grand piano purring like a pussycat.

Five days on and a weekend off became the pattern for Basil Willets's crew. Bob, a free agent, spent less time in the House and, in spite of pleas from Basil and Susan, struck out for the Lansdowne no matter how late the hour or how intense the bombing. He did not invite Susan to join him, for if she was injured or, God forbid, killed because of him he said he would never be able to forgive himself.

To compensate for his neglect, he invited her to lunch at L'Étoile, only to discover that Charlotte Street was closed; a solitary bay tree in a pot in the middle of the road bore a warning notice: 'Police. Danger. Unexploded Bomb'.

'We could go to Scott's, I guess,' Bob said. 'The oysters don't know there's a war on.'

'Too much of a man's club,' Susan said. 'I'm not dressed to impress.'

'You look just dandy to me,' Bob said.

'Do I?' Susan said.

'Sure you do.'

'Sometimes I wonder.'

'Well,' he said. 'Don't,' and gave her a kiss 'Hatchett's?'

'A little too far. I have to be back by three.'

'You work too hard.'

'Not as hard as you.'

'The point's moot,' Bob said. 'Hey, what's going on down there in the alley?'

In the lane at the rear of a characterless building a brace of cooks in white jackets and a chef in a tall white hat were fussing over a battery of pots and pans balanced on two Calor gas stoves while a couple of pretty young waitresses in traditional black and white dresses stood by to carry the dishes indoors.

The rich aroma of beef stew filled the alleyway.

'Good lord!' said Susan. 'They're cooking outside by the look of it. Now that's what I call enterprising.'

'Kitchen must be out of commission,' Bob said. 'What place is this and where's the front entrance?'

'Taylor's Hotel, I think, on Goodge Street.'

'Then that's the place for us,' Bob said.

The window table, set for two, provided a view of sandbags and rubble and, now and then, the blink of a bus going by, barely visible between the lattice of brown paper strips that all but covered the glass. The lights were off but some enterprising person had seen fit to place a fat wax candle in a saucer on each of the tables which, when lit, gave the low-beamed dining room a cosy air more suited to a winter night than a warm autumn afternoon.

Bob disposed of a Scotch and soda before the soup arrived and insisted on ordering an expensive bottle of claret to wash down the stew.

'You're drinking a lot these days?' Susan said.

'Steadies the nerves.'

'You don't have a nerve in your body, Mr Gaines.'

'Don't you believe it,' Bob said. 'I'm just as scared as everyone else. Well, maybe not everyone. I've been through this sort of thing before, remember.'

'In Madrid?'

'Yep, and elsewhere.'

'And you love it, don't you?'

He grinned, poured wine into her glass and into his own. He raised the glass and offered her a casual toast. 'You've sure got my measure, Mrs Cahill.'

'If it's excitement you're after,' Susan said, 'perhaps you should join the London fire service.'

'Ouch!'

'I'm sorry,' Susan said. 'That's unfair.'

'Nope, it's perfectly fair. How are they bearing up?'

'They?'

'Your folks. The widow. Your pappy.'

'Oh,' said Susan. 'They'll survive.'

'Sure they will. They're cockneys, oin't they?'

'Please, don't mock them.'

'I wouldn't dream of it,' Bob said. 'I've nothing but admiration for the way the poor are putting up with the vicissitudes of all-out war.'

'They're not poor,' Susan said. 'Whatever you may think of them, they're not poor.'

He reached out and touched her hand. 'Look, Susan, I didn't bring you here to argue.'

'Why did you bring me here?'

'To relax and enjoy yourself.'

'Not an easy thing to do these days.'

'A glass or two of wine might help.'

'I think not,' Susan said. 'Red wine and shorthand do not go well together.' She hesitated. 'How are things at the Lansdowne? Is Mr Slocum still throwing wild parties?'

'No, that's all come to a grinding halt,' Bob said. 'We're busy boys these days.' It was his turn to hesitate. 'It's not that I don't miss you. I do. But you're safer in Salt Street with Vivian. Goering's gang seems to have taken a special shine to Berkeley Square. We've been fire-bombed four times this week. An oil bomb put three apartments out of commission – ours not among them, fortunately – but the whole place stinks.' Another pause: 'You are okay at Vivian's, aren't you?'

'Yes,' Susan said wryly. 'I'm okay at Vivian's.'

'If you need a few bucks . . .'

'You're the last person I'd ask.'

'How come?' Bob said.

'Because I'm not a tart.'

'No, but I'm your friend and friends pitch in.'

'A friend? Is that all I am to you?'

'Damn it, Susan, I'm doing my best to be reasonable.'

'Reasonable?'

'Helpful. Helpful. I mean helpful.'

She stared at her untouched glass, at the hue of the wine, the shape of the candle flame showing through it. There were tears somewhere within her but she would not let them out, wouldn't let him see just how vulnerable she had become.

She said, 'Vivian made me a loan. I'll pay her back, of course.'

'What about your husband?'

'What about him?'

'Is he still mad at you?'

'Would you blame him if he was?' Susan said.

'I guess not,' Bob said. 'I just want to be sure if I do have to go away, you'll be taken care of.'

'Are you going away?'

'Maybe. God knows what's coming up next. If the *Union Post* decides it needs a correspondent in Cairo or Algiers . . .'

'You're their man.'

'Yeah, I'm their man. That's what I am. That's what I do. You knew it when you took me on.'

'Took you on? Really? I was under the impression you did the taking.'

'Now that,' he said, 'that *is* unfair.'

'English girls are easy; isn't that how it goes?'

'One thing you're not, kiddo, is easy.'

'That's good to know.'

'Oh, cut it out, Susie, for Chrissake,' he said. 'I don't know what's gotten into you.'

'Don't you?' she said. 'You should.'

He paused, head cocked. 'You're not pregnant, are you?'

'No, Robert, I'm not pregnant. If Cairo calls, or Libya, you may depart without a qualm. The only thing you'll be obliged to terminate is your contract with the BBC.'

'I don't much care for broadcasting, you know.'

'You are good at it, though.'

'That's what Quent told me.'

'Quent? Who's Quent?'

'Quentin Reynolds, the best journalist in the business. You met him once in the Lansdowne.'

'Did I?' Susan said. 'After a while all you journalists begin to look the same.'

'Like penguins?' Bob said.

She smiled. 'Yes, like penguins,' then, feeling marginally better, reached for her glass of wine.

31

The stallholders were packing up early. You never quite knew when Jerry would send over a few spotters and drop the odd incendiary just to spread a bit of panic before dusk settled in and the heavy bombers appeared in force.

It looked like any other weekday street market, a little busier than most, perhaps, for those folk who had been bombed out were in desperate need of clothing and, this being the East End, there were plenty of suppliers eager to meet demand.

Handcarts, donkey-drawn flat carts strewn with second-hand garments, penny-whistle men, scam-artists with three greasy cards and tables you could fold in a wink if a copper appeared shared the street with fruit sellers, pie-men, purveyors of drinks, hot and cold, and, bizarrely, one old woman with a washing basket filled with cracked mirrors and chipped vases that, to Breda's surprise, seemed to be selling like hot cakes.

Breda was on the scout for a warm second-hand coat to see her through the winter and a half-decent pair of boots that might fit Billy. She had seven shillings and eight pence in the pocket of her one and only dress, a floral-patterned cotton rag that she'd happened to be wearing on the night

Pitt Street had been hit. It was too light now for an autumn afternoon and had been made all the lighter by the amount of scrubbing she'd had to do to get the mud stains out of the material.

Hidden under a blanket in St Vee's were a pleated knee-length skirt, one respectable blouse and a sparc underskirt that her mother had retrieved from the bedroom in Stratton's, plus the underwear that Danny, without a blush, had bought for her at Crossland's. From various charitable sources Billy had acquired quite a decent wardrobe of cast-offs, including a brand-new pair of stockings. Unfortunately, he was still hopping around in shoes at least a size too small for him. She should have brought Billy with her but he'd been such a handful of late that she'd left him with Ma and had slipped out alone to search for affordable bargains which, up to now, hadn't exactly fallen into her lap.

Further up Fawley Street were the barrows of optimistic booksellers ridding themselves of 'damaged stock' which, as far as Breda could make out, was just the same old stock as it had always been: dog-eared copies of Dickens and Thackeray and cheap yellow-backed novels that fell apart as soon as you opened them. On the step of a bomb-blasted building that had until recently housed an insurance office an elderly gentleman in a top hat and a morning coat that had seen better days was loudly touting the miraculous properties of a pill that would settle stomach upsets, soothe the nerves and cure constipation which, at a shilling a box, seemed to Breda just too good a bargain to be true.

Pausing at the rear of the jeering little crowd to listen to the old charlatan's florid spiel, she felt a hand on her arm and the point of a knife blade prick her hip. Her first thought was that some swine was after her seven shillings and eight pence. She clamped her elbow over the pocket of her dress and opened her mouth to give the bugger a mouthful.

'Keep your trap shut, girly,' Vince said quietly, 'or I'll carve out your kidneys. Now, smile nice an' take a walk with me, all lovey-dovey, like. You got me?'

'Yeah,' Breda said. 'I got you.'

He palmed the knife and snared her arm. Breda had no doubt that if she made any kind of fuss he wouldn't hesitate to carry out his threat and leave her bleeding on the pavement.

'Where you takin' me?'

'Somewhere nice an' quiet where we can 'ave a little chat.'

'I thought you was in the army?' Breda said.

'The army's for mugs.'

He wore a rumpled battledress without regimental markings, a beret instead of a helmet and shoes, not boots. He had none of the sort of equipment Breda thought a soldier should have, no belts or pouches, not even a gas mask.

'Where's Steve?' Breda said. 'Why ain't he with you?'

'Steve's stuck in camp in bloody Durham pissin' his pants an' keepin' his nose clean case they call 'im to Harry King's trial.'

'Will they?'

'How the hell do I know?' Vince said. 'They might have Steve Millar by the balls but they ha'n't got me no more.'

'In other words,' Breda said, 'you're a deserter. They shoot deserters, don't they?'

'Only if they catch them,' Vince said. 'Won't make no difference to you what I am, not when I get through with you.'

'What you gonna do to me?'

Vince tightened his grip, knife blade flat against her arm. . 'I ain't had a woman in weeks,' he said, 'so what you think I'm gonna do to you?'

'You don't want me, you want Leo's money, don'cha?'

'That's the second thing on my list.'

'I don't 'ave it. I never 'ad it.'

'Lyin' bitch,' Vince said. 'You're the only person in the world that greasy little Eye-tie would trust with his loot. Well, I'm gonna make you squeal, girly, believe me, I am.'

Up ahead where Fawley Street split round the old clock tower, she caught sight of Ronnie's friend, Clary Knotts. He was in fireman's uniform and was walking briskly across the corner heading, she thought, for Oxmoor Road.

She wrenched at Vince's arm and opened her mouth to scream but Vince was too quick for her. He grabbed her, hugged her, thrust his face into hers in a mock kiss and, with the knife pricking her belly, pushed her into an alley between the houses and shoved her through an open doorway into what had once been someone's back parlour.

Gelid light from a broken window showed an iron grate spewing cold ashes, a battered armchair and a patch of torn linoleum littered with fragments of glass, ceiling plaster and broken bricks. The room had been used as a lavatory and stank to high heaven. Two brown rats that had been feeding on something unspeakable rose up, squeaking, and streaked between Breda's legs out into the alley. Breda let out a yell. Vince wrapped a forearm around her throat and, wasting no time, rammed a hand under her dress and dragged down her knickers.

Elbows pumping like pistons, Breda pummelled his

stomach and hips and tried to kick his shins. He pulled her closer, smothering her frantic attempts to defend herself, then dropped down, bent his knees and tossed her on to the floor. He disentangled her knickers from her shoes and threw them away, furled her dress up to her waist then sat back on his heels, grinning.

Breda said, 'I had it, yeah, but it got stole.'

He called her a filthy name, told her she was a liar, then, sliding his hands up under the top of the dress, yanked her brassiere over her breasts and stroked her nipples.

Breda said, 'Stole. All of it. They took it all.'

He leaned into her and brought his mouth close to her ear. Mention of money had distracted him, if only for a second. Breda spread out her arms as if to brace herself, to capitulate in what he was about to do to her and, groping, closed her hand round a chunk of broken brick.

'Who did?' Vince said.

'The rescue squad,' she said. 'Our 'ouse got bombed, bad. The rescue squad found the money in the debris an' stole it 'fore I could get there. It's the truth, Vince, honest to God, it is.'

'Yeah, an' I came up the Thames in a canoe,' he said. 'You willin' to die for a lousy three grand, girly? 'Fore I'm done with you, you'll be wishin' you *was* dead.'

And, Breda thought, they'll find me lying in this dirty hole, torn and bleeding and write me off as just another poor cow who lured a man here to earn a few bob; another corpse nobody cares about, like the girls they find in the corners of shelters, round the back of bombed buildings or floating, bloated, in the dock.

'You ask me,' she said, 'you're all mouth an' no trousers.'

'What you say?'

'You 'eard me, big boy. You gonna show me what you got or just brag about it?'

He removed his hands from her breasts, sat back and fumbled with his trouser buttons. He rose awkwardly into a half squat and dug his member from his underpants. He was short but very thick and very ugly. Breda had seen lots of men before Ronnie, some sleek and shiny, some large, some small, but all the same down there when roused.

Smirking, Vince glanced down and touched himself.

It was the moment, the one moment, her one and only chance. Breda cocked her knee to her chest and caught him off balance. He performed a little Cossack dance to right himself. Breda drove the heel of her shoe into the pale, upstart part that protruded from his fly and, more by luck than aim, struck the target head on. Vince roared and fell back.

Breda rolled out and away from him before he could recover and, on her knees, swung the half brick in a scything arc that caught him on the side of the head. Then rage overtook her, a great welling surge of rage at all the humiliations that had been piled upon her, all that she had sacrificed: Ron, her house, her daddy and damned near her mother and her son.

She raised the broken brick above her head in both hands and brought it crashing down.

It struck Vince midway between the bridge of the nose and the hairline. Blood started from his nose and his eyes rolled back in his head. He let out a cry that in other circumstances might have aroused her sympathy then slumped on to his side and lay motionless, legs drawn up and arms crushed beneath his chest.

Breda got to her feet. Rage still burned in her like a gas jet. She raised the piece of brick once more and was on the point of smashing it into his skull when sense took over. She prodded Vince with the toe of her shoe. Blood came from his mouth as well as his nose. Taking him by the shoulders, she flopped him on to his belly, face down, so that he wouldn't choke. When he spluttered and coughed she knew he wasn't dead but, to her relief, showed no signs of regaining consciousness.

Fear and rage drained out of her. For a moment she felt as if she might swoon. She closed her hands into fists and stretched her arms stiffly down by her sides to stop herself shaking.

'Right,' she said aloud. 'All right,' and fished about on the floor to find her knickers. She shook the knickers free of dirt and, still unsteady on her pins, carried them to the doorway and, leaning against the jamb, put them on.

The air that filtered down the narrow alley was cool and, clinging to the door jamb, she drew in several huge, deep breaths to clear her head. The odd thing wasn't that she felt bad but that she didn't feel worse. It was as if the sudden storm of anger had purged her guilt and released her from uncertainty.

She glanced round to make sure that Vince was still out cold, then, taking her time, brushed grit from her dress, front and back, tidied her hair and, spitting on her fingertips, gave her face a bit of wash to restore some colour to her cheeks.

She drew herself up, braced her trembling knees and walked down the narrow passageway and out into Fawley Street in search of a policeman.

It didn't take long to find one. He was hanging about the

kerb on the curve of the cobbled area in front of the old clock tower and he looked, Breda thought, quite bored.

She approached him boldly, doing her best to strut with a little of her youthful self-confidence.

'Wonder if you could 'elp me?' she said.

'Certainly do my best, miss.'

'Lookin' for a place I can send a telegram.'

'Post Office do that for you,' the constable said. 'The one up in Shannon Street's still open. Better get a move on, though, they closes at half past five.'

'Thank you.' Breda smiled, made as if to step off the kerb, then hesitated. 'By the way, Officer,' she said, 'ain't really none o' my business but there's a chap down there in that buildin' an' I don't think he's very well.'

'What makes you think that?'

'Saw 'im stagger in there bleedin' pretty bad.'

'Did you now?' the copper said. 'Soldier?'

'Yeah,' Breda said. 'I do believe 'e was.'

'Better see about that then, hadn't I?' the copper said and, with a nod to a good citizen, strode off towards the alley while Breda, letting out her breath, whisked round the side of the old clock tower and, in a flash, was gone.

'Are you sure this is the place?' Griff said. 'It doesn't look like a shady nook to me. Looks more like a farm track.' He put down a foot to brace himself and leaned into the handlebars of the bicycle. 'Mr Pell may have got it wrong.'

'Mr Pell never gets anythin' wrong,' Danny said. 'Anyhow, I've tried everywhere else an' there's not a bloody room tae rent within twenty miles of Wood Norton.'

'We've seen to that, I suppose. I mean, the BBC,' Griff

said. 'Between evacuees from Birmingham and bearded gentlemen from Outer Mongolia you'll be lucky to find an unoccupied rabbit hole. From what you've told me your friend from London isn't going to be too happy stuck up a farm track miles from anywhere.'

'There you're wrong,' Danny said.

'Is that what the telegram was about, the one that Harrison tossed on your desk with such contempt?'

'Aye, it was,' Danny said.

'Would it be stretching friendship too far to ask what it said? I mean, what's got you into such a lather?'

Danny paused. 'Well, if you must know, the telegram said, "Get me out of here."'

'Is that all?'

'Breda can be quite laconic when she's bein' charged per word,' Danny said. 'Somethin's obviously changed her mind about quittin' London.'

'Nightly air raids, perchance?' said Griff wryly.

'At least, she's seen sense at last an' I won't have to twist her arm to do the right thing. "Get me out of here," sounds pretty desperate to me.'

'Desperate or not,' Griff said, 'I still question if a big city girl will appreciate being totally cut off from civilisation.'

'Hell's bells, Griff, it's only a quarter of a mile from Deaconsfield,' Danny said. 'You can walk to the Pells' front door in ten minutes. Besides, farm tracks usually lead to farms an' unless I'm off beam the farm where Femi an' Ursula an' some of the other girls live is just across that field.'

'Femi?' Griff said. 'Now, if I weren't engaged to the loveliest girl on earth I wouldn't mind lodging with Femi myself. I assume you've knocked on every door in the village?'

'What do you think I've been doin' every spare minute for the last few days?' Danny said. 'I even asked the bloody billeting officer to see if he could help. He just laughed. Now if only you'd do the decent thing, wed Kate an' move into married quarters, I could bring Breda down to stay with the Pells.'

'Have you *seen* the so-called married quarters?' Griff said. 'In any case I've already arranged with Mrs Pell to shift you into Kate's room and Kate and I will have the one we're in now.'

'When?'

'November,' Griff said. 'By the by, I'd be awfully grateful if you'd be my best man. Harrison may not be keen to let us both take leave at the same time but if we give him plenty of warning I'm sure he'll come round.'

'Are you sure you want me for a best man?'

'It's either you or a sheep shearer from Brecon. A difficult choice, I admit, but beggars can't be choosers.'

'What does Kate have tae say about it?'

'It was her idea.'

'Oh!'

'So there you are, boyo. You can hardly refuse a request from the blushing bride, can you? In any case, it'll be good to get away for a couple of days and I guarantee the Cottrells will lay on a feast fit for a king.'

'It's not happenin' here in the Greenhill then?'

'Coventry,' Griffith said. 'Kate's parents are insisting on a proper church wedding. As they're paying for it – well, why not?'

'When?'

'November 15th. It's a Friday. Will you do it?'

'Of course I'll do it,' Danny said. 'But it'll cost you.'

'Cost me what?'

'Three quid for a new blue suit.'

'You could always turn up in your kilt, I suppose.'

'Very funny!' Danny said and, hoisting himself back on to the saddle of his bicycle, added, 'Now, if you don't mind, let's forge on an' see if we can find this place Mr Pell talked about.'

'Shady Nook.'

'Aye, Shady Nook,' said Danny.

32

It was a little after nine on Saturday evening when Vivian slumped over the desk and rested her brow on the typewriter. 'Done,' she said aloud, though there was no one in the room to hear her. 'Bloody well done.'

The book was finished and the top copy would be on its way to her literary agent, Charlie Ames, first thing on Monday. He had already persuaded *The Times* to publish an extract, though just how much attention an article on British injustice would attract when London was lying in ruins and half the population were living underground was debatable. Ted Carr, *The Times* assistant editor, had liked what he'd seen of the book but, as Charlie Ames pointed out, Ted Carr was a supporter of Joe Stalin and highly critical of Churchill's 'Collar the Lot' policy which he saw as a ruse to cleanse the country of Communist sympathisers.

Vivian didn't care. She'd done her best, more than her best. The book, Charlie assured her, had flair and passion, by which he meant piss and vinegar, an assessment with which Vivian was all too willing to agree. Now came the tedious slog of ensuring that her all footnotes were accurate and compiling an index. Even so, *An Enemy in Our Midst?* – she'd added the question mark at Basil's suggestion – would be published in the spring and some useful dollops of cash would flow into her bank account.

She wondered what sort of reception the book would have, where and by whom it would be reviewed and how many public appearances Charlie might be able to arrange on the back of it. Then she sat up. What the devil was she dreaming of? Charlie and Ted Carr and the publishing chaps might continue to ply their trades as if the future were as staid as the past but the Germans had other ideas. Long before *An Enemy* appeared in Foyle's window there might be no Foyle's, no publishers and no future at all for books like hers.

'Oh, bollocks!' she said and, leaping up, bundled the typescript into a box file and thrust the file into the small fire-proof safe that Basil had bought for the purpose. She closed the safe door, locked the handle, then, swaying slightly, stood in the middle of the room and listened to the wind whistling down the mews and the faint sound of gunfire and aeroplane engines that came riding along with it.

The raid had started at a little after eight.

Viv had ignored the warning and, absorbed in her work, had carried on typing. She had no fire watch duties tonight and, no matter how Basil fussed, would eat an unhurried supper, drop into bed for a good night's sleep, and be damned to the bloody Jerries and their policy of obliteration.

She lit a cigarette and wandered through the hall into the living room in search of her husband.

The blackout curtains were closed. Basil had left one light burning, the standard lamp with the big parchment shade.

The men were outlined against the light, Basil in shirtsleeves and waistcoat and his brother, Derek, in naval uniform. They had their backs to her and were looking down at Susan who was stretched out on the davenport fast asleep and showing rather a lot of leg.

Vivian cleared her throat. The men swung round.

'Enjoying the view?' Viv said.

Commander Willets was not in the least embarrassed.

'Every sailor's dream,' he said, then, coming forward, kissed Vivian on the cheek. 'The poor girl must be exhausted.'

'I'm sure she is,' Vivian said. 'Are you staying for supper?'

'Supper, yes, please. But I must be on my merry way as soon as the all-clear sounds. I rather expected to find you cowering in the cellar. It's pretty fierce out there tonight.'

'We're learning to ignore it,' Basil said. 'At least Vivian is. Didn't you hear the doorbell, dearest?'

'No,' Vivian said. 'I was otherwise occupied,' then to Derek, 'I gather you're just passing through.'

'I was my way to the station from a meeting at the Admiralty when the siren sounded. I hope you don't mind but I decided to seek shelter here instead of hanging about a railway station. If the worst comes to the worst there's an early train at five thirty. I'll make a run for that, come what may.'

'Well,' said Basil, 'however brief your visit, it is good to see you, old chap. Vivian, will you wake Susan, please.'

'Why not let Derek do it?' Vivian said, then added, smiling, 'But not with a kiss, old chap. Please, not with a kiss.'

In spite of, or perhaps because of the air raid it turned out to be one hell of a party, one whale of a party, the best damned party, Jake Tucker, linchpin of the United Press, declared since Chuck Rainer's farewell lunch at Horcher's in Berlin; a lunch that had lasted all afternoon and far into the night and had wound up with Chuck being arrested and having to bribe some snot-nosed gauleiter to call the American embassy to send someone round to bail him out before he wound up in Dachau.

There was no excuse for the party that took place in Pete Slocum's apartment that night. It just grew, like little Topsy, from a rowdy crowd of journalists and broadcasters who happened to be dining in the Lansdowne's restaurant so far below street level that you could barely hear the explosions let alone the whistle of any bombs that might be heading your way.

Bob shared a big table with Pete, Chuck and Tucker, some guy from the *Daily Mail* and three women, two of them young, that Pete had winkled out of the *Union Post*'s London office.

They began with lobster cocktails and aquavit, moved on through beefsteaks and breaded partridge, washed down with a nice selection of wines, and finished up with ice cream and macaroons. When, at length, Pete got up to leave, the others followed, not just the gang at Pete's table but half the guys of both sexes in the dining room, for it was Saturday night in London town and, raid or no raid, no one was going to bed before dawn.

George, the valet, kept his nerve long enough to pour one round of martinis, cut up lemons and fill a number of bowls with salted peanuts and stuffed olives. He even laid out coffee makings in the kitchen and a tray of fresh eggs for anyone who might be crazy enough to want breakfast. But when, shortly after midnight, one whistling scream was followed by a loud explosion and even the chaps who were shooting craps on the shag pile got up and galloped into the corridor, George threw in the towel, left the foolhardy idiots to get on with it and fled downstairs to the basement.

In theory you had ninety seconds' grace between the bomb leaving the bomb bay and the bomb striking its target. Ninety seconds was surely enough for any reasonable person to down a last martini, kiss a pretty girl or, if religion was your thing, mutter a prayer before you piled out into the corridor to put an extra wall between you and the blast in the hope that the Lansdowne wouldn't suffer a direct hit that would put you out of the game for good.

'Hello,' she said. 'I don't know if you remember me?'

'Sure, I remember you,' Bob said. 'Who could ever forget?' Leaning on the corridor wall, the girl looked up at him with big, round eyes. There was nothing innocent about her, Bob guessed, except that look, child-like and knowing at one and the same time.

'Tina, isn't it?' he said.

'Hmm,' she said. 'Hmm.'

And then she fell silent like everyone else in the corridor as the whistle of another falling bomb grew louder and louder.

The explosion was close and violent.

For a moment it seemed the building might crash down and bury them all. Later Bob would swear that not only did the ground move beneath his feet but that the biggest steel and concrete apartment house in the city swayed like a tree in the wind.

'Ooo,' the girl said, pursing her lips. 'Too close for comfort, wouldn't you say?' and, before Bob could stop her, insinuated herself into his arms.

★

They ate supper in the kitchen tucked away at the back of the mews house, sheltered from what was going on outside. Vivian did most of the talking. She was glad to have an audience, Susan guessed, for she was pleased with herself for 'polishing off' her book in double-quick time and chattered on and on about the relevance her exposé might have when it came to rebuilding Britain in a post-war world.

On that September night the post-war world seemed as far away as the planet Neptune but the brothers Willets were sufficiently considerate not to draw attention to the distinct possibility that Britain would be invaded, or to the raid that rattled the slates or the fact that in an hour or two Derek would be returning to convoy duty on the dark Atlantic.

When he had wakened her out of a deep, deep sleep at first Susan had mistaken him for Danny. Rubbing her eyes and yawning, she'd been quite unaware that her dress had ridden up and that she was showing not only her slip and stocking tops but bare thighs as well. Saying nothing, Commander Willets had leaned out of the light and, with finger and thumb, had tugged down the hem of her dress to protect her modesty.

For eighteen years she'd been governed by her father in the paradoxical security of a life lived an inch above the poverty line. She had been pushed out of the nest only to fulfil her father's promise to a mother she couldn't remember, pushed out into the world to prove that even a cockney crane driver could make a silk purse out of a sow's ear.

Her marriage to Danny Cahill had turned out to be less a romantic idyll than a vain attempt on her part to retreat into a world she'd left behind. And when the war had finally arrived and all the old verities had gone by the board how easy it had been to fall into the trap of equating uncertainty with irresponsibility, which had been all very fine and dandy until Ronnie had been killed.

'Look at the girl,' Basil said. 'She's still half asleep.'

'No.' Susan gave herself a shake. 'I'm listening.'

'Well, if she can sleep with a tummy full of your curry,' Vivian said, 'she's a better man than I am, Gunga Din.'

The curry Basil had put together was hot and tasty. The men and Vivian drank bottled beer and Susan drank tea. They all smoked cigarettes from a tin that Commander Willets had brought with him and talked not of the possibility of defeat but of a time beyond that, a brighter day when the victory Churchill promised had been secured and everything got back to normal, whatever 'normal' might mean by then.

'Will you stay with the BBC?' Derek Willets asked.

'If I can,' Susan answered. 'I doubt if the Corporation will continue to employ married women. It's stated in my contract, I think, that we married ladies will be out on our ear ten minutes after an armistice is signed.'

'That policy may change,' Basil said. 'Indeed, I'll be very surprised if it doesn't.'

Viv said, 'You've more faith in the establishment than I have, dear. With all the chaps coming back looking for jobs, you can bet that working wives will get short shrift.'

'Your husband's with the BBC too, is he not?' Derek asked.

'Yes,' Susan answered. 'He's placed with a unit in Evesham right now but I'm rather hoping he may be brought back to London quite soon.'

'Are you?' Vivian said. 'I thought . . .'

Basil cleared his throat and, under the pretext of stubbing

out his cigarette, avoided meeting Susan's eye. 'Actually,' he said, 'Danny won't be coming back to London after all.'

'Why? Did Rupert Talbot turn him down?'

'Quite the contrary,' Basil said. 'Danny turned Rupert Talbot down. Didn't he tell you? He's decided to stay in Evesham.'

'No,' Susan said. 'He didn't tell me.'

'You must be disappointed,' Derek Willets said.

'Oh, yes, I am,' said Susan. 'Very.'

One minute the priests were handing out wafers, wine and blessings in front of the altar and the next, or so it seemed to Breda, they were dishing out mail that had been left in a bag in the priests' house over on Pound Street and that no one had found until this morning.

It struck Breda as weird to be receiving letters early on a Sunday morning with the wind swishing through holes in the church roof and the altar boys in none-too-clean shifts running up and down shouting, 'Beidermeyer? Mrs Beidermeyer? You 'ere, Mrs Beidermeyer?' or 'McIntosh. McIntosh. Got a postcard for McIntosh,' as if the sacred precincts of St Veronica's had turned into a sorting office.

'That'll be from her daughter, Faye,' Nora said.

'What will?' said Breda.

'The postcard. Her daughter, Faye, in Nottingham.'

'What's Faye doin' in Nottingham?'

'Factory work. Very hush-hush.'

'Can't be that hush-hush, Ma, if you know about it.'

'I don't know what Mrs Beidermeyer's doing here, though,' Nora said, frowning. 'She should be at the synagogue.'

'Maybe Father Joe's converted 'er,' Breda said. 'Anyhow,

it don't look she is 'ere since the kid's put the letter back in the bag.'

Then: 'Hooper, Hooper. Lookin' for Mrs Hooper.'

'Hoy,' said Breda, heart thumping. 'That's me.'

There were three letters for Breda and one for Nora.

Sensibly, she should have taken the mail outside. Billy would no doubt be playing fast and loose with his grandfather who was in no fit state to chase a six-year-old round the buildings, but she couldn't wait to find out who had written to her and what news the letters might contain.

She slit the first brown envelope with her thumbnail, scanned the official letter from the Home Office and, glancing at her mother, folded it neatly and tucked it into the waistband of her skirt.

She paused and stared out into the church, at the altar, at the blank space on the shrapnel-pitted wall where the crucifix had hung and at the hustle and bustle of choirboys and ordinary women and men milling about in the aisles.

She didn't know what she felt or how to respond to the news that Leonardo Romano had been a passenger on the vessel, *Arandora Star*, that had been sunk by enemy action in the Irish Sea and that he was missing, believed dead. No explanations, no apologies, no expressions of regret, just a formal statement, grudging in the extreme, that wiped away her childhood, relieved her of guilt and – she glanced at Nora once more – set her mother free to marry again.

Breda swallowed the lump in her throat and said, 'What you got, Ma? Is that a letter from Auntie Mary?'

'No, it's from Molly.'

'Who's Molly?'

'Auntie Mary's daughter.'

'I didn't even know Auntie Mary 'ad a husband.'

'Well, she has. She had. She's a widow. Molly's your cousin. She's got brothers, a husband and three kiddies, and . . .'

'And?' Breda put in.

'She'll have us. She'll take us in.'

'Even Matt?'

'All of us.'

'Did you tell 'er Matt's a Proddy?' Breda asked.

'Won't matter, not to Molly.' Nora raised her eyes to heaven in a fair representation of ecstasy. 'Sure an' we're all going home to Limerick. Wait till I tell Father Joseph.'

Breda said, 'Why don'cha do that right now, Ma. I'm sure the father will be as thrilled as you are.'

'Yes,' Nora said, leaping up. 'Limerick,' and, waving the letter from Breda's long-lost cousin, set off down the aisle to buttonhole the already harassed priest.

Breda opened the second brown envelope. It contained a short handwritten letter from Mr Reilly, the station officer at Oxmoor Road, in which he expressed his sympathy for her loss and told her what a good fireman Ron had been and how much he was missed by his colleagues.

Breda folded that letter too and put it carefully into her waistband for safe keeping.

Then, sniffing and puffing, she opened the last of the letters, which came from Evesham, from Danny, and would change her life for ever.

The all-clear sounded early, at 2.41 a.m. At a little after four o'clock Commander Derek Willets took his leave and set off on foot to find out if the station had survived and what trains might be running to carry him back to Portsmouth.

There was nothing sentimental in his farewell. It was very matter-of-fact. He shook Basil's hand, kissed Vivian's cheek, gave Susan a nod and a wink and, wrapped up in a duffle coat that had seen better days, strode off into the darkness as if, Susan thought, he was just popping round to the corner dairy to fetch a pint of milk.

Soon after, with dishes and pans washed and dried and the kitchen all shipshape, Vivian and Basil said goodnight and retired upstairs to their bedroom to catch up on lost sleep while Susan, though she had a little cubby of her own with a bed in it, lay down on the davenport once more and, closing her eyes, tried to sleep too.

Sleep would not come, though. Her mind hummed with uneasy thoughts of Ron, of her father, of the bright little girl she'd been before she'd realised just how her daddy had shaped her to fulfil not some vague death-bed promise to a wife he could barely recall and had probably never loved but only to satisfy his vanity.

How disappointed he must be that he was still the man he had always been and she, the star of his show, had deserted him. She wished him no ill; he had lost a reliable son, as she had lost a reliable brother. Even so, she was relieved, vastly so, that he had taken up with Nora Romano who would look after him, body and soul, and who had Breda to rely on if things got out of hand.

She sat up suddenly and crouched on the edge of the davenport, pressed her knees together. She was restless, agitated, in need not of Danny, who loved her and might be retrieved at the tug of a heart-string, but of her incorrigible lover who knew what she was and what she wanted and was more than ready to give it to her.

Rising, she lifted a corner of the blackout curtain.

The first pallid light of dawn filled the crooked little street that backed on to the mews. It was windy too, a thin penetrating wind that blew dust and leaves before it.

Summer was over, the long hot Indian summer. The days were growing too short, the nights too long. Her restlessness took on an urgency that robbed her of will.

She hurried into the bathroom, washed her face, combed her hair, applied make-up and, within minutes, overcoat flapping and hat held on with one hand, she was trotting up Salt Street in the direction of Berkeley Square.

A bomb, one among the many that had fallen on central London that Saturday night, had ripped up Conduit Street and brought down some of the buildings there. Fire tenders and ambulances had spilled over into the square but, as far as Susan could make out, Lansdowne House had not been hit, though the façade was pitted by shrapnel and black stains marked the wall where, some nights ago, the oil bomb Bob had told her about had obviously taken its toll.

The commissionaire knew Susan by sight but a warden guarding the doorway insisted on inspecting her identity card and asking impertinent questions before he let her enter. Early breakfast was already being served in the restaurant. Three men and two women brushed past Susan on their way downstairs – the elevator was under repair – but spared her not so much as a second glance. In the corridor outside Pete Slocum's apartment several empty glasses and a dimpled bottle of Scotch, empty too, were scattered round the doorway.

Susan pressed the bell button and waited.

340

She hoped Bob would be asleep, that she could slip naked into bed beside him, waken him with an intimate touch and that, roused, he would make love to her, hot, forceful, indecent love before they fell asleep in each other's arms.

The door opened an inch or two and a haggard face peered at her through the gap.

'Ah, it's you, is it?' Pete Slocum said. 'Too late, Mrs Cahill. You've missed all the fun.'

He was naked beneath the dressing gown, a knee-length woman's dressing gown in pale yellow silk. Susan couldn't help but glance down at his lean torso and bony hips and the long, flaccid member that hung between his thighs.

She said, 'Is he here?'

'Yep, he's here.'

'Well, aren't you going to let me in?'

'You don't want to come in right now, Mrs Cahill,' Pete Slocum said. 'Take my word on it.'

'Oh, but I do,' Susan said. 'I most definitely do.'

Slocum sighed, knotted the tie of his dressing gown, pulled open the door and ushered her into the hallway.

She looked down it into the living room but could make out nothing but bare feet protruding from an end of the couch and a man in some sort of uniform curled up on the floor.

'Where is he?' she said.

'In his room?'

'Is he asleep?'

'Mrs Cahill . . .' Slocum shrugged. 'Never mind.'

She opened the door of Bob's room, slipped inside and quietly closed the door behind her. She began to unbutton her overcoat, then, drawing close to the bed, stopped in her tracks. The blackout curtain billowed inward as a gust of wind found the open window. Daylight played across the bed.

The girl, stark naked, sprawled across Bob's belly, her slender legs stretched backward, one foot, one toe, touching the carpet as if she had been struck down while practising some strenuous balletic move. Between Susan's shoe and the girl's foot a discarded rubber leaked fluid into the rug.

Susan clamped a hand to her mouth and squeezed her fingers into her cheeks. Bob hoisted himself up on an elbow. The girl stirred and, twisting round, stared at Susan without embarrassment or remorse. 'Do come and join us, darling,' she said. 'I'm sure Bob won't mind.'

'You bastard, Robert. You utter bastard,' Susan said, then, before he could stop her, fled.

33

Cloud covered the sun and the gusting wind that swirled dust in all directions made picnicking on the steps of St Vee's too uncomfortable to put up with for long.

Down in the crypt a team of volunteers were mopping the floor, airing beds and blankets and generally cleaning up. Priests and nuns went about their religious duties, and a WVS van, parked across the mouth of the lane, served tea and buns to those who had missed breakfast.

For many of Father Joe's homeless flock it would be a quiet day of rest and recuperation but for others, Breda and Nora among them, it was a day to make plans and the huge wood-panelled hall of the Dock Workers' Union, now functioning as rest centre, was an ideal place in which to do it.

Matt commandeered a table while Breda and Nora joined the queue at the counter to purchase tea, toast and a packet of the sweet oatmeal biscuits that Billy liked.

There were many familiar faces in the Dock Workers' hall that Sunday morning; too many. It required quite a bit of manoeuvring to keep Billy out of earshot of those who wished to commiserate with his mother and more than one white lie to explain why so many ladies wished to pat his shaven head and so many gentlemen pressed sixpence or a shilling into his palm until, without even trying, he had enough silver in his pocket to keep him in sweets and comics for a year.

When Matt shifted his chair round, stuck out his injured foot and held up his stick like a sentry shouldering a rifle, however, all but a very few took the hint and when papers were spread out among the plates and cups it was apparent that the family had private business to conduct and was best left to get on with it undisturbed.

'Old Leo – huh!' Matt scratched his nose with his forefinger. 'Old beggar beat me to it. Who'd 'ave thought he'd be the one to go first. Drowned like a rat in the Irish Sea. Makes you think, don't it? Never know what's round the corner, do yer?' He smoothed a hand over the Home Office notepaper. 'Seems like yesterday we was boys runnin' wild together, now—'

'Now you can marry my ma,' Breda put in.

'Eh?' Matt looked up.

'You 'eard me,' Breda said. 'God knows, you been rattlin' on about it long enough. Nothin' to stop you now.'

'I'm a Protestant,' Matt said, as if he had just discovered that fact about himself. 'I mean, will they let me marry a Catholic in Ireland?'

Nora said, 'Auntie Mary married a Protestant an' they didn't burn her at the stake. What they won't put up with is you an' me livin' in sin.'

Breda said, 'You don't seem very upset, Ma.'

'Upset?'

'About Dad, about Leo?'

'After all the trouble he brought me drowning's too good for him.' Nora glanced down at Billy who was seated by her

344

side. 'No, no.' She crossed herself hastily. 'I don't mean that. Sure an' I'm sorry he's dead. I'll even say a prayer for him.'

'An' light a candle,' Billy suggested.

'Yes, dear,' she said. 'And light a candle.'

'Who's Leo, anyway?' Billy asked.

'He was your granddad,' Nora answered.

'I thought you was my granddad,' Billy said.

'You got two granddads,' Matt told him. 'Everybody does.'

'Now I only got one?'

'Uh-huh,' Breda said. 'Now you only got one.'

'But I still got a dad,' Billy said. 'He's in the army. You don't get drowned in the army.'

'Nah, hardly anybody gets drowned in the army,' Breda said, adding quickly, 'How many of them biscuits you had?'

'Two.'

'Have another one then an' let the grown-ups talk. Okay?'

Billy agreed to the deal by accepting the biscuit his mother offered and, head resting on Nora's shoulder, bit into it.

Finger to her lips, Breda gave Matt Mr Reilly's condolence note and watched him read it. She expected tears or at least some evidence of emotion but her father-in-law just pushed the letter back across the table. 'I reckon you'll want to keep it.'

''Course I want to keep it. It's all I got left.'

'Be some money comin' your way, though,' Matt said.

'There might,' said Breda, 'but it won't be much.'

'Remember to leave them your new address,' Nora said.

'My new—'

'Molly's house in Limerick.'

Breda drew in a deep breath. 'Ma,' she said, 'I ain't goin' with you to Limerick.'

'You can't stay 'ere on your own,' Matt said. 'I won't stand for it, not with Billy the way he is.'

Breda took Danny's letter from her skirt and placed it on the table where both Matt and Nora could read it. 'Danny's found a place for Billy an' me in the country.'

'Damned if 'e has,' Matt Hooper said. 'You ain't goin', girl, an' that's flat.'

'Who's gonna stop me?' Breda said. 'Danny says it ain't much of a place he's found for Billy an' me but there's a school handy an' there might even be a part-time job for me in the canteen of a factory where 'is friend works.'

Nora said, 'I knew Danny wouldn't let you down.'

'Let 'er down?' Matt said. 'Ron gone not ten bleedin' minutes an' that Scotch bastard wants 'er for 'imself.'

'Shut up, Matt, just shut up,' Nora said. 'You'll be safe with Danny, dear. He'll look after you.'

'She'll be a lot safer with us in Ireland,' Matt said.

'Sure an' you've no say in the matter,' Nora told him.

'No, but I bloody well know who has.'

'Who's that then?' Nora asked.

'Susan,' Matt answered. 'Our Susan.'

Some of the boys and girls from the News Department were having a party of sorts in the canteen to celebrate the announcement that ferocious storms were due to pound the coast of Britain and that any plans Adolf might have to use the full moon and high tides of the 24th to launch an invasion would surely be swept away.

One stately newsreader had popped the cork on a bottle of champagne and the minions, Susan thought, were pretending to be merrier than they really were just to please the old buffer.

When they called out and invited her to join them, she forced a smile, shook her head and hurried on to buy a couple of sandwiches to eat upstairs.

She felt relieved, almost light-hearted now that the inevitable had happened and Robert Gaines had displayed his true colours. He had, she told herself, been just too good to be true, too good in bed, too good at the microphone but, in the end, not good enough for her.

Four or five years ago she would have blamed herself for his betrayal, would have believed herself to be inadequate, unattractive, lacking in sex appeal, a failure. She was not as she'd been five years ago, thank heaven, so unsure of herself that she would knuckle under and let some man, a virtual stranger, drain her of self-confidence as a vampire might drain her of blood. The fact that Bob Gaines had dared cheat on her only strengthened her belief that she deserved better.

In the end he was nothing but an opportunistic, fly-by-night foreign journalist who had caught her when she was at her most vulnerable – which, now she thought of it, was really all Danny Cahill's fault for leaving her alone in London in the first place. Nor was Vivian entirely blameless. And Basil, yes, Basil had positively encouraged her to embark on an affair for the sake of his blessed programme.

After the first flush of shock and anger had subsided she'd swiftly gained control of herself and, on the short walk through the windy streets from Berkeley Square to Portland Place, had begun to construct her defences.

Even before the doors of Broadcasting House had closed behind her she knew precisely how she would treat him, how her aloof indifference to his excuses and apologies would turn the tables until it appeared that *she* was rejecting *him*, that he, not she, was the fool.

She was hungry: a good sign, a sure sign that her strategy was sound and that whatever hurt Bob Gaines had inflicted upon her was already beginning to heal.

She carried the sandwiches and a mug of tea up to the third-floor office and placed them on her desk. The damaged window, under the metal shutter, had been repaired or, rather, replaced by a huge sheet of plyboard that cut out all the light. All to the good, she thought, for the transition from daylight to dusk was a melancholy time, even before the sirens sounded warning of the inevitable raid.

She cut the sandwiches into manageable quarters with a paper knife and ate them; egg and cress, not her favourite filling but palatable enough. At least the bread was fresh. She found a handkerchief in her handbag, wiped her mouth and fingers, lit a cigarette and sipped lukewarm tea. Her typewriter, the telephone, the wallboard with the week's schedule pinned to it, the tray on Basil's desk with letters waiting to be signed: all the comforts of home, really.

She finished the tea and the cigarette and, tipping back her chair, rested her head against the wall and easily, effortlessly, drifted off to sleep.

The persistent ringing of the telephone wakened her. She tipped the chair forward and blinked. Her neck ached and she had a bad taste in her mouth. She waited for the phone to stop ringing but it didn't. She glanced at the wall clock and realised that she'd slept for the best part of two hours. Small wonder, she thought as she crossed the room, that her neck ached.

She stooped over Basil's desk and stared at the telephone. She knew who the caller would be, the despicable Mr Gaines, no doubt, telling her what a mistake he'd made, that he'd been drunk, that nothing had happened, that he hardly knew the girl, that she meant nothing to him, that he . . .

She picked up the receiver and said, 'Well?'

For an instant, she failed to recognise his voice. Then it dawned on her that she had never heard him speak on a telephone before. He sounded different, hesitant and apologetic and, curiously, more refined, as if he feared that his call might somehow be broadcast to the nation.

'Dad?' she said.

'Is that Mrs Cahill? I'm looking for Mrs Cahill.'

'Yes, Dad, it's me. It's Susan.'

A pause, some muttering, a fumbling with coins, the clash of coppers as he found the right button, then, shouting, he said, 'Is that you, Susan?'

She was amused by his inability to deal with the implements of the modern world that were so familiar to her but she was also uneasy. The effort it must have cost him to enter a public telephone box and place a call to the BBC, the holy of holies in his book, suggested that something was seriously wrong: another death, another tragedy – Billy or Nora, perhaps – another problem she must deal with when she barely had time to deal with problems of her own.

'What is it?' she said. 'Is it Billy?'

'No, it's me. It's your father.'

'I know it's you, Dad. You don't have to shout. I can hear you perfectly well. Why are you calling me at work?'

'You won't get into trouble, will you? I wouldn't want to get you in no trouble. I told them it was urgent.'

'For God's sake, simmer down and tell me what—'

'He's leavin' you.'

Bewildered, Susan said, 'How do you know that?'

'Danny. He's leavin' you.'

'Danny?'

'Your 'usband.'

'I know who Danny is, Dad. What makes you think—'

'You gotter stop 'er, Susie. It ain't right.'

'I don't know what you're talking about. Stop who?'

'Her. Breda,' her father said, then, in a rush, 'They didn't want me tellin' you. They said you wouldn't be interested.'

'I don't understand.'

'She's goin' to stay with 'im in this country place.'

'Evesham. Is she? Does Danny know about it?'

'He told 'er to come. He's got a place for 'er to stay. He's even sendin' 'er money for the fares. I mean, Ron's wife, our Ron's wife goin' to live in a strange town with Danny Cahill. You ask me, the cow was at it behind Ronnie's back. Now Ron's not 'ere to sort 'er out it's up to me to do it for 'im.'

'Is Billy going too?'

''Course 'e is. She won't go without 'im.'

'I think Danny's just making sure Billy gets out of London. At least I hope he is. What about you, you and Nora?'

'Not invited.' He paused. 'Anyway, we're goin' to Ireland.'

'Ireland?'

'To stay with Nora's niece, least till me foot heals up.'

'And you want Breda to go with you, is that it?'

'It ain't right for Billy to be took away. It just ain't right,' he said. 'It's up to you to stop 'er, Susie. He's your bleedin' husband. You can put your foot down.'

'I'm not sure I can. I'm not sure I even want to.'

Obviously no one had told her father about her affair with Robert and that her marriage to Danny Cahill might be on its last legs. Now Breda, Breda with her swagger and her big chest, would finish it off for sure. Breda had one card in her hand that she could never hope to trump: Billy, the stubborn, pathetic little boy who was already more like her father in temperament than Ron had ever been.

'Susan?' her father said. 'Susie, are you there?'

'Yes.'

'I'm runnin' out of money 'ere.'

'Do you need cash?'

'What? No, pennies.'

'What about cash to get you to Ireland?'

'Nora's got some savings in the bank. She can get the money without 'er bank book, she says. The book went up in smoke but the banks know what to do about that. Susie, you there, Susie? What you gonner do about—'

And the line went dead.

She replaced the receiver and waited, motionless, for her father to ring back. A minute passed, then two. The phone remained resolutely silent, her father's final question hanging unanswered in the air.

'Shady Nook?' Kate said. 'I wonder who dreamed that up?'

'Someone with a great deal of imagination,' Griff said. 'They can call it Shangri-La if they like, it's still nothing but an old railway carriage.'

'How on earth did they get it here?' said Kate.

'Tractor, I expect,' Danny said. 'Once you're inside it's not as bad as it looks.'

'It couldn't possibly be as bad as it looks,' Kate said. 'I hope your friend knows what she's coming to.'

'My friend,' Danny said, 'won't care what she's coming to. Anywhere's better than London right now an' poor old Breda doesn't have much choice.'

'You're pretty cocky about all this, aren't you, boyo?'

'I'm not cocky at all,' said Danny. 'Somebody's got to look out for her now she's a widow with a kid an' nowhere to live. Her mother took me in when I was homeless, least I can do is return the favour.'

'This may not be time or the place – especially not the place – but what,' Griff said, 'does your wife have to say about it?'

Griffiths and Kate were leaning against the bicycles which, with pails, brooms and mops hanging from the handlebars and jutting out from the saddlebags, made them look like gypsies peddling hardware door to door.

Griff's sheepskin coat and patched old cords fitted the image of a rural mendicant, aided by a pair of Mr Pell's wellington boots flopping on his feet, which, Kate said, might endear him to the odd one-eyed milkmaid but would definitely not go down well in Coventry High Street, though she, in baggy slacks and rubber galoshes, with a beret pulled tight over her hair, didn't look much like a fashion plate either.

'Good God, Cahill!' Griff said. 'Don't tell me your wife doesn't know?'

'Know what?' said Danny.

'That you're setting up a little love nest for—'

'I think that's enough, Silwyn,' Kate said. 'It's really none of our business.'

'Given that Jock here has blackmailed us into sacrificing our valuable leisure time to skivvy for him,' Griff said, 'I believe I am entitled to ask, not,' he added hastily, 'that you, my dear old chum, are in any way obligated to answer.'

'Doesn't matter what my wife thinks.' Danny hesitated. 'She's been livin' her own life for a while now.'

'You mean she's still with the American bloke?'

Kate cut him short. 'Silwyn, enough!'

The railway carriage was securely propped on bricks and heavy wooden sleepers and to judge by the profusion of weeds that had grown up around it had been there for some time. The windows were smeared with grime and the paintwork on the sides of the coach was peeling, but the interior had been neatly partitioned off to provide two comfortable bunk beds, a tiny end kitchen with a Calor gas cooking ring and a little parlour with a coal-burning barrel stove. A lean-to hut with a chemical toilet inside had been added at one end of the coach and at the other a big wooden shed to store firewood and coal.

'Who lived here?' Kate said.

'Farm labourer,' Danny told her.

'What happened to him? Did he die?'

'Naw,' Danny said. 'He joined the navy.'

'He was probably a young cowman,' Griff suggested. 'Mr Pell told me that Gaydon, the landowner, got rid of his dairy herd when the war started and turned the land over to arable. How much is Gaydon rooking you for rent, Danny?'

'Three bob a week.'

'Highway robbery. But it isn't going to break you, is it?'

'Mr Gaydon seemed glad enough to get the place off his hands,' Danny said. 'When I told him it was for evacuees he even threw in a free load of coal. I've a feelin' Mr Pell might've put the elbow in. Gaydon an' he drink in the same pub.'

'How long has the place been empty?' Kate said.

'Six or seven months, apparently.'

'And when is your friend arriving?'

'Thursday.'

'In that case' – Kate detached a pail from the handlebars – 'we'd better not stand around chatting. Where's the water supply? We don't have to carry it up from the Avon, do we?'

'Naw,' Danny said. 'I doubt if Breda'd put up with that. There's a well round the back. Sweet water, Gaydon assures me.'

'A well?' said Griff. 'Good Lord!'

'You can make a wish, if you like,' Kate said.

'I wish I'd never got into this,' said Griff. 'Too late to back out now, I suppose.'

'Far too late,' Kate told him and, handing him the pail, sent him off to find water while Danny and she, armed with brooms, attacked the coach's musty interior to make it ready for Breda and her son.

34

On Sunday afternoon a small formation of German bombers flew into the Thames estuary only to be turned back by anti-aircraft fire before it reached London. The warning siren had been followed, ten minutes later, by the all-clear and Basil, on his way over from Salt Street, had barely broken stride. He had, he confessed, slept later than he'd intended and apologised to Susan who, he seemed to assume, had been at her desk for hours. Susan did not disillusion him.

When Basil asked if she'd heard anything from Bob Gaines, she shook her head and carried on typing in spite of the fact that her fingers no longer seemed to be properly connected to her brain. The call from her father had thrown her for a loop. His insistence that she put a spoke in Breda's wheel was motivated by pure selfishness, of course. He wanted to keep Billy for himself. She could hardly blame him for that; nor could she blame Danny for persuading Breda to quit London before winter set in.

She might write to Danny or try to reach him by telephone, she supposed, tell him she'd broken off with Bob Gaines and depend on Danny's sense of honour to keep Breda out of his bed. The alternative was to swallow her pride, forgive Bob his indiscretion, move into the Lansdowne and become 'officially', as it were, his girl. Forgiveness seemed like weakness, though; a step too far just to have a man in her life.

Basil said, 'Have you had lunch yet, Susan?'

'No, not yet.'

'Best go soon,' he said. 'Before you do, however, I'd be grateful if you'd put through a call to Gaines and see what the devil he's up to. I thought he'd be here by now to deliver his piece for Tuesday. It's going to be a scramble as it is.'

'Why don't you call him? At least he listens to you.'

'Doesn't he listen to you?' Basil said. 'I thought—'

'What *do* you think, Baz?' Bob Gaines said from the doorway. 'That Susie has me by the tail? You don't have me by the tail, sweetheart, do you?'

Leaning against the doorpost, hat tipped back and trench-coat belted tightly about his waist, he might have stepped from one of the gangster films that Ronnie had been so fond of. He spoke in a laconic tone of voice, as if he had rehearsed his lines.

In that moment Susan knew there could be no possibility of forgiveness.

Bob pushed himself away from the door and handed Basil a cardboard folder. 'That's your stuff for Tuesday,' he said. 'Timed to nine minutes but you may want to chop it down since I won't be reading it.'

Basil held the folder in two hands and pressed it to his chin as if he intended to open it with his teeth. He said, 'Just what's going on here?'

'I'm resigning.'

'You can't,' Basil said. 'You have a contract.'

'With an in-built, iron-clad separation clause,' Bob said. 'You should've paid more attention to the small print before you signed me up.'

'Tuesday, what about Tuesday?'

'I'll be on my way to New York.'

'You're going home?' Susan said.

'I sail for Lisbon tomorrow morning to pick up a ship for the States. God knows how long it'll take me but – yeah, I'm going home.'

'Why, Bob? Why?' Basil said.

'I've had enough of England, enough of the BBC and—'

'You've had enough of me,' Susan heard herself say.

'Too much of you, maybe,' Bob said.

'Are you taking her with you?' Susan asked.

'Who?'

'That – that girl?'

'Tina? Are you crazy? She was good between the sheets but that's an end of it. She knew it was just a fling. At least she didn't bore the pants off me.'

'What?' Susan got to her feet. 'What did you say?'

'She didn't try to lay her guilt on me or make me out to be a bastard because I couldn't fix her life for her. She knows how to have fun and let go. No boring pap about commitment. The only thing I'm committed to is my career and right here, right now in this sticky old flytrap you call the BBC, my career is foundering.'

'That,' Basil said, 'is one of the most ridiculous excuses for resigning I've ever heard. Whatever may be going on between you and Susan—'

'He's a coward,' Susan said. 'Don't you see, Basil? He's a moral coward. What will you do, Robert, when you can no longer remain uninvolved? Where will you hide then? Cairo, Marseilles, Casablanca . . .'

'Russia,' he said. 'The *Post* has promised me Russia.'

'Perfect!' Susan said. 'Ideal! When you pick up a girl in Leningrad you won't even have to talk to her.'

'At least she won't be made of ice.'

'I think,' Basil said, 'that's enough.'

'Go back to your husband, Susan,' Bob told her. 'That's all you ever wanted to do anyhow. Go back to your poor dim schmuck of a husband and play games with him. Me, I'm out of here.' He stepped to the desk and shook Basil's hand. 'I can't say it's been much of a pleasure, Baz, but I wish you well. I wish you luck, you and Vivian. Keep your heads down and stay healthy.' He turned to Susan. 'You too, I guess. You too,' and then, without another word, he was gone.

'Well,' Basil said, after a pause, 'that's a shocker, a real shocker. What are we going to do now?'

'Find someone else,' Susan said. 'Someone better.'

'Don't tell me you have someone in mind?' Basil said.

'For the programme?'

'Yes, for the programme.'

'Unfortunately not,' said Susan.

Susan was the last person Breda expected to see wading through the crowds in Paddington railway station that blustery Thursday morning. She was having a hard enough time coping with her emotions without having to face up to the woman who had married Danny Cahill. Ronnie had never been second-best, certainly not. She had loved her husband as much as she had ever loved anyone, but she had loved Danny Cahill too with a possessive kind of affection that her marriage to Ronnie hadn't dented but that Susan's marriage to Danny most certainly had. Now, by several ugly quirks of fate, she might have Danny all to herself again.

It had been a relatively quiet night with nothing much more than a shower of incendiaries sent down from Goering's assassins, though, according to Matt, who got all his news from the *Daily Express* these days, fires were raging in Berlin after a huge RAF bombing raid, and Hitler was having fits.

With money Nora had given him Matt had bought them breakfast at one of the vans and in shabby, half-ruined Fawley Street Breda had said goodbye not only to Shadwell but to her mother, her father-in-law and in a queer sort of way to Ronnie too.

Nora had wanted to accompany them to the station, to snatch a last precious hour with her daughter and grandson but Matt had said his foot wouldn't stand up to it; besides, she didn't have time, not when they'd be heading for Euston to catch a noon train to Liverpool to link with the night boat to Dublin.

So there in Fawley Street, not two hundred yards from Brauschmidt's high-class butcher's, where Ronnie had served his apprenticeship, not three hundred yards from the fish bar in which Leo had met his femme fatale and less than a mile from the spot where Breda's brother, Georgie, had been struck down in the wake of the Cable Street riots, there they parted, not knowing if or when or where they might all be together again.

Nora had wept buckets; Breda too.

Bewildered and truculent, Billy had butted his granddad in the belly when Matt had tried to hug him and, until they'd squeezed on to the bus with the other refugees, had growled, snarled and sulked. Only when he saw his grandma running alongside the bus with tears streaming down her face did he cry too, two big fat tears trickling down his cheeks, his bottom lip, no longer pugnacious, trembling like a raspberry jelly.

The government's scheme to evacuate as many women and children as possible from the East End before winter made living in shelters a serious hazard to health was in full swing. The major railway stations swarmed with young children and their harassed mothers and Paddington, just reopened after its recent pounding, was no exception.

With Billy trotting by her side and clutching two bundles containing their few belongings, Breda was in no mood for confrontation. She cut across the narrow concourse in the direction of Platform 4 which, a porter informed her, was where the train for Evesham would depart as soon as it was assembled.

The platform was already crowded with women and children, though just where they were all going, Breda couldn't imagine. There were soldiers, too, laden with kitbags and packs, a little troupe of RAF bandsmen awkwardly burdened with cornet and trombone cases and, in the same muddled group, a Guards' officer lugging a bag of golf clubs.

'Breda. Breda. Over here.'

She swung this way and then the other, bobbing her head, but it was Billy, at hip height, who spotted his aunt first.

Susie was standing not far from the platform gate and, Breda thought uncharitably, looked less like a million dollars than a couple of bent pennies. She wore an old tweed coat and a tweedy sort of skirt that was far too large for her and a knitted cap that would have looked better on a trawler man than it did on an employee of the BBC.

'What you doin' 'ere?' Breda asked.

'Danny asked me to see you off safely.'

'Danny? How did you—'

'He telephoned,' Susan said. 'Took him ages to get through, but he did in the end. He told me what train you'd be on and asked me to give you these.'

'What?' said Breda suspiciously.

Susan held out a brown paper bag. 'It's not much. Couple of veal and ham pies, some cut cake and a bottle of ginger pop. I had no idea it would be so busy.'

Breda shifted one bundle to her armpit and reached for the brown paper bag but Billy, stepping up, carefully detached it from his Aunt Susan's hand and, after peeping inside, pressed it securely to his chest.

'Yum?' Susan said.

'Yum,' Billy agreed and almost managed a smile.

'Is this a peace offerin'?' Breda said.

'I'm sure I don't know what you mean,' said Susan.

'Yeah, but I'm sure you do,' Breda said.

'Danny's not doing it for you. He's doing it for Billy.'

Breda sighed. 'Long as he ain't doin' it to get back at you, that's okay with me.'

'Danny isn't the spiteful type,' said Susan. 'He's far too down-to-earth to take revenge. Not,' she added, 'that I'd blame him if he did.'

'You still got your feller,' Breda said. 'Ain't one man enough for you, Susie?'

'My – my "feller" has gone back to New York.'

'Oh, really?' Breda said. 'Why didn't you go with 'im?'

'I have work to do here.'

'Does Danny know – about your feller, I mean?'

Susan smiled. 'I did rather make a point of telling him.'

'I'll bet you did.'

'Ah, yes,' Susan said. 'You may have – what do they call it? – territorial advantage but Danny's still my husband.'

'Ooo,' Breda said, smiling too, 'if there's one thing I love, it's a challenge.'

'I haven't given up on Danny just yet, you know.'

'Maybe not,' Breda said. 'The big question is, has Danny given up on you?'

'That's something we'll have to find out, isn't it?'

'It certainly is,' said Breda.

The piercing shriek of a train whistle cut across their conversation followed by a massive explosion of white steam. Stragglers on the concourse surged towards the gate, dragging small children by the hand and rolling behind them on trolleys all sorts of bits and pieces, from cribs to baby baths to wireless sets and electric fires, as if London had become the site of a rummage sale and they were making off with the spoils.

'Never gonna get a seat now,' Breda said. 'We better go.'

'Yes,' Susan said. 'You'd better.'

Breda watched her sister-in-law crouch, look Billy straight in the eye and heard her say, 'Be a good boy now and take care of Mummy,' before she delivered a kiss from which Billy did not flinch but, to Breda's surprise, returned in kind.

'Ain't you the lucky one,' Breda said.

'That,' said Susan, 'remains to be seen,' then, tugging down the knitted cap and wrapping the coat around her, turned and hurried away.